SUICIDE RUN TO ARCHANGEL

A World War II Novel Based on a True Story

CAPT. MICHAEL J. DODD

HELLGATE PRESS ASHLAND, OREGON

SUICIDE RUN TO ARCHANGEL

Published by Hellgate Press
(An imprint of L&R Publishing, LLC)

 This is a work of fiction based on a true story.

Hellgate Press
Ashland, OR 97520
email: sales@hellgatepress.com

Cover and Interior Design: L. Redding

ISBN: 978-1-954163-90-4

Printed and bound in the United States of America
First edition 10 9 8 7 6 5 4 3 2 1

CONTENTS

Author's Note

THE BATTLE OF THE ATLANTIC was the longest continuous campaign of World War II, stretching from 1939 to the end of the war in Europe in May 1945. The battle pitted Allied merchant ships and their Navy defenders against the German U-boats, naval ships, and the Luftwaffe. The critical job of the merchant ships was to deliver war materiel and supplies from the United States to England and Russia in their battle against the Nazis. For much of the conflict, the outcome was in doubt. Early on, Allied merchant ships were sunk at a rate faster than they could be replaced. At one point, England was reduced to only a few months' supply of food and fuel. British Prime Minister Winston Churchill declared "...the U-boat menace was the only thing I really worried about during the war."

The tide finally turned in the spring of 1943 with several epic convoy battles. How did the Allies achieve this victory? It hinged on the US conversion of its enormous industrial capacity to a war footing. Huge numbers of merchant Liberty Ships along with destroyers, battleships, and long-range bombers, were produced and gradually turned the tide.

The Liberty Ship was a 440-foot vessel which was standardized and manufactured rapidly at eighteen shipyards along the east and west coasts and the Gulf of Mexico. The average time to construct a Liberty Ship was reduced from 150 days to forty days. Some 2,700 were produced by the end of the war. In addition, thousands of long-range bombers were manufactured. These could track and protect the convoys.

The other game changer was new technology developed to locate the illusive U-boats. SONAR was improved to detect U-boats while underwater. RADAR was developed for surface tracking, and High Frequency Direction Finding (Huff-Duff) was invented to detect U-boat radio communications and pinpoint a vessel's location. Finally, the German secret code (ENIGMA) was cracked by the British. This breakthrough allowed analysis of the enemy battle plans and locations of U-boat wolfpacks.

The cost of the Battle of the Atlantic for both sides was horrendous. On the Allied ledger, some 35,000 merchant mariners and navy armed guards lost their lives. More than 3,000 Allied merchant ships were sunk.

The Germans lost 783 U-boats out of a fleet of about 900. During the last months of the war, a German crewmember boarding a U-boat had only a 5% chance of returning home. Some 30,000 submariners lost their lives. This was the highest loss-rate of any service of any combatant in World War II.

This historical novel is based on actual events that occurred during the war. The Liberty Ship *Esek Hopkins* delivered vital cargo to various international ports throughout the conflict. Its first voyage was from New Jersey to Archangel, Russia. The *Esek Hopkins* was one of forty merchant marine ships in a convoy which was given the code name PQ 18. The horrific attacks on PQ 18 by the German *U 408*, and other U-boats on September 13, 1942 were real, as were the ships struck by torpedoes. Following the U-boat attacks, persistent bombing of the convoy by the Luftwaffe terrorized the sailors on board and sank more ships. The harrowing journey during the last leg of the voyage to Archangel resulted in hundreds of casualties and enormous loss of vessels and supplies. All true. Remarkably, the *Esek Hopkins* made it to Archangel and back to Baltimore with no casualties.

The central character, Jack Dodd, was my uncle, and served on the *Esek Hopkins* as a deck cadet during that voyage to Russia in Convoy PQ 18 during the summer of 1942. The sequence of events outlined in this book is accurate and is drawn from my uncle's diary and letters home. After Jack's death in 1990, my cousin, also named Michael (but with middle initial "H"), pulled the data together and wrote a short private manuscript based on his father's notes and recollections. The manuscript was circulated only among family members. My thanks to Michael for giving me a copy, and for granting me permission to use his father's information to create this historical novel.

Jack Dodd and other family members named in this book were real people, as were the captains of *U-408*, and the Russian ship *Stalingrad*. Other characters, personal events and conversations are fiction. Based on my research, the events surrounding the attack on PQ-18 on September 13, 1942 are accurate.

The story that follows offers a view through a tiny window into the lives of some of the men who fought in the Battle of the Atlantic. This book is dedicated to all those who served in that prolonged nightmare.

Prologue

THE GERMAN SUBMARINE *UNTERSEEBOOT-408* jolted for a moment as a gush of compressed air forced a slender, smooth twenty-three-foot torpedo into the North Atlantic. The twin counterrotating props had begun spinning on command before the torpedo left tube number one. The generally reliable G7a TI torpedo carried six hundred twenty pounds of high explosives for a distance up to five thousand yards. The torpedo could propel itself at a remarkable speed of forty knots (about forty-five miles per hour). In addition, it was programmed to travel at a specific distance below the surface. In this case, the depth was set at fifteen feet. German navy men referred to torpedoes as "eels." Americans called them "tin fish."

On this Sunday morning in September 1942, the air was cold and the sky overcast in the North Atlantic. The U-boat target was a cargo ship in an Allied convoy of forty merchant vessels. The Germans had learned through their spy network that the convoy was given the code name PQ 18. The convoy had departed from Iceland with a destination of the port city of Archangel, Russia. Before Iceland, the convoy had come from the Scottish coast. It originated in Halifax, Nova Scotia. Prior to Halifax, the individual ships had loaded cargo from several ports on the East Coast of the United States. The journey from Iceland to Archangel was the last and most dangerous segment of the long and treacherous voyage of Convoy PQ 18.

Even though most of the ships in the convoy were American, the particular ship targeted by *U-408* happened to be a Russian cargo vessel named *Stalingrad.* She squatted deeply in the cold, choppy sea with her cargo of coal, fuel oil and military supplies. The depth of her hull was twenty-five feet below the churning waves. The German eel had a high probability of a strike.

But any good U-boat captain would not rely on a single torpedo. Captain Reinhard von Hymmen leaned against the periscope frame with a stopwatch in his hand. His crew remained perfectly silent in the cramped, smelly, two-hundred-twenty-foot steel tube, which carved its way silently through the frigid water some twenty feet below the surface.

A few moments earlier, Captain Hymmen had gazed through the monocular periscope and inspected the Allied convoy. He had picked out one ship at the edge of the convoy, recited to his officers the speed and distance, and ordered the scope down as the calculation was performed. An officer loaded the data into the torpedo gyroscope as the eel rested peacefully in its tube. Captain Hymmen had noted the target ship did not have the outline of a typical American Liberty Ship. He speculated that it looked like a Russian commercial vessel. So much the better. He detested the Russians.

Now it was time to launch the second eel. As he gazed at his stopwatch, the tiny, rotating secondhand arrow arrived at number three and the captain uttered, "*Rohr zwei los*" (tube two loose). The submarine gently jolted a second time. The bow of the U-boat lifted slightly as the three-thousand-three-hundred-ninety-pound eel departed from tube two. The U-boat elevator fins were adjusted to keep the vessel level underwater. Several crew members looked at each other and each gave a silent, subtle grin. They knew their captain rarely missed. This torpedo was set at a depth of eighteen feet. Hymmen glanced at his first mate as the secondhand continued its journey around the face of his watch. After another fifteen seconds, he said with conviction, "*Drei.*" A third torpedo shot into the sea. These were the first three torpedoes launched by *U-408* on this mission. Captain Hymmen had eleven torpedoes remaining.

Captain Hymmen knew there were risks of launching G7a TI

torpedoes at 10:00 a.m. on an overcast day. But he was no wilting flower. In this situation, the risk was worth it. Too many targets were cruising at a pokey nine knots directly before him. Things could change for the worse before dusk. He would take his chances now despite the fact that his torpedoes would leave a bubble trail from the chemical reaction that propelled them. And in his favor, he had seen no escort ships on this side of the convoy. In addition, the other captains in the wolf pack were all taking the same risk with their torpedoes.

The three G7a TI torpedoes raced toward the *Stalingrad* at a high speed. Captain Hymmen determined the distance the torpedoes must travel to detonation was fifteen hundred yards. At the given speed, the first torpedo should strike its target in one minute, ten seconds. The second should detonate in one minute, twenty-five seconds, and the third in one minute, forty seconds. The captain waited patiently to raise the periscope. He looked at the stopwatch in his right hand. After a thirty-second interval following the launch of the last torpedo, his voice broke the silence, and he ordered the periscope up. He rotated the scope and gazed with his right eye into the single ocular. To no one in particular, he instructed *U-408* to slow to three knots.

On the bridge of the *Stalingrad*, the second mate, Dimitri Novolov and Captain Alexi Sakharov had just finished a quick breakfast in the officers' quarters. The captain was surveying the starboard horizon with binoculars.

Suddenly he screamed in Russian, "Oh, Christ!" Then, "Stop engines! Full Reverse! Hard to port!"

None of these efforts would change the final outcome. Dimitri complied with the captain's orders, then gazed to the right. Even without binoculars, he could see the trail of bubbles projecting a line toward the midsection of the *Stalingrad*. The torpedo was traveling twenty-two yards every second.

The captain pushed the general alarm button to sound the klaxon as the ship grudgingly, incrementally began to slow; too late. Several deck hands also had seen the torpedo and were donning life jackets and running toward the port side lifeboats. On the bridge, Dimitri estimated he had first spotted the torpedo at about two hundred yards from the *Stalingrad.* He had practiced the math during his training. He quickly surmised the ship would be struck in nine seconds. The math was accurate.

The first torpedo from *U-408* passed twenty yards in front of the *Stalingrad.* It also missed other ships in the convoy and likely drifted to the ocean floor when all its fuel was expended. The second torpedo was on target to strike the midsection of the *Stalingrad.* The third torpedo missed its target completely due to a malfunction in the propellent. It traveled straight, but at a slower speed of thirty-five knots. It continued on its journey until it struck the steel hull of an American Liberty Ship, the *Oliver Ellsworth.* This ship was about four hundred yards behind the *Stalingrad.* It was an "accidental" hit. In a few short moments, two merchant ships were struck out of three shots from *U-408.*

Hymmen could not resist smiling as he observed the first explosion through the periscope. He calmly announced the strike to his men without moving his eye away from the ocular. Moments later, the dulled sound of the explosion on the Stalingrad carried under water and the tearing and screeching of steel was audible to all in the U-boat. The crew softly clapped and congratulated one another. There were still two torpedoes loose. Within fifteen seconds a second explosion occurred in the captain's left field of view through the periscope. It was an American Liberty Ship. He announced in German, "We have struck a second ship!" This time, just as the underwater explosive sound arrived at the U-boat, the crew let out a loud cheer, which the captain tolerated. It was not often that two ships were struck in such rapid succession. Not bad.

Since the first explosion was about fifteen seconds late, Captain Hymmen realized it was the second torpedo which struck the Russian ship. He concluded the first torpedo missed completely. And he correctly deduced that the third eel had defective propulsion since it missed the primary target and hit the ship behind the Russian freighter. It was a lucky hit of the American ship. But to all the crew, he had bracketed the underwater bombs nicely. To them, he was a genius, their genius.

Hymmen continued watching as fire consumed the *Stalingrad* and it began listing to starboard amidst thick black smoke. Clearly, the blow was mortal. The American ship was smoking, but not listing. Three torpedoes, two hits. One ship sinking for sure. He knew when they returned to the submarine pens on the French coast, he would be celebrated as a hero. In the distance, on the far side of the convoy, he could detect several other black clouds rising from the ocean surface. This day marked a successful attack by the wolf pack.

Thoughts drifted through Hymmen's mind as he gazed at the destruction before his eye.

It was nasty business. "My crew may appropriately be happy," he thought, "but there is incomprehensible terror on board those two ships." He did not allow himself to dwell on the topic. A little voice reminded him that one day the positions may be reversed.

Captain Hymmen's *U-408* was one of ten German submarines participating in the attack on PQ 18. This wolf pack had a title: *Tragertod*, or Tragic Death. The tracking of Convoy PQ 18 by German air and sea reconnaissance began on September 12. On this day, Sunday, September 13, 1942, the U-boats began picking targets and launching their deadly weapons.

On the *Stalingrad*, Captain Sakharov could not take his terror-filled eyes off the speeding torpedo. He could no longer speak. Dimitri had donned a life jacket and handed one to the captain just as the ship groaned with a huge, violent explosive shudder. The percussion knocked both men off their feet. The windows on the starboard side of the bridge shattered. An intense, bright flash had briefly illuminated the interior. Almost immediately, the ship began to list to starboard. Dimitri stood and inspected himself. He appeared to be in one piece. He helped the captain stand.

"Captain, we must get down to the lifeboats. There is no hope; the ship is sinking, and we do not have much time." Black, foul-smelling smoke filled the air. A powerful rumble deep in the bowels of the ship made the doomed vessel shudder again. Shouts and screams were audible from below and from the smoke-filled deck.

"Captain, the boilers have ruptured. There is no hope. We must save ourselves!" Captain Sakharov said nothing. The seconds peeled by. Dimitri helped him put on the life jacket. It was becoming difficult to stand on the bridge. The list to starboard was already about fifteen degrees. The second mate tried to pull him along, but Sakharov would not budge.

Finally, he said to the captain, "I will go down now. Follow me. We can go to the port side. I see the men lowering the lifeboats. Come." The captain shook his head and gazed into oblivion.

Dimitri left the captain and scampered down the steel stairs into the smoky confusion of the main deck and crashed into the first mate, Oleg. He had a bloody nose and deep cuts with glass shards poking from his skin. "Where is the captain?"

Dimitri coughed and gasped between breaths as he took in the mayhem and horror on deck. "He's in shock-on the bridge-he would not join me! I'm not sure you can help."

"So be it," Oleg shouted as he grabbed Dimitri's arm and they both struggled to walk up the steepening grade amidst the hideous smoke and chaos to find a lifeboat on the port side.

The scene below the waterline in the hull of the *Stalingrad* was horrifying. The G7a T I torpedo had operated perfectly. The torpedo exploded on contact with the steel hull and the six hundred and twenty pounds of high explosives erupted with extreme violence eighteen feet below the waterline. A ragged irregular hole ten feet in diameter was created through the one-inch steel hull. Coal bunkers were present near the explosion and caught fire immediately.

Within a few seconds, the third deck level was engulfed in flames. The fire soon reached the boilers one deck below, resulting in a second explosion, even as thousands of gallons of frigid North Atlantic water gushed through the gaping hole. Most of the bulkhead doors were not latched and the water passed forward and aft unimpeded.

Eight crew members below were killed immediately. Those who survived the blast were struggling toward the nearest ladder to get as high as they could, as quickly as possible. The boiler men always knew they would be the first to go when a torpedo hit. They were most anxious during the night when the risk of attack was greatest. This attack during daylight was a surprise and stunned them. Some searched for their colleagues in murky, freezing water, screaming names in vain. A few drowned while looking in desperation. Others were scalded with the flames and heat and could barely move. It was a scene re-created from Dante's *Inferno* in this tiny, unholy spot in the middle of the vast ocean.

The *Stalingrad*, a ship of 3,500 tons, sank below the surface in four minutes, her bow descending slowly, finally. Oil slicks clung to the surface, with some splotches catching fire. Anything capable of floating freely popped up, as screaming men struggled through the muck toward lifeboats and flotsam. Water swirled in little maelstroms, and demonic shattering and screeching sounds of steel fracturing in the dying ship echoed frighteningly to the surface.

Through his periscope, Captain Hymmen of *U-408* passively watched the carnage before him. It was traditional for German captains to observe the actual sinking of an enemy ship before they could count the success in their logs. In addition to the length of the ship, he estimated the tonnage–which often was exaggerated by German captains. If possible, the captains would attempt to confirm the name of the ship and its port of origin. Hymmen was a bit too far to make out the name *Stalingrad* on the descending, gasping bow of the ship.

Amazingly, of the eighty-seven crew and passengers on the Russian collier, sixty-six were eventually rescued. Captain A. Sakharov was the last man to leave the *Stalingrad.* He floated in the frigid ocean for nearly forty minutes. When his shivering, oil-coated body was fished up by a British minesweeper, he was the last pulled from the water on that horrible day. He survived the unforgiving cold and, remarkably, continued his career in the Russian navy.

The American Liberty Ship, *Oliver Ellsworth,* had been the victim of *U-408's* third torpedo. She was built in Baltimore and had been launched only three months prior. On this trip, her eight-thousand-ton capacity was maxed out with ammunition and aircraft. She sustained a direct hit on her starboard side and quickly filled with water. Since most of her below-deck hatches and doors had been secured, the water did not fill the ship completely and she did not list or sink. Her eight officers, thirty-four Merchant Marine crewmen, and twenty-eight Navy Armed Guards quickly got into lifeboats. There was considerable fear that the large quantity of ammunition on board would explode. But it did not. All the crew, except one Navy Armed Guard, were rescued. She sat forlornly in the ocean, stricken, and alone, but not dead. The water line was three-quarters up her freeboard. After an hour, she had drifted far behind the convoy. The British Admiralty determined she could not be recovered. Once her crew was rescued, the *Oliver Ellsworth* was fired upon by an Allied escort ship until she sank.

Slightly over one mile away, toward the center of Convoy PQ 18, cruised the Liberty Ship *Esek Hopkins.* Most of her crew gathered along the starboard side gazing in the distance as swirling, black smoke filled the air above the two stricken vessels. The men stood in silence.

They were mesmerized, stunned and angry. This was their first taste of war, and it was here, it was now, and it was clearly visible right before them. The powerful and violent destruction was all too real. Some of the men murmured a prayer as they contemplated their mortality and their insignificance in this massive global conflict.

Deck cadet Jack Dodd was among those who stared from the deck of the *Esek Hopkins* at the distant carnage. His body unwillingly shivered for a moment. A recurring thought twirled through his head, "Why, why am I doing this?" No one on that deck needed to be told the *Esek Hopkins* could be next.

Dinner that evening was somber. The officers came to the mess and tried to reassure the crew that every man on those ships who survived the blast was rescued. Yes, those who survived the blast. How many was that? The officers talked about the life vests, the fire drills, the lifeboat-launching techniques, and survival techniques in the water. Everything except how to deal with the deep, corrosive fear that inhabited their hearts with pounding, unending, unbearable horror.

All the men, including the officers, struggled with sleep that night. Jack finally dozed off after imagining those huge powerful, mortally-wounded ships rolling over repeatedly on their long journey to the bottom of the sea, with struggling, suffering men in states of panic, eyes wide open under water, trying to determine "up" in total blackness, as they used all their strength to escape, to gasp for one more breath, as their last thoughts contemplated their life's end, their loved ones, their meager existence. No one deserved to die like that. And yet…

Jack Dodd moved with a sudden jolt. The space he occupied rolled and swayed randomly. His clothes were damp with perspiration. He knew his eyes were open, but he could see nothing. Finally, his thoughts came into focus. He was on board the Liberty Ship *Esek Hopkins* as it moaned and groaned somewhere in the North Atlantic, rolling like a barrel in heavy seas. He had been sleeping deeply on the lower bunk. The room was dark with the portholes securely covered and all lights out. Irregular snoring noises emanated from his three roommates. This was reassuring. The nightmare of that horrific day was still frighteningly real. He could not get it out of his mind. He took a deep breath and tried to calm himself. He would never be able to get back to sleep. Somehow, when he started on this idyllic journey, he did not anticipate how close to death he would truly be.

Yes, Sunday, September 13, 1942, was indeed a bad day for the Allies. The crew of *Esek Hopkins* would never forget the shock and horror of that mournful day.

And that was just the beginning.

CHAPTER 1

A Decision

JOHN D. DODD, KNOWN AS "Jack" to friends and family, was a reliable son, a good brother, a fun uncle. All his nieces and nephews liked him. When children were first exposed to him, they withdrew somewhat into shyness, most likely because he presented a somewhat ominous appearance with his bushy, black, heavy eyebrows. But that was a family trait. His father and both brothers had the same bushy eyebrows. Once his nieces and nephews got to know his friendly personality and his interest in their own affairs and activities, they accepted the eyebrows and they quickly warmed to him. And with considerable irony, his nephews grew up to develop the identical trait.

Jack had a sense of humor that tickled the children. He sometimes carried a little toy or special coin in his pocket that revealed some magic or gag. One time, there was a rumor about his behavior after obtaining his driver's license that intrigued the children. Usually, no family member brought it up, but during one Thanksgiving dinner, his brother Howard dropped it suspiciously, surreptitiously into the conversation. Out of nowhere, Howard offered up, "What was the name of that nasty neighborhood kid who went home with a bloody nose, Jack? Remember? After he was pestering Gladys."

Jack bent over his plate and pushed his peas around, as a slight rubescent change come over his complexion, noticed even by the children. They perked up. This clearly was something interesting they did not know about Uncle Jack.

Mary Hogan Dodd, the clan's perceptive mother, said, "Now, Howard, why bring that up? Never mind."

Gladys, Jack's favorite sister, was never shy and picked up the thread. "His name was Freddie Wilson. He was one of the neighborhood bullies. Jack had just gotten his driver's license and was going to take me for a ride around town. Freddie spied us getting into the car and invited himself to join us. Jack grumbled, but how could he say no? Anyway, he wanted to show off his driving skills. Freddie seemed to like me, and he tried to squeeze into the front seat next to me, but I locked the door. Jack told him he had to ride in the back if he wanted the thrill of seeing Jack drive. We had gone only a few blocks when Freddie got rude and started using some…impolite language. Jack told him to knock it off, but, being the bully Freddie was, he persisted. He referred to Jack as a little punk. That did it. Jack pulled the car off to the side, got out, opened the back door and grabbed Freddie's arm and yanked him out. Freddie was a year older and a little bigger than Jack, but," Gladys paused dramatically, as she scanned the attentive faces of the nieces and nephews, "Uncle Jack did not like being called a punk."

Jack was uncomfortable and looked up. "Do we really need to go on? It's not that interesting."

Gladys ignored him. "So your uncle yelled at Freddie, 'No need to use language like that around my sister,' and he pushed Freddie hard. He fell to the ground after stumbling over some tree roots. Then Freddie jumped up and mumbled something like, 'You asked for it, punk,' and hit Uncle Jack on the side of his face. I wanted to get out of the car to see if Jack was hurt but I was afraid and watched with the door securely locked."

"What did you do, Uncle Jack?" asked Billy, the oldest nephew at the table.

Jack was chewing on a fragment of turkey meat. As all eyes stared at him, he muttered, "I took a swing and got a lucky hit on his nose. He took a swing, I ducked, then I hit him three times real quick, boom, boom, boom."

Gladys jumped in, "You should have seen the look on Freddie's face. He could not believe Jack Dodd was so full of fire. He turned and ran home with a bloody nose. And he never bothered us again." The children gazed now at their Uncle Jack with a new sense of awe and respect.

Jack and his siblings grew up on a peaceful street, in the quiet, southern port town of Baltimore on the Patapsco River, in the beautiful, majestic state of Maryland. Jack had always felt some attachment, some orientation toward the water. Its beauty, its calmness, its serenity somehow enticed him, seduced him. His brother, Bill, felt a similar attraction. This feeling made little sense and was difficult to explain to the unenlightened. Jack had a friend from high school with a small fourteen-foot sailboat—a model known as a Snipe—and they would, during the warm breezy months, go out for sails on the busy Patapsco River, the deep, blue River which oriented the city toward the outside world.

In 1940, as the war in Europe began to infect the world, Jack decided to volunteer for sea duty. After much deliberation and discussions with his brothers and friends, he elected to join the Merchant Marine, largely because it was a shorter route to get to sea compared to joining the US Navy. Six months of studies were required at the Merchant Marine Academy in Kings Point, New York. Graduates were given impressive pairs of khaki fatigues and blue dress uniforms nearly identical to the US Navy outfits. The look was popular with the ladies.

By now, Jack was a handsome young man with his still bushy, black eyebrows, and thick, dark hair that glistened in combed-back waves. He stood at five foot seven and had friendly, sincere brown eyes. His face gleamed with nicely aligned white teeth that promoted a friendly smile, which he used to his advantage whenever required.

Jack's father, William J. Dodd, had been a horseman and had

run the stables for the wealthy stockbroker, Alexander Brown, who established the first American brokerage house in Baltimore. William was a risk-taker and enjoyed gambling and was good at cards. He owned an assortment of fighting roosters to supplement the family income.

Jack's mother, Mary Hogan Dodd, was a second-generation Irish woman eleven years younger than her husband. The family lived in a large, three-story home on Ithaca Street in a middle-class Baltimore neighborhood known as Gwynn Oak. Jack had two older brothers and five older sisters. His oldest sister, May, was old enough to care for Jack as if she were his mother. Jack had a comfortable and enjoyable childhood despite the fact that his father died when Jack was twelve years old.

After attending a Catholic high school, Jack took on several jobs, most recently at a brick plant, to help with the family expenses. He considered college, but with no father to support that effort, he worked instead. Jack was the youngest of the brood and his mother was very protective of her "baby." Little did Jack know how rapidly and profoundly his life would change after he made his decision to jump into the fray.

Jack wrestled with the method and timing of informing his mother of his decision to participate in the war effort. First, he elected to discuss it with the oldest sibling, Howard. Jack held him in high esteem and valued his opinion. He invited Howard to come over on a Sunday morning while their mother was at church with the sisters still living at home.

Howard knew about Jack's decision to join the war effort and was glad he sought advice regarding notification to their mother. Howard was always neatly coiffured and wore a coat, tie, and vest during most of his waking hours. Howard bore a striking resemblance to the famous airman, Howard Hughes, and occasionally had been accosted in public by mistake.

Howard raised his familial bushy eyebrows and threw out some ideas.

"Well, I think you're doing the right thing joining the Merchant Marine," Howard offered. "If Dad were alive, he would be very impressed. And if I were not forty-five years old, I might join you," he said with a chuckle. He continued, "Mother, of course is another story.

She'll be quite upset. The idea of her youngest son going to war will tear her up. And the absence of your income to household expenses...well, you can imagine. She may not bring that up, but you know she will worry."

Jack noted, "The Merchant Marine salary is not bad. It's sixty-five dollars per month. A little less than I bring in now at the brick plant. So, I still can help with household expenses."

"I can chip in a little," Howard suggested. "Bill is still in medical training and with his new baby, he can't help much. But don't worry, we won't let Mother starve."

Jack asked, "Do you think I should present my plans to everyone at the same time or to Mother alone?"

"Don't present it to everyone together," Howard offered. "Our sisters will have a fit in front of Mother. I would find some time alone with Mother and present it to her first. Later, you can discuss it with the sisters. And you had better expect resistance. Think of convincing arguments ahead of time, both for Mother and the girls. I will support you."

"I've got the arguments laid out already," Jack replied.

Howard sat down on the comfortable sofa, crossed his legs, and said, "Okay, let's hear them."

Jack began slowly pacing around the carpeted living room, practicing how he might present the arguments to his mother.

He started, "So, the Merchant Marine is not a war-making service branch, like the Navy or the Army. The merchant mariners work for the owners of the private commercial ships and are just 'delivery boys.' They may get attacked, but they only defend themselves. And Mother knows I've always liked the sea, so it makes sense to get involved in something I enjoy."

Howard nodded in agreement.

Jack continued, "And I will sign up separately for each cruise. So, when I return to port and step off the ship, in theory, I can choose never to go back on any other cruise. It can be a little tricky to get out of the obligation, but it is possible, especially if you have some medical excuse. Each cruise is under a separate contract with the Commerce Department. And it's all volunteer. It's not like the Navy where you sign up for a two-year tour of duty. And the cruises usually last for only a couple of months."

Howard raised the infamous congenital eyebrows again and looked admiringly at his youngest brother. "I did not realize that. Your arguments make good sense."

"Yup. And there is no cost for my six-month training at the Merchant Marine Academy. Money was a big concern of Mother's when I was considering college."

Jack continued pacing and went on. "The Academy offers college-level courses with emphasis on ship maintenance, safety protocols, plotting courses, the physics of propulsion, and the like. After graduation, you get a nice diploma and a uniform and are assigned to a freighter as a deck cadet. I will have little control over my ship assignment or destination. Most ships go to Europe, but some go to South America, Iran, or even Australia. If a deck cadet goes on repeat cruises, studies hard, and passes all the tests, he can advance up the ladder. It's possible to get promoted all the way to captain. They sometimes refer to the captain as the ship's master. Can you imagine me being a sea captain in the Merchant Marine, Howard?"

"I'm glad you have done your homework and thought this through," Howard replied. "And yes, I could imagine you advancing to 'Captain Jack Dodd.' But first, you have to get past Mary Hogan Dodd and your sisters…"

Jack nodded and closed, "And finally, I can argue that I will see the world and learn so much more than I would at some college. And, by joining the Merchant Marine, I will avoid getting drafted into a much more dangerous service branch."

Howard observed, "As I said, I will support you. And don't forget to remind Mother that many American mothers are kissing their sons good-by all over the country these days. She can hardly expect you to remain behind or later get drafted into a service where your risk is higher."

"Thanks, Howard, I really appreciate your support," Jack said.

"Of course. I do have a few suggestions," Howard replied. "One: Pay attention in the classroom and soak up all you can. Your life may depend on it. Two: Treat all your colleagues and mates fairly and don't get caught up in any intrigues. Three: Make Dad proud."

Tears began to collect in Jack's eyes at Howard's last request. "I promise to heed your advice and I will make you all proud, Howard."

"When do you plan on discussing it with Mother?"

"This afternoon. The girls are going to the movies. They wanted me to join them, but I need to take care of this with Mother. That new movie has finally come to Baltimore; *Gone with the Wind.* It's almost four hours long, so that will give me plenty of time with Mother. I can see the movie some other time."

"Fine. Let me know if I can help."

They shook hands and Howard took his leave. Jack watched Howard skip down the porch stairs in his black and white wing-tipped shoes and saunter out to his luxurious midnight-blue Packard sedan.

Not thirty minutes later, Mary Hogan Dodd, and the three daughters, returned from mass.

Jack had set the breakfast table and started cooking sausage patties. Their mother prepared the pancakes. This was the traditional Dodd meal after church.

Gladys, Margaret, and Ginny pestered Jack all through the delicious pancakes and sausage. This time about the new movie. They insisted he join them. But he was adamant with his refusal. As excuses, he offered that he was trying to save money, he needed to prepare for work on Monday, and he needed to wash his clothes. What finally got them to accept his refusal was when he told them he wanted to take his lady friend, Gail, to see the movie, and they had a date next Saturday. They finally obliged, but then they started to tease him about how serious he must be with Gail. Jack was thinking how they never wanted to leave him alone. They always found some reason to pick on him. This was another reason to get out of the house for a few months in the Merchant Marine!

Jack helped with the dishes, then went to his room on the third floor to review all the arguments he would offer to his mother. He listened for the girls to leave. Once he heard them depart, he nervously went down the stairs and found his mother sitting in her favorite rocker in the center of the living room reading the paper.

As he came down the staircase, Mary looked up and said, "Here, Jack, come sit with me for a bit. I think you have something on your mind."

Jack was reminded of how preceptive she was. She knew something was up. And as he looked at her, he noted how lovely his mother was. She had a kind, sweet face and a happy, expressive disposition likely related to her deep Catholic faith. Her hair was nearly all white and she kept it short to display its natural curls. For her age, she had few wrinkles but retained occasional youthful freckles on her smooth skin. Her sky-blue eyes were intelligent and wise.

She remained slender, despite giving birth to eight children and dealing with her husband's death.

Mary seemed to know what was coming. Jack realized he might as well get right to it.

As he walked to the sofa, he said as calmly as possible, "Well, Mom, you know I have been trying to decide how I can best serve my country in this European war we are getting dragged into."

His mother nodded peacefully.

"So, I have decided..." He paused, looking into her intelligent, steady eyes, and wished Howard was there. "Well, I have decided to join the Merchant Marine and help deliver supplies to our friends around the world." Jack felt that was as mild a presentation as he could offer.

She revealed nothing in her eyes. He continued, "The Merchant Marine accepts guys as young as sixteen. I am twenty-two."

"I know, Jack," was all she offered. Then, "You remind me so of your father."

He was not expecting that. A curve ball. He needed to stay on course. He walked around the living room and continued, "I have been accepted at the Merchant Marine Academy at Kings Point, New York."

"I see."

"I will start in January. It's a six-month program. And there's no tuition since they need more recruits for all the new ships under construction," he announced with conviction. "There's no two-year commitment or contract like the Navy. I could walk away after I complete a single cruise. Usually. The cruises typically last only two or three months. And the pay isn't bad. And I can contribute some of it toward household expenses."

His mother replied mournfully, "I don't want you to go…" She suddenly looked very tired. "But I realize this is something you want to do with all your heart. And you feel a duty to your country. Which is wonderful. Your father would be proud. I pray for all my children, but I will pray especially hard for you while you are away. I will offer Sunday mass for you. I want you to come home safely to me."

What a woman. Almost tearfully, Jack replied, "Thanks, Mother. I greatly appreciate your sentiments. I will come home. I promise."

How could he keep that promise?

She knew better and replied, "I wish we all could be so sure. Now I want you to present this plan to your sisters when they get back from the theater."

"Okay, I will," he replied as he walked to his mother who stood and gave him a long, powerful hug.

"I will always love you, son."

"I love you too, Mother." He could not recall if he had ever said that to her before.

The girls would not return from the movie until about 4:00 p.m., so Jack decided to walk down to the local drug store to see who was hanging out at the soda fountain. Walking took longer than the streetcar, but he liked the exercise and wanted time to think. His mother asked him to bring home a quart of milk and a pound of butter.

The drug store was vacant. He made his purchase and started home. He thought about how much easier it had been to tell his mother privately. She took it better than he expected.

When Jack got home, his three sisters had returned from the theater. They were busy talking in the kitchen when he showed up with the milk and butter. They all turned on him together, squawking, "How can you do this to Mother? You are her last son! She needs your support! What did Bill and Howard say? If something happens to you, we will never forgive you!" Obviously, his mother had jumped the gun. She was likely tearful when the sisters arrived home and she told them his plans.

Margaret was the most vocal. She was spouting so fast, fine particles of spittle sprang from her mouth. Finally, their mother told them to calm themselves and sit down.

Jack now had a chance to speak and with a relaxed smile he asked, "So how was the movie? Did the South win this time?"

The joke was not a hit. More squawking.

Then, with conviction, he proceeded to make his points, which he did with improved eloquence after his earlier presentation to their mother.

The sisters barely listened. Finally, Ginny said, "Let's call Howard." This always was a good default position during a family feud.

And they did. Each of the three spoke separately to Howard. As the oldest sibling, Howard seemed to have a soothing, calming effect. But after they hung up, the sisters would not relent, despite Howard's logical and reassuring sentiments. At this point Jack got fed up and decided he did not want to share any more of the afternoon or dinner with them.

He announced, "I'm going to find Monty Dolan and enjoy a quiet meal with him. Mom, see if you can calm them down by the time I get back."

But Margaret would not let him off. "Jack Dodd, look at me! How can you do this to Mother? And us? We rely on you. Who's going to care for the yard and chores around the house? And what are we going to do if you don't come home?"

Margaret had freckles on her lower lip, at which Jack found himself staring with inappropriate amusement. She would not relent.

Finally, Jack felt his face flushing. "Margaret, stop it! You all act as if I am committing some crime or something. I'm not robbing a bank or murdering someone. I'm doing something honorable; I'm serving my country. If you can't see that, tough luck. And if I don't come home, that means I'm dead!"

He slammed the door as he departed.

Margaret turned to the others and burst into tears. She was always the most emotional of the sisters.

"He doesn't get. He just doesn't get it," Margaret sobbed.

Ginny and Gladys went to comfort her. Mary Hogan Dodd had seen it before. Margaret would get over it.

This time Jack decided to take the streetcar for the longer trip to the pool hall in search of his pal, Monty. As the trolley rumbled to a stop, he climbed up the three steps, dropped his Mercury Head dime in the metal coin box and nodded to the conductor. He took the nearest seat on the half-empty trolly. His thoughts digested the day as the electric streetcar rumbled and swayed noisily down the tracks. Regarding the sisters, the afternoon ended in a grumpy stalemate. But he knew they would get over it. They really had no choice. More importantly, Jack had the blessing and acceptance of his wonderful mother. So, on balance, the day ended well.

Jack did make a date to see *Gone with the Wind,* with Gail Robeson on Saturday. He had dated her on and off for about six months. He liked to call her GR. She was about a year older than Jack and they first met when they attended Forest Park High School. GR was a fraction more sophisticated in the sex department. When they first attempted clumsy relations, she supplied the protection. They did not plan to have relations on each date. It was time, and circumstance dependent. Jack knew she went out with other fellows, and she did not expect Jack to see her exclusively. Her short, blond, bouncy hair was the rage in the era. He was not certain if it was dyed. Her eyes were brown and pleasant to gaze into. She was as tall as Jack with long slender legs and shapely hips.

Gail and Jack took a streetcar downtown to Eutaw Street, where the high-end Hippodrome Theatre was located. Tickets were an outrageous fifty cents apiece. During the thirty-minute ride, Jack outlined his plans to Gail. He would likely not see her for the six months while attending the Merchant Marine Academy. As he was speaking, Jack surprised himself when he realized how it sounded like he was setting her up for lovemaking with a sympathy appeal. He even convinced himself that it was totally subconscious. It worked.

Gail liked him. Maybe more than he liked her. She was the one who requested they keep in touch by mail. He agreed. Not completely to his surprise, when he was at sea, it was Gail who aided with his self-rapture.

But even his feelings about Gail would change, along with so many other unpredictable adjustments in his life-experiences on his long and startling war-time journey.

CHAPTER 2

The Academy

JACK REPORTED TO THE STATELY Merchant Marine Academy campus at Kings Point, New York, on the first Friday in January 1942. A freezing cold wind out of the north greeted him and the other candidates.

The world had changed drastically since he decided to join the Merchant Marine three months before. On December 7, 1941—just a month before his arrival on campus—the Japanese Imperial Navy bombed Pearl Harbor and caused massive damage to the United States Pacific Fleet. Five days later, Hitler declared war on the United States. The Atlantic Ocean now became a shooting gallery for German U-boats. Their targets were the merchant ships delivering goods to England and Russia. Whichever ship Jack was assigned to, the Germans would be working hard to sink it. They might as well have painted a big target on the side of each ship.

This new dynamic started working on Jack. And his mother. He thought his sisters would never let him get out of the house. Once war was declared, they put increasing pressure on Jack to stay home. There were several family quarrels. But his mother remained serene and stately and began going to daily mass. Margaret refused to kiss Jack goodbye. His mother gave him a box of writing cards and encouraged him to compose short notes often. Jack gave her a warm hug and agreed to comply. As he walked out the front door, he wondered if he would ever see his family again. What had he gotten himself into?

Once he arrived at the Merchant Marine Academy, he would be out of the pressure-cooker that was his home. But now he would be in a different pressure-cooker; an academic one. He was determined to do well among his 146 classmates.

And so it began.

Jack slowly acclimated himself to the Academy rhythm. Each day started with 6:30 a.m. reveille, then breakfast for all students together at 7:00 a.m. There was a brief prayer before meals. After breakfast, classes began at 8:00 a.m. and continued until noon. After a one-hour lunch break, classes went from 1:00 p.m. to 3:00 p.m. Then students were expected to study in the library, work out at the gym, or engage in one of the intramural sports available.

Jack decided to take up squash, which caused an intense sweaty workout in a finite period of time. Dinner was at 6:00 p.m. followed by study hall until 10:00 p.m. Lights out at 11:00 p.m.

Weekends were open other than optional review classes and tutoring on Saturday mornings.

New York City was less than a two-hour drive from the Academy campus and many students tried to make the journey at least once a month for rest and relaxation. By mid-March, Jack felt comfortable enough with his studies to take off for a weekend with some pals. Ross Engles, Jack's roommate, and two other guys made the trip. They stayed in a cheap hotel in Midtown. With the country on a war footing, there were many military men roaming around New York. Jack and his buddies wore their dress uniforms in hopes of getting special breaks at restaurants and maybe attracting the attention of the opposite sex.

Local New York newspapers had begun to report on the sinking of merchant ships along the East Coast by German U-boats. The sinkings were adding up almost daily. Fireballs from exploding merchant ships were spotted from the shores at night. Debris, oil and bodies were accumulating along the New Jersey beaches and points south. Where was the Navy?

Jack and his colleagues were alarmed by what they were reading in the newspapers.

Clearly, the U-boats were not attacking boats in the middle of the ocean, but rather near ports of departure, where they were easy to locate. At this rate of destruction, there may be no merchant ships left to sail on.

After Jack and his three classmates checked into their hotel in New York, they found an Irish pub a few blocks away. They chose a table in the rear and ordered a round of Guinnesses. A group of three British officers asked if they could join them and pulled up additional chairs. The Brits were full of information and apparently felt a need to talk about it. In no time, Guinness loosened their tongues. Jack and Ross probed the men with many questions. One junior officer named Charlie Black claimed he had been on a ship sunk by a U-boat two months prior.

Jack pumped him. "Really, Charlie? What kind of ship were you on?"

Charlie took a long draw on the Guinness. "Are you lads buying the next round?" Jack nodded.

"Well, I was on a British ship with the unlikely name of *Cyclops.* She was a twenty-year-old freighter with no cannons or guns. We had nine thousand tons of general cargo on board.

We were alone and headed to Halifax, Nova Scotia. It was about an hour past sunset, and we were within a hundred miles of our destination when the first torpedo struck. No one spotted the U-boat or the pecker trail—that's what we call the torpedo bubble trail—in the dark. It was a complete surprise. Ironically, the damn thing struck the bow, just under the single eye painted next to the name *Cyclops.*"

He paused as the next round was placed on the table by an attractive redhead. She had a low-cut blouse which encouraged generous tips. Irish music began thumping in the background.

Charlie continued, "I don't think *Cyclops* would have sunk

from the damage done to the bow. No doubt the bastard U-boat captain reached the same conclusion. Within five minutes, a second torpedo struck just aft of the superstructure, exactly where the engine room was. That Kraut captain was a smart devil and a good shot. The ship started listing within minutes. Many mates were lost below. Fortunately, we were able to launch all four lifeboats. The Krauts turned on their searchlight and watched us climb into the lifeboats. They could not have been two hundred yards away. We feared they would machine-gun us. We were totally defenseless.

Eighty-seven of one hundred twenty souls were lost that night."

Jack shook his head in disgust. "How did you manage to get to land?"

Charlie nodded and responded after a gulp of cool stout. "The time-interval between the two torpedo hits gave us opportunity to send repeated SOS signals, which were picked up by a destroyer a few hours away. They located us before noon the next day. We were lucky the Krauts did not wait around and take a shot at the destroyer."

A second British officer, Ralph Chichester, chimed in. "My father fought in the navy in the first war. In those days, the U-boat captains would come to the surface a short distance from the freighters and slowly approach. The Germans would announce in English they were going to torpedo the ship and gave thirty minutes for all passengers to get into lifeboats. Then they would back up and torpedo the ship until she sank. It was more of a gentleman's game. Not this time around. And now they almost always attack at night."

Ralph took a big swig of the Guinness to keep himself going. "I, too, was on a ship attacked by the bloody Krauts not five months ago. By a miracle, they were not able to sink us. We were in a convoy in the Mediterranean Sea taking supplies to Malta. There were about twenty ships in the convoy. Shortly after noon, a U-boat came to the surface about five hundred yards on our port side. He had the audacity to make his appearance in the middle of all the ships on a lazy, sunny afternoon. The escorts were on the perimeter of the convoy and did not immediately see the threat. He must have been out of torpedoes. The U-boat crew quickly scampered on deck and manned their 105mm cannon. That's a powerful weapon; never underestimate it. I was standing amidships looking over the side with the second cook, enjoying the nice weather. As soon as we saw the U-boat, we yelled up to the bridge to warn the officers and they sounded the battle alarm. I was a fireman and already near my station. The German crew was quick to load the gun, take aim, and fire. Their speed surprised us. That was the last thought that passed through the cook's mind. Somehow, the shell struck the cook right in the head—blew it right off."

The Americans gazed at him in disbelief. Chichester nodded. "It's true. Standing right next to me. I will never forget it. There was a shrieking, whistling sound and a kind of wind and shock wave, then a snapping, thunking noise as warm matter splattered on my right side. All in an instant. At first, it was unclear what happened. Reflexively, I jerked my head and body to the left. When I turned to look at the cook, his headless body was flat on the deck, with blood squirting from his neck all over the place. In four columns. I threw up and ducked below the side. My impulse was to speak to him, but there was no 'him' to speak to. I was frozen kneeling next to him. Then I crapped in my pants. It scared me like nothing else in my life."

Jack was stunned and speechless. Horrible thoughts flashed through his mind. Ross Engles was the first to speak. "So, so… there was no explosion?"

Chichester gulped down another substantial swig and replied. "Nope. After hitting the cook, the shell must have passed through our rigging and by the mast and did not strike another thing. It likely splashed out in the ocean somewhere. That shell had a singular mission. It was God's will. I was just two feet from him. Everything was numb. The next thing I recall was a huge explosion. The miserable Krauts had gotten off a second shot which struck the third level of the superstructure. A fire started. This time,

I experienced a different kind of shock. The explosion numbed my hearing and added a new level of fright. A colleague ran by me and stopped. "Oh, Christ,' was all he could say, and he helped me up. I felt more dead than alive but, with his help, stumbled to my fire station on the deck level. Do you want to hear the details?"

"Whatever you feel like saying," said Ross quietly.

"Well, since you lads are buying, I'll have another round and keep talking," he laughed nervously.

"It was lucky I was a fireman. One of my buddies first arrived at the hose and was unwinding it. You can imagine what a mess I was. Vomit on my shirt, crap running down my legs. He was not sure what happened to me, but he took the hose, and turned it on low and sprayed me off. I signaled to my backside, and he understood, and put the nozzle inside my belt and let it rinse, until the third shot from the Krauts. This one hit the side of the ship just a notch above the water line. The explosion knocked both of us down on the deck. Now I was dizzy and could hear only ringing in my ears. I may have been unconscious for a time. Not sure. My next recollection was two mates lifting me off the deck. Then out. I woke up in a sick-room bunk. I was in some kind of shock state, but no 'serious' permanent injuries. At least not to my body." There was a pause as everyone took a drink. Jack spoke next. "What happened to the German sons of bitches?"

"Our gunners got to their weapons by the time the Germans got off their third shot and our boys started firing our 20mm guns. They claimed they hit the Krauts on deck and struck the con tower, but the U-boat submerged and was never seen again. Our fireman got the two fires out after about an hour. The hole on the port side was six feet in diameter, I was told. But they got it repaired in half a day. The cook's headless body was wrapped and after a short ceremony with the full crew, slid overboard into the ocean that evening. I was not permitted to attend. Just as well. Four other crew members were seriously injured, but recovered. Even the captain got some shrapnel in his leg."

Ross said, "What a mess. I guess the message is, never give the Germans an even break. They come at you with everything. We got to give it back with everything." Everyone nodded.

The Irish beat throbbed in the background. Jack took a long slug of the Guinness to calm his brain. Scrambled thoughts tumbled through his cerebrum. What was he thinking? Maybe his sisters were right. This was war; a first-class horror show; a trip through hell, not a joy ride. The merchant mariners may be "delivery boys," and not attack ships. But the Germans did not bother to make that distinction. To the Krauts, they were navy men and fair game. And our ships were carrying valuable cargo to German enemies. Too late to bail now. Jack was all in, like it or not. He thought about his lovely mother. Back in Baltimore, she and his sisters were probably reading the newspaper reports. He had not written in five days. Better send a note soon and tell the family all is good. Maybe these ship sinkings would stop before he got an assignment. Or maybe there would be no ships to go out on. Maybe.

The third British officer now got into it. His name was Mickey Aldridge.

"You see what the bloody Germans are doing, don't you? They are daring the US Navy to come out and attack. They keep sinking ships off your shores to draw out the Navy destroyers. Then, they will sink all the ships in the Navy. And all the merchant ships. War over. That bastard U-boat Admiral Donitz is no dummy. They say the new U-boats can sail for six thousand miles without refueling. That's across the ocean and back. For those with less range, they park tanker-subs in the mid-ocean called 'milk cows.' Some sense of humor, those Krauts… 'milk cows.' Then yesterday I was talking to a tugboat captain in New York Harbor. He was on the night shift docked at the terminal. Just looking out over the harbor. He swears that a U-boat popped up three hundred yards from his docked tug."

Jack yelled above the music, "I don't believe it. No German could be that stupid."

Aldridge retorted, "Stupid, is it? Don't you know there are no guns in the harbor. And only two destroyers, both docked. And they probably have no ammunition. And even if they did have ammunition, it would take two hours to wake up the crew and cast off. The tug captain swears he saw a swastika on the sub con with his binoculars. He could see three officers pointing and gazing at the lights. They must have thought the Americans were all nuts. Which they are!"

"Hey, wait a minute," Jack objected. "Don't make cracks like that."

Aldridge replied, "Why not? Who's in charge in New York? Why are all the lights blazing? Those guys in the U-boats can see the outlines of merchant ships sailing out of port. You might as well send the Germans an invitation. And there are no nets in the harbor. I believe the guy. He said they submerged after fifteen minutes. But I don't know if anyone else saw them. There was nothing in the papers."

The Americans at the table shook their heads and ordered another round.

Charlie chimed in. "It is not that far-fetched. We all know there must be a dozen U-boats out there, judging by the number of merchant ships they're sinking. It would not surprise me if some daring captain came into the harbor under water and popped up for a view in the dark. Something to brag about back in Germany. Useful propaganda showing why the Americans will lose the war. But I will tell you one thing: those Krauts must have damn good, accurate charts to pull a stunt like that." With grimaces, they all nodded.

Were it not for the four beers, Jack's heart would have been pounding. Still, he was distraught, dejected, and depressed. He had had enough for one evening. He bid his compatriots and the Brits farewell and headed back to the hotel room. The others decided to stay and watch the ladies.

The vile groaning of the ice-cold metal forced him to grit his teeth and tighten all the muscles in his non-athletic frame. In total darkness, he gasped as he inhaled the repulsive odor and texture of sulfur, oil and steam. He ignored the urge to vomit. Perspiration gathered on the skin of his face and arms. He was overwhelmed with abject fear. In the distance, a glowing visage emerged from the shadows. It was a hideous, headless human figure, with four columns of blood spurting and pulsing upward from the base of his naked neck. It walked with determination directly toward him. Then, a stupendous explosion filled the black space with intense light, heat, and pressure. His hearing was numbed as he was hurled backward through the thick, hot, putrid air. He was nearly sightless with burned eyes and skin. He seemed to be on his back surrounded by frigid liquid and screeching, oscillating metallic vibrations. He could barely respond or move. Cold engulfed him. He gasped for breath, but inhaled a foul toxic liquid and coughed and sputtered as he tried to sit up. As the freezing liquid surrounded him, he struggled to stand. The visage reappeared and strangely bowed to him…directing bitter-cold, pulsing, fresh red blood onto his face and torso.

So, this was hell.

His body was wet, his head pounding, his breathing rapid. Jack rubbed his weary eyes and collected his wits. Other people were in the room…in a hotel…in New York. Okay. What a dream…an absolute horror show.

Light peaked around the drawn blinds. He stumbled into the bathroom and evacuated his full bladder. A shower: that would bring back reality and freshen him up. It did.

His compatriots slowly stirred as Jack dressed. He announced to no one as he exited the room, "See you guys downstairs."

The lobby was already buzzing with businessmen, military guys, attractive females…some in the arms of service men, some alone. He picked up a copy of the *New York Times* and chose a comfortable chair near the perimeter to oversee all the action. The headline read: "German Forces Penetrate Deep into Russia." Jack had been hoping the article would distract him from his headache when a more interesting distraction appeared. His peripheral vision detected a feminine shape just above the top edge of the newspaper. He gazed up. An attractive woman, in a colorful shirt-waist dress, but with too much lipstick, looked down at him seductively. "Would you like some company, soldier?"

Jack thought she certainly gets right to the point. He quipped, "You want to talk about the German invasion of Russia?" She smiled, then sat down on the adjacent sofa, crossed her slender legs, and looked into his brown eyes. She purred, "I can think of more interesting 'invasions.'" She tilted her head a notch and slightly raised her left brow as she said "invasions."

Clever girl, thought Jack. *She might be interesting to get to know in different circumstances.* Thoughts swirled through his throbbing head. *Some day she will probably get married and have nice kids. Too bad she has to survive like this in these distressing times. He looked through her eyes. What sights? What emotions? What kind of childhood? Who were her parents? Her friends? How long could she do this? Does she care? Do the sun and the stars above care? But God will forgive her. If she asks. Does it matter? To her? To anyone? After all, we are biologic creatures. She serves some purpose. She may be good at what she does. If this is what she needs to do for survival, who can blame her?*

A loud car horn blared just outside the window of the hotel, startling both of them. Was she simply another machine– going through the mechanics of sex– another worker in another type of factory—going through the motions, day in and day out? Another cog in the human factory?

He thought of his sisters.

For some reason he was inclined to continue the conversation.

"I drank too much beer last night and I have a bit of a headache this morning," he offered as an excuse.

Like any true professional, she had a retort. "I know a sure cure for that headache. Want me to tell you about it?" She smiled. She had nice teeth.

Jack felt his pulse quicken. How do women do this? How was he going to get out of this? Did he want to get out?

She leaned back on the sofa. The buzz in the lobby continued. She stared at him. She started swinging her leg slowly, rhythmically. Perhaps she liked the challenge of resistance.

On the far side of the lobby, Jack saw his three compatriots exit the elevator. *Deus ex machina.* Jack stood, perhaps a bit too quickly, too rudely. He put the newspaper on the table and announced, "It is nearly ten o'clock in the morning, and I have not yet had breakfast and my buddies and I need a bite to eat."

She remained in a relaxed repose. "Too bad. One can have breakfast anytime. But an hour with me may be unforgettable." With a wink, she said, "Maybe next time."

Jack could not hold himself back. "Say, what is your name?"

"Melody. A never-ending melody."

Jack grinned. "Of course. Yes, of course." Soft siren music of "Offenbach's Barcarolle" began to drift through his mind.

Jack turned and walked toward the front entrance. His pals saw Jack end his engagement with the attractive set of legs. They followed him as he kept moving toward the hotel entrance and onto the street in search of a restaurant to satisfy at least one of his urges. The music played and teased.

Trotting behind, Ross said, "Hey, who was the chick? Maybe she wants to join us for breakfast. How do you attract these broads, Dodd?"

Jack responded without much thought. "Just my uniform, I guess. She doesn't want to join us." Other more immediate basic needs were on her mind, he thought. Just then Jack caught a movement in the periphery of his vision at the hotel front door. One of the hotel managers was escorting Melody out. She did not resist and stepped onto the street. She spotted Jack with his pals not fifty feet away. She stopped and looked at Jack. He sized her up again as she stood there, silently taunting, tempting in the clear morning sunlight.

Ross was standing next to Jack and said, "If she just got escorted out of the lobby, that means she's a pro. Let's march."

She waited, staring at Jack. He took a step in her direction. Ross grabbed his arm. "Not a good idea, pal."

The music played in his ears. What made her so enticing? Was it her unspoken accumulated knowledge? His mind explored. How would she manage in a different, more sophisticated setting? Did she speak the king's English? How would she be perceived in front of the captain? Or his mother? She maintained her gaze. The Melody persisted. Ross grasped his arm tightly and pulled. The other two mates moved him along. He turned back one more time. She was gone.

They found a busy neighborhood restaurant within two blocks and quickly placed their orders. The four men seemed fascinated with this woman named Melody. Had Jack set something up? No. Was Jack listening? No. Or had "Barcarolle" taken over? Yes. Once the bacon, eggs and hot cakes arrived, they got off the topic of the broad and switched over to the frightening conversation with the Brits the night before and their headaches this morning. Jack told them about his nightmare. They thought and analyzed, trying to find a silver lining from the depressing news about the U-boats swarming around the East Coast, the sinking of the *Cyclops*...and the dream of the headless deck cadet. The only tiny bit of good news they could come up with was that it was possible to survive a torpedo attack. A small comfort. Everyone agreed. Small comfort. Meanwhile, the music played on; the tune would not leave his psyche.

The curriculum at the Academy was rigorous, but Jack adjusted himself to the studies and did well, finishing in the upper third of his class. He made friends and acquaintances with many of his diverse classmates.

The one exception was a rather crude character from Chicago, one George Nowakowski. On the first day, he let it be known to all that he did not like to be called George. He preferred—no demanded—the moniker "Ski." He grew up on the tough side of Chicago and seemed to be angry with everyone. His grim facial expression was not particularly conducive to encouraging friendships. Ski struggled through the academics and at one point, Jack helped him with some course-plotting exercises. But Ski was grateful to no one and developed few friendships.

After class one day, there was a buzz of excitement in the student union building.

Newspapers were torn up and scattered on the floor with cadets yelling and whooping. Jack arrived there for study hall because of its quiet environment. He saw Ross in the middle of the mayhem staring at the front page of a newspaper and ran up to him.

"What's going on?" Jack yelled above the racket and chatter.

"Unbelievable," responded Ross as he tilted the headlines toward Jack. "We bloody bombed Tokyo. Look at this. Some guy named Dolittle flew sixteen B-25 bombers off an aircraft carrier and attacked Tokyo on April 18. We finally delivered a return surprise attack on Tokyo. Unbelievable!"

The country was aroused and for days, nothing else was talked about. After months of negative news, our armed forces finally punched the lousy Japs in the nose. All the men at the academy were perked up and more positive. The US was no longer just a punching bag.

Then, two weeks before graduation, Jack got involved in a little incident. By chance, he and Ski were sitting across from each other at lunch in the cafeteria. The students around them were talking about the fairer sex. Jack commented that he always liked to be nicely dressed when going out on a date. For some reason, this irritated Ski, and he pushed his tray against Jack's, splashing coffee on Jack's clean uniform. Jack jumped up, picked up his coffee cup and threw the remnants in Ski's face. Ski wiped his face, jumped up and approached Jack, who backed away from the table. Ski was three inches taller than Jack and outweighed him by forty pounds. This would not be an even match. That neighborhood bully, Freddie Wilson, flashed through Jack's mind. In his DNA, Jack had an Irish temper and did not like bullies, and he now determined to stand his ground, no matter the odds against him. They both put their fists up. Ski took the first swing. Jack ducked and the big fist grazed the left side of Jack's head as he leaned to the right. Without standing, Jack thrust forward with all his strength and slammed his right shoulder into Ski's midsection, pushing him among the chairs as they both fell to the floor. By this time two instructors ran over, and the other students wrestled to separate the fighters.

Fortunately, no one was seriously injured.

There was a hearing by the Board of Discipline the next day and based on the many eyewitness accounts, no formal charges were made. Both men were reprimanded and given demerits. This was just below the most severe punishment, dismissal from the Academy. They would be allowed to graduate.

A number of interesting outcomes followed the altercation. The accepted consensus was that Ski started the fight. This was of no benefit to his already sullen reputation. Jack, on the other hand, took on an aura of gallantry for having the audacity to take on the big lug. Jack did not dwell on the topic when it came up for discussion among his classmates. He blew it off as a minor misunderstanding.

But inside, Jack realized he could have been seriously injured if the fight had gone on.

And deep down, his troubled conscience recognized that he had already violated one of the promises he had made to Howard: 'Don't get caught up in any intrigues.' He wasn't even on board a ship yet. He must be more careful. All these geared-up, potent young men cramped into the small space of a ship, could ignite like a tinder box with a short fuse. He promised himself nothing like this would happen again.

Unfortunately, he was wrong.

CHAPTER 3

A New Home

AFTER COMPLETION OF HIS STUDIES and graduation from the Merchant Marine Academy, Jack was ordered to report to Hoboken, New Jersey, on June 6, 1942. His first assignment was on the Liberty Ship SS *Esek Hopkins.* This was a newly built vessel from the Fairfield Shipyard of the Bethlehem Steel Corporation in Baltimore. How ironic, he thought, his first experience in the coming challenge would be aboard a ship built in his hometown. He hoped this represented some sort of mystical connection. A good omen.

As he walked toward the dock, his eyes gazed in the distance for the first time on his new home away from home. The *Esek Hopkins* appeared vast in her four-hundred-forty-foot length and was all gray, but rather ungainly, with three large masts and multiple guns spouting fore and aft. Each mast seemed entangled with confusing, innumerable cables and pullies. In the center of the ship was a large, four-story, house-like superstructure, where the helm and most of the crew's quarters were located. The ship was launched on April 27, 1942, after which she was outfitted, tested, and the interior completed by the middle of May. She had been successfully operated and satisfied all the standards required by the Navy. She was as new as new could be. She had never sailed before, and the paint was fresh and clean with no signs of rust.

Squawking sea gulls glided in circles above as Jack approached the gray monster ship. Between the pier and the hull, he noticed the ubiquitous flotsam consisting of bobbing bottles, a blue shirt, fragments of straw and leaves and one dead bird, as gentle breezes encouraged the debris to collect. The words *Esek Hopkins* were clearly visible in white as they wrapped around the curved stern from the port to the starboard side. Printed below, in smaller letters, was the port, *Baltimore.* He noted the rudder post and the massive rudder itself which projected up about four feet out of the water. During his studies, Jack had learned that the single propeller on these Liberty Ships had four blades and was eighteen feet in diameter. But here, the tips of two of the four blades were visible above the waterline as the empty ship sat high in the water. He realized that when the *Esek Hopkins* was fully loaded, all this would be completely buried in the sea.

He looked up higher, above the railing, and the most prominent feature was a single large cannon, pointed aft and surrounded by a wide gun tub. This was a five-inch cannon used for long-range shots at airplanes and distant surface vessels. He had learned at the Academy that it could fire an exploding fifty-pound projectile as far as six miles. On each side of the stern were another pair of gun tubs, each containing a three-inch cannon that also was used against attacking aircraft and surface targets at distances of up to four miles. Just forward of these guns were two smaller tubs, each occupied with a single barrel, 20mm, Swiss-made Oerlikon machine gun. He had learned that the bullets for these guns were about one and a half inches in diameter and seven inches long. Even from his position on the shore, Jack could tell the guns were impressive.

They had two C-shaped steel shoulder bars. A gunner stood with his shoulders strapped to the bars and by moving his body left and right could aim the weapon. There was a circular wire device mounted at eye level with progressively smaller concentric rings. This aided the gunner in acquiring a target. Jack had paid strict attention during his training and decided these were the weapons he wanted to man during combat. They were most useful as short-range antiaircraft guns but could also be used to shoot at submarines on the surface. Jack was fascinated by these impressive killing machines. He knew that the operation of these weapons was the duty of the Navy Armed Guards on board. Since war was declared, the US Navy now supplied about twenty-five Navy Armed Guards to each merchant ship. The guards were in charge of firing and maintaining all the guns and cannons. Nevertheless, he made up his mind he would learn to fire these devices to participate in defending his vessel. He would not sit back, and watch things happen. He was determined to learn how to shoot the 20-caliber machine guns, by hook or by crook.

He could not help smiling as his imagination flirted with the vision of himself aiming and firing these beautiful, powerful weapons. He saw the fully loaded ship plowing through the blue shimmering waves surrounded by swarming bombers and fighters, her guns blasting away incessantly to protect her men and cargo. He would be at one of the machine guns, knocking attackers from the sky in droves. After they swept the enemy aside and arrived safely in port, cheering crowds and waving flags would welcome them. Heros one and all. The local mayor would pin metals on each crew member. Celebrations for days. Newspaper photos and interviews with the local press corps. He could barely wait for the initiation to begin.

He continued his stroll along the ship as fictive visions continued and flickered; pretty girls passing out flowers and toasts in all the taverns and restaurants. What a time they would have. Everyone back home would be envious of his military experience and world-travel status.

As he continued his walk forward, he observed the smooth, welded steel plates with no rivets. Next were two large lifeboats suspended on davits and tucked in and ready to be extended over the side and dropped in the sea on short notice. Even though as a deck cadet, he would be responsible for the maintenance and launching of the lifeboats, he paid little attention to them at this point, assuming he would never be in a situation where he might need to use one.

As he looked up at the superstructure housing, he noted two

more gun tubs with 20mm machine guns that were adjacent to the bridge, and one level above it. Another pair were positioned on the starboard side. Next was a long-suspended stairway hanging from the side at forty-five degrees. He noticed two officers engaged in a discussion at the top. He would have time to meet them later. For now, he wanted to continue his external tour. After all, for the next several weeks he would be seeing only the inside of this ship.

He looked up at the second mast, immediately in front of the helm station. There were multiple arms, cables, and blocks hanging from the top through a series of pullies. The purpose of the masts on board was to act as cranes to lower and remove supplies from the five large storage holds. The holds were about the size of a basketball court and were twenty-eight feet in height. Vast quantities of goods could be stowed in these enormous chambers.

As he proceeded forward toward the bow of the ship, he again saw the name *Esek Hopkins* painted high up on the side in white letters. Just above the name, there were positioned three more gun-tubs on the deck. The forward one had another three-inch antiaircraft cannon. The next two gun-tubs contained additional 20mm Oerlikon machine guns. Just forward of the name, he saw a large E-shaped anchor hanging from the side. Below the anchor was a vertical line of numbers. These started at zero at the level of the flat bottom of the hull and proceeded upward at one-foot intervals, indicating how deep the vessel sat in the water. As Jack looked down at the current level, it was at the eleven-foot mark. The ship was essentially empty and sitting high. He then tracked the numbers up to just below the anchor where the highest number was thirty. If the water level was at thirty feet, the ship was completely loaded. He had learned at the Academy that fully loaded ships were more stable in rough seas. The greater the mass inside, the lower was the center of gravity, which increased stability. As he stood gazing up at the thirty-foot level, he realized that with a fully loaded ship in rough conditions, the seas would easily wash over the forward deck. Hmm, he thought, not a good time to be on deck without a lifeline.

Jack was pleased with the clean, new ship to which he was assigned. His home for weeks at sea. She looked vast, healthy, powerful and surprisingly dangerous for a merchant ship. She appeared to be seaworthy and up to her task. He found it difficult to comprehend how a torpedo could penetrate the steel hull and sink such a vast ship. But maybe he was fooling himself.

Now it was time to get on board and meet some of his colleagues. He walked back toward the center of the vessel and looked up as he climbed the three dozen stairs to get on board for the first time. As he climbed, he counted in his head the number of guns available to kill an enemy. There were four large antiaircraft cannons, one forward, and three aft. As for the 20mm Oerlikon machine guns; he counted two aft, four amidships and two forward. Twelve weapons in all. Not bad for a Merchant Marine ship. He could not wait to get his hands on the 20mm.

As he got to the top of the stairs, the two officers he had seen earlier were standing next to the mast and pointing down into the hold. He approached them and introduced himself with a pleasant smile. As Jack looked at the stripes on the taller officer's sleeve, he realized he was speaking to the ship's Captain.

Captain Edward J. Gleason extended his hand and gave a hearty shake. "Pleased to meet you, Deck Cadet Jack Dodd." Jack immediately liked the Captain, who paid attention to Jack's name and rank. He even pronounced the last name correctly. So many folks said Dabbs or Dobbs or Dodds or some other iteration. The other officer was Second Mate Mark Williams, who then grasped Jack's hand. Jack was proud to announce that he and the *Esek Hopkins* were both from Baltimore, although Jack was a bit older. All had a good chuckle. Williams suggested that Jack walk around the deck and familiarize himself with the ship. He should then report to the second deck, look up Chief Mate Bruce Cockrell, and get his room assignment and duty roster. Williams wondered where Jack's gear was. Jack informed him that he had spent the night at a local hotel and would get his gear on board later that afternoon. The Captain smiled and told Jack there was no hurry since they likely would not depart from Hoboken for a few days. This would give the crew time to study the boat and get to know each other and the Navy Armed Guards.

The Captain added, "Dodd, congratulations, you are the first crewmen on board. But there is no door prize. Nice to have you as a deck cadet on the *Esek Hopkins* for her first voyage."

The Captain seemed pleasant and straight-forward. No frills, but no nonsense either. As Jack would learn, he was correct in his assessment of the master of the ship.

Jack located the chief mate, Bruce Cockrell, seated in the mess hall reviewing some paperwork. Jack noted that all the chairs and tables were bolted to the floor on sturdy steel posts, an indicator of anticipated rough seas ahead. Jack introduced himself and shook the chief mate's large, powerful hand. Bruce had a passive, neutral face, but a large muscular frame which could likely smash any adversary into a pulp. Jack wondered what it would take to set him off. Bruce searched the manifest and located Jack's name.

He looked at Jack and with a chuckle declared, "Well, Mr. Dodd, it appears you are on the right ship. Congratulations, you passed your first test. In addition, you are the first deck cadet to arrive. Would you like to see our magnificent accommodations?"

The smell of fresh paint surrounded them as they walked down two flights of stairs and along a corridor with small rooms on either side. The Chief chose one at random and Jack peeked in. The room was tiny and had two stacked bunks for four crew members. The steel-framed bunks were bolted to the floor. Small boxes were under the bunks for storage. One small chest of drawers was nailed against the wall. The walls were painted a dingy green tint. One small round port hole offered a modicum of natural light to the otherwise dismal scene. Jack decided not to make a wise crack but instead nodded with a non-committal, "Um-hm."

The Chief looked Jack up and down and commented, "Mr. Dodd, you seem like a nice lad and since you are the first on board, I will give you a small opportunity. Up one flight, there is a closet where we store paper supplies. We are one bed short for our crew, so we were able to squeeze a single bunk in the closet. So, if you would like the only "private stateroom" on board, other than the Captain's, I am happy to offer it to you. Sometimes it pays to be early."

Jack thought for a second, then turned down the offer. "I think I would like to meet some interesting characters while sailing across the ocean. Not so easy when bunking alone. I want the complete experience."

Cockrell chuckled. "Up to you, lad. But don't come back crying to me. Sometimes the snoring of three roommates can wake a dead fish. And if you would like one bit of advice, I suggest you take a lower bunk. When we are in the middle of the ocean, there is less swaying in the heavy seas when you are down low."

"Thanks, I appreciate that," Jack replied with a smile. "Any other suggestions for a first-time deck cadet?"

"Well," he offered, "you only get one storage box under the bunk for personal belongings. Pack your things and place it under your head, not your feet. Get a lock for the box. Sometimes things can disappear. When your bunk mate above you shows up, make arrangements where he can step up to get on top. You don't want his stinky feet in your face."

"Many thanks. Is it ok to call you Bruce?"

"No. Just call me 'Chief,'" Bruce replied. "A good rule for deck mates is not to become too familiar with the officers. Don't forget, you guys are the low men on the totem pole. And remember this: Captain Gleason and I run a tight ship. We don't tolerate any insubordination. Follow the rules and you will do fine."

Chief Cockrell then led Jack into his small office two decks above. There, he went over the duty roster and some other logistical issues with Jack. He informed him that he was fortunate to be on a

Liberty Ship with Captain Gleason. Bruce related that he had sailed with Gleason twice before, and the Captain was an excellent skipper. He knew his business and was fair and reasonable.

Jack asked the Chief, "Can I look at the crew manifest? I was wondering if any of my classmates from the Academy were assigned to the *Esek Hopkins*."

"No reason not to. You will eventually meet everyone on board," as he handed Jack the three sheets of paper.

Jack ran through the names. He recognized two names of classmates and one other when he got to the "Ns."

"Ugg," escaped from his throat.

"What is it?" asked the Chief.

"Oh, well, nothing," Jack murmured.

"Young man, I am your Chief. I am the first officer below the Captain. You do not want to cross me or deceive me in any way. If I find out you are hiding something, there will be hell to pay. Me and the Captain are the two most important people on this boat, and you had better be straight with both of us. Clear?"

Jack again thought of his brother, Howard's, advice. Then he replied, "Yes, sir. Well, sir, there are three of my classmates on this ship. Two I know and get along with fine. The third is George Nowakowski from Chicago. He and I got into a disagreement at the Academy." Jack stopped there.

The Chief bored into Jack's eyes with an intensity Jack was not acquainted with. "I think there is more—what else." Jack realized this man had experience leading men of all kinds and there was no sense being on the wrong side of him from the outset. So, Jack told him the story of the altercation at the Academy.

The Chief sat back in his chair. "Not that big a deal. Happens all the time. Maybe even more often on board a ship at sea where, for weeks, no one can escape for relief. This Ski guy sounds like a bully. I need that kind of information. I am glad you shared it with me. Keep your nose clean, Dodd, and you and I will get along fine."

Ultimately, Jack was relieved he had honestly unburdened himself with this information. But he was not comfortable with Ski on board the ship. Now, every time they crossed paths, some bad commerce would pass between them. Meals, work on deck, visits to shore. This new complication, along with all the other uncertainty of being a U-boat target, would be a constant source of anxiety. How many more stresses would add up on this voyage?

The Chief seemed to read Jack's mind. "You are wishing you were on another ship. Or that he was."

Jack nodded, "There will probably be many times we will bump into each other. If he wants to make trouble, there is nothing I can do."

The Chief frowned, "I am not so sure about that. Maybe I can help you. That is, if you are interested."

"Sure, what do you mean?"

Chief Cockrell started, "Boxing is a popular sport on many Merchant Marine ships. It seems to help relieve the crew tension. I used to do a little boxing on previous cruises. I got pretty good at it. So, I can offer you some tips if you get in a jam."

Jack said, "Please go ahead. I have only been in one short fist fight a few years ago."

"We are going to assume you are defending yourself, ok? Someone pushes you or threatens you. The first thing you should do is make fists. And make sure your thumb is on the outside of your fingers—not inside; otherwise, you will break your thumb on first contact. Second, crouch down spread your feet apart to give you good balance. Fists up, head down, feet apart. Third, plan on ducking a lot. Bob and weave. Watch your opponent carefully. Most people are right-handed and lead with their right fist. But some guys will faint with their left hand and move their left foot forward. That will throw you off guard. Then they will pull their right hand back, step forward with their right foot to add momentum and take a wide swing. If they land a solid punch, you are done. Anticipate this and duck. Then as you duck, charge forward before he recovers his balance and either ram your shoulder into his belly or drive a right uppercut into his belly with upward force directed at the solar plexus. If you happen to break his ribs, he is out of commission. At the very least you will knock the air out of his lungs."

The Chief had Jack stand up to give a demonstration. For a few minutes, Jack practiced bobbing and making uppercuts. He felt a little ridiculous but felt it was important to gain some experience from this knowledgeable fighter.

Cockrell continued, "You always want to keep a fight short. Less than fifteen seconds. You do not want a ten-round boxing match. You will get crushed. Ideally, you want to land one good punch on the face and hope that ends the fight. The best place to strike is a solid blow to the nose. If this punch does not knock him down, you did not hit hard enough. But even a mild blow to the nose will daze him. The nose has lots of pain nerves and blood vessels. Blood will fly all over the place, and guys do not like the sight of their own blood. The second-best spot to hit is on the cheekbone. A solid hit here may fracture the bone, which is very painful and causes lots of bleeding. He will swallow or spit out the blood. Again, most guys quit here. The third best place to strike is the lower jaw. This will usually knock out a few teeth and may fracture the jawbone. It is painful and bloody, who wants to see their teeth scattered on the floor? Don't waste time with body blows. This takes too much time and exposes you to head-punches. If you land a solid punch to the head on one of those three spots, the fight will be over quickly."

"Great information, Chief. Thank you. Any other advice?'

"Yes, do not start a fight. If people see you start a fight, they will bear witness against you, and you will be held responsible for any damage to the person or surroundings. And if you knock a guy down, don't walk away until you are certain the guy is not going to get up and continue. And if he has pals around, consider that they may attack you. Keep your fists up and stay in fighting stance as you look left and right."

Jack nodded thoughtfully. "It is obvious you speak from experience."

"As I said, I used to box on other merchant ships. But that was a controlled situation with a referee, and we wore boxing gloves. What we are talking about here is bare fist fighting. More painful and dangerous. That is why it is so important to get in the first punch. Incidentally, the Captain forbids boxing on his ships. Although it can be entertaining for the crew and lets off steam, he wants no part of it. And if some guy gets in the habit of quarreling on board, he will throw them in the brig. I hope that helps, Dodd."

"Yes, sir, thanks very much. And believe me, I don't want any trouble."

"I believe you; for now. And I will keep an eye on this Ski character. Now, you might as well collect your gear and get settled in your room. Then start to explore the vessel. She is new and beautiful. Learn every square inch. She is your home for the next few weeks. And don't bother to ask the destination. Even if I knew, I could not tell you. All right, Dodd, get out of here." Obligingly, Jack jumped out of his seat and saluted.

As Jack went back on deck and down the boarding ladder to pick up his gear from the nearby hotel, his mind was digesting all the issues facing him. On the positive side of the ledger, he would enjoy the benefits of a newly manufactured ship. And Captain Gleason and Chief Cockrell seemed like decent guys. He decided he must stay on the good side of both. And Cockrell just gave him an invaluable lesson. He decided he would practice the boxing stance and swings whenever he had any privacy.

On the negative side of the ledger was the unfortunate circumstance of his antagonist from the Academy showing up on the same ship, and of course, the German U-boats, and an unknown destination. Well, all his mates faced the latter two negatives.

Jack reaffirmed in his mind to ignore the negatives and concentrate on the positives. He would stive to be the best deck mate on the ship. And make no enemies. A worthy goal, but how could he accomplish that?

Jack got settled in his room and spent the next few days on board following what Captain Gleason and Chief Cockrell had recommended. Like a new kid in school, he explored the vessel and learned as much as he could about the huge merchant ship. He enjoyed spending spare time around one of the 20mm machine guns. He touched it, moved it, studied it.

As more men showed up on board, Jack attempted to engage everyone and remember all their names. He was quickly overwhelmed. One of the Navy Armed Guards, Ron Sewell, and Al Fitzgerald, another deck cadet along with Jack were assigned to Battle Station #4, the forward gun tub on the port front side of the superstructure, one level above the bridge. Jack and Fitz were supposed to keep the ammunition coming and change the gun barrels often to keep them cool. Ron was charged with firing the gun. That 20mm antiaircraft gun would be their baby for the entire journey. Jack let it be known that he wanted to learn as much as possible and help with firing the gun. Ron agreed to train him. Anyhow, it was good to have a backup in case Ron was wounded or…

Jack also enjoyed probing around the engine room and learning as much as possible about the ship's propulsion. The mass-produced Liberty Ship possessed a somewhat antiquated steam engine. But the engine was reliable and manufactured with easily replaceable parts. He had learned a great deal about engines at the Merchant Marine Academy, but he wanted to pull that information together to give him useful, practical knowledge.

The eventual encounter with Ski Nowakowski took place five days after Jack arrived on board. Jack had thought about it and decided to greet him cheerfully as a fellow graduate from the Academy and as a new shipmate. Jack was on the way to the mess hall for lunch when Ski and a few other mates were climbing the stairs with their duffel bags in tow. Jack spoke first. "Hey, Ski, how's it going?"

Ski looked at him and frowned. "So we end up on the same ship. What do you know?"

Ignoring the rudeness, Jack replied, "This is a great new vessel. All the comforts of home. And we have a nice group of officers."

He then slid past Ski who replied only, "Uh huh. I haven't forgot you, bub. You got off easy last time." Ski cast his chin up. "You might look nice with a couple o' black eyes," he said with an artificial smile revealing his poor dentation. Jack kept moving.

There was some good news. Jack was delighted to learn that Ski was bunked one deck above him: not far enough but still better than in the same room. And the three mates assigned to Jack's room seemed like good guys. One was Ross Engles, who was a classmate from the Academy and had gone to New York with Jack. The other two were Ralph Bonners and Alex "the Greek," Salamis.

As deck cadets, Jack and his roommates discussed and reviewed their jobs on the Liberty Ship, including assisting in loading and unloading cargo, checking equipment, inspecting lifeboats and rafts, sounding bilges, cleaning the decks, managing the lines, operating the engine, running gear, managing the anchors, and responding to any other tasks requested by the first mate or the captain. Jack learned through the grapevine that the *Esek Hopkins,* on this journey, would be carrying oil drums, ammunition, TNT, tanks, artillery guns, airplanes, a locomotive, steel bars and some fifteen miles of continuous cable which would be wound around in a large circle in one of the holds. All these supplies would be loaded on board at their next stop, which, for the time being, was kept secret. A mood of excitement surrounded the men. A first journey, a primal cruise, a practical exercise in all they had learned. But mostly it was an adventure at sea.

Once the crew got acclimated to the layout of the ship and their general duties, there were slow periods. During these periods Jack forced himself to engage in the requisite studies. As a deck cadet (also known as a nautical apprentice) he was considered a trainee who was responsible for learning all the duties of a deck officer on a merchant ship. To move up the command structure in the Merchant Marine, the cadet must complete prescribed sea time to qualify for the written exams for promotion from deck cadet to third mate. At the Merchant Marine Academy, one of his courses, known as Basic Safety Training, included survival techniques, firefighting, and fire prevention along with first aid. Another task assigned to Jack on *Esek Hopkins* was to dispense Vaco life suits to the officers and crew. The suits had a reputation for being life savers if you were forced to abandon ship. The insulation they provided was particularly valuable in the frigid waters of the North Atlantic. Boots were attached to the body of the suit and were waterproof. The sleeves ended at the wrists with tight elastic. A bright yellow hood was pulled up over the head and secured by tightening a cord so only the face was exposed.

In a spare moment during lunch, Jack and a few mates were discussing the name of the ship. No one had heard of *Esek Hopkins.* Who was this person? Jack asked the second mate, Mark Williams, about the identity of the man. Williams seemed to possess some knowledge of the topic. Mark explained that *Esek Hopkins* was a sea captain who was appointed by the Continental Congress as the first Commander in Chief of the nascent American Navy during the Revolutionary War. Then Jack asked Williams how they chose names for Liberty Ships. Williams informed him that names were chosen by the United States Maritime Commission. The Commission picked names of Americans who were deceased and had achieved some level of fame during their lifetimes. Later Jack learned that as World War II progressed, and more boats were manufactured, names were running short. So as a new source, contemporary sailors who had lost their lives in the Merchant Marine were chosen. Rank was not a concern. Captains or cooks had ships named after them. About one hundred ships were named for women.

By June 10, 1942, with basic provisions of food and fuel on board, the *Esek Hopkins* cast off from her slip in Hoboken. The journey had begun. Excitement filled the air. Somewhat clumsily, lines were untied from the port cleats and pulled on board. It was the first time for the crew to work as a team. Orders were barked from the side decks of the bridge. Black smoke poured from the single stack. Tug lines stretched to the breaking point as the bow was pulled out into the channel. The ship was sitting high in the water and when the prop began to turn, considerable splashing danced from the stern. Rumor on board claimed they were going to dock at another port in New Jersey to load thousands of tons of supplies and equipment, including two thousand tons of high explosives. This sounded hazardous to Jack, and it was. A spark during loading could set off a conflagration. And when sailing across the ocean, a single, well-placed torpedo strike to the hull could blow the ship to smithereens. But for now, they were off for the first time and after they had secured the lines and fenders, the crew scurried around the decks to find the best vantage point for watching the world slide by.

That evening, the *Esek Hopkins* pulled up at the end of a two-mile-long pier at Craven Point, New Jersey, directly across from Manhattan. The extreme length of the pier was to protect the population from an accidental explosion, should one occur while provisioning the ships. A good idea for the local population, but not encouraging for the men doing the work. For their first docking, the process went on with few problems. The men were struggling and learning to work as a team.

The process of loading a Liberty Ship was new to many of the deck cadets and Craven Point was where they learned. At the Academy Jack had learned that each Liberty Ship had five deep holds for storage. To load and remove equipment and supplies was a cumbersome task and took participation of a full complement of deck hands. Each hold was covered with a heavy canvas tarp which protected multiple wooden doors measuring eight by three feet.

When peering down, there was a second deck, known as the Tween Deck, which was ten feet below the main deck. The Tween Deck had the same wooden covers and after sliding these doors aside the full depth of the hold below was exposed. The distance down from the Tween Deck to the keel was about eighteen feet; near certain death to anyone who might fall.

On deck, next to the openings, were a pair of large steam-driven steel winches which spun the steel lifting cables. The steel cables rose up to the top of the booms on the mast, ran through pullies, and descended downward to be attached to whatever needed to be lifted. In this manner, large heavy objects could be carried from the pier and lowered to the bottom of the holds.

Jack and the other deck cadets spent the first two days becoming experts in the coordination and operation of opening and closing the holds and loading mostly boxes and crates of necessary ship supplies. They quickly became proficient and began loading heavy equipment, ammunition, and tanks on the third day. Through the loading process, Jack and Ski managed to ignore each other. Ski's main job was in the engine room as a "wiper." That job consisted of keeping the machinery well lubricated while underway. But when in port, the men who worked in the engine room also helped with any deck work.

After several days of carefully loading and positioning TNT, ammunition, aircraft parts, jeeps, and tanks in the holds, along with one locomotive on deck, the ship was sitting low in the water and was ready for the next stop on its journey. During the loading, Jack and the crew realized their ultimate destination was across the North Atlantic to Russia. Many of the crates loaded by the stevedores were labeled "Moscow."

Jack had a feeling of satisfaction and accomplishment once the first part of his journey was completed. And it was completed safely. His mates had worked as a team in relative calm toward their common goal. He only hoped that feeling of camaraderie would last the entire trip.

Jack had never seen New York from the sea and was mesmerized by the scenes before him. Ships and vessels of all shapes and sizes made their way in and out of the harbor and up and down the Hudson. He was fascinated by the Statue of Liberty. To his surprise, she appeared smaller than expected. He pondered about all the immigrants who had sailed here and looked forward to seeing Lady Liberty as a sign of freedom and opportunity. His father's ancestors migrated to the US from Liverpool, England and his mother's family from Cork, Ireland. He likely was not the first of his clan to gaze upon Lady Liberty from the deck of a ship.

All seemed in order as he contemplated the next phase and remembered his promise to his mother.

CHAPTER 4

Warnings

TO EVERYONE'S DELIGHT, BY JUNE 13, 1942, the *Esek Hopkins*, fully packed and engorged with everything she would need, carefully slid from her ties to land. A little red tug sounded a pair of brief toots as she recovered her line from the bow of *Esek Hopkins* and turned her attention to her next mission. The heavy Liberty Ship was now imbedded deep in the water. She looked and felt different; she puttered and bobbed along ponderously with swirling black smoke rising from her stack.

Jack and his mates retrieved the thick wet lines and secured the fenders in their proper places on board. He decided to remain out on deck for a few hours as the ship made her way out toward the Atlantic Ocean through the scenic Long Island Sound. Was it his imagination or were other vessels giving his ship a wide berth as she steamed to sea, knowing she was full of dangerous cargo? As he studied the pleasure boat movements and shoreline scenery passing by, he noted several of the tiny Snipe sailboats that he knew so well from his dreamy summer days on the Chesapeake Bay.

That first night out, the *Esek Hopkins* anchored at the east end of the Sound. Although Jack was not assigned to anchor duty, he watched the men with fascination as they artfully pulled leavers and released locks on the chain. As if having a mind of its own, the chain noisily and rapidly flew through the deck fittings. Everyone stood back. The anchor chain could rip off an arm or leg. Jack needed to know the drill, in case he was required to fill in.

After dinner in the mess hall, Jack started a personal policy of studying at least one hour a day. On the same deck as the helm, there was a small room designated as "the library" where quiet reading or studying was encouraged. On this first evening at anchor, he wanted to tackle the complexities of longitude and latitude. With his navigation book he took a seat in the corner and began reading. Not five minutes into his work, Captain Gleason walked by and spotted Jack.

"Hey, Dodd, what are you up to?" he inquired with a pleasant smile.

"Oh, just doing a little reading about latitude and longitude." Jack hoped he was not disturbing anything and would not be asked to leave.

"Good man. Join me at the helm and I will pass on what I know. I will try to make it more interesting than that dry book," Gleason suggested.

"Yes, sir." Jack stood, saluted nervously, and followed the Captain forward to the helm station. Jack wanted to make a good impression during this unusual opportunity.

"Pull up a chair," the Captain offered as he pointed to a table on the starboard side with a settee for three along with four chairs. Jack followed orders and placed his book on the table as he took a seat.

The helm station, or bridge, was about thirty feet long and twelve feet wide. The helm steering station itself was in the center with a binnacle and wheel and compass mounted forward of the wheel. There were six small square windows facing forward for the master to look through while steering. The view through the windows was somewhat restricted. They were intentionally made small for protection from enemy gunfire or steel fragments from explosions. On each side of the bridge were heavy steel doors. These lead out to covered observation platforms, which gave good visibility forward and aft. On the port side of the bridge was a small kitchen area with a second table, a refrigerator, and cupboards. Coffee and snacks were available twenty-four hours a day on the bridge. The outside walls of the bridge area were surrounded by a four-inch-thick layer of asbestos and padding. This would protect the bridge from all but a direct hit from a bomb or large shell. On the back side of the bridge room there were two parallel corridors which led to the officer's quarters.

"Would you like a cup of coffee, Dodd?" Gleason asked politely.

Jack was stunned that the Captain was offering to prepare coffee for such a low man in the crew. He responded tentatively, "No, thank you, sir. I had some with dinner."

Gleason smiled and said, "I am from Indiana and in the midwest we call the midday meal 'dinner.' The evening meal is referred to as 'supper.' Sorry to get off topic. Incidentally, my wife's mother was a Dodd. Her father was from somewhere in southern England. And not that common a name. So, anyway, Dodd, what have you learned about longitude and latitude?"

Jack pondered. *So maybe that's why the Captain immediately remembered my name when I introduced myself on the first day. Nice to know, but ultimately it means nothing. I am still a lowly deck cadet.*

Jack started, "Well, sir, the earth is nearly a perfect sphere. For navigation purposes it is important to divide the surface into manageable blocks or boxes. So, lines drawn from the North Pole to the South Pole are called lines of longitude. And the distance between the lines is never constant. The lines touch at the poles and are farthest apart at the equator. Lines of latitude start at the equator. They are parallel and always the same distance apart."

Gleason nodded, "Well stated. You must have had good teachers."

Just then, second mate Mark Williams and chief mate Bruce Cockrell entered the bridge from the port aft corridor. They both saluted and bid the Captain a good evening and nodded to Jack. "Sorry, sir, we did not realize you had company."

"No worries. Dodd and I were having a discussion about basic navigation. Pull up chairs gentlemen."

Mark reminded the Captain that he was there to report on the ship's operating condition.

Gleason told him to proceed.

Mark began, "All systems are in good working order after our first day under way with a full load. We are drawing twenty-five feet. We estimate our cargo at eight thousand, seven hundred tons. In theory, we could take on about one thousand two hundred more tons to reach our max. But she handles well with this load, and we got to eight knots with ease. All indicators from the engine room are excellent. All bilge pumps are functioning. The crew is accounted for. Our single anchor is secure for the night. Mild weather conditions with light winds are expected for the next twenty-four hours. I have left an order that all lights on board are to be extinguished one hour before sunset even though technically we are not yet in the Atlantic. All windows and port holes must be covered. Dim red lights are allowed only in the engine room, corridors, and the bridge."

The Captain nodded, "Very well. Thank you, Mark."

At this point, Jack stood up. "Sir, I think I should excuse myself. I am certain you have important topics to cover this evening with your officers."

Gleason replied, "Nonsense. Stick around, Dodd. You might learn some things."

Jack exchanged glances with Mark and the Chief with an expression of "I tried." He sat down and listened to every word. Like a dry little sponge.

Gleason began, "As we all know it is critically important that we make ourselves invisible to the enemy U-boats. All lights out, no smoking, all portholes covered—in fact, lets cover these six windows now even though the sun doesn't set for another hour and a half."

Jack jumped up, found the window covers and applied them securely to the six openings.

The Chief turned on a small red light at the floor level. The bridge was uncomfortably dark.

Gleason continued. "As we all know, the U-boats have devastated our merchant ships over the past six months. And right in our front yard. The Navy believes the U-boats could easily see the silhouettes of our merchant ships against the shore lights as they departed from ports at night. And the public will not turn off their lights. The ships were slow-moving targets as they left port. Like shooting fish in a barrel. According to the newspapers, our ships often are struck just a few miles offshore and the explosions and fire balls wake people up. Folks gather on the shores to watch the ships burn all night. Then oil, debris and bodies float up on the beaches the next morning. What a nightmare.

"So, gentlemen, we must assume that every hour of every day we are being watched by those cunning Germans. And, of course, we are most at risk of attack at night. On moonless nights we are difficult to see unless a light, no matter how small, is detected. A lighted cigarette is visible at one thousand yards in the darkness. The U-boats typically will shoot two torpedoes at their target to increase the likelihood of a strike. And this is made easier if the target ship is at anchor, like we are now. And, as you know, the U-boats come to the surface to launch torpedoes. In the dark, on the surface, they are nearly invisible since they are painted black. And obviously, their captains are quite audacious."

Jack decided to throw in a comment. "Sir, I heard a rumor that a U-boat cruised into New York Harbor at midnight. A tugboat captain saw the vessel come to the surface and the men on board were pointing to all the bright lights of Manhattan."

"I heard the same rumor, Dodd. I guess it must be true if we both heard it," Gleason observed with a chuckle. "That fellow Donitz, the chief admiral of the Kriegsmairne, is a very clever guy. I have been reading about him. He has a huge round head. Full of crap, I suppose. But he developed a diabolic and devastating strategy. His theory was, why waste time and fuel searching for freighters in the ocean when you can sink them as they leave port. He assumed our navy was not prepared and he was correct."

The Chief chimed in, "I wonder why that crazy Hitler would declare war on the United States after Japan attacked us on

December 7, last year? Didn't he have enough headaches fighting the British and the Russians?'

Mark responded, "He had a treaty with Japan. If either nation was attacked, the other would come to their aid. So, once we were at war with Japan, Hitler felt an obligation to join the fray. He probably thought he could knock us out of the war in a few months."

"He still might," offered Captain Gleason. "If he can stop our ships from supplying England, the British may collapse. Then he will direct his formidable war machine fully toward the Russians. Does anyone here want to learn German?"

Jack chimed in, "*Nein.*" Everyone laughed.

Bruce said he had been reading up on the German army in the *New York Harold Tribune.*

"The *Tribune* has a daily report from their London office. According to the newspaper, the German high command was shocked when Hitler suddenly declared war on us. Apparently, there was no discussion with his generals. The German army is bogged down in a cataclysmic war with the Russians in the east which is consuming vast quantities of German manpower, weaponry, and supplies. And the Germans are encountering fierce fighting on a second front in North Africa against British General Montgomery for control of Middle East oil. The German army does not need a third enemy."

Jack asked, "So is that how we got into the mess? To rescue the British?"

Gleason responded, "Right. As noted, if the U-boats can stop our shipments to Europe, the war will end quickly. So, the North Atlantic is the new battlefield. You all remember when the Germans invaded Russia last June to the surprise of the world. The Germans had a treaty with the Russians, and Stalin was stunned when the Germans attacked. The Russians were completely unprepared. Since then, they have been hanging on by their fingernails. The hope is that supplies from our convoys will allow the Russians to hold off the Germans until the Brits and our army can invade Europe...which may be years away."

The men gazed down at the floor in thought.

Gleason continued, "I am not at liberty to tell you our ultimate destination, but I will point out that there are only two ports on the north-western side of Russia: Murmansk and Archangel. And in winter, these ports are iced in."

Bruce and Mark silently, quickly glanced at each other. Identical thoughts flickered through their minds. Why was the Captain revealing this confidential information in front of a lowly, non-officer deck cadet? Did the Captain have some special plan for Dodd?

Simultaneously, Jack realized several things. Clearly the Captain trusted him. Jack knew this information was generally restricted to officers. Why did the Captain place such confidence in him? Also, Jack now had a second confirmation that the *Esek Hopkins* was destined for Russia. Finally, Jack concluded correctly that the revelation of this secret information was a test. Jack could not discuss this with anyone no matter how tempting it would be to possess "inside information." He must maintain the confidence of the Captain. As a corollary, Bruce or Mark could damage Jack if they desired, by leaking this information among the crew. Jack could be blamed. Perhaps this was an overreaction, but Jack must maintain a good relationship with the Chief and first mate. That should start soon. Jack recalled the advice of his brother, Howard: "Don't get involved in any intrigues." Jack did not ask for this, but here it was.

As if reading their minds, the Captain stated, "Dodd, this information is secret and must be kept in complete confidence. Is that clear?"

"Yes, sir. You have my word." Jack hoped this was the end of the discussion for the evening. He was already hearing more than he needed.

But the Captain continued, "By the way, our immediate next port-of-call is Halifax, Nova Scotia. It is about a three-day journey. We will join up there with more merchant ships and some escorts. And we may take on additional cargo. I am scheduled to attend a few high-level meetings on shore. At one of these meetings, I will get our position assignment in the convoy.

As you probably know, the location of a ship in the convoy is critically important. With forty ships there are typically four rows of ten ships each. Where you don't want to be is on either edge of the convoy. Those ships are the first to be targeted by U-boats. Typically, ships loaded with ammunition, like us, are placed in the middle of the convoy to offer a modicum of protection. But, of course, no spot in the convoy is completely safe."

Gleason paused, then added, "And you, gentlemen, will be happy to know there will be liberal shore leave. I suggest you make good use of it, for once we cast off from Halifax, we will not see land for about two weeks. Our plan is to depart from Halifax after just a day or two at anchor."

At this point, since these conversations seemed open-ended, Jack wondered what else he might learn. He was curious about enemy air attacks by the Luftwaffe, so he decided to prime the pump.

"Captain, do you think our convoy will be attacked by the German Luftwaffe?" he inquired innocently, already knowing the likely answer.

Gleason nodded and looked at Chief Cockrell. "Bruce, you did some flying early on with the Army Air Force. Can you answer that question? I would like to hear your opinion myself."

Bruce placed his cap on the table and sat down as if he might need to call forth all his energy to respond. "Well, sir, my guess is that yes, the Luftwaffe will attack us somewhere along our route; most likely as we get close to our destination. Wherever that may be," he added with a grin. In reality, Bruce knew it was not really a "guess." There was no doubt in his mind that the convoy would be bombed and strafed by the German air force. The last convoy had been shredded by the Luftwaffe.

He continued, "The Luftwaffe has good aircraft and competent pilots, although a large number of their best pilots were killed in the Battle of Britain during the summer of 1940. The Germans lost a huge number of fighters and bombers, but I read that most of them have been replaced. But the pilots take much longer to replace. So, I expect we may be kept busy with our guns. And, along with our escort ships, we will make the Germans pay."

Gleason lowered his voice and said, "I have it on good authority that we will have a small aircraft carrier cruising with our convoy. And it will carry those famous Spitfire and Hurricane fighters. So, any attacking Luftwaffe will be getting hell from those fighter planes. Keep that quiet, boys."

This was news to Mark and Bruce. Good news. Yet they were amazed how generous the Captain was with sprinkling around confidential information during this first evening at anchor.

Jack was simultaneously intrigued and anxious. He had never heard of a "small aircraft carrier." They all were huge in his mind. He would learn later that these were sometimes called "jeep carriers." They were converted Liberty Ships and held only ten or twelve single-engine fighter aircraft.

Also, the Captain's statement confirmed the military's expectation that the Luftwaffe definitely would be attacking the convoy. A little voice in Jack's brain popped up asking, "Why am I here? U-boats *and* bombers? How much more dangerous could this mission get? And keeping the promise to my mother may be more difficult than I assumed."

Gleason continued, "This journey will be no garden party. Once at sea, we can have another informal chat to discuss our Navy's strategy and our little ship's role in the plan. In the meantime, I would like to pass on to you gentlemen a bit of history which you may not be aware of." The Captain was clearly enjoying this session.

He continued, "As you all know, the Merchant Mariners are separate from the US Navy. We are commercial ships under the authority of the Commerce Department. Before the war, we could sail around anywhere in the world delivering cargo without interruption. But after Japan attacked Pearl Harbor last December 7, and Hitler declared war on us, our existence has changed completely. We now are considered open targets by the enemy. In the past, our ships had no guns for protection. Now, guns have been added to older ships and all new Liberty Ships being manufactured have a significant complement of weaponry for defensive purposes. Still, our ships are being sunk at very high rates. About four months ago the authorities decided to have navy ships escort us to England and then on to Russia. In addition, the British convinced us that we must travel in large convoys to enhance protection. Wisely, the Department of the Navy decided to add a separate crew on merchant ships to take control of all weapons on board. That allows us, the merchant mariners, to concentrate on our jobs operating the ship. As you know, they are known as the Navy Armed Guards. They have a separate command structure from our men. *Esek Hopkins* has twenty-five Armed Guards on board. I hope by now you have met them all."

The three men nodded.

"They are in charge of managing, maintaining and firing all the gunnery on board. They also help us with communications. And they supply the one medical officer on *Esek Hopkins.* He is not a doctor but has extensive first-aid training. Lest anyone forget, I am the Captain of this ship and take ultimate responsibility for the vessel. I have authority over the Navy Armed Guards as well. What I want to emphasize today is that I will tolerate no conflicts between our merchant marine crew and the Armed Guards. I know there are areas of disagreement which can pop up. Things like the fact that they get paid a little less than you do, and they don't get as much shore leave. But I will not tolerate agitation among the different crews. Bruce and Mark, make that clear to all on board."

"Yes, sir, we will," they responded. Bruce added, "I have already assigned a staggered meal program, since that seems to be a time when some crew members can stir up trouble."

"I have heard that from other captains. Excellent plan," Gleason replied. "And of course, the Armed Guards understand the merchant crew's areas of responsibly. Our boys are in charge of docking, loading and unloading, propulsion, cooking, running the mess hall, and keeping the vessel clean and functional."

The Chief replied, "Yes, sir, I believe both crews understand their areas of responsibility. I have also made it clear that during periods of conflict with the enemy, our crew members will aid with the gunnery duties. With that in mind I have initiated training exercises with all members of our crew who are not required in the engine room or on the bridge. For example, Dodd here has been assigned to our number four gun tub on the port side with Navy Armed Guard Ron Seward and Deck Cadet Al Fitzpatrick. They will operate the 20mm Oerlikon. I think your first practice is scheduled soon," he said as he nodded toward Dodd.

"Correct. Captain, I am anxious to knock some of those dirty Krauts out of the sky," Dodd declared.

Gleason smiled. "Good. Make every shot count."

"One other topic," the Captain continued. "Some merchant ships encourage boxing matches on board for entertainment purposes and to relieve tension among crew members. I do not tolerate boxing matches. I saw a man get killed when he fell on a steel cleat during a boxing match. Chief, please make that clear to the crew."

Gleason paused to let it sink in. Then he continued with another thought. "There is not much I can do when men on shore get into quarrels. And if crew members end up in a local jail, I am content leaving them there. And finally, it is the official position of this Captain to prohibit visits to houses of ill-repute. I am no fool and I realize there is little I can do in this personal area. But I need to take an official position, and that is it. I want to return home with a healthy crew, not one infested with various unsavory diseases. And please confirm that the medical officer is planning his talk on VD."

Chief Cockrell replied, "Consider it done, sir."

Dodd was thinking as the Captain spoke: *I want no part of any disputes. I am here to help in the war effort, and I will stay out of all crew conflicts and keep relations with everyone on an even keel. I know we are all living in cramped quarters for weeks in a metal container loaded with explosives and with danger all around. There are enough opportunities for stress dealing with the German U-boats, air attacks and the foul weather. I will be a helper, willing to do any tasks assigned to me for the good of the ship and the mission. And I will learn as much as possible. If this cruise goes well and I survive, I may well sign up for additional merchant marine cruises. After all, the pay is decent, and what better way to see the world and meet interesting people. Well, it might be more fun to see the world if there were no enemies out there trying to destroy your ship.*

Captain Gleason re-started his discussion on latitude and longitude. The Chief and Mark Williams chimed in with some pearls. Jack took notes and learned quite a bit that night. He grew weary by 2100 hours. He thanked the officers and excused himself from the bridge. The plan was to pull anchor early the next morning to start the next phase of their journey. Jack needed the rest. On this night, he got the best sleep of the entire trip.

CHAPTER 5

At Sea

JUST AS THE SUN PEAKED over the purple water and golden-sky interface on the eastern horizon, the *Esek Hopkins* weighed anchor and headed out into the Atlantic Ocean for the first time. There was a pulse of excitement on board, even at this early hour. The loaded ship was now officially entering the war zone. After breakfast, crew members roamed around in the sun engaging in animated conversation. Some stripped down to their underwear and began sunbathing as the steel decks warmed up.

Jack asked second mate Mark Williams if he could join him on the bridge as Mark navigated the ship and began joining up with a small convoy of fifteen merchant vessels.

"Sure, learn as much as you can, Jack," was his friendly reply. Their immediate destination was Halifax, Nova Scotia, a three-day sail from Long Island Sound. While under way, a minimum of two officers were required on the bridge. A third auxiliary was also required at certain times, like battle conditions or heavy seas. The auxiliary did not need to be an officer.

While Mark was at the wheel, the radio operator and communications officer, Manny Jackson, was acting as an auxiliary and assisting where needed. His popular name on board was "Sparks." His short-wave radio office was just down the hall from the bridge. Sparks was very knowledgeable and competent, and when not required to be on the radio, he would assist with helm duties. Sometimes the auxiliary person would stay outdoors on the observation deck of the bridge and the third mate on the opposite side. It was important to have those extra eyes looking aft and to the sides of the ship during approaches to ports, when anchoring or when sailing in crowded areas. In open waters the auxiliary man was not necessary.

On this day, Sparks was on the port observation deck recording the flag signals. The fleet commander's ship was signaling to the *Esek Hopkins* to give her a position in the convoy. Radio communications were forbidden.

Most of the new Liberty Ships, like *Esek Hopkins*, had a second helm. It was known as the "Monkey Island" and was located immediately above the main helm. The primary difference was that it was completely out in the open, with only a canvas cover to protect men from the sun. All the same instruments were present. On warm, calm days most officers preferred to operate the ship from this more pleasant outpost. On this particular day, it was a bit too windy.

The Captain's stateroom was the first room down the corridor behind the bridge on the starboard side. He was just a few steps away from the wheel if he was needed in an emergency. Each Captain had his own protocol regarding his time on the bridge. Gleason allowed his officers to operate the ship most of the time. He liked to observe them at the wheel and teach. Second mate Mark Williams had sailed with Gleason before and liked his style. Williams learned a great deal on the earlier cruises. He respected Gleason. So both the Chief and second mate had worked with the Captain in the past. A good, well-rounded team.

Jack enjoyed spending time on the bridge. And no one seemed to object. He soaked up every aspect of managing the ship. He paid attention to every nuance regarding speed, handling characteristics, course adjustments, course plotting and the quiet conversation among those in charge. Mark noted to Jack that this new vessel was very responsive at the wheel, and speed control was tight. He observed how well *Esek Hopkins* handled in mild wind and wave conditions. But stormy weather would be the true test, he said. Mark's last ship was difficult to manage in rough weather. The ship took a prolonged time to respond to the wheel. During storms it took two men to. Mark then told Jack about life on board a Liberty Ship during storms. Since this was Jack's first outing, he listened with awe and fascination.

Jack considered storms to be a sort of romantic part of an ocean crossing. But after listening to Mark, this changed his image to one of concern. Oh well, he would learn to deal with it. He would find out soon enough.

Other topics came up. Mark reminded Jack that crew members were not paid until they got off the ship in port. And they were paid in cash. Mark commented, "Jack, be very careful when you leave the dock. Your wallet is full of money and everyone in the surrounding neighborhood knows it. Petty thieves and pickpockets are abundant. Put your cash in a pouch and attach it to the inside of your belt. Don't let anyone approach you. That includes women and kids too. Walk with three or four buddies. Never venture out alone. Even cab drivers may try to steal from you. You have worked hard for that money."

Jack was appreciative. "I never thought of that, Mark. Thanks for the tips. I am sure that rule applies to any cash we have on board too. And at any port where we get shore leave."

"It does. Only carry money on shore that you plan to spend — and can afford to lose. One other thing, if you gamble or play cards, find a new hobby. I can't tell you who they are, but I can guarantee there are men on this ship who will rob you blind right in front of your eyes."

"Good to know. Thank God I have no interest in gambling. My father did some of that."

Captain Gleason appeared silently at the back of the bridge. "Don't let me interrupt, gentlemen. It sounds like an illuminating subject. But it is nearly lunch time. Jack, would you go down to the mess and ask the chief steward to send up lunch for six?"

"Yes, sir. I will take care of it," as Jack headed down the hall to the staircase, then stopped and looked back at the Captain quizzically. "Why six, sir?"

Gleason replied, "Third mate Lance Lockhart and the Chief are doing inspections but will be back in a few minutes. And I expect you to join us, Dodd."

Thirty minutes later Jack and the chief steward appeared with trays of sandwiches and drinks. Just behind them, the Chief and third mate Lockhart arrived. The food and beverages were put on the table and each of the six grabbed a bite and a drink and sat to see what was up. Was there a reason the Captain wanted them all on the bridge?

First, they discussed the weather and how that would affect their timeline for arrival in Halifax. Williams was still at the wheel and commented on the good performance of the ship so far. The tone of the conversation was casual, and anyone could chip in with their thoughts.

Gleason commented, "She is a new ship, I certainly hope she handles well." He took a generous bite out of his sandwich. The men felt he had something on his mind. He did. They stopped talking for a moment. When he finished chewing on his sandwich he offered a question: "So we are now officially participating in the war. How does it feel, boys?"

Jack kept a low profile but listened intently to learn any perspective from the officers.

No one wanted to start. Gleason looked directly at Jack, and said, "What do you think, Jack? Did Roosevelt do the right thing with the Lend-Lease program to help the British?"

Jack felt a blush developing. He stammered, "Well, sir, I am not sure I am qualified."

"That will never do, Deck Cadet Dodd. You are a citizen. You pay attention to the news. You volunteered for this hazardous job. I am sure you have thought about these issues," the Captain said congenially, but intentionally putting the heat on Jack. The officers observed Jack squirm, happy they were not on the hook for this one. Meanwhile, each one was framing an answer in the back of their minds, knowing they could be called on next.

The Captain *was* correct; Jack had thought about these issues. In fact, Jack had engaged in many discussions with his brothers over these exact topics. He quickly gathered his thoughts.

"Well, sir, I think Roosevelt did the right thing with the Lend-Lease program to help the British. We are not giving anything away. We loaned a bunch of destroyers to Churchill and in turn, Churchill granted us ninety-nine-year leases on various British ports around the world. Roosevelt described it on the radio like we were lending our neighbor a hose to help him put out a fire in his house. And Churchill declared they would finish the job, if we gave the British the supplies they needed. If we did not do that, then the Germans may have succeeded in invading England, and we would have to face the Germans alone—and face the Japs too. I think we are much better off having the English in the fight with us."

Gleason nodded. "Nicely stated. I suspected you were up on current events and paying attention. Anybody else have comments?"

Chief Cockrell added, "I think we have to admire our British 'cousins.' They declared war on the Germans after they invaded Poland in September 1939. So did the French, but the Krauts overran them in a few months. Under Churchill, the British have held out against the odds. Almost three years. Amazing." The men nodded in agreement.

The Captain wondered, "How do you suppose the Brits managed to hold off the Germans? The Krauts have a substantial navy and could have invaded the British Isles with their vast army."

Sparks chirped up. "Early in the war, like 1939 and 1940, I read that the Germans had a plan called 'Operation Sea Lion' to invade England. Goring, the Luftwaffe commander, promised Hitler he could wipe out the Royal Air Force. With no British air force, a naval landing would have been easy. But the British had good pilots and fighter aircraft equal to the Luftwaffe planes. They battled in the air through the summer of 1940 and by September the Germans had had enough. They could not destroy the Royal Air Force. There was no invasion."

Jack knew all this. He could have said the same thing. He felt pretty good about his knowledge level. Those previous discussions with his brothers were helpful. He decided to jump in again.

"In June of 1941, since they cancelled the invasion of England, the crazy Germans turned on their old ally, the Russians. That battle is still going on now, and the outcome remains in doubt. And the Krauts are also fighting the Brits in North Africa. Then Hitler declares war on us. I guess he thinks he can take on the whole world."

Gleason smiled. "Well, I just wanted to get an inkling of how much you all knew about the history of this conflict. I hope this perspective will help keep us all on target with our overall objective. We want to keep the Brits in the fight. Clearly, Churchill is not intimidated by Hitler. And we want the Russians to beat up the Germans until we can get our troops on the continent. So, our job is to get these critical supplies to our allies."

The second mate, Mark Andrews offered, "I just hope we have enough ships to keep this transatlantic pipeline going. We all know about the merchant ships sunk by the U-boats over the last six months. And I know we have a lot of shipyards cranking out the Liberty Ships, like our own *Esek Hopkins.* I guess no one really knows the math. How many produced vs. how many sunk. It is a scary equation."

"You are right, no one knows the answer to that," the Captain observed. "This war could go on for years. The outcome is certainly not clear. Only time will tell. The way I look at it is that we must do our absolute best all the time on our little ship in the ocean. With a little luck and hard work, we can deliver our cargo successfully and return home safely. That is our objective. I feel certain we can do it. We will do it as a team."

Everyone gently applauded. Gleason nodded. "I would like to

have an informal officers' meeting like this once or twice a week. Good to talk things over. Thanks, gentlemen, and good work."

The group broke up. Chief Cockrell took the helm and Mark Williams stayed on as the first back up. Jack had time and stayed on the bridge. The Captain retired to his room. Sparks went to the radio room.

Mark remarked quietly, "Gleason did something like this on the last cruise. I think it is a good idea. Like a little cocktail get-together without cocktails," he laughed.

The Chief agreed. "Good for morale. The officers get to know each other a little better in an informal arena. I suspect each meeting will get more casual and relaxed. Dodd, the Captain likes you. He put you on the spot, didn't he?"

Jack was puzzled. "You think he likes me? I thought he was trying to embarrass me."

The Chief replied, "If he did not like you, he would have ignored you. Your responses were pretty good. Tell me something, are you planning on staying in the Merchant Marines through the war?"

Jack smiled. "You mean if I survive this first crossing? Just kidding. Chief, I have not decided. I am from Baltimore, and I like the sea. But this is my first experience on a ship. So, there are too many unknowns to answer that. I can tell you my family is not keen on it. I am the youngest son, still living at home with my mother. My father is dead. I took a lot of crap when I took off on this adventure. I had to promise my mother I would return safely. Hope I can live up to that."

"Well, at least you are not married. If you had a wife you might have to take even more heat," offered Mark.

The Chief asked Jack if there were any new issues regarding his archenemy, Ski. "No, sir. I haven't seen him much," Jack replied.

Mark asked who Ski was, and the Chief filled him in.

Mark commented, "He sounds like a bully. Not the type of guy you want to have as a crew member. I will keep an eye out. Does the Captain know?"

Chief Cockrell looked at Jack as he replied, "Yes, I told the Captain. Don't worry, Jack. The Captain always wants to know if there are any problem characters on board. He needs that kind of information about his crew."

Still, Jack wondered if he should have told the Chief on the first day. *Too late now. The word may get out anyway. Two other crew members from the Academy knew about the altercation. Eventually, that sort of thing leaks out. Great. We might as well set up a secret boxing match between me and Ski for the crew to watch in some hidden location in the bilge. There would be no bets on me.*

The sun was drifting down toward the western horizon. Mark turned on the public address system and announced that it was now one hour before sunset and all hatches must be covered and all lights out. Mark turned on the dim red floor lights and turned off all the bridge white lights. Now, with lights out on all ships, strict attention must be paid to any vessel in front of *Esek Hopkins*. There were no running lights allowed on any vessel in the convoy. As nightfall surrounded them, the watch became the most important issue.

The good news was that so far, on this first day in the Atlantic, there were no U-boat attacks.

In spite of the snoring of his roommates in the cabin, Jack Dodd had a second consecutive night of fairly sound sleep. In the morning as he awoke, he wondered how many more of those restful nights he would have on this journey.

CHAPTER 6

Arrival and VD

THE MORE JACK DODD WORRIED about it, the more he was convinced that U-boats were following the *Esek Hopkins* and the other transports in their little convoy. He carried in his mind the episode of the British ship *Cyclops*, which was sunk just south of Halifax. He could not forget the frightening story told by Charlie Black in the Irish pub in New York. Jack had convinced himself that the same U-boat that had sunk the *Cyclops* was out there waiting for them. Finally, after worrying nonstop for hours, he concluded that obsessing about it was not healthy. He stopped.

The next day at sea they joined up with a second convoy consisting of thirty ships near Cape Cod. Somehow, the combined convoys now totaling forty-five vessels made Jack feel a little safer. In addition, there were several destroyers accompanying them on this first leg of their journey. Even so close to the Eastern Seaboard, U-boat watch had commenced. The second night out, there were several alarms indicating U-boat sightings. None of these were confirmed and there were no depth charges dropped and no merchant ships struck by torpedoes. Perhaps the crew on watch was trigger-happy and as paranoid as Jack. The convoy arrived safely in Halifax Harbor on June 15, 1942.

The harbor was enormous. As they arrived, there were already dozens of merchant ships at anchor floating casually like a vast garden party in the calm waters. The newly arrived fleet took most of a day to locate safe positions and drop their anchors. Since Jack was not an anchor deck cadet, he remained on the bridge to observe the process. Captain Gleason took the wheel on this occasion. Radio communication was allowed among the boats while in port. Sparks was busy informing the Captain of proposed anchor locations and coordinating with other merchant ships. To Jack, confusion seemed to reign, but the Captain concentrated on his task and the process was successfully completed without incident or controversy.

The sun was setting when the anchoring was complete, and the hungry crew headed to the mess for dinner. Corpsman Ralph Arnold, the Navy Armed Guard medical officer, planned to make a special presentation to the entire crew after dinner. He asked Mark Williams to make an announcement to that effect over the loudspeaker as the crew was eating. Once the meals were completed and tables cleared, Ralph entered the mess hall like a first-grade teacher, with easel in hand. Some of the crew moaned, since they now realized what was coming. He set up the easel in front of the room. This was the requisite lecture on venereal diseases and their prevention. Attendance was required so all crew members would hear the same story. On the easel were listed the names of common social diseases. At the top of the list was gonorrhea, then syphilis, then two other diseases most had never heard of. At the bottom of the easel was taped a small square packet. Inside the packet was a prophylactic, or as better known to the masses, a rubber.

Everyone in the group had some knowledge of these infections but often their ideas were primitive, naïve, or simply wrong. The medical officer hoped to straighten them out. The men sat in their seats, grinned, and whispered. They shifted nervously back and forth and hoped this would be quick. Corpsman Arnold was not well known to most of the crew since few had any reason to visit the medical clinic on board. After a few late stragglers arrived, Ralph bravely walked up to the easel and with a loud voice requested everyone's attention. He started with an amazing question: "Has anyone here ever had a venereal disease?" Men chuckled or grinned then turned their heads back and forth gazing at each other thinking no one was going to answer that stupid question. Was this guy crazy? After a long, deafening pause, a guy in the second row raised his hand. Jack was sitting next to him and was astonished.

He thought to himself, "This could be fun after all."

Ralph did not seem surprised that someone had offered to respond during this meeting, and he asked the courageous man if he could share his story. The man was not bashful and outlined how he was in port about a year ago and had relations with a local woman with "experience." Then two days later he developed "pain when I peed and got some kind of discharge." Without emotion he explained how he delayed getting medical attention, hoping it would go away. After a few days of increasing discomfort, he saw a doctor who gave him a shot and some pills, which he took for a week. He completed his story by stating that he now always carries a "rubber" with him in his wallet. His testimony was a perfect advertisement for rubbers. Corpsman Arnold was pleased. In fact, it was so perfect, some in the crowd wondered if he was a "plant" who was told to make his statement.

The group was initially amused but became more attentive as they heard the man's story.

Ralph thanked the man for sharing his tale. He asked if anyone else wanted to reveal an experience. To Jack's amazement, two other guys raised their hands and proceeded to relate their tales of woe. This meeting was turning into a public, collective confession. One guy had three episodes. Jack was beginning to consider himself fortunate. Did everyone have these diseases? Ralph then opened the floor to questions.

The only one offered was, "Do toilet seats pass on VD?" It was generally accepted by the masses that this was possible. In fact, on some ships, there was a designated toilet seat for men who were diagnosed with VD. It was painted red. Ralph had discussed this with some physicians, most of whom said it was not possible. Ralph explained this to the crew. A nervous murmur swept through the mess hall. The men were not convinced. And it was an easy excuse to explain how one got infected: "I got it from a toilet seat, honey."

The corpsman then gave a brief talk which included discussions of symptoms, treatments, and long-term side effects if the infections were left unattended. After about thirty minutes, Corpsman Arnold wrapped things up by reiterating the importance of the rubbers, which were offered free on board. He got a few laughs when he said, "I assume you all know how to use these." He then held up a cardboard box and said there were plenty of rubbers in the box, which he would place at the entrance to the medical office. Anyone was welcome to take a supply.

There followed lots of chatter and whispering. The meeting was adjourned and most of the crew members walked up and took a few "free samples" from the box. Not wanting to appear prudish in front of his mates, Jack walked up and took two and shoved them quickly into his pocket.

Jack later learned that many crew members had another purpose for the rubbers. Small personal items, like rings, tiny photos of loved ones, or cash were placed in the expanded rubber. They were then tied at the top to make them waterproof. When battle stations were called, the men would grab the novel container and stuff it in their pocket in hopes that if they died, the contents would be passed on safely to loved ones, preferably in a different container.

Jack was able to obtain shore leave and with several mates visited Halifax to see the sights and get some exercise. His colleagues were determined to locate a bar, but Jack wanted to explore, so he peeled off and made his way on his own. He was not impressed with Halifax.

The city was rather dismal and run down, and the dark, low, threatening clouds overhead did not help. Much of the city was perched on the side of a gently sloping hill, which extended upward for a mile or so. On the west side of the harbor, halfway up was a large imposing Citadel dating from 1749. As Jack explored the town, he learned there was a famous graveyard in Halifax. It was filled with the bodies of passengers and crew members recovered following the sinking of the Titanic in April 1912. Halifax was the closest port to the location of the sinking. What a sad legacy, he thought. He elected to skip the visit; he never enjoyed graveyards.

Jack decided to explore the Citadel. It still maintained a military presence and he saluted officers as they passed by. They appeared to be emanating from one point inside the fort and he traced their path. Lo and behold buried under the thick columns and walls, he found a small restaurant and pub with no signage to attract customers. Jack was in his blue uniform but obviously not in British mufti: nonetheless, two officers at the bar saw him lingering at the entrance and waved him in. The officers were Canadian and offered him a cocktail "on the house." They introduced themselves with a chuckle as Randy and Dandy. Jack calculated they were on their third or fourth drink. He extended his hand and said only, "Jack."

They quickly guessed he was on a merchant ship from the States. They announced they were stationed on a corvette which was in port for repairs. Jack asked what it was like protecting the convoys.

Randy laughed. "Bloody fun. Our corvette is half the size of a destroyer and almost as fast. And our Captain likes to run her at full throttle whenever in combat. He tears around like he is driving a sports car. The Germans don't waste torpedoes on us. They can't hit us. So, we are likely on the safest vessel in the ocean!"

Jack asked if they had seen much combat. Dandy took this one. "The busiest time was last spring. The Germans flooded the sea with their damn U-boats. They did a job on your merchant ships, didn't they? And right off your coast. No lights-out policy there. In bloody England all lights are out at sundown—if you have electricity. Ha ha. With so many targets around, we were throwing out depth charges like pennies popping out of a slot machine. I think we sank at least two U-boats and possibly another. The clever Krauts will sometimes eject garbage and clothing out of their torpedo tubes, so we think they have checked into Davy Jones's locker. But we know better. A real sinking has lots of oil. Got to see lots of oil...and blood...and limbs..."

Randy observed, "You Yanks on merchant ships have it tough. Not enough guns, but I hear the new Liberty Ships have more protection. And you finally are getting together in large convoys. We tried to tell you that last year, but your admirals wouldn't listen."

Randy pointed in the direction of the harbor. "There must be a hundred ships out there. If they sail together, they probably have five hundred or more guns. Even if you are lousy shots, you will knock out some of the bloody Luftwaffe planes. They like to strafe us with machine-gun fire. That's the only way they have a chance against a corvette. But we give it back. Our little ship has fifteen swastikas painted on the side of the bridge. And besides, you won't meet the Luftwaffe until you get closer to Russia. That is your destination, right?"

Jack pondered the question. He uttered the correct response, "Can't discuss."

"Right, right," said the one identified as Dandy. "Sorry for the question, mate."

Jack only nodded. No sense starting an argument. And he was still working his first drink and enjoying the Canadians. They both ordered another round. Their speech was becoming slurred. The bartender seemed to be acquainted with them and told them this was their last round. They made an act of protesting. The bartender shook his head slowly left and right, as if they were quite dense, and declared, "I am not cleaning up another mess after you clowns."

With stumbling diction, Dandy said, "Ya know, our admirals are pretty smart guys. They are trying to figure out how the German U-boats are so good at finding convoys in the middle of the bloody ocean. When they get close to land, their reconnaissance planes can find the convoys. But they don't have the range to find them in the middle. Do you know what the admirals came up with?"

Jack was smiling as he shook his head no. Dandy took another impressive gulp and put his elbows on the bar and leaned closer to Jack. He quietly uttered one word, "garbage," then sat back triumphantly.

Jack looked at Dandy then Randy and with a puzzled expression said, "You guys are funny."

"It's no joke," replied Randy, as he stared into his half empty glass.

Jack decided he wanted no more alcohol on this afternoon. He took a final swig and thanked the Canadians for their hospitality and bid his farewells.

Dandy grasped his sleeve, "No wait. You don't understand. This is…important." Randy slurred, "The admirals…may have figured it out. Listen."

Jack replied, "Gents, I must get back to my ship. I have duties on board. I am a deck cadet, not an officer. But again, thank you for the drink. If you come state-side, look me up. I am from Baltimore."

The Canadians together looked up and down at Jack's impressive blues, unclear what the difference was between the uniform of a merchant marine deck cadet and an officer. Jack began to turn away.

Randy said loudly, "It makes no difference. Please…come here for just one minute."

Jack turned. "Ok, but for just for a minute."

Randy said incongruously, "I am from Toronto. A great city. Not a little dump like here."

Dandy interrupted this wandering conversation and took over. "Captain Jack, the admirals have calculated…that with forty or fifty ships cruising across the ocean, there is lots of garbage you guys throw overboard. Probably a couple of tons every day. The boys up top suspect the Krauts may look for garbage trails in the ocean and track it to locate the convoys. That is the story." Dandy waved to the bartender with one finger up. The bartender shook his head no.

Jack's brow creased in thought. "Well, gentlemen, that certainly is an interesting theory. When I get back on board, I will pass it up the ranks. Thank you. Now you guys go easy on yourselves." He broke off despite their protests.

It had been a most fascinating afternoon. One can never know who one will stumble into. Their idea may be nothing, but who can tell?

Somehow, as he left the Citadel, it seemed as difficult to walk down the steep grade as uphill. He made his way to the city docks and waited for a launch. They were arriving at fifteen-minute intervals. Once back on *Esek Hopkins*, he would first mention this garbage idea to the Chief.

As the launch pulled up to the *Esek Hopkins*, Jack clamored up the ladder to get on board.

The ship was nearly vacant. But the ever-dutiful Chief was in his office with a stack of papers. Jack knocked on the door frame. Cockrell looked up. "Hey, Dodd. Halifax not so exciting?"

"Well not that exciting. But..." He related the story of the Canadian officers in the Citadel and their idea about the Germans tracking the convoy's garbage. The Chief was interested. He thanked Jack and said he would discuss it with the Captain. Jack saluted and headed back to his bunk for a quick rest before dinner.

Then there was the Captain's meeting.

CHAPTER 7

Anxiety

JACK WAS ON THE BRIDGE with second mate Mark Williams, when the Captain Gleason appeared. He had just returned to the *Esek Hopkins* from a conference with the higher ups in Halifax. He had a look of apprehension as he entered, like he had seen a ghost. Williams noticed the Captain's strained appearance.

"How did the meeting go, Captain?" inquired Williams with intended innocence.

"Lousy," snapped Gleason as he walked straight past them and down the hallway to his private cabin and slammed the door. Dodd and Williams exchanged glances.

Williams whispered, "I have never seen the Captain like that. And I have sailed with him on two cruises in the recent past. Something bad happened at that meeting ashore. Once he calms down, he'll let us know what is going on."

Jack nodded. Although he had known the Captain only briefly, Jack was a bit taken aback by his change in demeanor. Captain Gleason normally was cordial to everyone, even the lowly deck cadets like Dodd. They would learn soon enough.

That evening Gleason called the ship's four merchant marine officers to the helm for an informal gathering at 1700. Dodd was present on the bridge and though not an officer, the Captain invited him to sit in. By meeting time, Captain Gleason was in a better frame of mind. He smiled at his fellow officers as they gathered on the bridge. He nodded to Jack and asked him to close all the doors.

"To all present here, this meeting is strictly confidential. Is that clear, Dodd?"

Jack gazed directly into Gleason's eyes and said firmly, "Yes, sir."

Gleason took a seat and started. "So, this morning, on shore in Halifax, I met with the general staff and all the other captains in our convoy. The meeting went on for three hours and the discussion dealt with a variety of topics. A significant part revolved around our strategy and the capability of the enemy. An intelligence officer spent an hour telling us about German torpedoes. It was not pleasant."

The officers shifted in their seats.

Gleason continued. "The Germans are very clever and are excellent engineers. And, frankly, they appear to be far ahead of us in the sophistication of their weapons. Their usual torpedo, the G7a TI is known as a 'wet heater torpedo.' Its method of propulsion is from a chemical reaction which generates steam which in turn powers a compact four-cylinder engine. Some of you may have learned this in your training."

Second mate Williams raised his hand and Gleason nodded to him.

"Sir, we learned that those torpedoes have exhaust bubbles which leave a trail on the surface of the water and that allows their course to be tracked," he offered. Williams then turned to his colleagues and continued, "That bubble trail is referred to by the British as a 'pecker trail.' We have not seen any torpedoes yet, but I think we should use the term."

They all chuckled.

Gleason replied, "You can call it what you like. But don't forget, those underwater bombs travel at close to forty-five miles per hour. So, by the time you see the bubbles, there may not be much time to change course, or even put on a life vest."

Gleason continued, "Which is one reason I continue to insist all crew members wear life vests whenever on deck and of course during battle stations. Because of that bubble trail, the Germans typically attack at night. That is why we will observe a strict lights-out policy. No exceptions." He repeated those two words slowly. "We all know these regulations, but I have seen men on deck at night smoking and I have seen portholes uncovered. That will no longer be tolerated. The blackout policy may save our lives. Understood? And remind our navy colleagues. Remember, Williams, I want you to announce this policy over the loudspeaker system every evening one hour before sunset."

Williams nodded promptly. "Yes, sir."

"The Germans are working on another solution to the bubble trail problem. They soon will be using an electric torpedo which leaves no bubbles. They can launch these in daylight. Not good news for us. In addition, our intelligence indicates the Germans are not satisfied with the torpedo detonation devices called pistols. They are working on magnetic detonation devices which explode under the middle of the ships and lift them out of the water and crack the hulls into halves."

A few groans among the officers were heard. Jack Dodd raised his hand. Gleason nodded toward him.

"Sir, in the Merchant Marine Academy they taught us that the Navy was working on a process to de-magnetize the hulls. Has our hull been de-magnetized?"

Gleason responded, "Glad you were paying attention in school, Dodd. The process is known as degaussing. A net of thin wires can be wrapped around the hull of a ship to demagnetize it. The hull on *Esek Hopkins* has no degaussing wires. The Navy is still working on the details."

The officers looked at each other. Everyone was thinking how the odds were shifting toward the U-boats. They all knew these transatlantic trips were dangerous, but they wondered if any ships at all would get through. Perspiration collected under Jack's armpits.

"There is more, gentlemen," Gleason continued. "We now

think the range of the torpedoes may be as much as five thousand yards—a little over two and one-half miles. Quite incredible. However, the greater the distance, the less accurate. Based on the British experience, the ideal distance for an accurate torpedo shot is one thousand five hundred yards—a little less than one mile. For this shot, the U-boats come to the surface and launch two or more torpedoes to increase the odds of a hit. At this distance, U-boats coming to the surface can easily be detected with binoculars. I now expect watch twenty-four hours a day on port and starboard, fore, and aft. The only exception is foul weather. Every other captain in the convoy will be doing the same."

Chief Mate Bruce Cockerell raised his hand.

Gleason nodded to him, saying only, "Chief."

"Captain this will put a strain on our manpower. I can set up four-hour shifts, but we will need some stewards and engine room men."

"I don't care who you use. Train them, whip them into shape. And any ordinary seaman or able-bodied seaman who sleeps on his shift will end up in the brig," Gleason snapped.

Then, after a pause, he declared, "There is more. Intelligence has learned that the newer German torpedoes can turn. For example, they may travel straight for one thousand yards, and if no target is hit, they will turn in a circle to increase the odds of a strike."

The officers gazed at each other.

Mark Williams asked spontaneously without raising his hand, "So if we see a torpedo pass in front of our bow, we still are not safe. It could turn and hit us from the other direction?"

The Captain replied solemnly, "Correct."

Jack Dodd now wished he had not attended this officer's meeting. He could feel perspiration drops descending down his sides. He felt a gurgling in his belly and his heart was thumping. Before this meeting Jack felt he had a ninety-five percent probability of safely making the journey to Russia and back. Now the odds may have flipped. Keeping his promise to his mother may now be more difficult. He thought about all the ships which had been sunk along the East Coast of the United States during the six months he was at the Merchant Marine Academy. If anything, the Germans were even better now at sinking ships.

Captain Gleason interrupted Jack's thoughts. "That is not all. Our intelligence is good. They claim the Germans are close to making an acoustic torpedo. That means they can launch the weapon from thirty feet below the sea totally undetected. The torpedo has a sensing device in the nose which tracks the propeller noise of enemy ships. The torpedo will steer toward that noise and a single torpedo can destroy the entire aft part of the ship. These torpedoes could have a one hundred percent mortality. At the very least, the explosion would permanently cripple the ship.

"I think you all are aware of the German tactics. When their reconnaissance aircraft spot a convoy, they report the direction and number of vessels to the Luftwaffe base. The data is sent to all U-boats in the general vicinity. They gather in wolf-packs of four to six U-boats and wait. Incidentally, Dodd, I heard from the Chief about your discussion with some British officers about the possibility of U-boats tracking our convoy garbage. That came up this morning. They are still considering it.

"Typically, half of the wolf-packs align on one side of the convoy, half on the opposite side. They remain underwater and observe the convoy until they are ready to attack. Then they come to the surface, usually at night, and as a group, launch their torpedoes. They may repeat this attack mode several nights in a row. Early on, after the German declaration of war, our losses were staggering. You recall the successful U-boat attacks on our East Coast between January and July of this year when over three hundred and seventy-five of our merchant ships were sunk. And most within sight of our civilian population. Then we started using escort ships, like the British. The U-boats backed off and now confine attacks closer to the final destinations. We are up against a determined and clever enemy, gentlemen."

Jack caught the Captain's eye. Gleason nodded toward him. "Captain, several deck cadets on board, including myself, were at the Merchant Marine Academy during that period. We read about these attacks in the newspapers. Why did it take so long for our Navy to go after the U-boats?"

"Dodd, the answer to that question is beyond my pay grade. Maybe you can run for Congress one day and get to the bottom of it," he replied with a smile. A few laughs.

"Finally," Gleason continued, "as you know, the Germans have ports along the coast of France and northern Norway. From there they can launch surface ships to attack us. And the German Luftwaffe have airports in Norway, a mere one-hour flight time from where our convoy will pass. Their aircraft carry bombs, torpedoes, and mines along with high-powered machine guns."

Jack now understood why the Captain appeared so despondent when he returned from the meeting on shore. He could hardly blame him. He also understood why some of his mates had referred to convoys to Murmansk and Archangel as "suicide runs." How ironic, thought Jack, a suicide run to the city of Archangel.

Jack wondered if all the men on board should know about these newly outlined risks.

But he had sworn to keep quiet. Anyway, there was no reason to cause more anxiety among the crewmembers. They all had volunteered, they were trained, and this was their duty. Besides, everyone else in the Army, Navy, Marines and Air Corps was taking risks just as they were.

Jack widened his eyes when he saw Captain Gleason smile.

"Gentlemen, I will not leave you in a state of depression after all that negative news. There is some good news to balance things. First, the British have been fighting the Germans at sea since October of 1939. They have three years of valuable experience which they are sharing with us and we can use to our advantage. They have sunk many U-boats. And as you know, the Brits have determined that freighters and supply ships are best protected if they travel in convoys. Our convoy, soon to depart from Halifax, will consist of about forty freighters and liberty ships. Most of these ships have three or four long-range antiaircraft cannons. That means any attacking German aircraft will be facing over one hundred and twenty cannons. In addition, each of our liberty ships has eight, Swiss-designed, Oerlikon 20mm machine guns. That is a formidable force for any attacking aircraft."

The Captain now got up from his chair and began walking among the officers as he spoke.

"The British have significantly improved their detection devices for finding the U-boats. Their sonar is excellent, and we are improving ours. In addition, they have invented a system called Radio Detection and Ranging to electronically locate aircraft miles away and ships on the surface before they are in sight. You may have read about it. They call it RADAR. Each year the technology improves. Our ship does not have radar, but all our escort ships do. In addition, the Brits also use new radio direction finding instruments called Huff-Duff to triangulate U-boat radio transmissions and pinpoint the vessel's locations. And the US Navy has developed improved depth charges to destroy U-boats. As you may know, when destroyers attack U-boats they attempt to position themselves directly over them and drop a pair of depth charges aft, then shoot a pair from the sides of the stern, then shoot another pair from the beams. It is unlikely the depth charges will actually strike the U-boats. The hope is that each explosion and subsequent shock wave will jar the U-boat to one side, then the opposite side and crack the hull. As water fills the vessel, it will sink or be forced to the surface to be destroyed by gun fire. Now the British are working on new depth charges called Hedge Hogs. An array of ten or twelve of these Hedge Hogs or bomblets are shot simultaneously from British destroyers in a circular pattern. There is no underwater explosion unless they strike a U-boat. So, every explosion means a strike and every strike means a sinking."

Jack was fascinated with the level of knowledge pouring from the Captain's brain.

"And as you know, included with our convoy ships are many escort vessels. They consist of corvettes, destroyers, cruisers, and small aircraft carriers. Additional escort ships will join us as we approach the British Isles. They will be most useful as we cruise north around the Scandinavian Peninsula."

Jack shuffled in his chair but was breathing easier. The Captain was on an optimistic screed.

"There is one more fact to consider which is to our benefit. That is the bad weather of the North Atlantic. We will encounter fog banks, snow, high winds and vast waves. It may not be much fun on board, but it will make attacks on us very difficult for the Germans. Planes can't fly and U-boats can't find us. So, for those religious souls among you, pray for bad weather."

The officers chuckled. The relief was palpable.

"One last thing," the Captain added, "if U-boats are detected by our escort ships we can take evasive maneuvers. That means we can make a zig-zag course to confuse U-boat targeting and reduce the likelihood of a torpedo hit. Before we cast off from Halifax, I will review the mechanics of this program with you and how we coordinate with the other ships.

"Finally, I would like to remind you all about shore leave. We are here in Halifax for three more days. And we will have stops at other unnamed ports overseas. When on shore you must not speak to anyone about our schedule or destination!" he nearly shouted.

"You should assume the Germans have sympathizers and spies everywhere. No discussions with ladies of the night, girlfriends, bar mates, ministers or anyone, no matter how benign they appear. 'Loose Lips Sink Ships' is no joke. Make sure all the men under you have a clear understanding of this." Jack was proud he did not inform the drunken Brits at the Citadel of the alleged destination of the *Esek Hopkins.* Then Gleason looked at Dodd. "I suspect,

Dodd, that loose lips are more likely to aid the Germans in locating our convoys than our trail of garbage."

Jack responded only with, "Yes, sir."

Gleason closed out, "I think I have spent enough of your time this evening. I will end by saying that I will do everything in my power to protect you and the rest of the crew and to successfully deliver our cargo to the assigned destination…and deliver you safely home again. Now get down to the mess hall and fill your bellies."

All but Jack and Williams followed the Captain down to the mess hall. As the Captain clamored down the stairs, Jack heard Gleason make one final observation, "Don't forget, men: it was Hitler who declared war on us. Let's punch him out for good and send him to the grave."

"Hurah!" they shouted.

Jack was starting to like and respect Captain Gleason even more than before. But Jack remained in his seat and contemplated all he had just heard. Williams was at the helm, but he too was lost in thought. Jack was distressed, yet not despondent after the Captain finished up with a somewhat optimistic perspective. Still, it seemed every time Jack sat in on one of the officers' meetings with the Captain, his anxiety ramped up another notch or two. Why was the Captain exposing Jack to this level of tension and stress? It was just a few days ago, during that evening anchored in Long Island Sound, when the Captain was telling him about U-boat attacks at night, strict lights out, and aggressive German captains. Could the Captain be sending a different message? Get out of this dangerous business, Jack. You are in way over your head.

Was his sister, Margaret, correct? Sitting in quiet thought, Jack now made some important decisions.

First, he decided to start praying again. He was raised as a Catholic but was not a regular churchgoer and stopped his night-time prayers when he was about ten years old. He would start nightly prayers again. This would please his mother. No need to publicize it, just a few prayerful thoughts before sleep. Jack believed there was a God. Now, on this hazardous voyage, he came to the realization that his life or death was completely beyond his control.

Second, once the *Esek Hopkins* cast off from Halifax in the next few days, he would devote all his time and full concentration to performing at his best, to getting along with all his fellow crewmen, obeying his orders, following instructions and learning as much as possible. As a lowly deck cadet, he made no major decisions, but he would be the best deck cadet on the ship.

Third, whenever possible he would position himself in safe places on board and use utmost caution when on deck and performing his duties. He would take no unnecessary risks. If this ship was going to be hit by a torpedo, he wanted to be in a spot that gave him the best possible advantage for survival. After his terrible dream, he would stay out of the engine room, and stay as high on the ship as possible. Ideally, this meant spending more time near the helm. Fortunately, he was appointed to gun mount 4, which was one deck above the helm on the port side. He also would wear his life vest as often as was practical.

Fourth, he would keep a brief diary, even though it was discouraged officially. If he made it home, it would help him recall the dates and events which otherwise would soon be forgotten. If the ship was sunk, well…

Until this meeting with the Captain and officers, Jack had given little thought to how clever and determined the Germans were. Or how sophisticated their technology was.

Little did Jack Dodd know what horrors lay before him. Then there was the accident.

CHAPTER 8

A Problem

JUNE 16 PRESENTED ITSELF AS a clear breezy day in Halifax. The *Esek Hopkins* had weighed anchor early in the morning and was heading out to sea through the choppy, narrow channel to test her guns in the open ocean. The Navy Armed Guards and merchant crews were excited to initiate gun practice for the first time. Shortly after breakfast, Jack was in his room chatting with Alex when he felt the ship experience an unusual jolt which caused them both to stumble and fall. Within five seconds the klaxon general alarm sounded. There was a scheduled drill on this day, but Jack and Alex realized this was much more. As they raced up to the main deck, everyone was gazing over the starboard side of the *Esek Hopkins.* Alex went to the side and Jack ran up to the wheelhouse level. He looked over the side to see considerable debris floating past the ship toward the stern. He looked toward the bow and saw a massive barge jammed against the bow of the ship.

Just then, someone yelled "Man overboard," and a crewman threw a life ring over the starboard side. Jack saw two men amidst floating debris drifting rapidly in the strong tidal current. One was grabbing for flotsam; the other appeared to be unconscious in his life jacket. Without orders, several deck cadets began to lower a lifeboat, and Jack scrambled down to the main deck just in time to slide down the rope to join the other crew members in the lifeboat.

One of the ad hoc crew was Murray Wayburn, who was from Baltimore and attended Forest Park High School one year behind

Jack. They enjoyed commiserating about Baltimore at the dinner table. Murray was a husky guy who had played football during one of the high school's best seasons. He was manning an oar and pulled strongly while creating a rhythm for the other rowers. They plied swiftly toward the men who had drifted quite a distance away.

Luckily, two small private motorboats arrived to pull them from the water. No other victims were seen by the crew, so they rowed back toward the bow of the *Esek Hopkins* to ascertain what level of damage had been done to the ship. To their surprise, after gaining a better perspective, they gazed alarmingly at two damaged barges with a partially submerged, overturned tugboat with a single huge propeller projecting out of the water. There was steam bubbling up from the bowels of the tug, and Jack, Murray, and the rest of the crew decided it would be more valorous to row away to avoid a small explosion at the bow. And since the *Esek Hopkins* was loaded with ammunition and TNT, they were concerned more about a conflagration involving the entire contents of the ship.

This had already happened once before in these same Halifax waters. Jack recalled reading about that tragic day, December 6, 1917, during the First World War. It was a clear cold morning with no weather issues. Incredibly, in spite of perfect visibility, two ships underway collided in Halifax Harbor. One ship was loaded with munitions. No life was lost from the collision and after a struggle, with both vessels backing and maneuvering, the ships disengaged using their own power. Unfortunately, a small fire started on the munitions ship. The Captain realized the potential hazard and called for all hands to abandon ship. The injured vessel drifted toward shore and just after 9:00 a.m. the ship exploded with indescribable violence. An enormous fireball shot hundreds of feet into the sky. The shock wave rippled through Halifax and created a huge circular *tsunami* in the harbor estimated to be sixty feet in height. Many ships were overturned. It crashed on shore and forced its way up five street blocks into Halifax, destroying some sixteen hundred buildings. Over two thousand citizens were killed that morning and over six thousand were injured.

Jack whispered to himself, "None of that today."

They rowed back toward the superstructure the of the *Esek Hopkins* and Murray, with a booming voice, yelled up to Captain Gleason on the bridge, that there was no sign of fire or flooding, but a tug was overturned and sinking. Gleason had already notified the Canadian Coast Guard. He yelled that he was going to back away from the collision since the vessels were drifting closer to land. Under Gleason's watchful eye, the pilot on the *Esek Hopkins* reversed the engine and disengaged from the collision. Jack, and the lifeboat crew rowed closer and inspected the bow. They saw no sign of a defect in the hull structure. There was minor compression of the tip of the bow. They rowed back toward the bridge. Gleason yelled down. "Any sign of through-hull damage?" Murray yelled back, "No sir. Just a minor dent."

By now the Canadian Coast Guard vessel and another tugboat had arrived. Together the two vessels secured the barges and partially submerged tug, and slowly towed them to shore.

Then the Coast Guard vessel pulled up to the bow of *Esek Hopkins* and confirmed the findings. But as a precaution, they dropped a diver in and after fifteen minutes, the diver bobbed to the surface, removed his mask and confirmed an intact bow.

But still this was a major collision with the near sinking of a commercial tugboat and damage to a pair of barges. At this point, it was not clear if there was loss of life. The two men pulled from the water were on their way to the hospital.

Jack, Murray and the colleagues in the lifeboat paddled around a bit and then rowed back to the pullies hanging from *Esek Hopkins.* With some difficulty and awkwardness, the lifeboat was lifted to the main deck and repositioned on its rack. Jack realized this launching of a lifeboat was good practice for the crew. It was the first time one had been launched and retrieved. But the process took too long. Jack made a mental note to discuss this with the Chief.

Jack trotted back to the wheelhouse. The Captain, the Chief and Sparks were in an animated conversation with the pilot. When a break occurred in the heated discussion, Jack confirmed to the officers the minor damage he observed on the bow. The Chief pulled Jack aside and explained what he had observed from the bridge. According to Chief Cockrell, the tug was pulling the two barges side by side. It approached the *Esek Hopkins* from the port side, which gave the *Esek Hopkins* the right of way. The local pilot on board was steering the *Esek Hopkins* toward the narrow entrance channel. The Chief warned the pilot of the approaching barge.

When they both realized they were on a collision course with the barge, the pilot ordered the engine into neutral, then reverse, but it was too late. Clearly, it was the tug that should have altered course to avoid the collision. These barges normally carried ammunition, but on this morning, fortuitously, they were empty. The *Esek Hopkins* struck the barge amidships and pushed it up and over the tug, flipping the tug and destroying one barge and damaging the second.

Captain Gleason instructed the second mate to take a few deck cadets forward to inspect the inside of the bow of *Esek Hopkins* and determine what, if any, internal damage had been done.

Within fifteen minutes, Mark was back and reported there was no leak or internal damage. The barges and tug had been the recipients of all the force and damage of the collision.

By radio, the Coast Guard authorities cleared *Esek Hopkins* to leave the harbor. They informed Captain Gleason there soon would be an investigation.

With the same local pilot at the helm, the ship proceeded and safely maneuvered through the channel and out into the Atlantic to carry out the planned gun testing. Two deck cadets remained in the bilge area near the bow to be certain there was no leakage while underway.

There was none.

Most crewmen thought the collision was a sign of bad luck.

But Jack wondered if the collision could be the opposite for them—after all, they had suffered no significant damage. And this collision suggested that the ship was sturdy and well-constructed. In addition, none of their crew suffered any injury, other than a few falls and subsequent bruises. What's more, the ship was under the authority of the local pilot on board. There was no fault of any crew member or Captain Gleason. Blame for the accident would be determined following a thorough investigation by the Canadian Coast Guard and Port Authority.

Only much later would Jack learn just how fortuitous this accident was for the *Esek Hopkins* and her crew.

As the *Esek Hopkins* cruised out into the Atlantic, Jack redirected his attention to the task at hand. He was excited about this practice opportunity and anxiously manned the 20mm Oerlikon machine gun on the port side. The Navy Armed Guard crewman at gun tub number four was Ron Seward, along with a second deck cadet Al Fitzgerald. They reviewed in detail the operation of the weapon. Ron explained that the Swiss-made, single-barrel machine gun could fire an astonishing four hundred rounds per minute. The bullets were loaded into flexible belts or into a large round metal cassette known as a magazine. The bulky magazines held sixty bullets and weighed about fifty-five pounds. With continuous gunfire, all sixty bullets were expended in a brief eight seconds. To conserve ammunition, Jack was trained to squeeze the trigger in one-second intervals, which allowed only eight bursts if his timing was correct. But eight high-velocity bullets could take down an airplane.

Jack learned there were many alternative bullets available for this powerful weapon. Ron reviewed the types for Jack and Fitz. "The ones we are using in this practice session have green tips and are not explosive. Other bullets include red-tipped bullets which are incendiary, white-tipped bullets designated as explosive, and gray-tipped bullets which are explosive and have small amounts of phosphorus on the surface which causes them to glow after exiting the muzzle. These tracer bullets allow the gunner to see the direction of his fire and make his shooting more accurate. Finally, there are black-tipped bullets which are armor-piercing. Typically, the explosive phosphorus-tipped tracer bullets are placed in the magazine in every fifth slot." Jack and Fitz were paying strict attention.

Ron continued, "As you recall, the guns require three men to operate efficiently, and a certain rhythm is required. It is like a sort of lethal ballet. You two keep ammunition available and load quickly. You can alternate changing the hot barrels." They took a few minutes to practice loading belts and alternately, the magazine.

Ron then demonstrated how the shooter secured himself in the shoulder harness, then he moved his body left and right, up and down to aim. He then cocked the gun to load the first bullet into the breech. The final step before firing was to release the safety latch. The shooter then picked targets and pulled the trigger. Each man learned to perform all the jobs in case there was an injury. Ron reviewed how to change the barrels, which got so hot when in use, they had to be changed every few minutes. Jack and Fitz both removed the heavy barrels from two long metal tubes which were filled with water and attached to the side of the gun tub. They practiced unscrewing the barrels from the gun until they were comfortable with the process. Thick asbestos gloves were required during this part, which made the process cumbersome. Each gun had a total of three barrels. There could be no delay in waiting for barrels to cool. It took about thirty seconds to remove and replace the gun barrel. They timed each other during practice.

During a battle, thirty seconds could seem like an infinity, and no one could afford to be clumsy.

Jack and Fitz were now trained and ready! Jack wanted to shoot first, so he eagerly positioned himself in the C-shaped shoulder brackets and looped a belt around his chest to hold him tight in position. Ron helped secure him. By moving left and right he aimed the weapon. To aim up, he lifted his feet off the ground and by his weight the barrel of the gun rotated upward. To aim down toward the water, he pushed his feet hard on the deck. The gun was more massive and cumbersome than he expected, so Jack practiced kicking and pushing until he got the feel and rhythm.

The *Esek Hopkins* had arrived at the target area and was drifting leisurely in the moderate ten-knot breeze. There were a half dozen floating white buoys in the distance which were the targets for all the 20mm guns on board. Scattered rat-tat-tats began to fill the cool clear air as other guns blasted away. Jack was ready, although with more anxiety than he expected. Finally, with a casual air of nonchalance, cleverly suppressing his anxiety, he aimed slightly above one of the targets and squeezed the trigger for about one second. An impressive, powerful jolting rocked his body. The rapid, piercing rap, rap, rap accompanied the firing of each bullet. It was as if the machine had a soul of its own. The power of the device dominated Jack. He watched with fascination as the glowing tracer bullets accelerated toward the white target contrasted by the azure background of the sea. The eight splashes in the water could easily be discerned at the five-hundred-yard distance. His shots appeared to hit just above the target. Shots that close were considered a strike.

Ron raised his brows, pushed his cap back, and said, "Fine shooting. Good control. Nice grouping. You held the trigger for just about one second. Got off eight rounds. Must be beginner's luck."

Jack quickly responded with a chuckle and only half kidding said, "I am a natural."

He was impressed with the power, noise, and thrust of the machine gun. There was a thrill to the whole process, and he wondered how he would perform during a true threat situation.

Feeling overconfident, he blurted out, "I can't wait to knock some of those miserable Kraut bastards out of the sky!" Fitz and the Navy Guard chuckled.

Jack clearly was enjoying the experience. In fact, so far, it was the most exciting and enjoyable exercise he'd had as a deck cadet. Ron, Fitz and Jack alternated practicing on the powerful weapon. Not unexpectedly, Jack's accuracy dropped off as the practice continued. After his first success, he became overconfident and his shots fell short, or wide to either side. He became frustrated. Meanwhile, Ron and Fitz improved with their shooting as the day wore on. But on his last turn with the gun, Jack had a direct hit on the target, which gave him renewed confidence.

Ron declared, "I think you are ready for combat, Jack. Just remember, it will never be this easy again. Next time, others will be firing at you." Jack nodded and contemplated what that startling fact actually meant. Was his mother still praying for him?

That afternoon every gun on the *Esek Hopkins* was tested. The fore and aft antiaircraft cannons were the loudest. Their shells blasted out three to six miles depending on the color code on the shell tip. Jack watched in awe. A few seconds after the deafening crack of the cannon, there was an explosive spark in the distant sky followed by an audible thud after a six-second delay. A puff of black smoke slowly drifted in the distance. Jack could not imagine flying an aircraft into the heavy flak from a convoy of armed ships. Were the pilots brave or just crazy?

The day's exercise was successful—all guns were in good working order. The pilot turned the ship westward and proceeded back to Halifax Harbor to await its next assignment.

Dinner in the mess hall that evening was full of excitement and tall tales. Everyone had a story. Jack had learned a new skill. After dinner he went directly to his room and fell into a rapid sleep as soon as he hit the pillow, even as Alex tried to carry on a conversation.

The next morning at sunrise, the *Esek Hopkins* pulled anchor and again sailed out from Halifax Harbor into the ocean to join with twenty-five other ships in the newest convoy. This convoy, known as PQ 17, had one more destination in Canada before heading across the Atlantic. That was the city of Sydney, located on the eastern-most shores of Nova Scotia. The six-hour journey was uneventful, other than a single false alarm of a U-boat sighting. They arrived in Sydney Harbor on June 18.

Once anchored, Jack was granted leave and went ashore on a launch with a handful of colleagues. They soon learned from a local Sydney newspaper that there had been six men involved in the tugboat collision back in Halifax. Four men drowned and two were rescued. It was big news throughout Canada.

That same day, Captain Gleason was requested to attend a hearing about the collision and went ashore. Because of the accident and inquiries, the scheduled departure of the *Esek Hopkins* with PQ 17 was cancelled. They would be assigned to a new convoy. Jack and the crew were disappointed. Unknown at the time, this delay in their departure may have saved their ship and their lives. It was the beginning of the *Esek Hopkins* lucky streak.

The days wasted away as the number of sunsets mounted. The crew was itchy and bored and progressively agitated. Were fights on the verge of breaking out, below, quietly in the distant corner of some hold, out of sight and sound? A meaningless spark could set it off.

Everyone's mind was occupied with one thought; when do we depart from this desolate, intolerable port? Even for locals, there was little reason to visit Sydney by land, except to buy groceries or supplies, with its terminal location at the eastern tip of the barely populated province of Nova Scotia. And even less reason to visit by sea from foreign ports.

Eventually, the hearings regarding the tugboat collision ended. Now, at least there was hope among the crew that the Admirals were planning to get another group of ships together for the next convoy and departure soon would follow.

During the delay, Jack made several day trips to Sydney by water taxi. Like Halifax, he was unimpressed with the city. The city was a small, dingy port with no significant sights, no military fort, only a small yacht club. The Canadians called them Yacht Squadrons.

On the morning of July 4, as memories of his favorite summer holiday stirred his soul, Jack made another visit to Sydney, this time with a goal. To celebrate the holiday in his own way, Jack made a collect call to his family in Baltimore. He got through with his call and his mother's melodious voice was soothing, like a luxuriant salve on his roughened existence. His sisters made rounds on the phone, mostly with a perfunctory "Hi, Jack. All Ok?" Bill, the closest sibling to Jack in age, was a resident at Mercy Hospital and Jack caught him on his day off at home and they had a practical, but brief conversation.

Then Margaret grasped the phone, nearly shouting, "I hope you are happy, Jack Dodd! Things are not going well. Mother needs you here! We need…" Bill grabbed the phone. "All is fine here, Jack. You know how Margaret is. Say, I saw something in the papers about your Liberty Ship crashing into a tugboat in Halifax. What about it?"

Jack was surprised it made the Baltimore papers. "No worries on our end, just a few scratches on our bow. But four crewmen were lost on the tug. A bit of a mess. Because of that we got delayed for our crossing. Nothing else I can say now. Tell everyone I am fine. And, say, if you see Gail, tell her hi and I am thinking about her."

Bill seemed a bit surprised, "Ok. Mother wants another word."

She sounded tearful as she told him to write more often; they had only received one letter. He reminded her that while at sea, the letters both ways took much longer to arrive at their respective destinations. She said she loved him, and the call ended.

After hanging up the phone, Jack surprised himself with his soul-felt ennui. He remained standing by the dead phone, gazing at it, as it sat sadly on its hook, as if it had the answers he was searching for. He reviewed each word of the conversation. *Mother sounded ok. What did Margaret mean? No one else said there was an issue. Maybe I should not be here. Wasting time away. This ship may never deliver these goods to Russia. At the rate we are mov-*

ing, the war could be over. Most likely it was just Margaret being Margaret. Bill would have told me if there were any issues I needed to be concerned about. Bill seemed surprised that I sent greetings to Gail. I guess he forgot we had been seeing each other. Or...did he know something about her...? Maybe phone calls are not such a good idea.

He and the phone finally went their separate ways. No sense blaming the phone. Break the thought cycle. But clearly, he did actually miss them and the old homestead in Baltimore. The Fourth of July weekend was a big one for the Dodds, and Jack imagined all the fireworks and crowds at nearby Gwynn Oak Park. The scenes from the past drifted through his mind: holding Gail's soft hands, the cotton candy, the clattering roller coaster, the aroma of popcorn, the rays of the sun glittering off the paddleboat pond, the snapping sounds of the shots from the shooting gallery, the collection of colorful clowns prancing around, the taste of hot dogs and mustard, the taste of Gail's kisses after the sun disappeared, the interruption by the bright, persistent noisy fireworks, and then after...

But his reverie could not go on forever and he reverted back to reality and his duty on the good old *Esek Hopkins.* As the water taxi returned him and his navy mates from shore, he could not help but admire the colorful flags snapping in the breeze on his floating home away from home. Still, the nostalgic thoughts would not go away so easily.

The next morning, Jack busied himself with deck cadet rounds and inspections along with some studying. Chief Cockrell came looking for him and asked him to test out the Vaco life suit in a real-life situation. From storage in the "tween deck" he took the suit up to the main deck as ten of his colleagues gathered around to observe. The Chief stood by as an objective observer.

He told Jack to assume there was an emergency, and to don the suit as quickly as possible without assistance. His deck mates looked on with amusement as a small crowd formed. Jack was now a little nervous with all the scrutiny, but he unfolded the suit, put the leaden boots flat on the deck and with some difficulty, unzipped the front and let the suit drop. He struggled and wiggled to place his feet into the boots and was eventually successful. He pulled the suit up over his back and slid his arms into the heavy sleeves. He had to jump and jiggle a few times to allow the suit to encase him. He grabbed the large zipper at the crotch and pulled it up to his neck. He securely cinched the neck collar. A mate helped him don an external life vest. Once zipped up in the suit, Jack thumped clumsily to the side of the ship. He descended down the ship's exterior ladder and, two feet from the sea, he jumped into the cold water. He held his nose as he jumped, and for a few seconds, he was fully submerged. The suit had floatation, and along with his life jacket, he popped up quickly. Unfortunately, he did not cinch the neck collar tightly and a small amount of water entered the suit. His shirt quickly was soaked with the cold seawater. A lesson learned and shared with his mates as he awkwardly climbed back onto the ladder. The suit had built-in, small lead weights at the bottom of the boots to help stabilize the occupant in a vertical position while in the water. This made climbing ladders and walking difficult and rather clumsy. The mates got a good chuckle watching the only brave soul among them attempt this test.

Quietly, their admiration for Jack went up a notch. Ski was in the group and even he had a few laughs.

The Chief helped Jack onto the deck. He chuckled, "I have seen better things in a whore house. Men, I want everyone on board to do a practice run with these suits. You saw some of the difficulties. In an emergency, there will not be time to experiment. That is an order, men."

Still no word on a departure date. A minor fight broke out in the engine room between the indefatigable Ski and an oiler named Jake. It was quickly broken up by Chief Engineer Steve Littlejohn, who had experience in this realm. If Ski ever hoped to advance to Chief Engineer someday, this was not the way to proceed.

On another visit to Sydney, several days later, Jack decided to attend a class for signaling.

This task was an important skill and was usually performed by the first or second Navy Armed Guards. On *Esek Hopkins* that was Sparks. But as a deck cadet, Jack felt it would give him a leg up if he learned it sooner rather than later. The concept was simple enough and involved aiming a bright signal lamp at a distant ship and opening and closing a shutter to create signals. The difficult part was that each letter of the alphabet had a code. The code had to be memorized with precision so signals could be transmitted and received quickly. With emphasis on quickly. It took months of practice to become proficient.

While taking a break during the course, Jack heard rumors about the recently departed convoy, PQ 17. Jack listened carefully since that was the convoy the *Esek Hopkins* had originally been assigned to. The rumor was that the convoy was heavily attacked between Iceland and Russia. Sadly, there was a significant loss of Liberty Ships.

When Jack got back on board, he went directly to the bridge to see if anyone could confirm the rumor. The Chief, second mate Mark Williams, third mate Lance Lockhart and Sparks, along with the Captain were discussing that very topic.

"You may want to sit down for this, Jack," offered the Captain. Jack remained standing.

The Captain began, "Starting on July 1 and for two days, the German U-boats and Luftwaffe attacked PQ 17. Of the thirty-five merchant ships in the convoy, only eleven made it to Archangel."

"Oh, God," was all Jack could mutter.

"It appears that the losses were caused in part by an error of judgement on the part of the British Admiralty, the Captain continued. "British air reconnaissance had seen the German battleship *Tirpitz* docked at a Norwegian port. PQ 17 was underway from

Iceland to its destination of Archangel, Russia. Their projected course was relatively close to the *Tirpitz*, and the British command assumed the massive battleship soon would cast off and attack the PQ 17 convoy. Even though most of the ships in convoy PQ 17 were American, they were under the command of the British in this sector of the ocean. Air and U-boat attacks on the convoy were heavy. Convinced that the massive *Tirpitz* was cruising toward the convoy to finish them off, British Command ordered the American battleship USS *Washington* and the British battleship HMS *Duke of York*, and other protective ships, to leave the convoy and sail southwest in utmost haste to challenge the German battleship."

All Jack could utter was, "How could they do that? Everyone knows the escort ships are critical."

The Chief picked up the explanation as the Captain poured another cup of coffee. "The British had hoped to intercept and attack the *Tirpitz* after it sailed from Trondheim, Norway. Then on July 3, British Command issued the order for the convoy to break up and disperse with each ship ordered to sail to Russia on its own. Without the escort ships, the Admiralty felt it would be safer for the merchant ships to sail individually. This was a huge strategic mistake. Following orders, the ships did disperse. But without escorts, individual ships were easy targets for the U-boats and the Luftwaffe. The losses were staggering, the worst of the war. At least one hundred and fifty-three merchant mariners and Navy Armed Guards lost their lives. One can only imagine how many hundreds of vehicles, tanks, and aircraft were lost. And nearly one hundred thousand tons of food and supplies are now resting on the bottom of the sea. During the three-day onslaught the Germans made over two hundred sorties with six bombers and thirty-three torpedo planes. The miserable bastards lost only five aircraft."

The Captain followed, "To split up and disperse PQ 17 was a huge mistake, and the error rests on the shoulders of the British Admiralty. And as it turned out, the *Tirpitz* did not even leave port.

Apparently, the Germans were ambivalent about exposing this valued battleship. The *Tirpitz* was the twin of the Bismark battleship which was sunk by the British on May 27, 1941."

As Jack absorbed all the facts surrounding this debacle of the North Atlantic, it sent a quiver down his spine.

"And I don't have to remind you, Jack, that was the convoy we were scheduled to sail with," continued Gleason.

Jack almost shivered as he stated the obvious, "That collision in Halifax may have saved our lucky lives."

Lance spoke up. "Now, we will sail with the next convoy. And the Germans are even more experienced."

Here the Captain firmly stated his position. "I will not stand for any separation of our convoy from our escorts. That will not happen again. In fact, I will demand we have extra escort vessels before I sail." The Captain thought for a moment. Then he said, "I can even imagine that if I can't get adequate escort protection, we might run into something—like what happened in Halifax." He paused, then winked his right eye and smiled. They all looked at him, paused, then laughed out loud. *He couldn't be serious. Could he*?

What lay ahead with this new convoy…? How long would their luck hold?

It was a sunny clear, damp Friday morning on July 15 in Sydney Harbor. Jack was up early and quickly got to the bridge and gazed out to see more Liberty Ships collecting in the harbor. The *Esek Hopkins* would join them on a three-thousand-mile journey across the North Atlantic. He smiled and took a deep breath as his opportunity had finally arrived. The anticipation, the unknown, the danger thrilled him. He had never sailed across the ocean and had never seen battle. Pleasure sailing in the Chesapeake Bay had comprised his entire boating experience. Imagine, two weeks in the North Atlantic. What weather would they encounter? Would they see combat action? Would they suffer as badly as the previous convoy? Would he get a chance to fire the 20mm machine gun and knock some of those evil Krauts out of the sky?

Then, just before they pulled up the anchor, with the Chief at the helm and Lance and Jack as auxiliaries, Sparks ran to the bridge and announced he had just received a message from the Admiralty. The *Esek Hopkins* and three other Liberty ships would not sail with this Convoy. No reason was given.

Jack was despondent. Below the level of conscious thought, a groan involuntarily escaped from his gullet. Those on the bridge empathized with the sentiment.

Lance said, "The Captain is down in the mess. You better tell him, Sparks."

"Oh thanks, I get to break the news," was all he could come up with as he went on a search.

The mess was nearly full when Sparks found the Captain sitting with a few of the greasy engine room men in casual conversion, which he sometimes did to sense the men's sentiments. Sparks whispered in the Captain's ear. The Captain stood and announced to the crew that they would not sail on this day. An aggressive, loud groan erupted; cups banged on the table, feet shuffled, murmured cussing filled the chamber.

The Captain knew of no reason for the cancellation and he and Sparks quickly departed back to the bridge, as grumbling from the men echoed down the corridors. Ironically, a significant contingent was actually happy the orders had changed. Who wants to sail into a nest of submarines manned by bloodthirsty Germans? Others were tired of waiting and wanted to get to sea and end the delays.

Over the next few days at anchor, rumors aggressively circulated. Some shipmates returning from Sydney heard that one of their classmates from the Merchant Marine Academy was killed when his Liberty Ship was sunk after sailing out of Baltimore. Jack recognized the name, and did not know him well, but it was a shock, nonetheless. Another rumor was that a Russian submarine had struck the Tirpitz twice with torpedoes, but she did not sink. Rumors could take on a life of their own and the *Tirpitz* story alarmed everyone on board. The implication was that the *Tirpitz* was unsinkable. The mere existence of *Tirpitz* on the Norwegian coast had been enough to frighten the Admiralty to strip the last convoy of its escort ships with devastating results. That rumor was never confirmed. Another rumor avowed that all future convoys were cancelled. No one knew what to believe.

As if a warning to all on board who were excited to get into the fray, late that night, a deafening explosion rocked the entire crew out of bed. Everyone rushed to the deck, but there were no other explosions, no adjacent ships on fire or signs of anything amiss. Scrambled radio messages flickered among the anchored ships. The Captain, in his blue night clothes with white piping and hair disjointed, was up and standing next to Sparks in the radio room, trying to make sense of the scrambled messages. After a few minutes, the consensus was that a German sub had surfaced nearby and fired a pot shot in the direction of the anchored Liberty Ships and then scurried off. No ships sustained any damage, other than a little needle into everyone's psyche. The *Esek Hopkins* was anchored about a mile from the submarine net protecting Sydney Harbor. A Canadian Coast Guard cutter zipped out on a search but found nothing. Jack was now wide awake and curious enough to stay out on deck and roam around, searching for additional enemy action. Through the dim red glow on the bridge, he could make out the Captain engaged in the same ritual.

Troubling thoughts racked his mind as he strolled the dark decks alone and conversed with his troubled conscience. They had not even left port and the Germans were out there watching. The shot had been a message, a warning, an omen. U-boats were waiting just beyond the harbor safety net and could track you for the entire journey, with infinite time, picking and choosing targets, casually sinking ships as if playing a silly game of hide-and-seek.

Escort ships could not stop them from their grisly duty. Two weeks in the ocean was all the time in the world to sink forty ships in a convoy. In his mind Jack framed a picture of smelly, unshaven men, salivating as they targeted ships through their periscopes, laughing with each release of a deadly torpedo, chewing black tobacco and uttering guttural, incomprehensible orders, clicking their heals and saluting to anyone around.

After this episode, many seamen, including Jack, decided to sleep in their clothes and use a life vest as a pillow. No time to dress in an emergency. Some even left their shoes on.

Time slowed down, weary tension built again, as most of the crew was anxious to get moving and their exhaustion accumulated and wore on them. Their reserves were depleted, their training wasted, their lives slipping away. Jack and a small contingent of fellow merchant mariners were so bored they decided to drop a lifeboat over the side and sail around the beautiful coast of Cape Breton Island. This offered an opportunity to test the mast and rigging. The fishing pole they took along had little success, but at least it was a small, yet stimulating adventure. Jack taught his mates in the lifeboat the basic principles of sailing, and Neptune was kind enough to offer temperate breezes.

Other activities became more public on board. Gambling was allowed on merchant ships but was not encouraged. Small games in the privacy of staterooms were largely ignored. But now, gambling at cards was a constant on board, and more public. A subculture evolved where certain groups set up tables at one end of the mess or the other. The tables became the "house." Different games were offered and rotated on a daily basis. Three card draw, five card stud, blackjack, Texas hold 'em became part of the new routine, even with announced starting and closing times. The Captain and officers decided to tolerate these new standards as long as there were no fights. Gleason made an announcement on the public address system to that effect. He would shut down all gambling if a single fight started. The crew knew he would do it, too.

Aside from a few short-lived arguments and quarrels, there were no fist fights on board.

Even the cooks tried to make life more interesting. One day was Italian day, on another day they offered Southern food. However, the chefs could only do so much with the limited ingredients on board.

Jack hated to lose money gambling, so he occupied himself with reading, studying the famous Weems navigation books, practicing semaphore, reviewing charts, setting up and participating in fire drills, and showing his deck mates how to rig a lifeboat with a sailing mast.

New merchant ships began to arrive in Sydney Harbor. One was a Liberty Ship named *Patrick Henry*. She too had been built in Baltimore, and by chance, Jack had observed her launch on September 27, 1941. It was the first of the newly designed Liberty Ships launched. President Franklin Roosevelt had attended and given a nice speech. He had referred to Patrick Henry and his famous speech "Give me Liberty or give me death." Roosevelt claimed this new class of Merchant Marine ships would bring liberty to Europe, hence the name Liberty Ships. It was the first and only time Jack had ever seen the president of the United States in person. Even though Jack did not vote for him, it was a magical event.

The Captain finally allowed a more liberal policy for shore-leave. Even the Navy Armed Guard officers allowed their men to visit the boring port of Sydney more frequently. Word quietly spread that there were a few spots in town where friendly women could be located. Jack refused to partake in those amusements, and for good reasons. He did not like to cheapen male/female relations to a simple fee-for-service moment of pleasure. And his religious upbringing inculcated the immorality of such engagements along with the medical risks, so aptly pointed out in the medical officer's presentation. Finally, he held onto the memory of Gail. So why did he carry two rubbers in his wallet? For emergency use only, his conscious told him.

While sipping on a warm beer at one of the drinking holes in Sydney, Jack encountered crews from the other newly arrived ships. One mate informed Jack they heard that the *Esek Hopkins* had been sunk. Rumors again. It was a good thing Jack had sent off a letter home that very morning.

After another meaningless, dreadful week at anchor, a third group of ships departed without the *Esek Hopkins,* and the crew started to feel like an ugly spinster. Not all the convoys went to England or Russia. Other destinations included South America, the Mediterranean, and South Africa. Typically, the crews did not know their destinations, even when they heaved anchor and set sail.

On Saturday, July 25, the Captain returned from a conference on shore with news that they finally were going to cast off at four o'clock. the next morning. *Oh joy*! The bad news was they had orders to return to Halifax. *Who, under God's heaven, makes these bizarre decisions*? Jack had difficulty getting to sleep with the excitement and was up at 3:00 a.m. to observe the pulling of the anchor and motoring out. Although it was not new to him, he never tired of watching the departure process, and he always learned something. On time, they heaved the anchor and motored out of Sydney Harbor with five other ships and one corvette escort.

Within six hours of arriving at Halifax, the Captain was given new orders and the pilot boarded and guided the ship again into the Atlantic to join ships of a new convoy.

The new convoy, given the moniker PQ 18, consisted of forty merchant ships, and the *Esek Hopkins* was positioned in the third slot on the left in the second row. A lucky spot, Jack thought. Everyone on board knew they did not want to be on either outside row, an area referred to as "coffin row." Those vessels were typically the first to be struck by German torpedoes.

Seven destroyers escorted the merchant ships. Once underway, the word on the bridge was that the first destination was Clyde,

England. Jack noted the date in his diary; it was Monday, July 27. The speed of the convoy was set at a fairly brisk ten knots.

It did not take long for the excitement to begin. The first day out, just off the southeast coast of Nova Scotia, one of the Liberty Ships was struck by a torpedo. It was 7:30 a.m. when the watch on *Esek Hopkins* spotted two white rockets in the distance signaling a torpedo in the water. This was the German way of welcoming the newly formed convoy into the Atlantic war. Jack was stunned. The war was here sooner than he expected. He never learned which ship was struck or if she sank. He wondered if *Esek Hopkins* were struck, would anyone else in the convoy notice, or care? Yes, was the answer, of course. But it might take a day or so for the news to get around, because of the radio blackout. They would learn by Morse Code with light signals—the only way to communicate among ships during combat.

As they cruised east into the vast Atlantic, the winds were light, and the seas calm.

Whales could be seen blowing water ten feet into the air. Their calming effect belied the ever-present danger under the surface. While Jack and the first and second mates were on the bridge taking in the view, the Captain joined them. The discussion soon evolved to their ultimate destination. Captain Gleason informed them that they were expected to arrive at Clyde, England, by August 6 and then proceed to the Persian Gulf and ultimately end up in Australia. The journey might take up to half a year. Jack knew this was planned misinformation on Gleason's part. Jack had seen the boxes with "Moscow" printed on them. Playing along, Jack expressed how pleased he was to travel halfway around the world to warm weather—and get paid for it.

Early the next morning the crew was awoken by another huge explosion. Jack was a light sleeper and he flung himself out of bed, quickly put his shoes on and sprinted up to the bridge just as the ship's general alarm sounded. Well, if the crew wanted action, now they got it.

A nearby sister ship, the *Mary Luckenbach*, had first sounded her whistle with six blasts, meaning she had spotted a U-boat on her starboard side. She then fired her three-inch cannon at the U-boat. The loud report of the cannon had aroused Jack and most of the crew from slumber. There was no clear evidence of a hit. The U-boat disappeared. Within minutes a corvette appeared but elected not to drop depth charges. The Navy Armed Guards on the *Esek Hopkins* manned their guns for a while, but no other sightings were confirmed. The crew got back to their regular duties until 9:00 a.m., when, from the bridge, Jack spotted two white rockets on the horizon. Another merchant vessel was under attack. Chief Cockrell sounded the shrill klaxon, and the Navy gun crews, along with selected deck cadets like Jack, donned life jackets and raced to their weapons. This time they could feel the muted underwater "thunks" of far-off depth charges.

After an hour, the all-clear signal was sounded. Two ships hit in two days.

With the strict "lights out" policy for all convoy ships, on clear nights, it was very difficult to visualize your neighbor, unless the moon was bright. While Jack was on the bridge, he noted how eerie it was, knowing all those ships were out there all around you, but essentially invisible. On clear days, it was a different story. U-boats running on the surface, which they did ninety-eight percent of the time, could spot clouds of smoke from the merchant ship's stacks many miles away. Like fragrant flowers to bees.

CHAPTER 9

Wind and Waves

DURING HIS STUDIES ON BOARD, Jack learned that the first attempt at undersea combat occurred during the Civil War. A primitive, one-manned submarine tried to sink a wooden war ship, but the attempt failed. Large-scale combat with underwater ships did not develop until the First World War. During that war, U-boat captains would approach a ship before launching a torpedo. They would pull alongside and announce that they were planning to sink the vessel and allow passengers to get into lifeboats.

That all changed during World War II. The Kriegsmarine had improved its U-boats considerably and developed sophisticated strategies which made them highly effective for their grisly, morbid tasks. This time, it was all-out war, and there were no longer warnings to targets.

Jack's first inkling of this aggressive German strategy occurred while he was at the Merchant Marine Academy. As Jack was attending classes, a dozen German U-boats unmercifully attacked and sank hundreds of merchant ships directly along the East Coast and right in front of the US Navy during the six-month interval between January 1942 and July 1942. Clearly the Germans recognized that America had the ability to save England with a transatlantic pipeline of endless merchant ships. U-boats would be the ax to cut that American supply line.

Jack's second inkling was at the Irish pub in New York where the British Navy men acquainted him with the aggressiveness and brutality of the German U-boat commanders. Jack no longer looked at the war in abstract terms as a world-wide chess game for power. It was real, it was brutal, it was a life and death struggle, directly in front of him, and it was unrelenting.

And he now took it personally, viewing himself as a target. He was now counting on his mother's prayers to help. What else could he do?

Now on their third day at sea, Jack visited the helm after dinner to chat with the officers on duty. Chief Cockrell was at the wheel and Lance Lockhart was the auxiliary on duty. As Jack entered the helm station, they were involved in an animated discussion about baseball. Cockrell was an avid New York Yankees fan, and he was sure the Yankees would be in the World Series. Lockhart noted the St. Louis Cardinals were having a strong season and would likely battle it out with the Yankees in September. Jack chipped in that Baltimore had a minor league team named the Orioles, but they were not very good.

At this point Captain Gleason stepped into the helm station and the three men saluted.

The Captain asked no one in particular if it was time to go to blackout conditions.

Cockrell said unconvincingly, "Captain, I was just preparing to make the announcement."

Gleason smiled, accepting Cockrell's imperfections. He turned to the other officer on the bridge. "Lockhart, what is our speed and course?"

"Sir, we are cruising at nine knots with a course of eighty-two degrees. We are maintaining a three-hundred-yard distance from the ship in front and behind us, sir. The weather conditions show light winds and clear skies. The forecast is for increasing clouds tomorrow with ten to fifteen knot winds out of the west. The chance of rain is twenty-five percent, sir."

The Captain nodded. Lockhart hit a home run.

Gleason looked at Jack. "Dodd, how many propulsion systems do U-boats possess?"

"Sir?" he stammered. He collected his thoughts. "Um, they have diesel motors, sir. Two. They use these when traveling on the surface. When submerged they convert to electric motors." Jack inhaled slowly and stared into space. What could he have added? Speeds.

Predictably Gleason asked, "Which U-boat engines give the best speed?"

Jack had attended a lecture series on U-boat characteristics at the Academy. He scrolled through his mind. "Sir, the diesel engines are the best for speed. On the surface they can reach speeds of fifteen knots. But this consumes excessive fuel, so the ideal speed is ten knots."

"And the electric motors?" asked the Captain.

Jack could not recall. He knew it was slower. He guessed, "Five knots, sir."

The Captain nodded toward Cockrell, who quickly responded, "Sir, the standard model 7 C German U-boat can travel underwater with electric power at eight knots for brief periods. At four knots it can remain underwater for a maximum of eighteen hours. Their batteries will not last beyond that. In addition, their oxygen for their fifty-two crewmen will be exhausted by twelve hours."

"Dodd, why is it important for us to know this information about the U-boats' speed and endurance?" Gleason asked.

Jack was ready for this one. "Well, sir, the U-boats can spot our black smoke from twenty miles away. Since our convoy travels at the average speed of the slowest ship, which is eight or nine knots, the U-boats can outrun us on the surface. They can easily catch up when traveling at twelve knots. In a day or two they can position themselves ahead of our convoy on either side. Then our convoy, as if entering a pair of claws, can be attacked from both sides with torpedoes." Before the Captain could respond, Jack added, "And in addition to following our smoke trail, they may also track our garbage as we discussed earlier, sir."

Gleason replied, "Your analysis of the German tactics is correct, Dodd. By the way, I have been thinking about that garbage idea you learned from the Brits in Halifax. It's a very interesting idea. The more I think about it the more sense it makes. Our convoys are over a mile wide. And forty ships unload a lot of garbage. And we have to include the escorts. Some of the trash sinks but fruit and paper products float on the surface. Maybe for days. Cockrell what do you think? Can we estimate how many tons we unload during our two-week voyage? We should think about this. Maybe we should only empty trash at night, so it has time to sink before daylight. Or maybe we can figure out how to compress the trash into small compact packets which are heavier than water. Or could we burn up the light material and dump the heavier waste? Chief, I would like you to study alternatives and speak to the head cook, what's his name? Determine exactly how we dispose of garbage. Interesting pick-up, Dodd. Was your discussion with the Brits in a bar?"

"Well, yes sir, it was," he responded sheepishly. No need to pass on how drunk the Brits were.

"Nothing wrong with that. Always a good idea to keep your eyes and ears open. Never know what you might learn. All of you," said Gleason as he glanced at the men. Cockrell had no heart in the idea and never got back to the Captain. And other factors overwhelmed the Captain, and slowly pushed aside this interesting idea.

Gleason then returned to the original topic. "So we were talking about U-boats. In the past, we discussed that clever Admiral Donitz. His motto was, 'advance, attack, sink.' He wanted his U-boat captains to be aggressive and use creative strategies. The captain who sailed into New York Harbor that night a few weeks ago was one of the aggressive ones. They have been known to surface in the middle of a convoy and discharge torpedoes from the bow and stern. And our three-and five-inch cannons cannot aim low enough to hit them. Only our 20mm Oerlikon machine guns can aim that low. But their range is only about five hundred yards. So, the U-boat captains have learned that and know they are safe if they stay beyond that distance. Clever boys. Also, you gunners must be careful when firing at U-boats. If they are between our ships, you may hit one of ours with friendly fire. But I am sure the Navy Armed Guards all know this."

The men nodded. Lance offered, "And I think we all know that most U-boats have a potent cannon and two machine guns on deck. The cannon can fire quickly and is powerful enough to sink a ship."

Jack took a deep breath as he recalled the story, told by the Brits in the New York bar, about the U-boat cannon fire on the British merchant ship. Three shots, delivered quickly and accurately, severely damaged the vessel, blew a crewman's head off, and created a sickening nightmare Jack still could not get out of his head.

Gleason agreed. "Correct. And never, never underestimate the aggressiveness of our German foes. I read that the most aggressive U-boat captains never return to port with any torpedoes remaining on board. On every outing, they expend all torpedoes; otherwise, they view their mission as a failure. And always watch for periscopes. Scan the horizon with binoculars. Every man on board needs to know that they must immediately report any periscope sighting. And they should estimate distance and compass direction."

"They all have been told, Captain. Even the cooks and engine room men," offered the Chief.

"Good. And we all know that we are subject to U-boat attack at any point along our journey across the ocean. On the other hand, the Luftwaffe can attack only when near land. Thank God the Germans don't have any aircraft carriers."

Jack had a question since they were continuing with this U-boat discussion. "How do U-boats manage in severe storms? Do they stay on the surface and get battered around?"

Gleason looked at the Chief. "Want to answer that one for Mr. Dodd?"

"Yes, sir," the Chief responded. "U-boats can't stand to remain on the surface during rough weather. They get knocked around too much. So they submerge to avoid the turbulence and putter along at three or four knots to minimize battery use. But as we discussed, they must come to the surface to operate their diesel generators so they can recharge their batteries and take in oxygen for the crew. Storms can last for days, so when oxygen runs low, they come up despite the foul weather and hold on for dear life as they bounce around. Recharging may take three or four hours. Once they submerge below thirty feet, all is calm. While surface ships like us are tossed around like little corks."

Soon Jack would learn exactly what it was like to be a little cork in the endless ocean.

Three days after departing from Halifax, the *Esek Hopkins* and the ships of PQ 18 entered a thick fogbank. Neighboring vessels were no longer visible at a distance of one hundred feet.

Normally, a ship in dense fog is obliged to ring its bell or sound its horn at regular intervals. But this was not done in wartime—for obvious reasons. From the ship's helm, even the bow was not visible. It was a strange sensation, powering along at nine knots with nothing discernable in front of the ship. Some of the crew never got acclimated to this strange sensation and made a conscious effort to stay below. The fog was good news in terms of protection from U-boats and aircraft, but bad news in terms of possible collisions with other friendly ships.

On Captain Gleason's orders, Jack and three other deck mates dropped a fog buoy off the stern and let it drift into position three hundred yards aft. The fog buoy offered a method of safely keeping vessels in line during foggy conditions. Secured to the stern of each ship by a line, the five-foot vertical floating buoy shot water up about six feet in the air as it was dragged along. Once it was dropped from the stern of the lead ship, the captain in the following vessel paced himself to keep the buoy adjacent to the pilot house. In this fashion the Captain knew that the lead vessel was always three hundred yards straight ahead. This simple arrangement was a huge aid in avoiding collisions. Unfortunately, it did not work in stormy conditions.

Jack watched the buoy and line disappear into nothingness after only fifty feet.

Ironically, after the fog lifted the next day, they learned that somehow, during the night, they had unwittingly passed the ship in front of the *Esek Hopkins* without mishap. Jack learned a basic seaman's lesson: no scheme works 100 percent of the time.

On the first day of August the breezes increased and an unwelcome cold, heavy, skin-prickling rain commenced. This was the first foul weather the *Esek Hopkins* and the forty ships of the PQ 18 convoy had encountered on their journey across the Atlantic. As the day advanced, blistering gusts accelerated to gale force and waves rose to alarming heights. Some peaked as high as the ship's masts. As the waves climbed to their maximum height, the brutal wind blew white showers off the top of the huge pyramids of seawater. With wave direction and winds out of the northwest toward the back of the ship, the stern swayed slowly back and forth, making steering very difficult for the man at the helm. Jack learned this was known as "broaching" and it was the most difficult situation for controlling the ship's direction. A straight course was nearly impossible. Steering the ship in these conditions was exhausting.

As the *Esek Hopkins* powered up and over the peak of each huge wave, and precariously descended, it seemed to accelerate down into a trough where the bow buried itself in a valley of seawater. When watching this process from the helm, it was hopeful speculation and an act of faith to assume the bow would rise up again. The entire forward end of the ship was not visible to the helmsman, with the sea washing all the way to midships. As much as half the ship could be underwater. The military tanks and a single locomotive lashed to the deck of *Esek Hopkins* were awash with seawater during these dives. If a chain holding a tank on deck were to break, havoc could ensue. A loose tank could slide all over the deck on a destructive mission. The best outcome would be for the tank to burst through the side rail and cast itself overboard.

In addition to the forward and backward pitching, the vessel also rolled from side to side because of the fifty-knot winds battering the ship's beam. This motion may have been the most disorienting for the crew. One had the sensation that the ship would roll over and not right itself. The combination of these variable motions created havoc in the human inner ear. Even experienced sailors could not prevent vomiting. Fear creased the faces of the crew. Food intake was impossible, and water intake difficult. It was too distressing and disorienting for anyone to look out windows or portholes. Only the officers at the helm forced themselves to watch the alarming turmoil. They were required to. At night the psychological stress was nearly unbearable, with the up and down motion, lateral rolls, and no visual cues in the total blackness, the disorientation was complete. Only the compass could guide them. Captain Gleason required all officers to stay on the bridge, no matter the state of their gastrointestinal tracts. For stress relief, Gleason allowed the officers to alternate at the helm on an hourly basis, not at the usual four-hour terms.

It seemed endless, an infinity of waves and wind. All around the skies were dark, wet, foreboding. Ascending and descending the ship inched forward. Only rarely could one catch a glimpse of the mast of a far-off neighboring ship. The gray monotony, the repetitiveness, the constant up and down, the never-ending loss of balance and horizontal perspective wore down even the toughest sailor.

The safest place for all crewmen to attempt to rest was flat on the floor. Resting in bunks was out of the question, unless a seaman could rig a series of straps to hold him in. And only those sleeping on the lowest bunks would try this. Even on the floor, it was not possible to actually sleep because of the rolling. No one was permitted on an outside deck unless there was an emergency.

And no one could imagine what emergency would draw them out there. All hands remained inside, packed like sardines and tossed around as if in a blender. The vomiting was epidemic, with no cure. Even if a rare crewman had an appetite, it was not possible to prepare meals. Dishes flew in all directions and spent more time on the floor than in cabinets.

Novice sailors fared the worst with the rolling and pitching of the ship, especially on the first day. By the third day, the human body seemed to get more acclimated to the chaos. As a novice, Jack could not get out of his mind a premonition which started on the first day of foul weather. When at the helm, early during the storm, he watched with horror as the ship descended into the valleys adjacent to the huge waves. He grasped and held on tightly to the binnacle or onto the table bolted to the floor. He felt certain the ship would never come up. He broke into a sweat. Captain Gleason noted his pallor and the shocked look on Jack's face.

"Take it easy, Dodd, we will get through this," said the Captain as the ship creaked and groaned and the wind and dark seas churned and whipped around the *Esek Hopkins*. Jack was unable to reply.

Two days into the storm, crewmen stumbled around zombie-like. Protracted conversations were nil. Brief greetings to colleagues were about all a man could get out. No coffee with a morning chat group; no card games or checkers or chess; no reading or studying. The time was consumed by watching the hours slowly tick by. Some wondered how all the other ships were holding up through this abysmal weather. But each man, in spite of all the misery, kept the one pleasant thought in the back of his mind: this weather was keeping away the German U-boats and Luftwaffe. Some men averred that they prayed for the bad weather to persist throughout the entire voyage.

As Jack observed the repetitive, unrelenting horror show before him, he contemplated what to do in the event of an emergency, a real emergency. He resolved how he personally would deal with disaster like the ship rolling over and sinking. He decided to wear his life jacket whenever he walked around the ship, even to the toilets. He was not the only crewman on board with the same idea. The life jacket served dual purposes: if he crashed into a bulkhead or railing as the ship rolled, the life jacket would act as a cushion to protect his body. And if the ship went down, he would avoid the effort of having to find and don a life jacket in an emergent situation. Still, this was a small psychological remedy for the horror of that first day experiencing the vile and incomprehensible tumult.

During storms, using the toilet turned into a vigorous workout. For number one, Jack learned he had to spread his feet and place his hand against the wall while directing the line of pee with the other. If the ship healed over twenty or more degrees, there was a significant curve to the urine trail. With some effort and practice, he could improve his aim and avoid decorating the floor. With number two, at least he was sitting. The crew's bathrooms had eight toilets adjacent to each other with no intervening walls for privacy. To stay on the can during a storm, Jack had to spread his legs and hold onto the toilet seat with both hands as best he could.

Finishing up required waiting until the ship was relatively level, then doing a quick wipe.

At least vomiting into the toilet was performed while kneeling with your head "in the head." In this case, there were fewer accidents because the distance was shorter. Still, that did not make it fun. None of it was fun.

It was next to impossible to shower during a storm. In normal weather conditions, the crew could only take brief group showers since fresh water was in short supply. But even that was not available during the worst of the weather. If a storm lasted a few days and no one could shower, collective body odor became a problem on board with no good solution. Deodorant could do only so much.

By the third day, Jack was visiting the bridge several times daily to see how the officers were holding up and if he could assist. All the officers' attention was directed to steering and remaining on course, as the ship tormented the men with repetitive, nauseating regularity, swinging awkwardly, unnaturally from side to side, up and down with the whim of the waves and irregular gusts of wind. Even though the conversation was somewhat truncated, he forced himself to remain on the bridge in spite of the frightening view of the enormous waves. Mother Nature was in a foul mood.

As the storm slowly dissipated by day three, he got more acclimated to the chaos and turmoil. After days of pounding, Jack believed what the Captain had said, and accepted the prediction that the ship would survive the elements. The only real reason he forced himself to stay on the bridge was to become acclimated to the terror. He knew that if he wanted to remain in the Merchant Marine, he must learn to accept and tolerate these horrible conditions. So he stayed.

The other issue that everyone listened to, but few wanted to discuss was the groaning, creaking, and snapping sounds within the ship's hull. Jack, and anyone paying the least bit of attention, could sense the minute twisting of the steel as the pounding waves torqued the welded metal hull. He recalled his first view of the *Esek Hopkins* in port at Hoboken and the absence of rivets on the hull plating. All the plates were welded together. Rumors abounded that some of the first Liberty Ships constructed had instances of cracks developing along the welds. In fact, it was said those defective ships were made in California at a Henry Kaiser shipyard. They were given the moniker "Kaiser's Coffins." Jack was aware of at least one story regarding a newly built ship tied up at dock which developed a split along a welding seam below the water line, and quickly filled with water. As water accumulated, the entire hull split in two. Amazingly, the ship was hauled out and repaired within twenty-four hours. These ships were built quickly and not designed to last forever. Still, Jack had sense enough to recognize that by far, the greater danger to sinking was the enemy.

Still, everyone wondered, even the officers, how much punishment the hulls could endure. The Captain and a few of the officers had been informed that the engineers had established that on rare occasions, the hulls of some Liberty Ships could crack under severe strain. As a solution, the engineers decided to add heavy-duty, eight-foot curved steel brackets to the top corners of each of the five holds. The authorities certified that this additional support would fix the stress problem and stabilize the hulls. One of the jobs delegated to Jack and his fellow deck cadets was to make rounds below deck and inspect these brackets daily. Jack never liked this part of the hull inspection because he was unsure of what to look for. He and one other deck cadet would stare up into each corner of each hold and shine a light on the brackets. There they were. They all were welded in place. During rough weather, during his inspection, Jack and his colleague could hear creaking and groaning sounds emanating from some of the brackets. But there was never any sign of damage. Each day, they reported their findings to the Chief, who simply nodded and grumbled something incoherent.

Another job for deck cadets was to inspect the bilge area throughout the length of the vessel to watch for water accumulation. There was always some water in the bilge, but large volumes of water were a sign of a significant leak and the source had to be found and repaired. The Chief had assigned Jack and six other deck cadets to carry out this daily inspection. These inspections were particularly difficult during storms. The walk-through included the evaluation and testing of all twelve of the ship's bilge pumps. Fortunately, there was no significant evidence of leakage in the *Esek Hopkins*, even after the horrendous storm, or even after the accident in Halifax. And all bilge pumps remained operational. Still…one could not help but wonder. What was the tolerance of these steel hulls in rough seas with a full load of cargo?

During the storm, Jack spent plenty of time paying his dues to Neptune by hanging over the toilet and evacuating his stomach. Over time, for some reason, his nausea lessened. The storm-created disorientation reminded him of the roller coaster at Gwynn Oak Park in his neighborhood, a ride which never resulted in his vomiting. But this wild ride in the Atlantic was clearly different.

The one thing Jack found he comfortably could do in these extreme conditions was to push himself tightly into a corner booth in the mess area and sew. All the stools and tables were bolted to the floor and offered a good level of stability in spite of the surrounding chaos. He and one of the bosun's mates figured this out. They hooked up one day and spent time during the storm sewing canvas covers for the ventilator shafts. While immersed in this mundane activity, at one point, Captain Gleason stumbled by, looked at the pair, immediately recognized the merit of their concept, and sat down to assist with the sewing. The three enjoyed a brief chat. After a few minutes it was obvious the Captain's skills lay elsewhere.

Before he gave up and departed, Gleason noted, "Forecast from Sparks says we will get clearing tomorrow with twenty-knot winds. Hopefully, then we all can start eating again and stop losing weight!"

As he continued silently sewing, Jack thought of the age-old wish for boaters to have "smooth sailing." Now that phrase had real meaning for him and was no longer simply a figure of speech.

But nothing lasts forever, and the weather, as Sparks predicted, along with other more significant issues, was about to change.

CHAPTER 10

The Race

Finally, the winds calmed to ten knots, and the seas leveled to a one-foot chop. After three days in a blender, *Esek Hopkins* was running smoothly on a level plane, a journey so quiet and peaceful for the men, they wondered if they were moving at all. Sister ships were visible around them. A few were still being accounted for but there was a new lease on life with sunshine leading the way. A whale spouted in the distance. The mood on board was happy and uplifting as if something they had done somehow justified a celebration. Their only real accomplishment was survival. But that was something. Judging by the gaiety of some crewmen, hidden liquor must have appeared and was performing its magic.

Jack arose late from his bunk amidst his smelly, snoring compatriots. He placed his feet firmly on the stateroom floor, documenting there was no annoying swaying. He remained in place for a moment to confirm this was not simply a brief respite. Barefoot, he easily strolled toward the exterior wall. He partially uncovered the single round porthole to observe sunlight sending its warm rays like a smiling god across the sea. His roommates rolled in their bunks and groused about the irritating brightness, so he quickly covered the port. After dressing quietly, he did some stretching exercises and shadow boxed in his stocking feet. He elected to make his daily rounds before breaking his fast. His morning duties included inspecting the bilge and the twelve pumps, looking at the brackets in each hold, checking the lifeboats and their respective lines, peeking in the engine room, and walking on the main deck to assess the status of the steel chains holding all the hardware and tanks in position. Before proceeding to the mess hall, he jogged up the external staircase to the bridge. He stuck his head in to see who was at the helm. It was Lance Lockhart and he was alone.

"What's going on Lance?" he asked.

"Can you believe the weather? Like we died and went to heaven. It is so calm they left me here by myself. They must think I know what I am doing…At least I am maintaining course and have not hit anything," he chuckled.

Jack walked in smiling, "Well, I feel safe. Where is everyone?"

"The Captain is in his room with the door closed. He has not slept much and is trying to catch up. Sparks is my backup and is in the radio shack. I think Chief and Mark are chowing down. By the way, the Chief wants all the officers on the bridge at 1000 hours for some kind of meeting. He thought you might like to attend," he continued.

"Sure, I can be there. I just completed deck rounds, and all is good. It is a good thing we pulled the lifeboats inboard and double-secured them before the storm. I can find no broken lines or damage. Unless the Captain says otherwise, I am inclined to keep them in this position. In an emergency we just have to cut one extra line to get them over the side. I am heading to the mess."

Lance nodded. "Mention it to the Chief first. Gleason has a lot on his plate. See you up here at 1000."

In the mess hall, Jack saw his roommate Alex "the Greek" Salamis consuming a vast breakfast of grits, eggs, sausage, and bread. Jack grabbed a tin tray and proceeded through the short line filling his tray with lesser quantities of the same choices. The cooks would be busy all day.

As Jack sat, Alex was in a friendly mood and groused, "Hey, pal, you woke us this morning. Our butts were tired after that hell Poseidon put us through the past three days."

"Sorry, man, I tried to be quiet. Hey, I thought Neptune was the god of the sea."

"You Americans. You can't keep the ancient gods straight. Neptune was the Roman god of the sea. Poseidon is the Greek god," Alex retorted.

"Okay. I will keep them straight. A defect in my education, I guess. Say, where are Ross and Ralph?"

"They decided that sleep was more important than food at this point, in spite of your best efforts to wake them," Alex replied with a grin.

At this point, Ski approached, with tray in hand, wearing soiled jeans and displaying a grumpy expression. He chose a seat at the table adjacent to Jack and Alex. He nodded as he sat and grunted some inarticulate sound.

Jack wanted to maintain a positive disposition around the inadequate man and said as cheerfully as he could, "Hey, Ski, how is it going? We finally got some beautiful weather."

Ski pushed his food around, as if he had not heard the question, and loaded the eggs with salt and pepper. With pretentious nonchalance, he shoved a large glob in his mouth and while chewing, got out, "Okay."

Jack decided to get more specific to see if a more profound response could be elicited. "You work in the engine room, right?"

With apparent effort, Ski nodded. "That's right. You know that. I am the chief wiper. I keep all the drive shafts and gears clean and oiled. I keep this damned vessel moving. And don't you forget it. It is not the cleanest job in the world, but we keep this damned vessel moving," he repeated. "And we do it twenty-four hours a day."

Alex raised a brow as he gathered more eggs on his fork and said with the inherited wisdom of the ages, "I think about you engine-room guys all day. Working down there, day and night, in the heat and grease. I don't know how you do it. We go nowhere without you. We deliver nothing to nobody without you. And you know how to fix broken things. You guys are the pulsing heart of this ship."

Ski looked at Alex for the first time and with some suspicion in his eyes. Was he making fun of Ski's job?

Jack thought Alex was laying it on a bit thick. He hoped Alex would back off. To intervene, Jack threw out, "At least in the cold weather, you guys stay warm. While we deck cadets are getting wet, boiling in the sun or freezing in the snow." Alex got the message and said nothing more.

Ski observed, "You deck cadets may have it tough in the cold weather. But you are not outside all day long. I seen you hanging around the bridge quite a bit, Dodd. Up there kissing ass, making good with the Captain. Some think you act like an officer."

Jack started to stand, but Alex quietly, without being noticed, placed his hand on Jack's thigh, holding him down. Jack glanced at Alex, then gazed at Ski.

"The Captain has requested my presence on the bridge. I like to learn, and he likes to teach. Anything wrong with that?" Jack said, making a sincere effort to keep his tone of voice normal and level. He was glad he had been practicing his boxing stance and shadow-boxing when alone in his room. Once Alex had seen him air-punching and he also offered to assist Jack in his training. At the same time, Jack hoped he would never need to use the information and training Chief Cockrell had given him on that first day on board.

Ski shoveled in his last bites and commented as he stood, "No time to yack. Work to do."

Jack spoke quickly as Ski started away. "Thanks, Ski." Ski threw back a Parthian glance but did not slow his pace.

Alex let out a light belch and observed, "There is a lovely fellow. Isn't he the one you had a quarrel with at the Academy?"

"Yup. I am trying to avoid any repeat."

"I'll watch your back, Jack," said Alex, followed by a delayed chuckle. "Get it, 'your back Jack.' And we should keep up with your exercises and air-punching. You may need it."

Jack arrived at the bridge fifteen minutes early for the meeting called by the Captain.

Chief Cockrell, Mark and Lance were already present. Mark was at the helm, getting acclimated to the somewhat unique feeling of steering in smooth seas. One other crew member arrived shortly after Jack. The Chief introduced him to everyone, saying, "Gentlemen, for those of you who have not met him, this is Chief Engineer Steve Littlejohn."

Jack walked over and offered his hand. So, this man would be the boss of Ski.

Littlejohn looked the part. He wore coveralls with thin blue and white stripes which proceeded upward from his greasy black boots to his chest-high bib. Oily gloves were hanging from his rear pocket on one side along with a red cap on the other side. As Jack walked over to shake hands, it appeared the superficial grit had recently been washed away from the surface of the skin, but the black grease under his nails would never disappear. The only anomaly in his appearance was the perfectly combed and precisely parted, neat brown hair and the aroma of Vitalis about him, which somehow overcame the engine room smells. The officers seemed to know him already, but they all decided to replicate Jack's politeness and shook his hands, even if somewhat reluctantly.

"Well," started Captain Gleason, "thank you all for joining me for this little informal meeting. First, let me announce that no one is in trouble." He chuckled as he sensed the look of concern on his colleagues' faces. "I have asked the cooks to bring up some coffee and donuts shortly," he added.

Jack scanned the officers. The Captain's words did not offer much relief. Blank looks occupied their faces. Why were they anxious?

"Let's all sit," requested the Captain. "So, I have invited Chief Engineer Littlejohn here because of his background and experience. Before taking on the job as chief engineer on *Esek Hopkins*, Mr. Littlejohn worked at a manufacturing facility on the West Coast. Not just any facility, but at a shipyard that designed and constructed Liberty Ships. So, I have asked Mr. Littlejohn to share some of his experiences and insights surrounding the construction of Liberty Ships."

Littlejohn started reluctantly. "Sir, I am not much of a public speaker."

Gleason reassured him, "Relax, we are fellow crewmen. Let's start with who employed you."

"Yes, sir. I worked for the Henry J. Kaiser company. They were builders of hydroelectric dams in the Pacific Northwest. Before the war, Kaiser's only interaction with boats was that he was a minor partner in the Todd Shipbuilding Company in Seattle. He never built a boat in his life."

Littlejohn was pleased with his answer and looked toward the Captain for additional encouragement.

Gleason said, "So President Roosevelt was looking for someone to manufacture merchant ships and had met Kaiser. What do you know about that?"

"Well," he started, "Kaiser was a great salesman. Somehow, he convinced Roosevelt he could build large numbers of merchant ships and build them fast. That was the most important issue; build them fast; faster than the enemy could sink them. He used the Henry Ford method of mass production. And he built the ships in sections, twenty-one. Once the keel was put in place, huge cranes delivered the pre-built sections in exact order. Each section was put in position and welded to the next. Walls, pipes, electrical conduits were all built into each section. Like putting a giant puzzle together. Once all the sections were in place, an army of men and women crawled all over the ship and did the finishing work. Another thing they did was to cancel the use of rivets. Using rivets to bolt the steel hull plates together took too long. So, instead, they welded each huge steel plate together. It was amazing," Littlejohn declared with obvious pride.

Gleason jumped in. "What was your job at the plant, Littlejohn?"

"I was foreman of a welding team. Fifty men—and women—worked under me. And believe me the women were damned good. And reliable. And they never showed up drunk."

The officers exchanged glances and grinned.

Littlejohn noticed no resistance, so he got into it. "At first it took one-hundred and seventy days to complete a Liberty Ship and dump it in the water. Within six months we cut the time in half. Amazing. There were eighteen shipyards all over the country building the exact same ship. Identical parts. Transferable. If one yard was short, they could ship parts in two days from across the country. It was a beautiful thing. I worked at the Portland, Oregon, yard. It got so big, Kaiser built a city of thirty thousand next to the plant. Complete families lived there. It had everything. Schools, grocery stores, restaurants, churches, etc. He even built a hospital for everyone. He called it Kaiser Permanente. Buses took the workers to plants and the kids to schools. Two of my three kids were born there. I left eight months ago, but I heard they were having races among the shipyards to see who could build a ship the fastest. The last I heard, they finished one in two weeks."

Littlejohn paused to see if the men were bored yet, but Jack and the officers were fascinated. Captain Gleason posed a question. "I wonder why Kaiser is successful. Does he have a secret?"

"Well, sir, in my opinion," Littlejohn said, "Mr. Kaiser is a pretty smart fella. He told us every day on the loud-speaker system that if we had an idea how to improve things, we should go to our managers to tell 'em. At first no one believed it. But some went to the managers with ideas and, by god, they started doing it. They took ideas from anyone, even the clean-up folks. Some fella suggested they run the plants twenty-four hours a day, three-hundred-sixty-five days a year. No one ever did that before. In two weeks, they had it going. Each worker still had eight-hour shifts. They did break the rule in the Bible, though. We ended up working seven days straight with the eighth day off. The workers actually voted on it. And it passed by a small majority. That made it difficult for us to keep track of what day it was. And some of the churches started having services every day. Damn, they are still building those boats like crazy. We all could step off this ship tomorrow and jump on a new one, and everything would look the same and I could crank up the engine just like that." He snapped his fingers.

Gleason smiled. He enjoyed hearing inside stories. He had one more question for Mr. Littlejohn. "So as an expert welder do you have complete confidence in the hull strength of these Liberty Ships?"

Littlejohn responded without hesitation, "Yes, sir. Yes, sirrrr. The welding techniques were tested for weeks. They would weld two large steel hull planks together and then see how much pressure it took to break them apart. They were just as strong as the riveted planks. Those rare ships where the planks cracked were made during the first month, before the welding was perfected. And all ships have some play in the steel during storms. That is when you hear the groaning. Don't forget *Esek Hopkins* struck a barge and tug in Halifax. There were no issues with our hull. And hey, I am on this ship, ain't I?"

The coffee and donuts arrived. A general discussion ensued. Chief Cockrell threw out the idea that these Liberties were designed and built for only one trip across the ocean.

Littlejohn looked at Cockrell, "You asking me?" Cockrell nodded.

"Well, no one told *us* that. We assumed these ships would last for many years and in all kinds of weather. I'll wager they are around long after the war is over."

CHAPTER 11

Land of the Scots

AROUND 6:00 A.M. ON A cool dark morning in August 1942, the *Esek Hopkins* slipped quietly and slowly into the Firth of Clyde in Scotland amidst the thick, heavy moisture of a cold rain shower. Lockhart was at the helm as the Captain observed and threw out suggestions like, "Neutral now. Hard to port. There is a spot. Lower thrust. Not too close there. Depth is safe at forty feet. Drop it here."

Once safely anchored, a small skiff appeared with bagpipes wailing, a fitting welcome for the Americans as the sun peeped over the horizon decorated with puffy gray-white clouds. The haunting sounds echoed through the quiet anchorage like a sublime scene from a movie show. Jack half expected Clark Gable to hop from the skiff and onto the *Esek Hopkins*. The entire crew was delighted and impressed. Additional Liberty Ships followed in and anchored as the haunting music wailed on. Later, the clouds spread their wings, and the sun found a few more spots to shine through, revealing a beautiful hilly shoreline. The slopes were covered with emerald summer grass illuminated by the misty rays of sunshine. Small, neat houses dotted the coast, with tiny specks of sheep confined by miniature stone fencing, sprinkled amidst the green felt landscape. A small, single castle was observed midway up the hill. Captain Gleason had maneuvered the ship into a bay known as Loch Long at the base of a moderate-sized mountain whose peak was partially obstructed by billowy white clouds casually drifting by.

Other ships from their convoy appeared and were scattered at anchorages around the waterways. Captain Gleason decided to allow shore leave beginning the next day for half the crew, each day alternating. Jack was in the first group, and the next morning they departed on a launch whose destination was the only town nearby; a tiny port known as Gourock.

The fifty-minute trip by launch had an exciting turn. As they sped toward shore, Jack perceived in the hazy distance an enormous gray-brown shadow in the water. They were approaching the British passenger ship the HMS *Queen Mary*. She had just arrived through the mist and recently anchored. It was a spectacle to behold. Jack and the mates in the launch marveled how huge she was.

The captain of the launch was acquainted with her and gave a little dissertation as they sped toward the docks at Gourock. He started, "She was converted to a troop convoy ship a few years ago, and they pack some sixteen thousand troops and crew on her. They sailed from New York Harbor five days ago. After the war started, they painted her in camouflage gray so the bloody U-boats would have trouble spotting her. Henceforth, she became known as the Gray Ghost. She has made trips all over the globe. An entire army division can crowd on board. They say Hitler offered an Iron Cross and $25,000 to any U-boat captain who could sink her. So far it has not happened and likely won't. She can travel at a speed that no submarine or surface ship can equal. Flying along at twenty-eight knots makes her the fastest ship in the seas. She also uses a zig-zag course to avoid torpedoes. They will never hit her. She is more than twice the size of those four-hundred-and-forty-foot Liberty tin cans you lads sail on, and yet she flies along like a sports car."

Jack and his colleagues listened as the young man continued. "Last October, she was fully loaded and sailed to Gourock, just like now. There was a light cruiser escort with her, the HMS *Curacoa*. Somehow the escort ship did not appreciate her speed and cut in front of the Queen. She crushed the smaller ship like a little toy and cut her in two. Cut her right in half, she did. She sank quickly. Sadly, three hundred and thirty-one British crew members of the four hundred and thirty-two aboard the escort ship were lost. There were no casualties on the *Queen Mary*, and the bow was only slightly damaged." As he completed his interesting tale the launch arrived at the Gourock dock.

The tiny town had about fifteen hundred residents and was at the tip of a small peninsula.

There was bus service to Glasgow and, after wandering around Gourock for a while, Jack decided to take the one-hour trip to the big city. He carried only a small overnight bag. As the bus coursed through the lovely hill country, Jack saw evidence of considerable destruction by German bombers. Since large numbers of Allied troops were transported from ships inland, the Germans hoped to do whatever damage they could to the roads and infrastructure.

It was late in the day when Jack arrived in Glasgow. He searched in vain for overnight accommodations, but the town was filled with troops, and all the hotels, inns, and hostels were full. While grabbing a pint at a busy pub known as The Wishing Well, he encountered a young lady who, without being asked, identified herself as Penny McNeal. She said she lived about twelve miles outside Glasgow in the little farming town of Kilsyth. Jack was intrigued. She had cheerful, sparkling green eyes, which flickered gleefully when she spoke. Freckles decorated her smooth skin and no lipstick coated her attractive pink lips. She glowed when she smiled, and he noted slightly misaligned incisors, which gave her a suggestion of impishness. After chatting with Jack for a bit, and learning he had no accommodations, she offered to have him stay with her and her two sisters, Irene and Alice. She was amiable enough and spoke the King's English, although with a heavy Scottish accent. Jack accepted. The fact that she had a house and lived with her sisters, and gave her full name, strongly mitigated against her being a professional. He recalled his interaction with that pro at the hotel in New York with the fictitious name of Melody. That conversation had started with; "Would you like some company, soldier?" This young lady in Glasgow was clearly not in that class. Yet, why was she in a bar looking for male companionship? War changed people in strange ways, Jack thought.

Penny had a two-seater, canvas top, green Morgan sports vehicle which she drove more rapidly than Jack thought appropriate, and with scattered bomb craters, the ride was irregular and bumpy. The car was not an inexpensive one, suggesting Penny was not impoverished.

Conversation was somewhat difficult, with the noisy exhaust pipes and bouncy, rough ride. After about twenty minutes, she pulled up a quarter-mile driveway and parked in front of a prototypical English cottage complete with a steeply inclined roof which included a pair of dormer windows. On the first floor a large bay window projected out toward an ample lush, green garden. Fifty yards away was a huge barn which expelled the bleating of sheep. Straw was scattered about. The cottage looked solid with irregular stone sides painted white. Faint wisps of brown smoke twirled from the chimney in the light breeze. The sun had recently gone to rest behind a nearby hill.

Penny hopped out of the right side and said with a giggle, "Well, Jack Dodd, here is my little home. Alice and Irene are likely preparing dinner. Let's go in. We can prepare an extra table setting."

Jack squeezed out of the sports car and stood stiffly and stretched and groaned. "Where is the great mansion I expected?"

"No complaints, young man. We have hot running water and a shower and tub. Our ice box works most of the time. And our little garden keeps us happy with numerous vegetables," she replied.

Jack smiled at her agreeably and pulled his overnight case from behind the seat. She started up the walk toward the bright red front door, giving Jack his first view of her legs and behind. She was svelte and walked with a surprising level of sophistication for a "country farm girl." She wore casual brown loafers common in the era. Her legs were slender and proportioned. He liked what he saw. This sure beat his smelly, oafish compatriots on the *Esek Hopkins*. He looked around at the lovely evening countryside and had to pinch himself to recall he was in the midst of a world war.

Penny was leaning out of the doorway and called, "Come on, pokey. I want you to meet my sisters."

For some reason, Jack was slow to move. He liked the outdoor scene he was immersed in. Perhaps it was such a radical difference from the never-ending sameness of the open sea that he wanted to absorb more. Or perhaps he was a bit anxious about what would happen inside the lovely cottage. Or perhaps he was responding with suspicion to the apparent kindness and sincerity of Penny. Thoughts of his mother and sisters flickered through his mind. Then Gail.

Go on, Jack. Don't come across as a bore or a slug. Jump in with both feet.

A determined march up the walk, and an accompanying bright smile, brought him toward Penny. "I was so enjoying the beautiful scene here and contrasting it with the monotonous ocean I have become acquainted with," he declared. As he went through the doorway, he was greeted by two pleasant women. They exchanged introductions.

"Come in. It is so nice of you to join us," said Alice, who appeared to be the oldest. "We don't often see Americans in this little corner of the world," said Irene. "Please sit down in our humble parlor. Would you like something to drink?"

"Sure. Whatever you have is fine. Beer, wine, whisky?"

Alice said, "We have a good supply of red wine. Will that do?"

"Yes, of course. That would be fine. I hope I am not the only one drinking," Jack replied.

"I think tonight we all will imbibe," offered Irene.

Jack took a seat and in a few moments, Penny appeared with four glasses of red wine on a small silver tray with someone's initial embossed in the center. Each took a glass and Penny quickly took the floor and offered a toast. She raised her glass and said with surprising determination and intensity, "To a complete and crushing victory over the Germans and their nasty, barbaric race!"

Jack raised his bushy eyebrows and his glass at the demonstrable intensity of her hatred, and said in British fashion, "Hear, hear. I will drink to that all night!" And he nearly did.

To his surprise, Jack enjoyed the dinner with the three sisters. Perhaps the third glass of wine pushed him over the edge and made him sense things with a different perspective. And everyone seemed more congenial. Penny had put on lipstick and some eye makeup and looked quite lovely, Jack thought. In the middle of the meal, fueled by the wine, Jack could not hold back his curiosity and he asked Penny if she was married. She did not respond verbally, but shook her head no. She looked at him pensively and posed the same question to him. He said no. Did she turn her eyes down demurely? Did everyone at the table take a breath? Did the conversation then perk up? There seemed to be just a notch more gaiety at the table.

The wheels turned in Jack's mind. Why was she not married? Was there something wrong with her? How could an attractive young woman have stayed single so long? He would figure it out, eventually.

The simple meal of fresh vegetables and chicken was small, but tasty. Jack wondered how these three women were surviving. Perhaps a flock of sheep brought in some revenue. Perhaps there was another source of income. They did not appear impoverished, but neither were they well off.

As the meal continued, the discussion centered on the war and the importance of the merchant ships Jack was crewing. Then to more mundane topics as Alice did most of the talking.

"The farm was left to us by our late father," she explained. "Mother died in the bombing of London on July 10, 1940. We three had been living in the London suburbs and we collected here at the farm when our father died from typhus a month later. You may recall, London was heavily bombed in the summer of 1940. Irene and I had government jobs but were laid off following the destruction of our office building. It was a horrible mess. Our husbands joined the army and are both now serving in North Africa under General Montgomery. We have not seen them in six months, but they write regularly. Penny, explain your story."

Penny took a sip of wine and smiled as she turned to face Jack. "I was a student at the University of London, in my third year," she began. "I was studying art history. As Alice said, after both our parents died, we moved to this old farmhouse which had been in the family for many generations. We fixed it up. I think it turned out right well. We have a tenant farmer who does an excellent job managing the sheep for us. He has been doing so for many years. I hope to continue my studies after the war. For now, I am a farm girl…"

Jack now had an inkling of how angry the residents of the British Isles were with the Germans. All that made perfect sense. But he still had a feeling there was more to Penny's story. This was not the time or place to get into that topic. Perhaps later.

Jack observed, "You are now in the second massive, destructive war with Germany in two generations. And this little family has had horrible losses. I can understand your bitterness and anger. The Germans must be stopped. I am happy to do my part in some small way."

A piece of butter cake was offered for dessert. Alice asked Jack if he would like a dram of Scotch whisky with the cake. He replied, "I would never refuse such an offer while present in the ancestral home of Scotch whisky."

Jack added after a moment, "We in the United States have felt very little impact from the war. Our economy is now booming following the long economic depression, and women are joining in the war effort. But we recently started rationing gasoline and sugar. However, no one is bombing us or destroying our cities. And we want it to stay that way."

After a few more minutes of small talk, Jack announced, "Ladies, it has been a most delightful evening and I thank you so much for the camaraderie and wonderful meal. It has been too long since I have spent any time with the fair sex. But I have had a long day. Penny, would it be possible for me to take a quick shower before bedding down?"

Penny affirmed, "Of course, Jack. If you get your bag, I will show you the guest bedroom upstairs. The shower is down at the end of this corridor. I will leave towels there."

Jack enjoyed the warm shower immensely. He was in a private shower with a face cloth, a bar of soap, warm water, and a large towel. Such a contrast from the ship showers. He tried to be quick, but the pleasure was beyond description.

As he exited the shower room, Penny was standing in the hallway in a bathrobe. "Good night, Jack. Sleep well and there is no rush to get up early tomorrow," she said.

"Thank you so much for such a lovely evening, Penny," he responded, then added, "I will see you soon." How did that pop out? She smiled and turned to her room. Did her brow elevate just a notch?

Jack quietly ascended the creaky stairs and entered the small cozy bedroom. He folded his clothes and gazed out the dormer window. The night was crystal clear with stars twinkling, while a quarter moon sent subtle rays and alternating shadows along the verdant hillside. He closed the bedroom door but did not latch it. He crawled into a clean, soft, fresh bed for the first time in weeks. Was this heaven?

He was out in five minutes.

A gentle rustling. Warmth. Softness. A whisper…a faint whisper close to his ear. "Don't say a word…please." The warmth and softness enveloped him. It was so natural. So normal. So good. He responded quickly.

"But, no protection."

"Shhh…I have."

Soft, moist lips on his face…his mouth. Slowly. She bit his lip. Inserted her moist liquid tongue. He joyfully responded but made no sound other than rapid breathing. He was ready, but he wanted her to touch him forever. Slowly. He could feel her breath on his face.

Could she hear his pulse throbbing? She descended on him, silently, slowly. He closed his eyes and relished the warmth and natural sensations, all so innocent, so fresh, but not time enough.

She gasped for breath in ecstasy, just as he did. Then the softness of their warm bodies embracing enticed them into a delightful, comfortable, artistic sleep.

The next morning Penny was smiling and chatty at breakfast. Porridge was served with hot coffee. The sisters encouraged Jack to fill up since Penny was planning to take him for a long walk in the Highlands. The two sisters politely refused to join them. The sun was peeking over the lush green hills as they started out. They carried only walking sticks and a water pouch. Penny led the way through hills and dales, over streams, up cliffs, and across lovely moors dotted with heather. They encountered many sheep roaming about. The view of the sea was spectacular. In the distance Jack could pick out his ship anchored innocently and peacefully.

The scene was so quiet and harmless in appearance that he imagined he was gazing at a children's Christmas Garden. He felt lucky to be on land and wondered why he had chosen to go to sea. Especially as he sat in the heather with this lovely freckle-faced, green-eyed Scottish young lady who seemed to enjoy his company. So far there was no talk of the night before. Was it all a dream?

Penny moved closer to Jack. She took his hand and looked into his eyes. "You are not upset about last night, are you?" She already knew the answer.

"No, of course not. It was lovely. I almost thought it was a dream. I slept so soundly after, I don't recall you leaving," Jack replied.

"I slipped out before sunrise. And with difficulty, I might add. You are a delight to sleep with," she said.

Far in the distance, an airplane engine droned.

"I am not totally comfortable asking this, but how did I end up here? I mean, how did we meet?" he asked with some reluctance.

She maintained her cheerful disposition, seemingly no matter what the challenge. She gave a straight response, "You are wondering if this happens often. Do I frequently pick up men in bars? The answer is no. About six months ago I became involved with a man who was an RAF pilot. Sadly, he died in combat over Sicily. It is nearly impossible during wartime to meet people. So, frankly, many women here hope to meet someone, somewhere, somehow. Hopefully, someone who can take them away from this tragic war we are trapped in. I am certain you Americans know this. One way is to 'turn professional.' Not acceptable, of course. The other is to date, then marry someone. It is not unusual for American GIs to marry good women from London or other cities. Glasgow is the only place which offers any opportunity. I go to town twice a week to shop. While there I watch. I think I am reasonably good at judging character. I saw you in town searching for accommodations. I watched you go into the bar. I picked you."

Jack was surprised but even more impressed with her honesty. "How did you pick me out of all the men in town?"

"Intuition. Was I right?"

The aircraft noise drew closer. Then a deafening sound echoed throughout the hills as a low-flying fighter plane buzzed immediately over their heads. Jack impulsively grabbed Penny and covered her with his body, expecting an explosion any second. To his surprise, she laughed out loud and wrapped her arms around him. She kissed him on the cheek and explained, "That is a Spitfire, not an enemy aircraft. I recognize the distinctive engine sound. They buzz over the hills a few times a week on practice runs."

Jack grinned sheepishly, "You might have told me that in advance. That pilot scared the crap out of me." He started to sit, but she held on. She pulled him closer and kissed him on his lips. She placed her hands behind his head and kissed him with passion. She then ran her soft hands along his cheeks as she teased him with her tongue. The lovemaking in the heather was magic. She truly was an artist.

Penny got up slowly, took Jack's hand, and they continued their walking journey. She told Jack there were some shepherds nearby. She knew every inch of these hills. After about thirty minutes, they came to a small, charming wood and straw hut. Penny called, and out came the shepherd, his wife, and a small young girl. They greeted Penny warmly and she made introductions. Penny and Jack were invited into the hut and offered a glass of buttermilk. Since they had worked up an appetite, they anxiously accepted the nutritious beverage.

Ian, the shepherd, was full of questions for Jack as an American. Jack had to pay strict attention to the variant of English he was not accustomed to hearing. Ian inquired about Jack's home, his family, and the ship he was on. The shepherd then told of the dreadful bombing by the Luftwaffe a few months prior. The bombers came from three different directions in waves for two hours. There were no guns available to fire at the Luftwaffe. The Scotts had no air force in the vicinity. All the Spitfires and Hurricanes were preoccupied in the Mediterranean and protecting London. Many homes were destroyed, and roads pulverized. Jack was amazed how these wise, humble people somehow seemed to maintain an optimistic and positive attitude.

They seemed to know, in their bones, that they were in the right and, that ultimately they would prevail.

As the sun arced across the sky and cast shadows amidst the hills, Penny suggested they should head home. They bid farewell to their friendly hosts and began their trek back to the cottage. The conversation between them picked up where they left off, as if no time had intervened.

"So Jack, did I choose well?" she asked with a gentle laugh.

"You know I can't answer that. Only you. I am glad we met. But you must understand I will likely cast off in a few days for...

for a foreign port. And the journey could be dangerous. In fact, the next airplane that flies over my head will not likely be a Spitfire."

She stopped walking, took Jack's hand and turned to him, looking into his eyes as the sun disappeared behind him. "I know. But I refuse to give up living. And…and there is one more thing I must tell you."

She seemed strangely serious to Jack. So unlike her.

Penny gazed down in thought. She was gathering words. "I must tell you…I am married."

CHAPTER 12

The Negligee

JACK STEPPED BACK AND COULD utter only, "What? But yesterday at dinner you..."

She interrupted, "In the spring of 1940, I married a young barrister from Glasgow named Bill McNeal. He had done legal work for the family. Within three months, he joined the British navy and ended up being shipped to the Mediterranean for duty as a second officer on a corvette. A year ago, his ship was attacked during the siege of Malta. The navy told me that a Stuka dive bomber made a direct bomb strike on their vessel."

Her eyes were slowly filling with tears. Jack shook his head and held up his hand, but she continued, "The ship was destroyed and sunk. There were no survivors found, no ID plates, nothing. They told us all were lost. So technically, I am still married. By Scottish law, in this type of circumstance, we are not free of the bonds of marriage for one year. That date is next month, October 1, 1942. Sorry I did not tell you earlier...but it was not easy for me to talk about, and the best time was not clear."

"I see," replied Jack with sincere empathy and sadness, then added, "another reason added to the list for despising the Germans. I am so sorry. What a tragic experience. The war casts an evil cloud over the entire human race all over the earth. No one is safe; everyone is affected in some way. And who knows how it will end? If we lose to the Germans, it could be a very different world."

She brushed his analysis aside, as she blotted her lovely eyes, and looked into his face while his black hair blew around in the mountain breeze, "So, you are not angry?"

Jack replied, "You have done nothing wrong. I see no reason to be angry. Besides, I can't imagine being angry with you. You are a lovely, intelligent, vivacious young lady. You and your husband had a life of happiness before you, but it was snatched away. What a tragedy. Now you still have every right to be happy as you make your way through life."

He paused for a moment, then said, "We have known each other for only a day. A delightful day, but only a day. It is not clear where this relationship can go..."

"I understand," she interrupted before he said something she did not want to hear.

"Thank you for understanding. Let's enjoy our time together and hope things will work out for the best."

She took his hand, and they continued their walk back. They were silent in their thoughts until they were near the cottage. Irene was working in the garden and waved as she saw them walking down the hill.

Thoughtfully, Penny asked, sounding almost as if she had known him much longer, "Jack, can you stay here again tonight?... With us," she added to make it sound like there were multiple reasons for him to stay.

"No. As much as I would like to, I am required to check in with the ship to determine when we cast off. I am allowed to stay off the ship for more than one night, but only with the Captain's permission. And he must know where I am staying. And the general rule is that you must be back on board within two hours of notification. But I will take your cottage phone number anyway. Who knows, our ship could be here for two days or two weeks."

They went inside and Jack recovered his clothes and satchel. As he came down the stairs, he thanked Irene and Alice once more and got into the green Morgan, which Penny had warmed up. The sisters had packed sandwiches for them to eat on the journey.

Penny was quiet as she drove Jack through Glasgow and all the way back to Gourock. They arrived in time for Jack to catch the last launch back to the *Esek Hopkins* that evening. Penny left the engine of the car running as Jack got out. He walked around to the driver's side as Penny opened her door and stood to bid him goodbye. She wrapped her arms around him and kissed him firmly on his mouth. Jack enjoyed it and responded.

"So, since you can't stay here tonight, can you stop by tomorrow for a visit again?"

Jack smiled warmly, "Unless the wicked Germans knock me off, I will make it back to Glasgow. Likely around noon. Can you pick me up at the pub?"

"Around noon. I will see you there," she said enthusiastically. She wanted to say more, but the words did not come to her, and people were milling around.

Jack turned and started toward the launch at the end of the mole. Once aboard, his mind was already full of fond memories of Penny as the launch motored back to the *Esek Hopkins.*

How lucky could a guy be to encounter such a lovely young lady? He was treated so well by Penny and her sisters. Almost like family. And her lovely soft body and artful love making. He could not get his mind off one cute Scottish lass, one Penny McNeal. Dark clouds moved in, and heavy rain began just as the sailors boarded the Liberty Ship.

Jack climbed the ladder and made his first stop in the mess, now referred to as "The Forum," where a small group was having coffee. Rumors were circulating again. This time they were about U-boat attacks against another convoy. But several U-boats were reported sunk.

Jack then heard that the Liberty Ship *Patrick Henry*, anchored not far away, was firing her 20mm machine guns at an aircraft that appeared to be attacking her. It turned out the airplane was a British Spitfire. Jack wondered if it was the same Spitfire that buzzed him and Penny on the hill. Apparently, the pilot was showing off. But he paid for his hubris with a few holes in his fuselage. Fortunately, he landed safely and was not injured.

Jack decided to obtain clearance for his next visit on shore from Chief Cockrell rather than Captain Gleason, who was typically busy and not always easy to locate. Jack went up to the Chief's office where he was working through the paperwork which he never seemed to complete. Jack tapped on the doorway. The Chief looked up with disinterested curiosity.

"Hey, Dodd, what's up? I thought you were staying in town."

Jack was delighted his absence was barely noticed. "Good evening, Chief. I came back to see if we have orders for a departure time. And I would like additional shore leave for two days starting tomorrow."

"No orders yet. But the Captain thinks we will cast off in three days. So, I will give you two days' leave. Where will you be staying if we need to reach you?"

Jack had prepared for this and memorized the phone number at the farmhouse.

He replied innocently, "Belmont 42861. It is a little guest house outside of Glasgow." Cockrell handed Jack a clipboard with the names of all the crew.

He grumbled, "Here, write it down next to your name with today's date. Get your ass back here in two days, I don't care how pretty she is!"

Jack smiled but decided it was best to remain silent, and he scribbled the phone number in barely legible handwriting, in spite of his typical tendency to be conscientious with his penmanship. By the time he uttered, "Thanks, Chief," he was halfway down the hallway.

Jack jogged down the metal stairs to his room. Only Alex Salamis was there, legs crossed, two pillows under his head on his bunk, trying to read in very dim light. "Why aren't you on shore, Alex? Looks like half the ship is."

Alex threw it back, "Why are you on board? Nothing going on? I heard there are not many girls around. And the town is filling up with that massive mob of troops from the *Queen Mary*. You have any luck with the ladies?"

Jack replied as he stripped down for bed, "I was given one night on shore. I came back only to see if we had a departure date. The Chief told me we would likely cast off in three days. And yes, the town is crawling with guys. So, slim pickens. But I did meet a young lady."

As Jack crawled into his bunk, Alex was snoring, with the book comfortably laying open on his chest.

The next morning, Jack was up at six o'clock. He decided to wear his blue uniform with the white hat but took along a casual change of clothes in his bag. He wolfed down a big breakfast in the near-vacant mess hall and waited on the port side of *Esek Hopkins* for a launch. He felt a tinge of excitement, like a teenager in heat, as he climbed down the ladder and stepped onto the launch with only two other deck cadets on board at this hour. The sea was still, so the skipper of the launch opened her up and they arrived at the Gourock pier in only thirty-five minutes. Jack nearly trotted from the pier to the bus station. What was driving him? He could not recall the last time he was this excited about a date, a woman, a soft, cuddly woman, a special woman. The bus ride seemed interminable; the scenery was quite lovely, but it meant nothing to him as his mind could only think about one thing. Finally, the growling diesel bus pulled into the station in Glasgow. After a ten-minute walk, he strolled smartly into the Wishing Well Pub by 11:00 a.m. with considerable anticipation.

He was early, but he learned in training there could always be obstacles to one's objective. He rarely drank at this hour, but he could not stop tapping his feet at the little table he chose in a dimly lit corner. He needed something, even something just to fiddle with, so he ordered a pint of Guinness, instead of a coffee, and waited. Would she even show? Doubts crept in.

Why is time so slow when you want it to speed up? The beer did not taste right at this time of day. He aimlessly sipped, as if it was coffee, but the taste was all wrong. He was not good at waiting.

I should have come late. And let her wait. It was five to twelve. Yesterday, her exact words were, "around noon." Give her some leeway, Jack. Wait a minute, what if she doesn't show?

His thoughts were colliding with themselves.

She wouldn't do that. She actually likes me. But there are a lot of distractions. Officers and doctors wandering around. I am just a measly deck cadet. Did she really choose me? What did she see? Could this all be a sham? She could tell every guy that story. She probably had important things to do today. Farm work. Pushing hay around. What if she had car problems? She might not be able to make it at all. No way to contact me. How long should I wait? How long before I look like a fool? One customer had already had a coffee and left while I have been sitting here… alone. Relax, Jack. If she doesn't show, she doesn't show. Hardly the end of the world. Her freckles are cute. I could walk around town. She liked to kiss. Do a little shopping. And cuddle. Get something for Mother. And my sisters. But not Margaret. She was so soft. Why am I having these crazy thoughts? Do I really care if she shows up? Big deal. She is only a woman. Right, just a woman. And anyway…

His side vision picked up a motion near the bar entrance. He stopped staring at the fluffy suds floating near the top of his beer glass. At a distance, in the poor light, for just an instant, there stood someone he wished he knew. Her presentation was that of a slender female, in pleated tan slacks, which created an illusion of tallness. As she paused by herself, her hair appeared short, almost boy-like. Yet a certain formality was suggested by the pressed white blouse with top button ajar which suggested just a hint, a temptation, an offering of her balanced chest. Her cleavage, noticeable even at this distance, was enough to hold a viewer's prurient interest. In her hand she held a smart leather bag and on her arm was draped a blue cardigan sweater, creating an illusion of class and a hint of sophistication beyond her youthful appearance. She had an air of casualness, yet maturity, an ability to handle herself, a knowledge of how to manage her affairs. He wanted to know her. She examined the room, quickly at first, then slowly. She stopped on Jack, then a smile appeared, and she started toward him. It *was* Penny! In an instant she was no longer that illusory visage he had first squinted at. For a split second she had been a puzzling mystical someone else, now she was…his. A distinct thumping of his heart confirmed this was real. He smiled and stood as she approached. His smile was genuine, from the heart, uncommon. For some reason he did not want to appear too anxious to see her, even as his heart belied it. She looked so…different. His honest smile remained on his face, a joyful smile as he reached out to hug her and she reciprocated with a long hold.

She spoke silently into his ear. "It has only been a few hours, yet I missed you. More than I expected." She stepped back and appraised him in his impressive blue uniform, which was created specifically to impress.

It was his turn, "You look lovely. I almost didn't recognize you. Your outfit is smart. I like it." She slowly rotated to show it all. As he watched this sensuous display and observed her near-perfect figure, he wondered how he could be so lucky to have connected with such a unique woman. Then she stepped up to him, carefully placed her arms around his shoulders, and kissed him slowly, teasing him with her soft lips, then passionately, as if they were the only people on earth. Jack let her continue as long as she wanted. He was responding as nature had intended.

She felt his increased breathing and reluctantly stopped. She enjoyed having some control over him.

They sensed a new background silence in the pub. They

separated and looked around at the dozen or so patrons who were enjoying the romantic scene playing out. Penny blushed.

Several customers smiled and gave a gentle little wave of their hands. "Well, perhaps we should sit and order something," she suggested.

They sat as Jack gazed at her countenance and continued smiling but could not think of a word to say. Her appeal increased as he soaked up her visage. Penny started with a grin, reminding Jack of her slightly tilted incisor, and said, "I am happy to see you, Jack Dodd from Baltimore."

He laughed out loud. She added, "I thought about you last night. I missed cuddling. You should have stayed."

Jack leaned across the round table and whispered secretively, "I missed your warmth and softness." That was more than usual for the introverted Jack Dodd to acknowledge. It was becoming clear to him that this woman was getting under his skin and having more than a casual effect on him. Whenever he allowed himself to think this, it was followed by the unhappy thought that, because of the war, this relationship was not likely to go anywhere and any joy he felt with her was bracketed by a finite time frame. Why was life like that? But he forced himself to push that aside for now and enjoy the rare moment.

Eventually, the waiter appeared. He smiled at them as if they were celebrities, and as if he actually was happy to have them as customers. Without much thought, they ordered fish and chips. Jack told her that he was granted two nights' leave and could do whatever he desired on shore. Delight danced on her expressive face. Then the bad news: the *Esek Hopkins* would cast off in three days.

With her typical positive demeanor, she said, "Well, Jack, we shall just have to make the best of it."

"Agreed! Let's start by taking a walk in town and do a little shopping. I would like to get something for your sisters—and my sisters." Jack suggested.

After lunch they went to the Morgan sports car and stowed his bag and cap. Penny put on her cardigan and held his hand as they strolled through the center city like they were on Fifth Avenue in the Easter Parade, like they were alive, like they were in love. They talked, small talk, nonsense talk, while an unspoken sexual tension reciprocated between them as they pretended they were interested in the goods for sale in the store windows. Jack purchased a few small items for his mother and sisters; small enough to pack in his suitcase.

He asked, "What can I get for your sisters?"

"Something that is difficult to find. Let me think about it," she responded.

They continued their stroll, hand in hand.

"What shall we do tonight?" Penny asked the question they both had been silently contemplating as she gazed in the next window acting interested in the contents.

"Didn't you want to go back to your cottage?"

"No," she said casually, but a little too quickly, confirming she had already given thought to the issue and how to resolve it. "Let's get a room here. We can go out to dinner, then...get to bed early," she suggested. Her tone was somewhat seductive, but with a certain indescribable youthful innocence which somehow diminished any hint of naughtiness.

"Your sisters would prefer not to know if we were sleeping together in your ancestral home, is that it?" Jack asked politely.

"Well, yes. They would prefer we not. So, if we want to be comfortable and relax, we should stay here in Glasgow," she responded in a matter-of-fact fashion. "We can find a hotel. There are lots of them. On second thought, the ones in the town center may be full with all the troops here. Let's look for a small hotel as we walk. We can try some side streets."

Jack was fascinated by how quickly she made up her mind and her determination. She really did choose him. And why should he object? Except, too far, too fast? Departure in three days. The more time they spent together, the more difficult at separation time. He reminded himself, enjoy each moment; there may not be many remaining. Besides, why not let her drive this campaign? Let her have control. It was kind of fun. Something he was not used to.

For several hours, they wandered through many of the narrow, winding, streets of Glasgow, ignoring any garbage and odors and meandering denizens, who may have been drunk or simply too tired to walk straight. Time skittered past them. It seemed so easy, like pleasantly drifting through unaccounted space with her warm hand in his. He told her stories about the ship and storms and crew and their journey so far. Jack ceased counting how many small hotels he ventured into and repeatedly was told no vacancy. As they got farther from the center of the city, the options diminished. At last, they found a small inn with an elderly white-haired woman at the desk, sporting an untidy bun in her hair and blessed with a tiny, pointed nose. Penny waited outside. He signed in with the intentionally poorly scribbled names "Jack and Penny Dodd" as he noted mentally the absence of wedding rings on either left hand. It occurred to him that he had never engaged in this kind of deception before. Optimistically, and without telling Penny, he signed up for two nights and paid in advance.

As they climbed the stairs together, he realized how obvious their tryst appeared. He had left his bag and white hat locked in the Morgan and the only item they climbed the stairs with was Penny's large purse. Oh well. Certainly not the first time for the pointy-nosed lady, nor the first time in this war.

The room was small with a tiny bathroom but no shower or tub. A shared shower was available down the hall. Shadows descended on the window. Penny pulled the curtains closed, enveloping the room in darkness. Before Jack could turn on the shaded lamp, she approached him, held him, and kissed him. She paused, "I want to make love to you…all night long. Can we start right after an early dinner? Does that work?" He accepted the idea of a shared decision.

"Sure. I can barely wait to feel your warm body next to mine.

Whenever you want to start is fine with me." He lied; he wanted to start now. "It wouldn't hurt to fill up our stomachs after all that walking today."

Now, at least, there was a plan. As they clunked down the wooden stairs, they asked the pointy-nosed lady to suggest a restaurant nearby. She gave the name of a pub that Penny knew, The Artist's Loft. As they stepped outside and walked into the darkness, Penny noted, "I recognize this neighborhood now. The pub is known for good food and is just four blocks away. I used to know the owners, the Mackenzies. It should not be too crowded this early."

Penny was right on both counts: the Mackenzies still owned The Artist's Loft, and when they arrived, it was not yet crowded. They got a table along a wood-paneled wall which was festooned with tartans and pennants of all sorts and adjacent to an iron-clad knight, holding a long, wicked pike. The waiter promptly delivered menus and took their order for two glasses of Guinness. When he returned, they ordered without delay, both wanting to get to their appointment in bed. So far, to all appearances, they were managing to temporarily suppress their shared primitive urges. Just then, the lights were dimmed to near complete darkness in the pub to obey the "lights out ordinance" in wartime Glasgow. Jack was acclimated to eating in the dark on the ship, so he had no problems and dropped not a morsel. Penny, on the other hand, was engaged in more significant thoughts, wondering if Jack would appreciate the white negligee she stowed in her bag and wondering how long she would keep it on, and whether she should start the evening wearing the accompanying panties…or simply leave them off.

CHAPTER 13

The Bar Room Floor

AS THEY CONSUMED THEIR DINNERS with subtle, restrained animal urgency, the noise volume in the bar increased as more warm bodies stumbled in from the streets of Glasgow.

Simultaneously, they concluded it was time to depart, no dessert—that was to be served in bed—just locate the waiter. A group of British troops from the *Queen Mary* had collected at the bar and they were in a festive mood, since this was their last night before casting off. Most were well on their way already. Some began singing, which only increased the festive mood and rowdiness. Someone yelled out, "Sing the one about the mouse!" Others agreed, "Yeah, yeah, the one about the mouse." Two men started, others joined in:

Oh, the beer was spilled on the bar room floor,
And the bar was closed for the night.
When out of his house came a little brown mouse,
And stood in the pale moonlight.
He lapped up the beer on the bar room floor,
And that was the end of that.
And all night long, you could hear him roar…
Bring on the god-damned cat!

Cheers and laughter erupted. Jack and Penny stood and clapped. That ditty got everyone going. More songs erupted, each one bawdier than the next. Finally, Penny said, "Time to go. Can you find the waiter, Jack?"

Jack nodded in agreement and made his way toward the bar. He got the attention of a bartender, who with some difficulty found his check amidst the increasing crescendo of noise of laughter, songs, and doggerel. A man standing next to Jack began reciting a limerick to no one in particular:

There once was a lady from France,
Who decided to take a chance,
She let herself go, for an hour or so,
And now all her sisters are aunts!"

Jack chuckled to amuse the man, but wondered, what an ironic coincidence. Why had this man showed up at this particular moment in time and space to plant that seed in Jack's mind? And Penny has two sisters…but she is definitely not French.

Jack paid and turned to find Penny. Someone's shoulder struck his with a considerable jolt, perhaps too hard to be accidental. He turned left and found himself face to face with Ski.

Ski said sarcastically, "Sorry, bub. Well, look who it is. Good ol' Capt'n Dodd. Saw you sittin' there with that little lady, Capt'n. Makin your way with the local girls, eh."

Jack offered a false smile. "We were just leaving. Enjoy yourself tonight, Ski."

Ski lifted his chin. "Why don't you buy me and Fred a beer, Capt'n? Bein' that we're all mates on the same ship." Ski was close enough for Jack to smell the beer on his breath.

Penny approached from the side. Jack said, "Some other time. Like I said, we are on our way out."

Ski developed an ugly grimace on his absurd face as he uttered "What's wrong, punk? No charity for your mates?" and hit Jack on the left shoulder, hard, with his palm. The background chattering noise was increasing, throbbing. No one noticed. Jack looked at Penny. She was expressionless. The imbedded flash of Freddie Wilson bothering his sister Gladys and calling Jack "punk" entered the reptilian locus in his brain. In a second, Jack advanced and pushed Ski aside.

"Excuse us."

Jack suspected this would result in a swing and he was not disappointed. There was no space for a wide roundhouse arc, so Ski fired a jab with his right hand toward Jack's left cheek. Time slowed instantly. Jack anticipated the shot and jerked his head right, so most of the blow glanced along the left side of his face and nailed his ear. In the instant when Ski was recovering his balance, Jack analyzed whether to go for the face or abdomen. His brain said face, but his conscience said solar plexus. Jack went for the latter. As he quicky, reflexively made his fist, with thumb outside, he initiated the right upper cut and made good contact with Ski's blubbery belly just as he was recovering his balance. The jolt knocked him back into another sotted customer—unfortunately for Ski, a woman. The large man talking to her was quite upset by this rude interruption and reached out and spun Ski around, demanding an apology. Ski was busy bent over catching his breath. Jack was preparing to nail him on his right cheek and jumped into his practiced stance. As this scene was working its way to a conclusion, Ski's pal, Fred, was preparing to take a shot at Jack, who was not paying attention to other confederates, as Chief Cockrell had warned him. Penny quickly visualized what was about to happen and intervened by giving a swift, devastating kick to Fred's groin. Jack turned to see Fred bent over in considerable pain and watched as Penny boxed him on his left ear with her fist, knocking him in slow, suspended animation to the soggy floor crowded with feet and legs.

Ski, in the meantime, was unable to speak, much less apologize. He allowed himself to drop to the floor and tried with desperation to catch his breath. The man assumed Ski was faking, so he grabbed his coat and pulled him up, yelling, "Apologize. Apologize to—" He turned to the woman:

"What's your name?"

Clasping her drink close to her chest, she said, "Maria." Then she turned to explore other options.

"Yeah, Maria, apologize to Maria," he barked.

Jack grabbed Penny's hand and pulled her in the direction of the front door. But it was packed with uniformed men in a rowdy disposition. Penny turned Jack toward the left side of the bar. "I know another way out." They hurried down the corridor in the direction of the loo, but turned left down a staircase, past storage rooms for beer kegs and bottles and supplies, to an outside door, which Penny unlatched, as if she owned the place. They climbed the stairs into the chilled night along a side street with people milling about, waiting to participate in the fun inside. As they walked away, they heard cheers and a considerable commotion.

After a block of rapid, silent walking, Jack stopped, turned to her face, barely visible in the darkness, and gazed at her silently.

She spoke first. "What?"

"Exactly. What? What happened back there? You knocked that guy out of commission. Where did you learn to do that? Were you in the military?"

She replied, "Are you ok? For a moment I thought he was going to knock you out."

She turned his head with her pale, soft, delicate hands and inspected the left side. There appeared to be a small amount of dried blood around his ear. She pulled a kerchief from somewhere, spit on it, and gently wiped the blood away. He liked the attention; liked being mothered.

"I am okay, really. Thank God we got out of there when we did." The raucous noise and excitement could be heard echoing down the alley. "And how did you know how to get out the back way?"

She ignored him, pulled his hand, and they started walking quickly again as several couples passed them, heading in the direction of the action. Many people were carrying flashlights to find their way in the streets. Some blackout. For enemy aircraft above, Glasgow would be an easy nighttime target. But it had been months since the last bombing.

Penny started, "Well, as you saw, unlike the Wishing Well Pub, this place is off the beaten trail and caters more to locals. I went to school with Angus MacKenzie, one of the owners, and my husband and I used to frequent the place. So, I know the geography of the pub pretty well. It is unusual to see fights there, since the locals usually get along, and on Thursday nights, they even recite poetry and readings of Robert Burns. And occasionally, late in the evenings, someone may recite that mouse ditty. But when ships unload, and the crowd overflows away from the city center, we get invaded, as we say. Most of that crowd was already drunk by the time they got there."

"And your fighting skills?" he asked.

"Oh, really that's nothing," she assured him, pronouncing "nothing" as "no thin."

She continued. "With three girls, my father decided to keep us active and taught us to play many sports and wrestle, and I even took private boxing for a while. He wanted us to be able to take care of ourselves. I played football, or soccer as you call it, through secondary school and our team played in the finals during my senior year. I am quite a kicker."

"I saw that nicely demonstrated. I certainly will not forget it," he laughed. "Well," he continued, "the guy who pushed me was that guy Ski I told you about. He is a rotten apple and I try to avoid him whenever possible. Yet fate seems to bring us together for some reason."

They finally arrived at the inn and went through the unlocked door and climbed easily to their room, with erotic fantasies replacing the thoughts of the bizarre activities of the early evening. They were on a mission. Jack changed first in the tiny bathroom and jumped under the covers in his shorts. Penny took her time and elected to include her panties in her attire. She preened her hair to perfection. She was ready. She flicked off the light switch in the bathroom, tip-toed to the bed, and softly peeled back the sheets. It was not until she climbed next to his warm body that she realized Jack was quietly snoring in a deep slumber.

Jack woke up first, just as daylight nudged its head above the horizon. He scurried down the hall to evacuate his bladder. Then he washed his face and brushed his teeth in preparation for a relaxing day in port with his lovely accomplice. He would make a sincere effort to stay out of trouble. He went to the bed and saw Penny sleeping on her side, half covered with sheets, in a sensuous, transparent white negligee. Last night he missed the boat. But, this morning, he rolled her over as she flickered her eyes open, and he inspected this goddess before him. They caressed and kissed and enjoyed what thousands of years of evolution had prepared their bodies for, this time with particular warmth, affection, and beauty, pleasing to the stars.

As they dressed for breakfast, Jack told Penny not to pack. A warm, sensuous glow spread across her face when he told her he had reserved the room for two nights. After breakfast, they roamed around Glasgow in no particular direction, with no particular goal. She with a level of happiness not experienced since her life with Bill. And Jack, not with anyone he could recall, not Gail, not anyone. Without discussion, they silently, mystically formulated a method to avoid the topic of the morrow. They unconsciously drifted past The Artist's Loft. Clean up was underway. A few broken chairs were on the sidewalk. They peeked inside. A policeman was conversing with a man, who Penny identified as her friend, Angus MacKenzie. Penny thought it would best to back away, but Jack was curious. They stepped in.

With the sunlight behind them, Angus at first did not recognize his old classmate. He declared, "Sorry, we are closed for two days."

"Angus, it's me, Penny McNeal. What happened?"

He held his hand up to diminish the incoming light, and squinted. "Oh, hi Penny. Let me finish with the officer here, and I will be with you in a few minutes."

Penny nodded as Jack looked around, surprised how different the pub now appeared. The medieval knight was sprawling on the floor in several pieces; a few pictures were broken along with several mugs, while unbroken chairs and tables were stacked against the wall; the odor of spilled beer infiltrated the space.

Jack whispered to Penny, "Do you think Angus saw us last night? If so, we better play down our involvement." She nodded.

Angus stepped over as the policeman took photos. Penny introduced Jack.

"It got a little rough last night," Angus understated. "One of the boys said he served you dinner here last night, Penny."

"We were here early, but got out when the pushing started," she replied.

Angus said, "Not sure how it started. Makes little difference. A room full of drunk, hot-blooded young males just coming in off weeks at sea, makes for a combustible mixture. Half the bars in town likely had the same thing happen. My insurance should cover it. But I may hire some guards." He turned to Jack. "You call 'em bouncers in the States, right?"

"Exactly, bouncers. Taverns and bars hire the biggest guys they can find. Sometimes there is nothing for them to do, but if a fight starts, the bouncers hurl them out in the street," Jack replied, sounding for a moment like he spoke from experience.

Penny added one thing. "We could not get out the front door, so we went downstairs and out the back door. It may be unlocked."

"Thanks. I searched the place early this morning and locked it. I guess it's good you remember the layout, Penny," he replied with a wink. Jack noted it but discarded the flirt. Stay positive, he reminded himself.

They bid their goodbyes and ventured back into the street. A few blocks away they passed a grocery store. Penny suggested Jack purchase some food items as gifts for her sisters. He bought a few oranges, bananas, coffee, and hard candy. They decided to make the fifteen-minute drive to Kilsyth in the Morgan to deliver the perishable gifts to Alice and Irene. Jack agreed to stay for lunch, but he reminded her they would spend the night back in Glasgow, not with her sisters at the cottage.

As they pulled up to the cottage, Alice and Irene were both working in the garden, their heads ensconced with huge, enveloping tan hats. Once greetings were exchanged, they went in to enjoy a quick lunch of sandwiches and buttermilk. As they sat at the kitchen table, Jack presented his package. He thanked them for their gracious hospitality and kindness. Alice took the initiative and opened the package as her sisters looked on. They were delighted. The items he gave them were difficult to find, especially the coffee, and were quite expensive. Irene and Alice expressed their delight with a big hug for Jack.

After lunch, Jack and Penny took another walk in the hills behind the cottage. Neither wanted to discuss it, but it was the elephant in their minds. No avoiding it. Tomorrow Jack would be gone. They clearly were very attracted to each other. Perhaps in love. Neither would yet admit it. Too costly. Were the bonds of affection of the three days sufficient to hold them through what might lie ahead? And what if he survived? Even so, he would end up back in Baltimore. Forever. The war could go on for years, decades. Could they keep in contact?

Would they? Absent a firm commitment? What would be the point? Could she find someone else? A man who was not in the military? Not a risk? They barely spoke as these thoughts swirled in their minds. At the top of one of the hills, with views into the misty scenery of green hills and gray water, with wind sifting through their hair, with the heavens gazing down approvingly, she looked up at him and squeezed his arm. "Jack, I think I am in love with you."

He looked into her eyes and smiled peacefully. "It has been a wonderful experience, Penny. I feel great affection for you. But I am not sure it is love. Too quick. Too soon. Too risky."

"But I know what I feel. And I think you feel the same. You are not going to die, I know it. I could save money and come to Baltimore when your commitment is over. I could meet your family. Pick up where we left off here, and if we decided to get married, I would give up my life here." Her face was glowing, furtive, full of enthusiasm and verve. She was hard to resist. Jack was tempted. He wondered if she could be correct. Precisely on target. He felt it.

Then his logic unit clicked in and overtook his emotional unit. Too much risk, too many unknowns. And ultimately unfair to her. If her long-shot dream failed, she would have wasted a year or more. Critical time for her —to meet someone—who could give her what she wants and deserves. She wanted to be loved; perhaps too desperately.

"Let's head back," Jack reluctantly suggested.

"One more kiss for me to remember on this beautiful spot," she asked and without waiting for a response she grasped his head and engaged in a tender, soft, long kiss which they would never forget.

They trekked back to the cottage in silence. She recognized this battle was probably lost.

But she remained cheerful; they still had twelve hours to continue their affections. They told Alice and Irene that they would spend the night in Glasgow again.

The sisters were noncommittal. Silently, they wondered if Penny could be successful against all odds.

North Sea clouds moved in and gray, cold rain started as they drove into the city. They returned to the Wishing Well Pub which was full but not overcrowded. Jack saw a few of his mates at the bar and waved, feeling no urge to introduce Penny, since this was their last morsel of time together. After they sat at a distant table, Jack's roommate, Alex, with beer in hand, spotted them and came over.

"So, it looks like we cast off tomorrow, Jack," he said as he sized up Penny. Jack introduced her to his Greek roommate. Without invitation, Alex grabbed a chair and joined them. Penny and Jack each ordered a Guinness.

"What a shame we can't stay longer," Alex offered, hoping the comment would unravel how Penny fit into the scheme of things.

She did not look like a woman of the night, but you never knew. "Are you local, Penny?"

"Yes, I live in a little town a few miles from here." She smiled in response, thinking this was not an ideal time to meet new shipmates. "I live with my sisters, who have husbands serving in North Africa." Defensively she added, "and my husband serves—-" she paused; the verb was in the wrong tense— "in the British navy." Somehow, she felt this would clean out any nefarious thoughts from this gentleman's mind. It seemed to work.

"So, you guys are enjoying the town?" he asked, then paused. "Say, did you hear about the fight last night in some joint called The Artist's Loft? I, personally, was not there, but Jack, your old pal Ski was there. He got pretty bashed up. Spent a few hours in the hospital. Cut forehead took twelve stitches; got a pair of black eyes, a tooth missing. I saw him returning on board this morning. Looks like he got the worst of it. His engine-room buddy, Fred, also got hammered. And are you ready, Ski says you were there and started the ruckus. That's what he told the Chief. I could not imagine you bashing him up like that, but I did not get all the details."

Jack and Penny gaped at each other. Truth and lies. Alex quickly perceived it was true, at least some of it. Alex sipped on his Guinness thoughtfully and waited in silence.

After a pause, Jack let out, "That son of a bitch. Yes Alex, we were there having a nice quiet dinner. But Ski started it. We got out before things blew up. I'll be sure to relate the true details to the Chief."

Penny nodded to confirm.

Alex shrugged his shoulders and took a slug of warm beer. "Not my concern. Glad I missed it. I likely would have gotten a few broken ribs," he said with a laugh. He inspected Penny with more than simple curiosity. He said, "So your father named you Penelope…wife of Odysseus." Alex turned to Jack and winked. "Do you think Jack will make it back?" as if he were addressing Odysseus, otherwise known as "No Man." Alex gazed into the distance in thought. "Don't forget, I got your back, Jack," he laughed. Penny's annoyed expression matched Jack's fatigue with his roommate.

"Hey, Alex, we were trying to have a quiet dinner. We won't be insulted if you excuse yourself," Jack stated firmly, but politely making his wishes clear. Jack liked Alex and wanted to keep him on his team.

"Okay, Jack, my man. I am off. Penelope, it is a joy to make your acquaintance." He gave her an especially pleasant smile, his best. He then stood, bowed his head, and with beer in hand made his exit slowly toward the bar, now rapidly filling with thirsty customers wanting to enjoy the last night in town.

Once Alex was out of earshot, Jack noted, "He sleeps on the bunk above me. Usually not quite so obnoxious. Some guys get wound up with too much booze on board."

"No problem," Penny replied. "Not sure what he was getting at with the name Penelope. I know it is an old Greek name. Anyway, back to us. I am exhausted. Let's go back to the hotel after we eat. And hopefully, we can stay out of any brawls this evening. I would love to cuddle up…again."

Her wishes came true, and they enjoyed each other's sultry bodies one final time. Her white negligee was a popular item on the agenda. Afterwards, tears silently collected on her cheeks as together, entwined in each other's arms, they descended into a comfortable repose.

Morning came too soon. Jack took an inadequate shower down the hall, with too little hot water and too little water pressure, reminding him of life on board the *Esek Hopkins.*

Anxiety now dominated. They had little to pack. After checking out and bidding farewell to the pointy-nose behind the counter, they had a quick breakfast, where they exchanged mailing addresses, and walked to the Morgan. As Penny sat with the key in her hand, unable to start the car, she began to cry, selfishly letting out all her frustration and feelings of loss and separation. Her scene made Jack more despondent and added to his frustration.

"Let's go, get on with it," was the best he could do.

She dried her eyes. She started the car. She could not look at him or speak. She maneuvered the jazzy sports car through the narrow streets, around the clustered, unhappy, tense troops, past the waiting buses, toward the highway to her nowhere. There was nothing to talk about. Time passed as if it was meaningless. And cheap. She drove slowly. Jack toyed with his large formal white hat resting peacefully, uncommitted, on his lap. His thoughts flipped back and forth between her and duty; her, duty, her, duty…an endless loop with no resolution.

They disembarked at Gourock a few blocks from the pier. She walked with him along the mole. They stopped short of the launch. She took the initiative and hugged Jack, then kissed him on the lips. Tears ran down her face. She was speechless and powerless and could only turn her head from side to side, indicating her sadness and frustration and inability to make it right.

Jack, doing his best to hold it together, said, "Let's not make this difficult. Goodbyes are never easy. Thank you for all you have done for me. I can't tell you how much it means to me and how I have enjoyed my time with you, Penny McNeal. I promise to keep in touch. But live your life as you must." Tears began to collect in his eyes. It was time. He slowly turned and walked away.

As he distanced himself, her last words came out clumsily and weakly: "Remember to write, Jack Dodd. Remember to write." It was the best she could do. She waved as he walked on, but he had already determined he could not look back.

Darkness slowly enveloped the scene as he stepped aboard the launch and asked the helmsman, "Am I the last one on board for this trip?"

The helmsman looked at Jack, then toward Penny, then his watch, as three inebriated crewmen slouched and gurgled on the floor of the forty-foot vessel. "It appears you are. Would you like to stay a bit longer?"

Jack returned a smile to the helmsman, turned back to see slender Penny wisely walking toward the parked Morgan, and said,

"No. All is good here. It is time to go." The forty-five minute return trip to the *Esek Hopkins* was calm and lovely with no moon, no wind.

One of the chaps, full of whisky, and reclining in the bilge, was known to Jack. His name was George something. He had observed Jack's kiss goodnight. "Looks like you made a good strike, Captain Jack."

"Don't you start, George!" Jack bellowed.

The helmsman frowned. "He don't mean no harm. Likely jealous. Give him no mind."

Jack consented and went to the bow of the launch and concentrated on his fond memories and watched the black sea swiftly slide by with the tiny sparkle of nonjudgmental stars glistening on the surface as they approached the faint, unlit shadow of the *Esek Hopkins.*

CHAPTER 14

Departure

AS SOON AS HE CLIMBED back on board *Esek Hopkins*, Jack's demeanor changed as if someone had flicked a switch in his brain, a switch which he did not even know existed nor did he desire it to be switched. In fact, he felt somewhat guilty about how quickly his thoughts of Penny had redirected themselves toward matters on the ship. His first duty now was to find Chief Cockrell and straighten out the details of the bar fight. After dumping his overnight bag in his room, he made his way to the Chief's office. Cockrell's body seemed fixed to the same chair, looking at the same stack of papers. Jack wondered if he ever moved from that spot.

Cockrell turned his gaze toward Jack as he approached.

"Just the man I want to see. Come here, Dodd," he groused. "And remain standing; this may sound like an interrogation, and it is. First, I thought I told you to stay out of trouble. So, what the hell happened at that bar in Glasgow?"

Jack remained at attention, now wishing he could have stayed forever on shore with Penny. He relayed the story in detail to the grumpy Chief, who occasionally nodded imperceptibly.

"I got better things to deal with on this ship than this crap," was the first thing out of his mouth when Jack finished. "So who cut Ski's head and gave him two black eyes?"

"I have no idea, sir. All I did was hit him in the belly. Then my lady friend and I left. By the way, she kicked Fred in the nuts and as he bent over, she nailed him on the side of his head, knocking him to the floor. After I saw that, I was real careful with her," Jack chuckled.

"And, sir, look here at my left ear." He leaned over and showed the Chief. "That is the cut from Ski's hit. I bobbed and weaved just like you instructed me. But I was not paying attention to his buddy, Fred. That was when Penny booted him like a soccer ball."

"Okay, Dodd, your story has no inconsistencies with the police report. And your name didn't even come up, since you were not there when the police arrived. Nobody else claims you were involved—except Ski and Fred. By the way, Fred forgot to tell anyone about the broad kicking him where it hurts. Ha! The nice thing about a kick in that spot is, there is no evidence. And it knocks 'em out of commission. The police said they were quite drunk. I will write up my report and pass it on to the Captain and a copy will go in your file. Goddamn it, Dodd, I told you to stay out of trouble. Now I am doing paperwork on you, and I hate paperwork."

"Thank you, sir. In my opinion, sir, Ski is the problem. He started by pushing me; he was looking to start a fight. And I told you about him when I first got on the ship. I really don't want to ever see him again, but we are trapped here. By the way, thanks for your advice regarding the fighting part. It was very helpful. And I kept my thumb out of my fist."

Cockrell slammed his huge hand on the desk. "Get out of here, Dodd! And for the last time, stay out of trouble!"

Jack saluted with a "Yes, sir" and quickly scampered down the hall, down the metal stairs, and to his room. He unpacked, crashed, and thought about something pleasant, something warm, something friendly, a someone named Penny.

The next day, Jack learned that they were not yet departing from Scotland as planned. And no one was talking about a new departure date. Jack had used up his shore leave, so there was no way he could get back on land. He busied himself with deck cadet duties, but he also thought about Penny more than he expected or desired. It was so easy to remember their soft moments, her smiles, her freckles. Stop it, Jack. But it was so easy.

On those uncommon occasions when he bumped into George on board, he correctly anticipated winks and nods and teasing about his "date" with the comely Scottish lass. Rumors had already spread on board that he was in love. This was a motivation for him not to get upset about his reduced shore leave. Still…

One opportunity did present itself and Jack took it. Captain Gleason invited Jack to join him to attend gunnery classes on shore, along with the first and second mates and three Navy Guards, including Ron Sewell.

The Captain winked, "Now, no sporting around town, Jack. You must attend the classes." Obviously, the Captain had heard the rumors. Jack immediately answered in the affirmative and promised he would not miss a class.

The three classes were held on one afternoon at a warehouse in Gourock. There were several speakers, and Jack learned quite a bit more about loading, aiming, and firing the 20mm Oerlikon. It was an excellent review of what he had learned earlier, and he picked up many new tips. He also was taught how to fire the three-inch and five-inch antiaircraft cannons, should an emergent situation arise and those gunners were incapacitated. The program provided a valuable exercise which came in handy a few days later.

After Jack's return to the boat that afternoon, the crew was going through the lifeboat launch drill when one of his colleagues burned his hands trying to slow the rapid descent of the stern end of the lifeboat. Jack wanted to see what the treatment was, so he escorted the fellow to the medical clinic. Jack watched as the medical officer wrapped the man's hands in an ointment-saturated dressing. One never knew what skills could be required in the future. This came under Jack's category of learn everything you can.

While trapped on board at their anchorage, the men were tantalized by wild rumors which arrived almost as a daily ritual. One cadet said he had heard from good sources that they were headed to the Persian Gulf. That would be agreeable to all on board with the warm weather and gentle seas. The next day, another rumor directed them to Archangel, Russia—a dreadful thought. Rough seas, cold weather, and sub attacks were in store for them. Jack and many deck cadets already knew this was their true destination since they had seen the boxes labeled "Moscow." They also knew when heading to Russia they would pass around the northern coast of Norway where the huge German battleship *Tirpitz* was docked and ready to attack any convoys passing by. Then another alarming rumor surfaced. This one declared that some goofball, up the command structure suggested that six Liberty Ships might go out ahead of the convoy to draw the *Tirpitz* out of port. Meanwhile, the rest of the convoy would pass north and avoid any confrontation. The *Esek Hopkins* was said to be one of the six guinea pigs! Jack realized this was just another rumor. No one could be that crazy.

While in the mess, digesting the latest Forum news emanating from the unsettling rumor mill, there was a sudden terrifying event. It was 5:45 p.m. when someone yelled "fire," just as the screeching, throbbing fire alarm blared. Jack dropped his fork and sprinted up to the bridge to get instructions from the Chief. Captain Gleason was there with Sparks. The Captain pointed to smoke in the foredeck area and directed Jack and any other hands in the vicinity to start spraying water all over the forward deck and find the source. Jack rushed to the forepeak, where the swirls of gray smoke were pouring from a vent. Several deck cadets were unlatching the hatch closest to the vent. As they lifted it, a gust of smoke exited, forcing them back. The fire appeared to be localized to a small forward compartment. But everyone knew that fires on ships could spread rapidly and become catastrophic. No one needed to imagine how close the ammunition was.

Other than torpedoes, a fire on board was the most feared catastrophe. A cadet ran up with a large portable fire extinguisher, but clearly that was inadequate. Three cadets in the fire brigade, including Murray Wayburn from Baltimore, were running toward the smoking hatch with the heavy, clumsy brass nozzle attached to the thick canvas hose. Some Navy Guards ran up and one had a gas mask. Men were standing gaping toward the hatch, fearful of descending into the unknown. Jack grabbed the gas mask and quickly donned it as he started down the ladder into the smoking hatch. Murray grabbed Jack's arm before he disappeared into the smoke. He wrapped a rope around Jack's chest before he descended. He likely saved Jack's life.

In the room-sized hold, Jack could see only gray smoke swirling with an occasional glimpse of flames flickering in the forward point of the space. As he stepped from the six-foot ladder onto the deck floor, the cadets passed down the hose. He aimed the hose in the direction of the flames and screamed to turn on the water. To his surprise, the water pressure was so great that the hose literally lifted him off his feet and forced him back against the steel bulkhead, knocking his gas mask off his face. Fortunately, it remained attached around his neck. Jack repositioned it and, through the smoke, searched for the hose. It was flipping around uncontrollably. He grabbed the body of the hose and pulled it toward him. He braced himself against the bulkhead until he was able to get control of the powerful nozzle. He aimed at the source of the densest smoke, but soon he was overwhelmed and coughing from the smoke despite his mask. He dropped the hose and worked his way to the ladder by pulling on his lifeline. As he was half dragged up on deck, he gasped for air, and between coughs, tried to explain what he observed. He requested a new mask and assistance. Another deck cadet, Rich Osborn, encouraged that Jack had survived the initial fray, put on a gas mask and together they both descended into the smoke-filled room. As a team they were able to grasp the hose and direct the force of the water toward the fire and slowly, over fifteen minutes, the fire was finally, totally, happily extinguished.

By this time, the Captain and other officers appeared at the open hatch. Jack and Rich were standing in two inches of water as the Captain and Chief climbed down into the blackened chamber and searched for the source. Gleason looked at the two dirty, soaking men and said only, "Good work, men." With their masks in place, he did not recognize them. He then sloshed forward toward the source. All they found was a charred tarpaulin, floating sawdust, rope fragments, and a few bobbing paint cans. The tarpaulin had been used a few days earlier for a painting project. The fire was a case of spontaneous combustion.

The Captain looked at Chief Cockrell, as the cold dirty water sloshed around their ankles. "Put together a search team to look for other areas on board where paint and rags may be stored.

Put signs around the ship warning the crew to properly dispose of any paint products. And within the next two hours, I want to make an announcement on the loudspeaker."

Left unsaid was that only ten feet from the fire was the number one hold with too many tons of TNT to count.

The fire episode was the talk of the ship for some time. Captain Gleason learned within an hour that Rich Osborn and Jack were the men who put out the conflagration. He summoned them both to the bridge and thanked them for their courage "under fire." The men both expressed to the Captain that they were just doing their jobs and had been lucky during the episode. The Captain ordered them to take a shower and get cleaned up. Both were grateful for the extra shower time.

As Jack stepped into the shower, the only private one he took on board, he was thankful that the Captain did not bring up anything about the fight at the bar. Jack hoped that his efforts to extinguish the fire would be written up and also make its way to his file. Thoughts of Penny percolated in the back of his mind. She would have been proud, as would his mother. It then struck him that he thought of Penny before his mother...

By 2100, the Captain made an announcement on the loud

speaker. He thanked Rich Osborn and Jack Dodd by name for extinguishing the fire. He warned the crew about leaving any fire hazard unattended, especially paint products. He then informed the crew that two new guns were to be loaded on board the next day. He explained that they looked like mortars and were used to shoot into the sky a grenade attached to a thin wire. When the grenade reached several hundred feet of altitude, it exploded, and a parachute was released. With the ship under way, the parachute would hang in the sky by the wire and entangle attacking enemy aircraft. At least that was the theory. They also had "barrage balloons" for the same purpose while at anchor. The balloons were attached to a winch on the mast.

The next day, the tempo on the *Esek Hopkins* changed when winter equipment and clothing were loaded on board, along with the two new cannons. Now it was obvious to all that they were headed to Russia, not the Persian Gulf. This was going to be no picnic, and everyone now knew it. Each man on board was issued long woolen underwear, sheepskin-lined helmets and face masks, and long woolen ski socks. They also received heavy turtleneck sweaters, long leather jackets lined with sheepskin, fur-lined gloves, and rubber boots. Extra woolen blankets also were included. It was good that the service did not want its Merchant Marine and Navy crews to get cold. They would have multiple other issues to deal with.

Now that the crew was provisioned for the cold Russian weather, and the ship full of fuel, the *Esek Hopkins* heaved anchor and headed out toward its next destination. Jack had written four letters that morning to make the last mail delivery to shore. Three were addressed to Penny. Jack continued to think about Penny more than he expected. Perhaps the farther away he was, the more he longed for her. He realized that from the hilltop, she could see that all the ships remained in the harbor for two extra days before their departure from Gourock. But at the same time, she must have realized that leave had been cancelled for all sailors, so there was no chance of Jack seeing her.

Cold rain came down in sheets as they steamed past the little port town of Gourock one final time and out into the Firth of Clyde. Jack gazed at the spot where Penny stood on the mole, tearfully bidding him goodbye, bringing forth all the soft memories. The act of heaving the anchor, the black smoke trailing from the stack, the waves gracefully sliding away from the bow, all offered additional evidence to the uncomfortable realization that he may never see her again.

The emotion this elicited was more powerful than he anticipated. He stood on deck in the cold rain and stared at the spot on shore where they kissed goodbye.

The ship joined thirty other vessels that made up a new convoy. The next stop was Loch Ewe, Scotland, where they anchored two days later. More ships arrived during the afternoon, filling the loch with such a crowd they could barely swing at anchor without striking an adjacent ship. It was another spectacularly beautiful anchorage. Jack noted how breathtaking the surrounding mountains were on those occasions when the clouds dissipated.

That evening he wrote another letter. It started:

Dearest Penny,

I miss you terribly. Even with all the distractions on board, I think of you always. No need to explain in detail...

He went on to outline the events on board. Then he dawdled on her, perhaps excessively, realizing he was not very good at it. He surprised himself with his finish:

With much love and affection, Jack.

Maybe he was, after all, in love with her.

The next day, some British naval men came on board by launch and were scheduled to check all the cannons and machine guns. Jack and his mates followed them from gun to gun and listened to all they said. There was a clear message in that exercise. They would most certainly be using the guns on this next leg of the journey.

The remaining days at anchor were filled with fire drills and lifeboat drills. Jack knew them cold. The Brits were certainly intent on preparing the crew for whatever may happen.

After the drills, Jack busied himself on the bridge by studying navigation and instruments—again. Captain Gleason made one last trip to shore and when he got back and settled on the bridge, he related a story where someone on shore was asking if he knew Captain Dodd of the *Esek Hopkins*! Everyone on the bridge got a laugh but the name stuck, in a light-hearted fashion.

The next few days on board were a recycling of numbing boredom for the crew. There was no town of any substance in this desolate part of Scotland and no shore leave was granted. Everyone occupied themselves with cards, checkers, chess, studying, reviewing drills, fishing, cleaning equipment, exercising, writing notes to girlfriends and family, and just trying to maintain a level head while trapped on board and anticipating their uncertain futures. One crewmember taught Jack how to splice wire cables. Times were tough.

During one evening at mess, Jack saw Ski at a distant table. His face was still black and blue with a dressing decorating his colorful forehead. Jack almost wished he had be the creator of that mess. And if Ski was telling others that Jack did this, so much the better. No one would bother Jack, if this is what he could do to one of the tough engine wipers. And all Jack had to show for it was a scratch on his ear.

During periods of boredom, the rumor mill cranked up even more than when in port. One day, the old rumor spread again that they were not going to Russia after all, but to the Persian Gulf, again. A strange rumor indeed, Jack thought, since they were so far north and had just been issued heavy woolen clothing. Some folks just liked to live in a fantasy world or enjoyed disturbing the peace and agitating.

Captain Gleason returned to the ship with some local port

authorities. They searched the ship for stowaways. The crew was surprised. Why would someone want to leave Scotland and make a dangerous trip to Russia? Perhaps they were searching for some crewmen's hidden "wives." Perhaps they feared a crew member might bring a female on board for the voyage. No stowaways were found.

On September 1, in the afternoon, four corvettes approached the quiet convoy and dropped anchor. This was the tipoff that they soon would head out. The next day, at 5:00 p.m., the *Esek Hopkins* heaved anchor and started the next phase of her journey. As they sailed out of the loch, ships took their assigned positions to form the convoy. Jack was on the bridge and observed and learned as the ships came together.

This convoy kept the name PQ 18. Jack was astonished at the number of escort ships accompanying them. He observed thirteen destroyers, along with multiple corvettes and submarines as well as a hospital ship. In addition, there were two heavy anti-aircraft cruisers and the HMS *Avenger*, a small aircraft carrier with twelve British Hurricanes and three Swordfish sub chasers on board. Jack learned this four-hundred-and-ninety-foot flattop was built in Chester, Pennsylvania, as a merchant ship. She was converted into an escort carrier, sometimes called a "jeep carrier," and transferred to the Royal Navy under President Roosevelt's Lend-Lease Program. Her aircraft could act in three modes. Their most important task was to disrupt Luftwaffe air attacks. They could also search for U-boats and bomb them with depth charges. Finally, they could act in a reconnaissance capacity. Jack was mesmerized as he watched the aircraft practice takeoff and landing exercises on the relatively short flight deck. Captain Gleason was particularly happy with the presence of the escort carrier and her fighter aircraft. They significantly improved the odds of survival and success for the convoy.

This trip would be anything but boring.

CHAPTER 15

The Stage Is Set

A LIBERTY SHIP'S POSITION IN the convoy was determined by the British Admiralty. By an earlier agreement, the US Navy had no say. This was not an insignificant issue. All the men on board knew how important their ship position was and how their survival may depend on it.

Those vessels assigned to the outer perimeter of the convoy were invariably the first attacked by U-boats. They were easy targets. The ships in the inner rows of the convoy were relatively safe from the devastating torpedoes, although there were exceptions. If a torpedo missed a ship on the perimeter, the eel could stay on its course and strike a ship inside. And the officers knew that the clever Germans developed torpedoes which could go straight then turn in circles, increasing the odds of a strike if the first target ship was missed. And when it came to Luftwaffe air attacks, there was no safe spot in the convoy.

U-boat captains who perceived themselves as dashing or reckless would come to the surface in the midst of the convoys. This daring move gave some advantages to the U-boat. It gave them the opportunity to make a point-blank torpedo shot at one or more merchant ships. They could launch torpedoes from the bow or stern of the U-boat. No wasted torpedo shots.

Also, it made it difficult for the escort ships to rush in to attack the U-boats amidst the convoy vessels. The clever U-boat captains realized one final advantage; the large cannons on the Liberty Ships were designed and positioned as antiaircraft guns and lacked the ability to aim below the horizon. The only weapons available to shoot at the U-boats were the Oerlikon 20mm machine guns. Their range was limited, and the Germans quickly realized how far from the ships they could safely attack. In addition, the U-boats had their own potent cannon on deck along with two high-caliber machine guns. The U-boat cannon was often successful in sinking ships when they aimed at the waterline.

The merchant ships inside the convoy had one other issue which jeopardized their safety. When the Luftwaffe bomber aircraft attacked the convoy, they often would direct their bombs at the ships in the middle of the convoy. It was a target-rich environment. Or, they could line up over the long rows of ships and drop bombs on one ship after another. For those pilots who were daring enough, after they exhausted their bomb load, they could return and fly in low between the rows of ships and direct machine guns at the vessels from both sides of the aircraft. The gunners on the ships often held their return fire because they may strike their fellow adjacent vessels with friendly fire.

The *Esek Hopkins* was assigned to the position of the fourth ship in the third row in the convoy. This convoy was four ships long and ten wide. Jack and the crew talked among themselves about how fortunate they were to be in such a "safe" spot.

Once the *Esek Hopkins* heaved anchor and the convoy was formed, the crew learned they were cruising first to Reykjavik, Iceland. Jack wondered if some of the officers might be the source of the false rumors about destinations. It kept the crew confused and talking. It was likely a good strategy. If the crew had false data, any loose talk on shore would be useless to German agents or spies.

The speed of the convoy was usually determined by the speed of the slowest vessel. In this case they were cruising at seven knots. German U-boats could travel at a maximum speed of fifteen knots on the surface. Destroyers could travel at speeds over twenty-five knots and the smaller corvettes at twenty knots. But torpedoes won the race; they could top forty knots.

On the first day out, Jack was on the bridge, and he noted that the barometer began to fall sharply as dark clouds moved in from the west and the wind picked up. By early evening, gale-force winds were howling, and waves were building. The *Esek Hopkins* and the convoy were on a northwest course from Scotland to Iceland. The westerly winds and waves were striking the ships on their port sides and causing the vessels to roll excessively. Waves crested and broke over the bow and sides with dramatic force and power. No human was safe outside.

Incomprehensibly, the ship rolled as much as thirty degrees. The first few times this happened, everyone on board thought the ship would never right herself. But, against all odds, she did. And repeatedly. As did all the ships in the convoy. None were lost in the storm.

During this second Atlantic storm encountered by the *Esek Hopkins*, Jack was quickly reminded that there was no safe place on board. He secured his gear as best he could. He tried to write letters home, but even with bracing himself in the corner of the bed, writing was nearly impossible. At one point the trash can careened out of the cabin into the corridor and down one flight of stairs to the deck below. To sleep Jack wedged himself between a life jacket and pillows against the wall. One deck below he heard china crashing in the galley. No one would sleep well .

At 6:00 a.m., as the ship pitched and rolled, Jack struggled to dress and make his way to the bridge. As he stumbled up the stairs, he suspected the rolling had somewhat diminished. Or was he getting acclimated to it? He had no appetite.

Captain Gleason was on the bridge, and he informed Jack they had lost track of ten neighboring ships. It was not infrequent that ships got off course during storms; the more alarming issue was a possible collision and sinking. But within the next hour they all were sighted and accounted for. Then the Captain reminded Jack to inspect the cargo in the holds. He collected eight other deck cadets for the difficult task. It took them the better part of four hours to struggle down in their bulky life jackets as the ship pitched and rolled. Some holds were packed with jeeps and Sherman tanks, others with supplies and ammunition. After sustaining an assortment of bruises, they determined that all was secure.

During the next twenty-four hours, the wind diminished, and the storm slowly subsided. A hazy appearance of the sun overhead was a welcome sight. Sparks, the wireless operator, got a report of a British ship being bombed near the coast of Iceland. Then, to set off everyone's nerves even more, a ship nearby shot one of its guns. The klaxon alarm was sounded on the *Esek Hopkins* and everyone ran to their stations. But after thirty minutes all were told to stand down. No reason was given for the gunshot. As the ships were approaching Iceland, nerves were on high alert.

The next day, Monday, September 7, 1942, was Labor Day. Jack engaged in pleasant thoughts of being with friends back home on the warm Eastern Shore beaches. Young men and women from Baltimore, Philadelphia and Washington poured into Ocean City, Maryland and Rehoboth Beach, Delaware to take in the sun and surf for the long weekend. Penny would fit in nicely, he concluded. Interesting, he thought, how he often tried to fit Penny into any situation back home...Sadly, neither Jack Dodd, nor Penny McNeal would be in attendance this season. Maybe next year.

That afternoon, as Jack made his way to the bridge, he saw the rocky coastline of Iceland for the first time. A short time later four British escort ships peeled away from the convoy and signaled by Morse Code, "Cheerio, good luck." Jack somehow felt a little naked as he watched them depart. He realized how you barely noticed them until they were gone.

About an hour later, Jack, the Captain, and the first mate relaxed a bit as they watched fifteen additional merchant ships and escorts sail out of Reykjavik to join their convoy. Then Captain Gleason told a story about how he considered Labor Day a lucky omen for him. On this holiday one year ago, he was captain on a merchant ship departing from Puerto Rico with two other ships and no escort vessels. Torpedoes struck and sank two of the ships. His ship was not struck and completed her mission. They all hoped his luck would hold for the *Esek Hopkins.*

As the convoy puttered north at seven knots, Jack appreciated the jagged, rocky cliffs of the west coast of Iceland. That evening, September 8, the peaceful state of affairs was interrupted by the screaming klaxon battle station alarm. Through binoculars, Jack saw men on an adjacent merchant ship hoist a flag which indicated enemy aircraft were approaching. The ship carried a single British Hurricane fighter plane which was immediately launched from a catapult. This was no false alarm. But the enemy aircraft were not bombers or fighters, but German reconnaissance planes. The PQ-18 convoy had been discovered and was now being watched.

On September 9, the convoy completed its turn around the northern tip of Iceland and headed east at ninety degrees. Their course now took them just within the Arctic Circle. The temperature had been dropping steadily for the past twelve hours. Their course to Russia would pass south of the island of Spitzbergen and north of the coast of Norway. Once beyond Norway, they would turn south and enter the Barents Sea. The Russian port of Murmansk is on the western side of the Barents Sea. The port of Archangel is further along the Russian coast and is tucked in the White Sea. From German ports and airfields in Norway this region between Iceland and the White Sea was the most fertile for air and sea attacks on Allied convoys. They were entering the "hot zone." And everyone knew it.

Before noon there was another battle station alarm on board. But again, it was a German reconnaissance aircraft. The tension was slowly mounting among the crew members.

Even though technically it was late summer, they now were dressing for frigid weather. The thought of being cast in the freezing water if their vessel was sunk, even with the protection of Vaco waterproof suits, was unbearable.

When Allied convoys to England and Russia first started in

May 1940 with PQ 1, before Germany declared war on the US, there was essentially no opposition from the Kriegsmairne. Once war was declared, attacks on the convoys began in earnest. By May 1942, German action against PQ 16 had increased to the point where nine of thirty merchant vessels were sunk.

Jack recalled that the next convoy, PQ 17, had catastrophic losses. He knew the *Esek Hopkins* was scheduled to be in that convoy but was delayed because of the collision in Halifax Harbor. The Allies were determined to avoid additional catastrophic destruction of ships with these priceless cargos. The Admiralty created the largest escort service ever assembled to protect this convoy, PQ 18.

Tensions on board mounted that same day as Jack and a few mates lunching below heard a loud "thump" and felt a shock to the hull. They thought the ship had been struck by a torpedo and rushed up on deck. Word quickly spread that the shock was explained by a nearby depth charge. Very nearby! Okay, good news, but depth charges meant there must be a U-boat in the vicinity. If there was, it got away and there was no further action, other than three corvettes casting about the choppy sea behind the convoy.

The next day it was foggy in the morning. Good news for the convoy. But the wind picked up and the fog cleared by 1:00 p.m. A small plane flew near the convoy and was shot at by a merchant ship. The plane was friendly and fortunately it was not hit. Itchy trigger fingers. To further raise the temperature, Captain Gleason got a rare radio message from the British admiral saying to be prepared for a German attack in the next two days.

Standing on the bridge, Jack blurted out loud, "Hell, we have been expecting an attack since we left Scotland!"

On Saturday, September 12, there were three battle station alarms starting just after noon. The first two were false alarms. The third alarm was because a German Heinkel was circling far in front of the convoy. Four British Hurricanes took off from the HMS *Avenger* in pursuit. The Heinkel got away while all the crews stood on deck freezing by the guns in the chilly wind.

They were still ten days from Archangel. The crew consensus was that they would get hammered the next day. The Germans certainly had been watching them long enough.

Jack wondered if everyone was truly ready.

CHAPTER 16

Showtime

SUNDAY, SEPTEMBER 13, 1942 WAS a day which no crew member on any ship in Convoy PQ 18 would ever forget. Jack had not slept well but when the piercing battle alarm sounded at 9:00 a.m., he was on his feet in an instant and wide awake. He was the first of his three roommates out of his room. His heart pounded. In sixty seconds, with electrified nerves, he had dashed up to battle station number four, one deck above the bridge level. He quickly secured his life vest and helmet as he prepared to man the Oerlikon 20mm machine gun. Station four was a round gun tub ten feet in diameter. The circular wall was four feet high and consisted of double-plated half-inch steel with asphalt and gravel between the plates to prevent bullet penetration. In the center of the tub was a sturdy steel mount for the powerful Oerlikon. The machine gun barrel was centered between two rectangles of steel plates to protect the gunner. From this position the gun could maintain fire in any direction, except across the ship due to the obstructions of masts and rigging. It could aim down at targets in the water close to the ship. This gun tub was one of four built at each corner of the ship's superstructure. As Jack had noted when he first inspected the *Esek Hopkins*, the ship had two additional 20mm gun tubs forward and two aft. Her other protective guns were the big three-inch antiaircraft cannons on the bow and stern along with the single five-inch cannon facing aft. On this day, they would be firing all their weapons; frequently.

Jack gazed down at the helm station, one deck below, where Brice Cockrell and Capt. Gleason were steering the ship. The occupants of the bridge were protected by walls consisting of four-inch-thick, fire-proof, absorbent asphalt and gravel material. It was the safest spot on the ship.

Moments later Jack was joined at the gun tub by his pal, Navy Armed Guard Ron Sewell.

Jack was reviewing in his mind the many tips he had learned in the gun class on shore with Captain Gleason and the earlier experience he had shooting the gun off the shore of Halifax. Jack knew his job and was ready. Ron started at the gun. Fitz, the third assist, trotted up as he tightened his life vest, secured his helmet, and asked, "Is this the real deal?"

No one dared respond. They searched the sky. No aircraft were in sight. Within thirty minutes the all-clear signal sounded. Unable to determine if they were happy or unhappy, they shrugged their shoulders and returned to their bunks. No sooner had Jack flopped on his bed than there was a distant explosion, and the battle alarm annoyingly sounded again. He raced to the main deck and saw a dense column of smoke rising in the sky on the far side of the convoy to starboard. At the base of the smoke was a merchant ship. She could be seen listing to starboard just moments after a torpedo hit. Clearly, the vessel was terminal. So it began.

On the *Esek Hopkins,* the crew collected on the starboard side, piling up next to Jack and gaping at the spectacle in the distance. The second mate, Mark Williams, trotted up. He recognized the ship because of her position on the right edge of the convoy.

He announced, "I think that is the Russian collier named *Stalingrad.*"

His impression was accurate. The *Stalingrad* was struck by the second torpedo from *U-408*, compliments of Captain Reinhard Hymmen. Flames flicked from the deck, and smoke shot at least one hundred feet in the air. Random scattered gun-fire erupted from different sources around the *Esek Hopkins.* Distant depth charge shock waves reverberated below their ship, creating numbing concussions under the crew.

Moments later there was another explosion. Captain Reinhard Hymmen had scored his second torpedo strike. This ship was also to starboard, but just aft of the *Stalingrad.* Williams commented to the surrounding crew that he was sure that was the *Oliver Ellsworth*, an American Liberty Ship.

Williams observed with disgust, "Those bastard U-boat captains are out there picking off the ships like fish in a barrel. Where are the goddamn escorts?"

No sooner had Williams spoken the words than a destroyer was seen racing toward the explosion. More distant shock waves from depth charges rattled their feet from below the *Esek Hopkins.* The *Stalingrad* was rapidly sinking, and a rescue craft was already collecting survivors.

Jack said to no one in particular, "God, at this rate we all will be sunk by sunset."

Williams, no longer mesmerized by the frightening scene, shouted to the men, "To your battle stations—now! The entire convoy is under attack!" All the crewmen scattered.

The *Oliver Ellsworth* was not sinking. It took about thirty minutes for the crew to evacuate that stricken vessel. She was no longer under way, while the convoy continued moving ahead. The Admiralty took the position that it would not be wise to allow Germans to board any ship after she was abandoned. The Admiralty made a decision to sink her. An Allied destroyer approached and shelled *Oliver Ellsworth* until she slowly disappeared beneath the waves.

Now distant explosions were heard far off toward the left side of the convoy, and billowing smoke climbed into the sky. The U-boat commanders were having a grand day. The wolf pack concept was very effective. They were methodically eliminating targets on both sides of the convoy.

Then the Luftwaffe joined the show. Jack was positioned at gun tub number four watching the horizon and speaking with Ron and

Fitz when the deafening battle alarm sounded again, causing the three men to jump. The alarm was much louder when one was standing on deck. Ron and Fitz tightened their helmets as Jack brought more ammo into the tub. They searched the sky. Someone from the aft cannon yelled, "There they are, coming toward our starboard bow!" Jack, Fitz and Ron jerked their heads around to the right.

Jack squinted. "I see them. God help us. There must be a hundred!"

There were about thirty German Heinkel (He 111) bombers and twenty Junker (Ju 88) fighter-bombers approaching on this attack. A smaller group of four-engine FW Condor heavy bombers were barely visible at a higher altitude and lagging behind the faster fighter-bombers. The He 111 bombers each were loaded with a single torpedo, while most of the Ju 88s carried multiple smaller bombs. The aircraft descended into attack formation and split their forces. The twin-engine He 111 bombers swung around to approach directly toward the starboard side of the convoy to increase the odds of a strike by aiming at the sides of the ships rather than head on.

But the swift Ju 88s arrived first. These twin-engine fighter/bombers were designed to fly at speeds fast enough to outpace the fighter planes of the era. They attacked the convoy from the left side.

Ron yelled, "God, look how fast those damn things are moving. We will have to aim way in front of them!"

The escort ships along the outer perimeter of the convoy first opened an intense rate of fire as soon as the planes were in range.

Jack gazed at the turmoil in the sky and observed, "God, it looks like the bright lights on Broadway."

Fitz yelled, "It looks like unholy hell to me!"

A pair of bombs from nowhere exploded with a frightening burst just adjacent to the *Esek Hopkins,* and a tall column of ocean descended on deck. Sea water splashed on Jack, Ron, and Fitz; their first "injury" of the battle. Where did the bombs come from? There were no aircraft in their immediate vicinity.

Ron looked overhead, pointed straight up, and said, "Directly above us. A Condor bomber. So high you can't even hear it."

This was the first day of the convoy's engagement with the enemy in the sky. The inexperienced escort gunners were not so accurate. But the heavy barrage of gunfire ultimately achieved some success. The port engine of one of the Ju 88s was struck, and the trio followed the crippled aircraft until it slammed violently into the distant ocean, flinging wing fragments around, and making secondary splashes, before descending into the depths.

Ron shouted gleefully, "Goddamn it, one down!"

As more attacking aircraft got through the escort ship's barrages, the three-inch and five-inch cannons of the *Esek Hopkins* began pounding out shots as rapidly as the Navy Armed Guards could load them. The fast Ju 88 engines screamed as they got nearer, sprinkling their lethal cargo on random ships. They were getting closer to the *Esek Hopkins* and the trio readied themselves as each reviewed in his mind his immediate task. No faltering; no screw-ups.

Ron started on the 20mm. He was strapped into the shoulder braces and had been practicing aiming by jostling back and forth. Jack was in charge of moving and loading the heavy ammo magazines. Fitz had already donned the asbestos gloves and would exchange the hot barrels.

Soon enough, a Ju 88 in the distance turned toward them for a bombing run. The first gun to fire at the bomber was the forward three-inch cannon. It made a tremendously loud crack as it unloaded its fifty-pound shell. The aim was off to the right. Next, one of the forward 20mm Oerlikons erupted, but the gunner fired too soon, and his shots fell short. Ron waited for one or two more seconds, then took a bead and squeezed the trigger for the first time in anger.

He had aimed high, but the tracers indicated not high enough. All the bullets fell under the blistering fast fighter-bomber. Two bombs released from the aircraft wings. All eyes fixed. The pilot's timing was off. The pair of bombs zipped over the rigging and exploded one hundred and fifty yards past their ship, flinging tons of water upward in a pair of white spouts.

As cannon cracks and machine gun fire rattled in the background, Ron screamed out how amazed he was at the speed of the Ju 88s. He turned to Jack and yelled, "We need to shoot way in front of the bombers so they fly into the stream of bullets; just like they told us in training."

Jack nodded that he understood. Still…

A vessel two over on the starboard side of *Esek Hopkins* was the next ship struck. She was the Liberty Ship, *John Penn.* She took a torpedo dropped from one of the He 111s. The explosion was terrific, and the three men felt the shock wave and thunderous sound sweep across the *Esek Hopkins'* deck. Jack checked periodically and saw that the *John Penn* did not sink immediately, but slowly drifted out of formation. He saw rescue vessels approach and begin fishing crewmen from the cold ocean. Later the ship was intentionally sunk by an Allied destroyer. More waste.

The intense fireworks flashed in the sky for what seemed like forever. Explosions surrounded Jack. Gunfire in all directions seemed to be unceasing. The intense cracking of the four large cannons and the never-ending rat-tat-tat of the eight 20mm Oerlikons were stupefying and exhausting. Fitz seemed to be changing the gun barrel of their 20mm every two minutes, though no one was keeping time. Hot bubbles gurgled up from the water-filled cooling tubes each time Fitz exchanged the blistering-hot barrels.

It was difficult to be certain they actually were knocking aircraft out of the sky. But they were making hits. There was no time to watch a suspected hit to see if it later crashed somewhere on the horizon. They were too busy picking up new targets whizzing by. More bombs crashed and exploded in the water from nowhere. These pesky high-altitude, four engine Condors were out of range of the *Esek Hopkins* cannons. The only way to destroy them was from the long-range cannons on the escort ships or by the Allied fighter aircraft.

Another shattering explosion and shock wave assaulted the gunners. It was the American Liberty Ship *Oregonian.* She was positioned in the first row, tenth spot—which was the most right-hand point in the convoy. Although that position was vulnerable to U-boat attacks, the *Oregonian* was struck by another He 111 torpedo and sunk. She was probably a half a mile from the *Esek Hopkins* when she was hit, but the explosion was frightening, and the stunning shock of the percussion was absorbed by everyone on deck. These shock waves and deafening explosive sounds were a surprise to Jack. He had no inkling how the violent explosions could be sensed when so far away. He wondered what impact it had on the men on board the ships who survived in the midst of the explosions. He did not dwell on the topic.

But he commented out loud, "Damn, what is happening to all those crew members?" Fitz was having similar thoughts. Ron shook his head and broke up the discussion by asking Jack to bring over another ammunition magazine. Fitz blessed himself.

There was a brief respite in the bombing and strafing as the Luftwaffe aircraft flew out over the expanse of ocean to regroup.

"Do you think that's it for the day?" Ron asked Jack optimistically as he attached the next magazine to the 20mm and wiped the sweat from his face.

Fitz offered, "No way. Hitler expects those pilots to sink every ship in the ocean. They will be back."

"Who knows?" Jack replied, shrugging his shoulders. "Sink every ship or lose every airplane. I got to give it to them, those Germans are pretty determined."

Jack wondered what type of men these pilots were. Did they have families, go to church, pray to the same God? And what motivated them to risk their lives, and to kill on such a massive scale? The sun, stars and moon make no judgement on this man-created horrific scene here in the vast ocean. It was a strange reality. It had meaning only to silly, mortal men.

Jack looked down toward the ship's bridge. He saw no sign of damage. Crew members started walking from their stations. Some ran for toilet breaks, or perhaps vomiting breaks.

Empty 20mm cartridges rolled around the gun tub noisily as the *Esek Hopkins* serenely, innocently plowed through the light chop.

Deck hands around the three-inch and five-inch cannons were throwing the large empty shell casings overboard. A surprisingly large number of shells were rolling around the deck.

Other hands moved ammunition from storage boxes to the gun tubs.

Just then someone yelled, "Here they come from the port side!" At that instant the battle station's alarm sounded again making everyone on deck jump. Jack, Fitz and Ron were on the port side, and they locked in the ammunition magazine and wiped down the gun barrel. They stared off at the horizon and watched the dots get larger. The *Esek Hopkins* was the fourth ship in, third row –a good spot for protection from U-boat torpedoes. But no ship was safe from the Luftwaffe torpedoes and bombs. All eyes and guns were directed to port. The escort ships along the perimeter started firing at the enemy. Then the battle station's alarm went off again, once more making everyone jump. As if they weren't already at their battle stations. Someone on the bridge had itchy fingers. Then, ugly words from the speaker system: "Enemy aircraft approaching from the stern!" It was the second mate's voice. He unnecessarily repeated it. The sky lit up with antiaircraft fire from the escort ships behind them.

Since the trio was positioned on the port side, Ron commanded they would concentrate on the aircraft coming in from the port side first. He yelled something about knocking out all the planes on that side, then they would direct their attention aft. Hopefully, the aft guns would temporarily protect the stern. Hopefully.

In the distance, the trio could see an He 111 bomber drop what looked like a little stick. The torpedo was directed toward one of the ships on the far-left edge of the convoy. Apparently, the pilot was wide with his targeting. The aircraft images got larger as the seconds ticked by.

One bomber was closing on them at a ten-degree angle from

the port bow. Jack shuddered for a moment—the *Esek Hopkins* was the target. Flak from other ships was zipping past the plane, but the pilot kept on. The three-inch cannon on the bow erupted, discharging shells every ten seconds, but missed repeatedly. The aircraft was too far for their 20mm; but not for long. Jack held his breath waiting for that torpedo to drop. Ron grasped the gun firmly, leaned back and down, and aimed high, hoping the plane would fly into the stream of bullets from his gun. He waited and waited before squeezing the trigger. Other 20mm guns from the *Esek Hopkins* were firing but missing with tracers falling short and under the plane.

Jack yelled, "Shoot, shoot for God's sake!"

Ron waited one more second, aimed forward, then squeezed the trigger. The tracer bullets marked the rounds hitting the wing just to the left of the cockpit. The short burst appeared to do little harm. In a second the plane was over top of them as they strained to see what would happen next. In an instant, they observed the twenty-three-foot torpedo release from the belly of the He 111. With their eyes, they ignored the plane but followed the torpedo as it slowly, majestically, gracefully carried itself forward with twin props spinning, and eventually was absorbed into the cold, disinterested ocean with a surprisingly small splash. They squinted to see which ship was at the end of the extended line of the underwater bomb. They waited and waited for an uncomfortably long time.

Ron looked at Jack, "They missed."

Not a second later there was a bright flash from the ship one row behind them and second from the right edge of the convoy. The three men reflexively blinked, pulled back and watched in horror to see a frightful disruption of the side of the ship, with fragments of spiraling metal and debris shooting into the air, followed by a gushing mushroom cloud of black smoke. It was a mere two seconds before the powerful shock wave blew past them followed by the crushing, deafening sound of the explosion. Jack grimaced as he imagined the confusion and terror on the burning, smoky decks, with screaming, scrambling men making instantaneous decisions which may save or doom each of the sixty crewmen. Men just like Jack. Why them? Why had that pilot not targeted the *Esek Hopkins*?

Fitz uttered, "Hail Mary."

Ron quipped, "If I were you, I would skip Mary and pray directly to God!" He extended his arm and lined his eye with his index finger pointing to the He 111 which had dropped the torpedo, escaping in the distance. "I got the bastard!" he screamed amidst the turmoil.

Ron's bullets had struck the starboard engine, which was leaving a sputtering trail of gray smoke. The plane was losing altitude. They did not dwell on the stricken bomber, but Ron screamed, "Got you, Kraut bastards. I hope you all burn in hell!"

They learned later that the ship which was torpedoed was a Panamanian steamer, the *Africander.* The single torpedo which struck her eventually sank her. Excruciating terror for the *Africander* crew.

A nearby splash from a single bomb piercing the water surface exploded next to the *Esek Hopkins* and once again, they were covered with cold sea water. The bomb missed the ship by a mere fifty feet and exploded beneath the water's surface. The ship was rocked by the explosion. The three gave each other a wary smile, thinking how lucky they were...again. Ron looked at Fitz. "Keep praying. It seems to be working." Now, Jack was joining in with silent prayers.

The battle raged. The planes kept coming. A seeming never-ending procession of enemy aircraft swarmed over the convoy. Ron, Fitz, and Jack reloaded ammo magazine after magazine, cocked the gun and searched for targets and fired away. They were developing a rhythm.

Meanwhile, the bow and stern Navy Armed Guards were firing off three-inch and five-inch cannon shells at a rate of four or five per minute. The background crack of those cannons and the overwhelming clatter of the eight 20mm machine guns made it difficult to think or pause or contemplate. All was reflex. All was exhausting. It became surreal. A dream. Motion, countermotion. Look, aim, shoot. No time for thinking. No time for prayers. No time for anything. Just do.

Next on the growing list of mortalities was another Panamanian steamer, *Macbeth*. She was on the far-right side of the convoy just in front of the *Stalingrad*, the first vessel sunk on this dreadful day. The *Macbeth* was sunk by another He 111. Jack and Ron were so busy fighting off the Luftwaffe, they barely noticed the explosion. About twenty minutes after the strike, when they glanced around the deck, they saw the smoke rising from the *Macbeth* carcass in the distance.

The battle was not one-sided. Jack began to count the number of Luftwaffe planes that were knocked out of the sky. But he was so busy, he lost track after eight downed planes. Not until a few days later did they get the final tally. Still, if one plane could sink one ship…

There were breaks in the action. During one break, some of the galley hands came up on deck to deliver some coffee, water, and sandwiches. Some crew members grabbed at the coffee and inhaled the sandwiches, while others could not even look at the snacks. Jack took a long slug of water. Ron tore into a sandwich. Fitz wasn't interested and just watched the sky.

Everyone looked around the deck of the ship. So far, no dead bodies lying about. Not even a sign of blood. Shell casings littered the gray surface. They all gazed about, looking for friendly faces in the crew. Something, anything familiar was somehow reassuring that they were still human, still alive, still sane.

Jack glanced at his watch. It was 3:00 p.m. The fireworks had started shortly after 9:00 a.m. What a day. His body was spent. His shoulders felt like liquid and were clumsy and difficult to maneuver. His legs felt irregular, ridged and flimsy. Unrealistically and out of character, he told Ron he was going down below for a quick nap. Ron reminded him they had not sounded the all-clear yet. Jack ignored him. Just as he got to the exterior door, however, the battle alarm sounded. Normally, Jack would have sprinted back to station number four. This time with deliberation, he stopped, turned thoughtfully, and slowly, clumsily made his way back toward the gun tub like a casual stroll down Gwynn Oak Avenue back home. As he joined Ron and Fitz, they were exchanging a hot gun barrel for a cool one, and confirming the magazine was in proper firing position, they heard a powerful explosion. They looked forward to starboard and saw a lifting trail of black and gray smoke. This Liberty Ship was in the front row, far right corner. She was occupying the spot of the *Oregonian*, sunk an hour earlier, the most dangerous position in the convoy. And the U-boat captain was a good shot. They learned later this was a British merchant ship, the *Empire Stevenson.* The now-familiar explosive shock wave surrounded them, followed by the ear-shattering explosion. A distant underwater thud of depth charges was heard and felt beneath their feet.

Time became dense during the attacks. It seemed an hour before the next air attack. In reality it was about fifteen minutes. This time the attackers came head-on. Heavy firing from escort ships at the front of the convoy could be heard as cannon rounds popped with black smoke and exploded high in the sky. Jack and Ron searched around a full three hundred and sixty degrees to be certain they were not attacking from two or three different directions. It appeared all the planes were coming toward their bow. Since their 20mm could not shoot straight ahead because of the ship's rigging and booms, they angled the gun forward as much as possible and fired at any aircraft flying past them on the port side. Now, with no more bombs, the Ju 88s were flying very low and firing their machine guns at ships on either side. With Liberty Ships across from them, there was a chance any friendly bullets which missed the aircraft might strike their colleagues on adjacent ships or strike them. Because of this, many Navy Guards manning the 20mms held their fire. In the meantime, Ju 88 gunfire was strafing the deck of *Esek Hopkins.* Each shot created a sharp clanking sound as it struck the steel. The German gunners aimed at the superstructure and helm station in hopes of killing the captain and officers. Since the trio were positioned just one level above the helm, they were taking many of the rounds. Ron and Fitz got as low as possible in the gun tub. By now, Jack had had one turn at the 20mm and felt he was a good enough shot and could more accurately lead the bullets so the aircraft would fly into them. Risking his life, he stood up, strapped himself to the shoulder brace, and cocked the fully loaded weapon. Fitz peeped above the edge of the tub as bullets clanked about, and watched as Jack placed his tracer bullets far ahead of the amazingly fast Ju 88s. In that brief time frame, of the eight or so planes they targeted, Fitz thought Jack hit at least four, although he could not document a kill. What was not known was, did Jack strike any Liberty Ships across from the *Esek Hopkins*? And how had Jack dodged all the bullets and survived?

Again, during the firefight, another thunderous explosion overwhelmed the noise of cannon fire and shells clanking on the deck of the *Esek Hopkins*. It was a Liberty Ship two ahead of them in the front line. The ship was sunk by a direct hit from a Ju 88 bomb. It was another British merchant ship, the *Empire Beaumont*. Captain Gleason had to turn the *Esek Hopkins* sharply to port to avoid the injured ship. The *Empire Beaumont* sank below the surface within fifteen minutes. The *Esek Hopkins* slid past many of the screaming crew bobbing and thrashing in the water. By established orders, Liberty Ships under way were prohibited from stopping to rescue sailors in the water. The two reasons given were that a stopped vessel was an easy target and that smaller rescue ships could do a better job of recovery. Still, it was impossibly difficult to watch as fellow seamen struggled in desperation. Jack scanned the waters in horror. As he gazed at the turmoil, he made a mental note that he could see no men in a Vaco wet suit. He realized it took too long to climb into them.

Jack wondered, “How long can this go on? And how long can I stay lucky?”

The day was not over. As Ron and Fitz were watching the horizon, some movement caught their side vision. Fitz pointed to a spot in the water about one hundred and fifty yards off the port stern.

"A goddamn periscope," Ron shouted.

Jack rotated the 20mm and took a downward bead on the moving periscope. Once he was on the target, which was quickly zipping away from the *Esek Hopkins*, he cocked the gun and began to fire. His first shots fell short, then over the moving target. The periscope retracted below the surface in a few seconds and was not seen again.

The second mate, Mark Williams, came running out of the helm station and yelled, "What did you see in the water?"

Ron yelled back, "A U-boat periscope. I doubt we did any damage."

The second mate yelled back, "I will report the location. Good work, men. I hope it was not a friendly."

Jack looked at Ron, "Maybe it was a friendly…"

Fitz eased their minds. "Don't worry. There is no way a friendly would be lurking around in the middle of the convoy." They nodded in agreement.

The intensity of the Ju 88 attacks had slowed, but not ended. The final sinking of a Liberty Ship on this dreadful day occurred just as the sun was setting. It was a Russian steamer, the *Sukhona.* She was struck by a bomb from one of the last Ju 88s in the attack. The ship was on the far-right side of the convoy. Ironically, she had been behind the *Stalingrad* earlier in the morning. On this day, four ships were sunk on the right perimeter of the convoy.

The British escort carrier HMS *Avenger* had been very busy throughout the day. Of the twelve Hurricane fighter planes on board, eleven made it through the long battle. Those fighter planes were manned by excellent, brave pilots, who broke up many of the German attacks on the convoy. They shot down a number of Ju 88s and He 111s along with several of the high-flying Condors. As bad as the allied convoy losses were, they could have been much worse.

The Germans paid one final price that day. A Ju 88 appeared from nowhere and was streaking in low, below the radar, toward the HMS *Avenger* in one last attempt to put the escort carrier out of action. The German pilot clearly recognized what a disruption her fighter aircraft had been to their attack plans. The *Avenger* was about one-half a mile off the *Esek Hopkins'* port bow. Their three-inch cannons started firing along with about four other ships in the vicinity.

The *Avenger's* formidable array of guns also unleashed their barrage. The Ju 88 got close, but finally her port wing was struck and disintegrated, causing the low-flying bomber to flip down and hit the hard ocean surface and shatter into pieces. Everyone on the *Esek Hopkins'* deck cheered!

Finally, after another thirty minutes, the all-clear alarm went off, and everyone took a collective sigh of relief and headed for the doors to get some water or go to the heads. Ron, Fitz and Jack decided to wait for the crowd to subside. They stood by their gun and gazed at each other and inexplicably, gently laughed. They took off their helmets. Grit, grime and sweat covered their clothes and skin. But all their body parts were intact. They looked out over the vast Atlantic at the diabolical scene before them. In the distance were several points of faint dark smoke emanating from the water's surface at the site of sunken or near-sunken vessels. Debris, including timbers, furniture, papers, life jackets, oil slicks, and empty rafts bobbed in the waves as the *Esek Hopkins* glided past at eight knots. They could identify a dead body in a life jacket some distance away. There were several small boats picking up survivors as the sun set on the ominous, surreal scene.

"How can man do this to his fellow man?" Jack wondered out loud.

Ron gazed off at the destruction and, after a long pause, said, "Yeah, I guess both sides are responsible for this mess. But little Adolph, with his goofy moustache, declared war on us!"

Fitz observed, "That is why they train soldiers and sailors to do this. No member of the public would ever tolerate this chaos; this mess, this horror."

Jack thought of his mother. Maybe her prayers were helping. Then Penny.

Slowly, exhausted, without another word, they turned to go down below.

CHAPTER 17

Horror

IN THE MESS HALL, THE chatter was loud and incessant, as expected in any Forum. As tragic as the day was for the convoy, everyone on board the *Esek Hopkins* had survived. It was their first day of true combat, and they felt they had acquitted themselves well. Jack and Ron were seated next to each other at a table for twelve. Fitz had no appetite and gone off to crash in his bunk. Ron bragged about Jack to the other fellows at the table. He related how Jack kept firing the 20mm at the Ju 88s like a wild man, in spite of their return fire. Some of the group applauded. Like most crew members, Jack shyly retorted that he was "just doing my job."

The group therapy of talking and boasting was very helpful for all. As he scooped up dinner with his fork, Jack noted that his hands were trembling. This was new and quite distressing. No issue in his life had ever invaded his psyche enough to cause a tremor. As an attempt at distraction, he thought about Penny. He wondered what she was doing now. For sure, she had no worries, no anxiety, no tremor. She must have seen his letter by now. Did she still "love" him? Compare his life now to his three days in Scotland. Oh God, what a contrast. In any case, he got through his first day in real battle, tremor or not. He slyly looked around at his shipmates to see if anyone else had the shakes. One or two did.

Many stories, both real and imaginary, circulated in the mess hall that evening. There was laughing and tears and back-slapping. It was good to feel human again. God only knew how many men died in the convoy that day. Crew members began peeling off to bed as fatigue overwhelmed them. Jack included. He had not eaten much, and he was unconscious as soon as he hit his bunk just before midnight. Everyone needed rest.

The Earth continued its rotation beneath the sun. It was September 14 at 2:00 a.m. when the ear-numbing battle station alarm exploded in Jack's brain. He and his roommates leapt from their bunks and struggled to dress, in Jack's case with a clean shirt, trousers, and socks. His grimy clothes from the previous day were piled invisibly somewhere in the corner of the pitch-black room. He managed to get his low-cut boots on and tie them clumsily, not with his usual finesse. There was no conversation with his roommates, just incoherent grumbling and stumbling around. He shook his head left and right like a wet dog, as he walked into the poorly illuminated, red-light tinted corridor and struggled up the metal stairs in the direction of battle station number four. Jack could barely discern that Ron was already at the 20mm gun with helmet and life vest in place. As Jack arrived, Ron noted sarcastically that it was going to be tough to shoot at aircraft in the pitch-black starless sky. They gaped into the blank darkness as their eyes adjusted. Like the other ships around her, the *Esek Hopkins* had no lights on except for the faint red glow from the bridge. It looked like third mate Lance Lockhart was at the helm.

Fitz stumbled up, more asleep than awake. "What are you guys looking for? It's black as hell."

"Don't the bloody Germans ever sleep?" Jack asked Ron rhetorically.

They busied themselves finding and moving extra ammo boxes into their gun tub and affixing the first cassette into the 20mm. Below, on deck, shadows seemed to be wandering aimlessly, wondering what to do. Why did they wake us? Aircraft don't attack in this blackness. And there was no evidence of any U-boat activity.

Then, an extraordinarily bright flash erupted behind the *Esek Hopkins.* With their eyes dark-adapted, the light was so overwhelming, they squinted and held their hands up as shields. For an instant it seemed brighter than the sun. Seconds later an intensely powerful shock wave knocked off Fitz's unlatched helmet and caused Jack to lose his balance and nearly fall. Then the ear-pulsing explosive noise. All the dazed crew's eyes squinted and gazed aft as the night sky was aglow with an enormous conflagration on a ship a mere two vessels behind them. They knew the ship; it was the *Atheltemplar*, a British tanker filled with fuel oil. She had followed behind the *Esek Hopkins* from Iceland. As leaking oil coated the ocean surface, flames soon licked the sea and reached up into the black sky, extending a mysterious yellow cast onto many toy-like ships gliding along innocently in the vast ocean. The trio could feel the radiant heat.

Jack turned away for a moment and glanced at his mates as they stared and blinked, mesmerized by the horrifying nighttime spectacle. Their faces and bodies had a rippling, unworldly yellow cast.

As Jack gazed at the destruction, in complete horror, he could see men jumping from the side of the dying ship. Many jumped directly into the flaming sea in desperation. None of the men had time to don those cumbersome Vaco suits. Again. Some did not even have on life jackets. The crew instinctively knew they must abandon ship quickly. Should she explode, there would be zero chance of surviving. There was no ship behind her as she drifted farther back from the Convoy. Rescue ships approached and began scooping up the bobbing, floating, struggling mass of black oil-coated humanity. Depth charges reverberated in the distance in spite of the physical hazard to men in the water from the intense shock wave. Jack learned later that some of the men fished out of the water, later died from the underwater shock of the depth charges. They had internal injuries to their lungs and stomachs. He made a mental note to ask Ralph Arnold, the medical officer, about this.

Suddenly, Ron yelled, "Look!" as he pointed directly behind

and to the right of the *Esek Hopkins.* He grabbed the 20mm Oerlikon, cocked it and swung it back, without bothering to strap himself to the weapon. In the flickering yellow glow of the burning ship, Jack could make out the conning tower of a U-boat which had appeared from nowhere. The swastika was clearly visible. It was pointed in a perpendicular position across the wake of *Esek Hopkins.* Without the least hesitation, Ron squeezed the trigger, and the loud, powerful 20mm began spitting bullets. Tracers glowed in the darkness and nicely made a path toward the U-boat. Ron was not making one-second bursts. He was holding the trigger and going through the entire magazine in a protracted eight seconds. The bullets were falling short and he quickly pointed the Oerlikon higher, but still could not reach the U-boat. Everyone on deck was startled and watched with fascination as the tracers splashed in the water near the odious U-boat. Men began moving quickly on deck. A second Oerlikon, this one near the stern, began firing. Again, the U-boat was just beyond the five-hundred-yard range.

"Is that a bubble trail of a torpedo in front of the U-boat?" Fitz screamed, already knowing the answer. Jack was stunned by the rapidly changing events before his eyes. Then he saw a second bubble trail extending from the stern of the U-boat. "Look!" he shouted, "another torpedo from the stern!"

"Goddamn it," Ron shouted, "get me another magazine and get a fresh barrel ready!" Jack unlatched the first magazine as Fitz mounted another. The barrel was hot to touch but not yet ready to be exchanged. Then an explosive crack erupted from the stern with an intense flash of light. The three men jumped, at first thinking their ship had been struck by a torpedo. It was one of the three-inch cannons now firing at the U-boat. The cannon was level with the ocean and was not able to aim lower. The shot missed and splashed harmlessly in the distance. The U-boat slowly descended into the safety of the dark ocean; even as other Liberty Ships began firing harmlessly. Everyone waited for another torpedo strike of a fellow ship, but both torpedoes missed. Everyone was shocked at the audacity of the U-boat captain. There would be lots of discussion in the officer's mess that night and in the Forum with the crew.

The burning *Atheltemplar*, still extending an eerie circular glow around her, was falling farther behind the convoy. Two corvettes finally showed up. Then a destroyer. Apparently, they decided to drop no additional depth charges until all the men were pulled from the sea. That took over an hour.

It was difficult to stop staring at the flaming wreck as she drifted far back into the distance. She would not sink. In fact, she burned for hours, well into the light of day. Even as the convoy had progressed for many miles, the crew could still discern the flames on the distant horizon.

Jack learned from Sparks later, that after some ten hours, the fire burned out, and the British attempted to tow her, but were not able to save her. She eventually rolled over and drifted in the open sea. The British then tried to sink her but gave up, deciding it was a waste of ammunition. Sixty of her crew members were rescued. One was unaccounted for. Sixteen men later died from their injuries related to inhalation of hazardous fumes, skin burns, and acoustic shock waves from the first depth charges.

Ironically, a day later, she was sunk by an unlikely vessel, the German *U-408*. She came upon the stricken ship and sank her with her potent deck cannon. This was the same U-boat captained by Reinhard Hymmen, now somewhat infamous among his colleagues for sinking the two merchant ships the day before. He could chalk this one up as number three. Was he the audacious captain who appeared from nowhere and got off two unsuccessful torpedoes? Or was it another reckless captain?

The trio was exhausted and hungry when suddenly two starshells exploded in the sky ahead of the convoy. The shells had been launched from a U-boat somewhere in the distance. As if miniature suns, they gave off intense light sufficient to illuminate all the ships in the convoy and all the escort vessels. They hung by parachutes in the sky for at least five minutes. Typically, this was the prologue for torpedo attacks, since the U-boats got a good view of all the ships. Great anxiety swept through the convoy as everyone felt like they were like targets in a shooting gallery. In this case, perhaps that was the goal. If any torpedoes were launched, they all missed. Or perhaps the Germans wanted to count how many vessels they had sunk.

Darkness eventually enveloped them once again, and after thirty minutes, the all-clear klaxon sounded. The trio were tense and charged up. Each took a deep breath, and silently departed from the gun tub and worked their way down to the mess for a quick snack at 4:30 a.m. It was difficult to eat with only dim red floor lights illuminating the scene. Unknown to them, it would be their last meal of the day. They retired to their bunks, but Jack was unable to sleep.

At 5:30 a.m. the battle alarm sounded again. Once again, Jack dragged himself up to battle station number four. This time it *was* the Luftwaffe. The eastern horizon had just turned a beautiful orange before the sun peeked up. The bloody Germans were coming out of the east.

First the U-boats, now the Luftwaffe.

Jack gazed eastward and observed, "In a few minutes the glare of the sun will be in our eyes. Clever boys."

This time, as Fitz arrived, he tightly latched the chin strap on his helmet.

Uncharacteristically, Ron dragged himself up last. They all were exhausted and the day was just beginning.

As usual, the German planes were attacking toward the right side of the Convoy since they were taking off from Norway. Jack and Ron were on the port side of *Esek Hopkins*, so they would have to shoot across the boat. No easy task with all the rigging and masts in the way.

They were instructed to shoot above the rigging. Don't waste shots trying to get through the steel cables. The three discussed how the planes would have to be very close before they could begin firing upward above the rigging.

Jack declared, "Good; better chance of hitting the bastards."

Ron estimated a combined number of forty Ju 88s and He 111s; each with a full load of torpedoes and bombs. They filled the sky. Soon, the second ship to be hit on this eternal, forlorn day was the Liberty Ship *Wacosta.* She was the fifth ship to be sunk on the right side of the convoy in the same slot where the *Macbeth* had been sunk the day before.

Jack commented, "That is the coffin-corner over there."

"Glad I am here—I guess." was all Fitz could come up with.

As the sun offered the first glimpse of dawn, the three could see the bombs dropping and torpedoes splashing in the water as the aircraft swarmed over the convoy. British fighters had been launched and were beginning to engage the Luftwaffe planes. Jack had a bad feeling in his gut. He gritted his teeth. He looked at his hand. It was shaking.

"Come on, you bastards! I dare you! We can give it back too," he shouted in the ageless spirit of all warriors.

Ron was re-checking the ammo magazine and getting the gun ready for a long day. He asked Fitz to confirm the other two spare gun barrels were nearby, along with additional ammo boxes and magazines. Ron asked Fitz if he wanted a turn at the machine gun. He had been trained.

He casually replied, "No thanks, it's against my religion."

It was unclear to Jack and Ron if he was serious or not. They assumed he was.

"Besides," he added, "you guys are doing great. Much better than me. No sense wasting bullets, right?"

The intense antiaircraft gun barrage had started from the escort ships far to the right. The air was filled with exploding shells and tracer bullets. Planes were getting hit and dropping out of the sky. But not enough. Still, they came. Soon the loud cracking of the three-inch and five-inch cannons on the *Esek Hopkins* filled the air. With the seven Navy Armed Guards working in unison, they could now fire an incredible six rounds per minute. Jack could hear the shell casings clank on the deck forward and aft. He was mesmerized by the black puffs of smoke where each round exploded in the air, thousands of yards away. Some exploded very close to the aircraft, but they kept coming. Quickly, there was too much going on all at once. Too much to comprehend. The cacophony of pounding noises of all the guns firing at once was overwhelming.

The diabolic-looking four-engine German Condor heavy bombers wandered high above.

Jack glanced up occasionally. At one point he saw several British Hurricanes attacking the Condors, and at least two were hit and came spiraling down into the sea on the far horizon.

Ron yelled and pointed to the port side. In the distance, two Ju 88s were on a straight line heading toward the *Esek Hopkins.* As Jack watched in horror, he sensed the vessel slowing. Ron was ready at the Oerlikon with a full belt of ammo. The first Ju 88 released two bombs.

Jack could not take his eyes off them as they seemed to drift in slow motion toward their ship. He heard Ron letting his 20mm rounds go at the plane as it swept over the ship. The pair of explosives zinged just above their masts and blew up harmlessly in the dark sea beyond. Jack heard the familiar clattering of enemy machine guns as the second Ju 88 opened fire with its nose-mounted weapons. Bullets spattered across the deck striking armored tanks and the locomotive. Two crewmen jumped behind the locomotive for protection. This Ju 88 dropped a torpedo just after passing over the *Esek Hopkins.* He was targeting the ship to their right, but apparently missed. A third Ju 88 was tracking toward them. He let his two bombs go a fraction of a second too soon. They just missed the ship's bow, helped no doubt by Captain Gleason slowing the vessel. Ron kept a bead on the plane as it passed over the bow. He squeezed the trigger at just the right time. The tracer bullets showed strikes around the cockpit. Jack was certain he saw blood splatter on the windshield.

"You hit the bastard, Ron. You got the pilot," Jack screamed. He watched as the plane rotated violently into the sea before fifteen seconds elapsed. Jack could see the Nazi Swastika on the tail, slowly descend below the waves. That was number three.

Ron swiveled the gun around to port and yelled out, "Okay. Who's next?"

There was a brief halt in the action. Jack told his mates he needed to take a leak. He ran down to the main deck. He stopped. A Ju 88 was in the distance heading very low toward the ship from the right. Jack needed to run across the deck to gain some protection. As he looked ahead, he saw a deck hand hurrying toward him with his head down. Apparently, he was not aware of the potential danger approaching the starboard side of the ship. The Ju 88 was in range with her twin machine guns. The 20mm Oerlikons started firing at the Ju 88. Jack yelled, but the man could not hear him and on impulse Jack charged across the deck, heading directly at the deck hand. By the time he was halfway across the open deck, the man looked and saw Jack charging at him like a bull. Jack crashed into him and, with his momentum, pushed him back behind a bulkhead, just as high-caliber bullets from the Ju 88 clanked and clattered on the deck. The two safely collapsed in a pile. Jack felt a jarring yank on his right foot as they hit the deck.

"Sorry, pal, but you did not see that Ju 88 coming at us," Jack said as he looked into the man's face. Both men were startled and pulled away from each other. The black eyes and sutured forehead revealed Ski. Likewise, Ski was astonished to see it was Jack.

Ski's initial reaction was that of anger and he pushed Jack away, barking out, "What the hell?"

Jack was stunned as well. For an instant, the thought flashed through the archaic reptilian part of his brain that he could have solved the "Ski problem" by running past him and protecting only himself. But that would never do, as his higher brain centers correctly confirmed the valor of the maneuver he carried out.

Jack yelled, "Ski, you didn't see that Ju 88 coming at us. Those shots could have killed you."

The picture quickly came together as Ski realized Jack had probably saved his life. He stood up and brushed himself off, saying, "Hey, man, thanks. Thanks a lot. Who could ever imagine you, of all people, saving me from getting shot."

Jack struggled up, a little off kilter because of his wrecked boot. Ski extended his hand. Without hesitation, Jack shook it. Jack's right foot felt wobbly. He put a hand on Ski's shoulder to steady himself and lifted his foot. The right heel was missing with part of the boot shattered.

Jack declared, "God. A bullet must have hit my boot. Good thing that pilot was a lousy shot." Jack watched Ski laugh for the first time.

Ski said, "Get out o' here, man, before I hug you."

"All this trouble just to take a leak," Jack tossed out as he walked away with a limp.

A voice from the bridge yelled above the background noise, "You guys okay?" They both turned and gave a thumbs-up. It was the Captain.

Jack evacuated his bladder successfully. But as he rinsed his hands his tremor reappeared, only this time worse. He took a deep breath and turned on his good heel.

Jack made his way back to gun tube number four. Ron asked, "Where the hell have you been? You missed all the excitement. Right after you left, a Ju 88 buzzed over us with guns blazing. I led him by a hundred feet and nailed him. He lost altitude and hit the ocean about a mile away."

Jack could not hold back a smile as he replied, "Good. Nice shooting. I am sure he deserved it. For you, that is number four today. Way to go."

Jack was standing off kilter. Fitz looked down and saw his boot was damaged. Fitz laughed, "What happened to your boot?"

"As I was running across the deck, one of that Ju 88's bullets hit my boot; destroyed the heel," Jack replied, lifting his foot to show them. "I hope they have some extra boots on board, otherwise I will send that pilot a bill."

Ron retorted, "Not likely. That pilot has a new address: it's spelled H-E-L-L."

What they saw next left a visual imprint on their brains, that never left them. One of the He 111 attackers dropped a pair of bombs on the Liberty Ship *Mary Luckenbach.* It was a perfect direct hit. The Liberty Ship was filled with TNT, ammunition, and tanks; much like the *Esek Hopkins.* She was the fifth ship to the right; the unforgiving side of the convoy.

Even in the morning sunlight, the flash was indescribably bright. The shock wave that followed nearly knocked Jack off his feet. Ron's loosely strapped helmet blew off. They held onto the steel wall of the gun tub as the hurricane-like wind ripped past them, tearing on their clothes. They stared in disbelief as large metal chunks of the ship twirled high into the air as if shot from a cannon. Fiery sparklers flew in all directions and a dark mushroom cloud quickly engulfed the space the ship had occupied. Repeated explosions continued. The vessel was gone. Vaporized. Nothing remained. Chunks of metal and debris dropped from the sky for ten or fifteen seconds, splashing into the sea. Jack himself saw two enemy planes knocked from the sky from the shock wave, including the one which dropped the bombs. They both slammed violently into the sea.

The ship closest to the *Mary Luckenbach* was the Liberty Ship *Nathanial Green.* Jack learned later that the *Nathanial Green* was severely damaged by the explosion. The cargo on her deck was largely destroyed. Most doors, port holes, and the steel freeboard were damaged on the starboard side. The ship's medical clinic was damaged. One crewman was blown overboard, and seven others were severely burned. Her compass was knocked out of commission. But no damage was done to her powertrain, and remarkably she continued her mission to Archangel.

The *Nathanial Green* was three hundred yards from the *Mary Luckenbach* at the time of the explosion.

Jack turned to Ron, who was still staring at the destruction. "That could have been us!"

Fitz could not utter a sound. For the longest time, he stared in disbelief.

Ron rotated the trigger-grip of the 20mm toward Jack. "Let's get on with it. You take over for a while."

Jack strapped himself in, checked the half-empty magazine, cocked the gun, and searched for targets. He mumbled a few prayers as his hand tremor started up.

The early morning Luftwaffe attack had been destructive for both sides. Many planes had been knocked out of the sky. Finally, the remaining Luftwaffe aircraft flew off toward the eastern horizon. But not for good.

The loudspeaker came on with irritating static. It was Captain Gleason's voice: "Good work, men. All hands remain at your stations. We expect a second attack." Click.

Jack readied himself. In the gun tub there were twenty-five boxes of ammunition magazines, a few gun belts and two extra gun barrels. His life jacket was secured, and his steel helmet was strapped tightly in place. He was ready, but now filled with terror. In a matter of minutes, he nearly got his foot blown off and then he witnessed the complete destruction of a four-hundred-forty-foot American Liberty ship filled with fifty or sixty men, men just like him. Men with families. Men with girlfriends. Men with children, nieces, nephews, relatives, neighbors. Yet somehow, *Esek Hopkins* was spared, he was spared. This time. Maybe Penny would be incorrect. He really might not survive. He wished he was with Penny. In her safe, warm arms. That seemed like another world, a different universe, so different from the one Jack now occupied. Could he be living two diametrically opposed lives simultaneously on the same planet? Why was he even out here in this absurd, bloody war, in this bloody ocean on this bloody ship? *Yes Jack, why*?

Some men said they were happiest during actual combat. Jack did not understand that concept, until this day. At least during the intense action of combat, your mind was fully engaged. Fear was temporarily overcome. Ignored. After the battle, the mind starts working. Working in destructive ways; mental anguish, contemplating death, wondering why God spared you while others were sacrificed, thinking you are unworthy…

Jack whispered to himself, "Bring 'em on. I want to pull this trigger and pay you bastards back."

On and on it went.

They searched the sky. Which direction? Jack hoped they would attack from the port side. In that case he would have a direct shot, head on, as they approached. They waited, in silence. The ship was quiet except for the wave sounds lapping against the hull as the bow glided through the three-foot chop. The smell of cordite and spent gun powder was inescapable; it was imbedded in their clothes. One man scurried inside for a quick visit to the crapper.

Otherwise, there was no movement on the decks.

On this day, PQ 18 was supported by twenty-eight surface escort ships. They were mostly destroyers and corvettes. The antiaircraft cruiser *Scylla* and the escort carrier HMS *Avenger* remained with the convoy. HMS *Avenger* had proved extremely valuable the day before. Today, she was far astern, and it was difficult for Jack to see her launching the Hurricane fighters. Another antiaircraft cruiser had joined them from Iceland, the *Ulster Queen.* She was packed with every known type of weapon invented by man to knock aircraft out of the sky.

Jack's thoughts drifted to the fleet plan for defense. Although he was never involved during the inception of the plan, he had observed it in action the day before. When Luftwaffe aircraft were first seen on radar, the Hurricanes were launched from the *Avenger* as quickly as possible. They were the first line of defense and were very successful in disrupting Luftwaffe flight patterns and shooting aircraft out of the sky. The German pilots were trained as bombers and strafers, not fighter pilots. The British fighter pilots outclassed them and had sustained only one aircraft loss, so far. And even that British pilot was quickly scooped from the water by a corvette.

The next layer of defense was the outer perimeter of escort ships. Once the enemy aircraft were in range, the escort ships, including destroyers and the two cruisers, opened up with intense antiaircraft fire. Then, as the enemy got closer, each Liberty Ship filled the air with flak from the three-inch and five-inch cannons followed by the 20mm machine guns against any aircraft who survived the onslaught. Jack liked being part of the last line of defense.

Meanwhile, Allied vessels opposing any U-boats included the quick and nimble corvettes and the fast, slender destroyers. Destroyers were aptly named because they had the simultaneous duties to knock aircraft out of the sky and to track and destroy U-boats.

During training, Jack learned that Liberty Ship cannons used large shells with three different colored tips. The green-tipped ones were designed to explode at four thousand yards, the blue at two thousand yards, and the white at one thousand yards. It was estimated that the shrapnel from an exploding shell would be destructive within a fifteen-yard radius, and do severe damage withing a thirty yard radius. If enough shells were put in the air, they would knock planes out by simple probability. It was all based on probability. The same probability which affected Jack and his shipmates. The same probability that destroyed his shoe, but not his foot, or his brain.

This multi-layered defense system was a work in progress, but here and now, it was fine-tuned and knocking Germans out of the sky. There would be no repeat of the losses sustained in PQ 17. The Luftwaffe was paying a high price this time.

The merchant ships in this combined convoy started with forty vessels, eleven of which were British, twenty American, six Russian, and three Panamanian. It was obvious to the crew members that not all ships would make it to Archangel. Several had already been sunk. But if your ship was sunk, there was a high probability you would be rescued if you survived the torpedo or bomb explosion. It was all a matter of "good old probability," or luck. For those with religious faith, it was God's will. Under attack, everyone became religious.

As horrific and dreadful as these battles were, with each attack, the men grew more confident, their aim steadier, and their shooting more accurate.

Soon enough, not wanting to disappoint the men on the convoy, the German planes reappeared, this time from behind. On the *Esek Hopkins* the battle station alarm sounded, as if stating the obvious. The Captain's voice on the loudspeaker squawked: "Pay attention to the stern but keep watch in all directions!"

Jack was thinking as the tiny dots grew in size behind the *Esek Hopkins*, "This is one hell of a way to make a living. I wonder what my sisters are doing back in Baltimore. If they could see me now. Mom would have a fit. Were Dad alive, he would ask how many planes I shot down. Howard would be full of questions. Bill is likely delivering babies and too busy to worry. And where am I? I am sitting in the middle of the freezing ocean, shooting at bloody Germans who are trying to kill me; oh, and getting my foot shot up! And Penny, yes, Penny, Penny. She would hold me in her arms and…"

Jack felt the ship movement change. Captain Gleason slowed the *Esek Hopkins* again and turned sharply to starboard. Jack guessed he wanted to allow the ship's neighbors on either side to continue ahead and avoid friendly fire. Jack looked aft and saw that the *Esek Hopkins* was leaving a curvaceous wake. This would make torpedo targeting difficult and disrupt the airplanes' bombing patterns. Smart.

This attack began with Ju 88s flying in low in the lanes between ships, firing from both sides. The same pattern as the day before. Tiny lights flickered from prickly aircraft guns as invisible enemy bullets clanked around them. The German gunners were targeting the ship's bridge again. Jack heard whizzing sounds on two occasions as bullets zipped past his head. This made him even more determined to knock one of the Kraut planes out of the sky. He saw how far Ron had led the tracer bullets ahead of the planes and Jack quickly tried to replicate. But it was not as easy as it appeared, and his first rounds still fell behind the swift, noisy fighters.

"Damn, those things are fast!" he screamed above the racket of battle.

"Lead more!" yelled Ron. "And don't worry about getting hit. If your time is up, you will get hit; if not, you won't." Not very reassuring.

The wait was not long. This time, Jack aimed at an imaginary point ninety degrees off the side of the *Esek Hopkins.* He squeezed the trigger when the plane arrived at the level of the ship's stern. Tracers shot straight out, and as planned, in a half a second, the plane flew directly into the bullets. Jack released the trigger and watched. Nothing happened. The plane kept going.

"I know I hit the damn thing!" Jack screamed.

"Maybe you hit someone inside, Ron offered. Every strike does not take down a plane." Bombs dropped from nowhere and splashed about one hundred yards from the *Esek Hopkins* on the starboard side. The explosive burst scattered tons of white water fifty feet toward the sky. It was another bomb from the diabolic-looking Condor heavy bombers wandering high above. Jack glanced up occasionally. At one point during the day, he saw several British Hurricanes attacking the Condors and at least two were hit and came spiraling down into the sea on the far horizon. Those Hurricanes were invaluable, but they were unappreciated since they often flew so high that few crewmen noticed them.

Ron wondered out loud, "Maybe we took out the best pilots yesterday. These guys today don't seem to have the experience."

Jack threw back, "Don't count on it!"

The exhausting attacks continued by air through most of the

afternoon. The ferocity seemed less, and as the day wore on, there were definitely fewer planes. After the nighttime sinking of the *Atheltemplar*, there were no more U-boat attacks on September 14. The escort fleet and British fighter planes were proving their value every minute of every day. Jack could not imagine what it must have been like for the Liberty Ships of PQ-17, which gave up their escort ships and had to fight the Germans alone. This was nightmare enough.

By 4:00 p.m. the all-clear alarm had sounded, and Jack stumbled back to his room. He had no appetite. In spite of the cold air his shirt was wet with perspiration. His mind was an exhausted blank. Before crashing he took time to write down in his diary one brief thought; "We've been to HELL so many times, the devil calls me by my first name."

CHAPTER 18

A Tribunal

THE DETAIL WAS FINE, INCREDIBLY vivid, with sharp contrasting colors. The clarity of the sound was clear and crisp. The enormous aircraft carrier motion was barely detectable. Only the visible sea outside suggested movement. Jack found himself in his whites with a perfect, pristine, new officer's cap in place. The vast, vacuous space was teeming with men in military uniforms in perfect, sharply defined, wide, quiet rows. No aircraft were present. At one end of the space was a huge dais elevated two stories high. Jack squinted to discern the three seated figures. Suddenly, Jack found himself walking up the center isle with a disheveled man proceeding in front of him. The man was barefooted and in no hurry. Jack occasionally pushed him along. When Jack touched his shoulder, his hand met little resistance. It seemed to be partially absorbed by the shoulder. The pushing had little impact on Jack's desired goal of moving him along. Jack finally stopped doing it.

As they arrived in front of the dais, the man turned toward Jack and extended his cuffed hands. Unwittingly, Jack clumsily shook them. Jack had no key. The man was a mess, with bloody perspiration running down his face onto his dirty white robe. For the first time, Jack noticed a preposterously large crown of thorns on his bloody head with curly reddish-brown hair matted beneath it. Jack could discern every individual hair in the man's twisted red beard. His eyes were black and deep-set as if emaciated. He smiled at

Jack. His teeth were cracked and brown, with dried blood on his lips. Jack stepped back. The smile penetrated him. The man then sat on a comfortable red velvet chair which seemed to appear from the vapors.

Jack looked up at the dais. Seated there were the three somber men. All in suits. In the center was President Franklin D. Roosevelt. On the left side of the dais was Joseph Stalin and on the right side, Winston Churchill. Jack became an all-seeing eye.

In a slow, but firm Southern drawl, Roosevelt addressed the witness, "Before all here present, please identify yourself." Every soul on board heard every word.

"I am Jesus, the Christ."

There was no sound in the huge space packed with human beings.

Roosevelt continued, "This is not a trial. No repeat of that business two thousand years ago. I prefer to call it a tribunal. There will be no verdict or sentencing. We are simply here to comprehend why we are here."

Christ raised an eyebrow and looked suspiciously up at Roosevelt.

Roosevelt was taken aback by the power in the man's gaze. "I mean it," was his response. He continued, "Do you have any famous relatives who may be known to us?"

"Yes, my father is well known."

"And who is that?"

"He is known to you as God."

Stalin was no longer present on the dais.

The lawyer in Roosevelt continued with fact-gathering questions. "The same God who created the universe, the earth and man?"

"The same."

"The same God to whom men and women all over the world pray?"

"Yes."

"Does God hear prayers from Germans, French, Italians, Russians, Americans and all citizens of the world?" Roosevelt asked.

"Yes."

"And in this conflicted era of uncontrolled slaughter, all-encompassing war, many of those prayers are for each nation to go on to victory?"

"Yes, your observation is valid."

Roosevelt, who now sat alone on the dais, looked down at the witness and inquired, "How does God decide which side gets their prayers answered? Who will be victorious?"

For the second time Christ smiled and answered calmly, "It is beyond your comprehension. Although in one sense you already know. It is the side which is the less evil. Can you decide?"

Roosevelt ignored the question and continued, "In this battle before us here and now, incomprehensible destruction of human life is seen everywhere. Powerful weapons explode arms and legs into the air, splatter brains about, spill guts on the ground, vaporize aircraft, ships, etc., and traumatize the living along with the dead. Survivors drag home their broken bodies and fractured psyches. Why must there be so much evil in the world?"

A strange foul odor filled the vast space. Irregular motion engulfed the area along with unworldly crackling noises. The steel floor began to undulate. All was vivid, keen, hypersensitive. The humans stirred and became restless. The witness remained settled.

At this point, out of nowhere, Jack's mother, Mary Hogan Dodd, began walking up the aisle. She approached the sitting Christ. He seemed to recognize her. Roosevelt watched. Jack watched. The mass of humanity watched. She knelt before him, and he gently took her hand with his bloody hand. She spoke to him. But Jack could only discern, "safely home." Christ leaned close to her and whispered something in her ear. Then she rose and walked toward the open side of the ship and disappeared. Jack felt no remorse.

Howard, Jack's brother, then appeared from the back of the vast space. He was in a sharp, crisp, tailored suit and bright necktie and was walking backwards up the center aisle in his brown and white wing-tipped shoes, gesticulating with his hands. Only Jack seemed to notice him. Jack was disturbed, and wondered why Howard was here. He vanished before he got to the dais. Christ looked at Jack.

Then, a completely naked young woman appeared. She casually walked up the aisle. She seemed familiar to Jack, but no matter how hard he tried, he could not focus on her face.

As she got close to Christ, he smiled for the third time. She knelt before him, and he put his hand on her shoulder. She slowly disappeared in front of him.

Christ then looked up toward the dais and said, "To answer your question, Mr. President, there is a true evil force in the universe. You can smell it. And to counterbalance that evil there is free will."

Unfazed by the procession of the three phantoms, Roosevelt pondered, then asked, "Is free will necessary? Why gift it to mankind if conflict and hideous war is the result?"

"Perhaps man must learn to control his appetites," was the response.

Roosevelt persisted, "Why must there be evil? Would not the earth and universe be much more enjoyable without evil?"

Christ gazed out toward the mass of humanity and observed, "Who is the decider of what is evil? Man? Is he qualified to be the judge?" Could life be a test of character? Those worthy, will pass the threshold. Other places in the universe have not had the same problems you have experienced on earth. All civilizations have a maturing process. But earthlings have been slow learners."

At this point Jack noticed his own visage, uncontrolled, walking up the aisle toward the dais. As he looked at the Christ, the crown expanded on his head and became enormous. Then, in an instant it disappeared. At the same time, Christ's appearance changed radically. His face was clean, with no beard and short combed hair. He was in a military outfit with pins and metals all over his chest. Around his neck was a blue ribbon holding a large medallion made of gold and embossed with the word, "GOD" clearly visible in sparkling diamonds. Only Jack seemed to notice the change. Jack saw himself carrying sheets of paper in his hands as he marched up the aisle. On the papers were thousands of names. Jack extended his arms as he approached Christ. He seemed to be expecting them. He said to Jack, "You have done well," as he accepted the papers. In an instant, Jack flickered back to the all-seeing eye.

Roosevelt then asked with growing concern, "So, this will go on and on for mankind?"

Christ seemed to be breaking into tiny fragments. His last words sounded like, "afraid…robots…mechanical…"

Jack opened his one eye not buried in the pillow. His bunk mate Alex was walking in darkness toward the head. He heard Jack stir, turned and whispered, "Sorry to wake you. I need to take a leak. You crashed last night in reversed position on the bunk. So, as I stepped down, my stinky foot on your mattress may have aroused you."

Jack was perspiring and breathing hard.

CHAPTER 19

Persistence

HOWEVER UNSOUND THE FEW HOURS of sleep may have been, Jack was fortunate to squeeze in what he did. The first alarm aroused the entire crew at 5:00 a.m. It was Tuesday, September 15, two days after the German onslaught had begun. As he dressed in the dark among his stumbling roommates, and started up to his station, he felt the rumble of several depth charges from the deep. As he arrived at his station, there were no aircraft seen or heard, or evidence of torpedoes. At least not yet. After thirty minutes, in cold breezes and darkness, the all-clear alarm sounded. He knew he could not get back to sleep, so he went to Sparks' stateroom with Alex and had a few cigarettes while they exchanged some amusing sea tales. Jack decided to inform his colleagues about his bizarre dream.

Sparks said, "I been reading about this guy Freud, a shrink in Austria. He thinks dreams are some kind of subconscious thoughts bubbling to the surface. So, who was this chick in the dream?"

Jack smiled and thought, *Of all the weird segments in the dream, Sparks is interested only in the naked chick.* Jack knew it must have been PM even though her face was not visible. Or possibly GR. The soft body looked familiar, but not exact. What was so interesting was that Christ seemed to know her. Well, he knows everyone. Jack wondered if the dream meant she was okay for him. But which one? Or was it just his "subconscious" playing with him? And yet…

Jack laughed aloud and replied, "I don't know, man. Could have been someone I knew years ago. Or just the lovely, idealized woman all men desire." They chuckled. Humor was important and all too infrequent during these stressful times.

Then Alex quietly said he heard a story which was circulating around the ship that two mates were suffering from battle fatigue and had threatened to kill themselves. Not exactly a surprise. Everyone was under incredible stress. No names of the two mates came up. One threatened to jump overboard, the other to kill himself with a knife. Jack hoped they were confined to the infirmary and being watched by the medical officer. He gazed down surreptitiously at the tremor in his hands. Movement seemed to hide it. Unconsciously, he tapped his fingers. He began to wonder…about himself…with the strange dream, lack of sleep, stress of exposure to gunfire, the periods of absolute terror, mates considering suicide, the tremor.

Sparks was one of the few men on board who kept track of the date since he had access to the ship log and made daily notes. For most of the crew, time meant little, and it did not make much sense keeping track. The primary measure of time was how many days until they got to Archangel. They were supposed to arrive there in six days. If they made it at all.

As sunlight made its appearance, Jack was developing an appetite, so he and Sparks went to the mess to chow down. The tables were nearly full and talk in the Forum swirled around the two sick crew members. Amazing. So far, no crew member had been injured during the battles. Only Jack's shoe. He had replaced it with a spare.

Then, to talk about something other than concerns about suicide or the bloody Germans, one mate asked Jack how Ski got the black eyes in Glasgow. "Is it true you beat the crap out of him?"

Jack quickly responded, "No. He got rolled in a bar fight by a bunch of drunks. But I did punch him in the belly when he pushed me for not buying him a drink. After I belted him, he fell on the floor and I departed. I don't know who hit him in the face. I have no more comments on the topic."

The next topic to percolate up was the destruction of the *Mary Luckenbach.* The total, instantaneous vaporization was haunting to the weary men. Many closed their eyes at the thought of the explosion and immediate death of all on board. Everyone nodded and agreed, they were just one bomb away from the same fate. Some of the men at the table knew folks on the ship. It appeared to be all a matter of chance…or God's will. Jack pondered God's will. What did it really mean?

Then his dream, which merely posed the question but offered no clear answer to the question of evil. Jack wondered what Christ said to his mother in that dream. He finally realized he was spending too much time dwelling on that strange mental anomaly.

He retreated to his room but could not sleep. His tremor was more noticeable. He got up and started his daily rounds with other deck cadets. He and they needed company with each other. No way to get through this type of experience with no human interaction.

Around noon the wretched, piercing battle alarm sounded. Each dreadful blast now represented the sound of terror. The German He 111s had reloaded at the airfields in Norway and, with plenty of bombs, they inched forward through the bright sky toward the floating, bobbing convoy ships to deliver their lethal cargo. Just like a delivery service…a very deadly delivery service. How absurd was this entire play? The pulses of every man on board quickened as they speculated about their remaining time on earth.

Soon enough, the activity at station number four got very busy. For a period, Jack and Ron were firing the 20mm with such intensity that Fitz was changing the gun barrel every two or three minutes. On one of Jack's turns, he hit the starboard engine on a Heinkel bomber. She peeled away and turned eastward toward home with a trace amount of dark smoke trailing as far as they could track. Jack chalked it up as a kill. Ron and Jack were becoming somewhat blasé. Jack mentally confirmed that the thoughtful period following a battle was worse than the battle itself. During the battle there was no time to think. The live attacks under fire were so consuming that all other thoughts or analysis had no time to enter one's mind. On this day, the attacks seemed to become more routine now that the gunners grasped the form and order of the episodes. The men also grew in confidence with their performance as they became more acquainted with what was expected. And their aim and timing had improved. The aircraft were finite physical objects which were exceedingly dangerous, but whose behavior could be predicted and defended against. Planes seemed to have trouble targeting the ships during this attack. Miraculously, no ships were struck by bombs. Neither were there any successful U-boat attacks. They wondered whether the German's best pilots had been taken out. During breaks in the action, Ron and other crew members felt comfortable enough to make fun of the Germans and crack jokes at their expense. No one minimized the danger, but somehow their collective psyche was learning to deal with it. Still, the underlying tension never left them. Nor did the evolving sense of comradeship, which was characteristic of warriors since the beginning of time. An indefinable bonding was taking place, without anyone realizing it. Even they could not define it. And certainly, no outsiders could. It welded these men uniquely, like no other bonding could. It bonded even those who barely knew each other. It was a strange cement and it lasted forever.

One new German threat revealed itself. Sparks conveyed a rare radio message to the Captain on the bridge. It warned all ships in the convoy that the Luftwaffe had dropped large numbers of mines into the ocean. The convoy was now approaching that area. Chief Cockrell warned the crew on the loudspeaker. Navy Armed Guard spotters with rifles were stationed on the bow of the ship. Occasional shots rang out, but there were no explosions. The lesson was this: there was no weapon the Germans would not use to stop convoys from reaching Russia. All the supplies which the convoys were delivering were having a significant impact on the war effort.

During one break in the action, Jack heard the mine spotters call a warning to the bridge. As he gazed over the port side, he saw a mine floating not twenty feet from the side of the vessel. It was too close to shoot at.

"Good God," he said to his colleagues. "Another example of life and death really depending on simple probability"

Somehow the *Esek Hopkins* survived another day at sea. Tuesday merged into Wednesday, September 16. The early hours were characterized by the usual depth charge jolts. Jack, like most of his mates, was at a stage where, when he woke up with a thump from a depth charge, he just rolled over in his bunk and tried to get back to sleep. After several attempts, he was unable achieve his goal and finally stumbled out of bed, dressed, and decided to get a bite. In the dim red glow of the mess hall, as a sleepy Jack spilled his coffee, an announcement came over the loudspeaker. The third mate on the bridge read a telegram from the British Commodore, Admiral Boddam-Whittam. In part it said, "Thank you for the great effort you have made." All the mates looked around at each other and nodded. Then back to the chow. Perhaps someone out there was actually paying attention.

During breakfast, Jack noted his tremor was increasing in frequency and extent as he shoveled his eggs to his mouth. Others were noticing. At least the hearty meal perked him up. He went out on deck to see why things had been quiet enough for him to have such an enjoyable, peaceful meal. As he stepped out through the steel door onto the deck, dawn had broken, and he observed a heavy mist enveloping the ship. He could barely visualize his gun tub twenty feet above or the bow of the ship which was lost in the haze. Great news. Perhaps a day of rest after three days of attack.

Jack wandered up to the bridge to engage the officers on watch. Chief Cockrell, Mark Williams and Sparks were manning the helm. Jack had had no time to visit them during the past three battle days. Even though they could see nothing ahead, they were in good spirits with the fog impeding further attacks. Jack asked if anyone had an estimate of how many German planes the convoy ships had shot down. Second Mate Mark Williams threw out an estimate. "I heard the entire escort and merchant fleet, including the Hurricane fighters, downed forty German aircraft over the past three days. A fantastic job, gentlemen. Congrats to all. The Luftwaffe cannot afford to lose pilots at that rate. The Russians should serve us caviar every night when we arrive in port!"

Jack staked his claim. "Damn, that is incredible. We made the Krauts pay alright. Mr. Williams, I think I knocked at least one out of the air and hit another three or four.

Williams smiled at Jack. "We all saw you firing that hot pistol out there. Nice job. How many did Ron get?"

"At least four kills and another five or six hits. But he is a trained Navy man. I just started practicing on that 20mm a week ago. And sometimes it's difficult to confirm a definite kill," Jack stated proudly.

Mark Williams nodded and smiled. He changed the topic of the conversation by noting, "Impossible to see through this foggy muck."

The third mate, Lance Lockhart, was outside on the helm observation deck watching the spouting fog buoy which was barely visible at fifty feet on the starboard side. The *Esek Hopkins* was keeping pace and staying in line.

The Captain quietly appeared on the bridge. Jack figured he always approached quietly so he could listen in on the scuttlebutt of the officers. The officers had figured this out and rarely spoke of anything controversial while on the bridge. The Captain fixed himself a cup of coffee and looked at Jack. "Jack Dodd, I haven't seen you up here lately. You been busy?"

"Yes, sir," Jack replied. "Ron, Fitz and I have been keeping that number four gun barrel hot. I think we hit six or seven aircraft, but not sure how many went down. We were too busy to follow them."

Gleason thought for a moment then added, "Good work. Our Navy Armed Guards have been very busy with the big cannons too. They can now get off at least six shots a minute. That is unbelievable. They must have knocked down quite a few planes. You would think the Germans will eventually run out of pilots and crews." Gleason was thoughtful for a moment, then said, "Dodd, was that you on the deck two days ago trying to get yourself shot?"

"Ah, yes sir. Well, sir, I was not actually trying to get myself shot," was all Jack said as he tried to suppress the tremor in his hands.

Williams, still at the wheel, adjusted the course for a moment, then looked at Jack. "What's that all about? I heard nothing of this."

Jack addressed Williams. "Well, sir, there was a little break in the action, so I ran down to the main head to take a leak. As I arrived on the deck, I saw a Ju 88 off to starboard making a low run on us. Across the deck was a mate coming at me. He didn't see the Ju 88. So, I ran at him full speed and sort of tackled him. Just then the bullets started flying. One smashed the heel of my boot. That's it."

Mark said, "Well done. You may have saved the guy's life. Who was it?"

"He works in the engine room. A wiper. Known as Ski. It's good we both had our life vests on. It softened the fall," was all Jack added.

Gleason stared straight ahead into the fog through the moistened window and said nothing.

The next day, Thursday, September 17, the breeze picked up and cleared the fog but the skies remained troubled, ominous, and overcast. Remarkably, there were no attacks. However, German observation planes could be discerned through occasional cloud openings circling high above near the eastern horizon. They were probably observing that some of the convoy's escort ships were peeling away. Rumor had it that the British escorts were going to start covering another convoy departing from Russia and heading back to England. That would be PQ 14 and some ships from PQ 17, whose ships had recently unloaded their cargo. Even though those convoy ships were empty of supplies, the Germans still attacked them to reduce the number of viable ships in the fleet. Russian escorts were supposed to pick up coverage for PQ 18 after the British ships departed. No sign of them yet.

Miraculously, there were no pesky alarms that night. Maybe the Germans really were short of aircraft and pilots. But Jack did not sleep well. He was worried about his tremor. And his conscience was bothering him during the hazy zone before sleep. Had he been affected by the horrors he had witnessed over the past five days? Was he a different man? He had killed other human beings. True, they were his enemy. And they were trying to kill him. Still, how would that affect him? Would he be different in front of his family? In front of Penny? Was he even worthy of Penny now? He was a different man than the one who knew Penny. Perhaps she deserved better. Perhaps. Finally, he drifted off.

He got up on Friday, September 18, rested but not feeling good about himself. He observed that his tremor was absent as he came out of sleep, but it started once he was conscious and alert. He recalled that this day was the three-month anniversary of the *Esek Hopkins* departing from Hoboken, New Jersey. The three months had been anything but boring. He pondered how naïve he had been when he departed from Baltimore. Any romantic notions he had about the sea-faring life were now thoroughly wiped away. Clearly this journey had changed him significantly.

He went up to the mess hall and tried to shake out of his funk. He had a leisurely breakfast with his mates. Everyone seemed cheerful; mainly because Archangel was only one day away. They would get a chance to stand on solid ground again. And there was the mystery and excitement of a foreign port. Plus, those bloodthirsty Germans would not likely attack the convoy in a well-protected Russian port. And someone said they heard the two mates who were ready to commit suicide had been released from sick bay on sedatives. All good news.

Everyone seemed more relaxed.

The *Esek Hopkins* continued her cruise toward Russia at eight knots as four-foot waves slapped against the hull in a constant rhythm. Jack wandered up on deck to start his rounds. He tried to concentrate on his duties and strolled around more casually than usual, inspecting the cargo, pulling on the tight chains holding the locomotive and jeeps and tanks. Keep busy, he thought. With six other cadets he went to the holds to check for water leaks and confirm the bilge pumps were operational. He looked at all the supplies stuffed into the enormous holds. Soon all this cargo would be lifted off the ship and sent on its way to help the Russians push back the Nazi war machine. Every crew member on this ship and in this convoy contributed. And many had lost their lives in the effort. Jack allowed Penny to wander into his mind. He could feel a smile form on his face. She was worthy, but was he? Then he thought about her prediction. He hoped she was right.

Around 10:00 a.m. the unexpected shrill blast of the battle alarm caused Jack to literally jump. No wonder he had a tremor. He looked around the sky but saw nothing. Men were cursing as they scrambled out of the steel doors onto the deck and trotted to their battle stations in the cold air with their puffs of hot breath preceding them. Jack ran to the stairs and jumped up two at a time. Once at the gun tub, he looked around. Other mates were putting on their life jackets and helmets. He reluctantly followed, still not convinced this was not a false alarm. Ron and Fitz soon joined him.

With Ron's good eyes, he saw them first and pointed northwest off the port side. "There they are!"

Jack looked at Ron. "Let me start." His aggressiveness reminded him that he was a different man. The three initiated their well-practiced routine and locked in the 20mm cassette as they opened ammunition storage boxes. Fitz collected the two extra gun barrels. Jack strapped into the shoulder brackets and pulled tight on the canvas belt to keep his frame securely in position as he rotated the gun toward the port side. All the other gunners on board were replicating the process. Jack could now discern the steady pace of the aircraft as they closed in on the numerous targets available to them in the convoy. He wondered how the pilots chose to pick a particular ship. Another random event, he figured. The more he thought about it the more he calculated they all were going to bomb the *Esek Hopkins* since she had not yet been hit. His pulse quickened. He pulled hard on the cocking latch and readied the weapon.

Gunfire from the escort ships erupted with spark-like midair flashes followed by booming thuds permeating the air. He could see the explosive shells in the distance bursting around the German aircraft. One took a hit and spiraled into the sea in a violent splash of water. Surviving planes discharged little dots toward the ships below. A strike. A Liberty Ship one row ahead and four rows to port was hit. A flash, debris and smoke in the air, then a shock wave, then the lagging loud frightening sound of the energetic explosion.

Ron shouted, "I think that is the *Kentucky*! God help them!"

The three-inch and five-inch cannons on the *Esek Hopkins* began hurling shells thousands of yards into the distant skies. Jack still wasn't acclimated to the extremely loud crack of the cannon fire, but he could hardly complain. Everyone else had to put up with the extreme noise from those vital cannons which likely did more to protect the ship than Jack's machine gun.

Some of the crew manning the cannons wore ear protection. Must investigate that, he thought. He readied the 20mm. He would not rush. He now had enough experience to judge distance and wait until they were in range. No point wasting ammo like an amateur. His tremor disappeared.

One He 111 put a bead on them. The three-inch cannon on the bow was flinging shells at him but missed. As the lumbering aircraft got into range, Jack aimed high and squeezed the trigger. He watched the tracers hit the lateral starboard wing. He moved the 20mm gingerly to the right to keep up with the aircraft. His goal was to move his tracer bullets closer to the fuselage to strike the pilot and crew.

His conscience whispered: *You are a different man now; a killing machine.*

In no time, with multiple one-and two-second bursts from the loud, jolting, spewing, weapon, Jack emptied the magazine.

A little voice countered*: But this is self-defense; it is me or them.*

As if to confirm that thought, two bombs splashed and exploded in the water just beyond the *Esek Hopkins.* The explosion drenched the bow in a rainbow of white sea. There were multiple sharp clanking sounds as bomb fragments struck the hull. Jack thought they had bought the ticket.

You see? They want to destroy you and your friends. You must kill.

But the rational Jack thought, *God was with us again.* Hail Mary…

He followed the plane, but she was not mortally injured. Yet, he knew he hit her. No time to contemplate.

Ron moved in and declared, "My turn; you had your fun." Jack freed himself from the restraining straps and Ron tethered himself to the shoulder bracket. Fitz unscrewed the hot gun barrel with his asbestos gloves and put on a fresh cool one. Jack readied another magazine full of ammo.

Does Ron have these feelings? his little voice asked.

A second group of German planes was forming in the west. The three watched as a single British Hurricane was launched via catapult from a ship behind the *Esek Hopkins.* He got in the air quickly and tracked west. He flew high and fast, then peeled around to attack the incoming aircraft from behind. These German planes were carrying torpedoes. As they lined up for their drop, the Hurricane started firing and forced them to split up and seek other targets.

Still, one veered toward the *Esek Hopkins* and was ready to drop his load when, with an intense explosive eruption, all the guns on board opened up. A shot from the aft five-inch cannon struck the bomber at close range. Its wing blew off and the unbalanced aircraft pulled violently to the right and spiraled into the sea with an enormous, explosive splash of white ocean. Jack got a good look at the panic-stricken pilot trying to save the aircraft and himself. As the plane smashed into the concrete-like water, a few steel fragments of the aircraft spiraled into the air and struck the *Esek Hopkins* and scattered on deck. The tail of the plane, decorated with its red, black, and white swastika insignia, rose up for a moment; then, as its momentum stopped, it settled in the sea, finally descending below the icy, blue waters. No survivors from that one.

With anger and spite, Ron had unloaded a few bursts of 20mm bullets at the plane as it descended within fifty yards of the *Esek Hopkins'* stern.

The three gunners at battle station number four jumped in the air, and threw up their hands screaming, "Gotcha! You God-damned German bastards." Jack yelled, "Come on, come on, who is next?"

This is not really you, Jack.

He suppressed the distant little voice.

It was like a sporting event, rooting for your home team. Other gunners on the boat joined in the celebration.

Later that evening in the Forum, Jack would brag that the plane was so close he could tell the color of the pilot's eyes. They were red with panic, he declared. Hyperbole never hurt anyone.

Behind the trio, to the starboard side, was another explosion. It was three rows back and to the far right. Whatever was on board, it was not enough to cause the ship to vaporize or sink. A cloud of smoke shot into the sky. The ship lost power and fell behind. No crew were seen abandoning her. They learned later she was a Russian ship and was later salvaged. Still, two hits in less than an hour. The Kentucky was stricken but did not sink. She later had to be sunk intentionally. Maybe the Germans found some more experienced pilots since yesterday. Or maybe they just got lucky.

High above, Jack saw the ugly, diabolical four-engine FW Condors circling once more.

Where did the Germans get all these airplanes? A group of bombs slapped in the water all around them. The *Esek Hopkins* crew could do nothing. Fortunately, the high altitude of the aircraft reduced the accuracy of their bombs. Flak from the British antiaircraft cruiser could be seen bursting high above the battle. Where were the Hurricanes? They were difficult to spot, but they were there. Within minutes five Condors were hit; three descended into the sea and two turned east with black smoke trailing. None of them made it back to their base in Norway. The Hurricanes had the advantage with their speed, maneuverability, and nine-yard-long belts of explosive bullets firing from six wing-mounted machine guns. Still, during a thirty-minute interval, bombs rained down before the Hurricanes attacked in force. Incredibly, there were no direct bomb hits of any of the ships of Convoy PQ 18 on this day.

The He 111s and Ju 88s had expended all their bombs and torpedoes with only two bombing runs. But they continued to circle around and come in for strafing attacks at forty or fifty feet above sea level. These attacks kept the gun crews very busy on the *Esek Hopkins.* It seemed that all the Liberty Ships were firing simultaneously and nonstop at the German aircraft during the attacks. The intensity and noise were overwhelming.

Jack could not get over what a determined bunch the Germans were as he squeezed the trigger and watched his tracer bullets damage the tail of a passing Ju 88.

No time for that little voice.

German bullets, clanking all around the steel gun tub, the hull and superstructure of the ship, were paralyzingly frightening. Yet somehow, none of the men on board were struck.

Finally, late in the afternoon, with the sun drifting behind linear clouds in the west, the ugly, day-long attack subsided. The remaining Luftwaffe planes limped off to the east. The men at the gun stations were exhausted. The all-clear alarm sounded, but only a few gunners went below. The silence was startling. After six hours of constant stress, the men were sweaty, dirty, disheveled, and stunned. They looked around at their fellow man. All were startled with the reality they were experiencing. How long could they sustain themselves? What was the purpose of all this? On some level it was a complete absurdity. Humans trying to kill each other with complex, sophisticated murder-machines. Why? Was there some underlying reality which their feeble minds could not discern? How long could this torment go on? Then came more basic thoughts. Would they ever see their loved ones again? Did it matter? Would this horrific new reality change them forever? Could they ever go back to whatever was "normal"?

Jack, you know the answer.

Slowly, more of the gunners peeled away from their weapons and made their way below to evacuate their bladders, bowels, or stomachs.

Ron looked at Jack and Fitz. "Well," was all he could come up with, and he left the sentence unfinished.

Jack stared down at the deck. "I guess we made it through another one." Hardly profound, but what else could one say?

Fitz mumbled a silent prayer as the trio shuffled, amidst the hundreds of spent 20mm shells, toward their rooms.

CHAPTER 20

Arrival

IT WAS CERTAINLY ANTICLIMACTIC. AND so silent and subtle that one's senses barely perceived it. The main thing noticed out of the ordinary, for those up at the early hour, was that they could see land; barely. As the *Esek Hopkins* turned south to exit from the Barents Sea, she headed through a wide channel with land visible on either side. This channel was the entrance into the White Sea. As the convoy entered the channel, they would turn eastward for about twenty miles then southward toward the port of Archangel. The city was just outside the Artic Circle and located on the northern side of the Dvina River.

Jack woke up with a start around 5:00 a.m. on Saturday, September 19. Good news for the start of this day; no ugly dream. Perhaps his conscience had sorted things out. At least for now. Confirmatory evidence of how important sleep is.

He wondered if he had missed the docking at Archangel. He dressed quickly and scampered up on deck. The stars were uncharacteristically bright in the sky. He walked to each side of the ship to search for the lights of a city. There were none. As his eyes acclimated to the darkness, he could discern the dim, black, featureless outline of a low, flat shoreline. From both sides of the ship the images were identical. Where were they? Archangel was their expected destination today. This morning they were to tie up and begin unloading their cargo. It was bitterly cold on deck, so he climbed up to the bridge, which still was illuminated with faint red light. Mark Williams, the first mate, was at the helm. Sparks was snoozing on the settee. Mark smiled as Jack walked into the warm, quiet room.

With a twinkle in his voice, Jack whispered, "Did I miss Archangel? Are we in England?"

With a low chuckle, Mark replied, "Good morning, Jack. You missed everything. We are pulling into New York!"

Jack smiled, "That can't be right. It's too cold for New York."

Mark took a final swig of his cool, bitter coffee and brought Jack up to date on their location. "We are puttering along at two knots in the White Sea. There are Russian minefields ahead, so we are killing time until daybreak and waiting for the Russian pilot to board and lead us into Archangel, which is about fifty miles southeast. You should grab a bite to eat, then come on back up. The Captain should be here shortly."

Jack followed the sage advice. When he arrived back on the bridge, Captain Gleason was present, and the faint hint of daylight gave a better picture of their location. Several convoy ships were now visible around them. Dark gray land was discernable in the distance through the morning haze. Friendly aircraft were audible high above. Throughout the lazy day the convoy arced in large circles to nowhere. By late afternoon the winds stiffened. The fleet Admiral decided to halt the cruise to Archangel because of a weather front moving in. All ships were instructed to drop anchor. The burrowing cold winds from the hinterlands quickly picked up to gale force as eight-foot, white-capped waves pounded against the hull and rocked the ship like a bobbing cork. It took nearly an hour to direct the four-hundred-and-forty-foot *Esek Hopkins* into the wind and waves, while dropping two anchors simultaneously. Other ships were performing the same exercise and Captain Gleason, being the excellent helmsman he was, carried out the exercise without controversy. Jack paid attention and learned much as he watched the Captain at his job.

Sleep came with difficulty for the entire crew that night. The ship bounced up and down throughout the night as blistering, howling, frigid winds whistled past the masts, cables, and port holes and swirled around the lonely deck. Mixed sleet and snow pelted the anchored ships. No place for man nor beast. The anchors held.

The next day was Sunday, September 20. As Jack woke up, he whispered a silent prayer that they would safely unload their dangerous cargo in Archangel. If nothing else, this journey had impressed upon him how faith could sustain and aid him during the stressful periods. Then he noted with curiosity that when he prayed, his tremor disappeared.

The wind and sleet died down by noon and the skies cleared. But the fleet remained at anchor until late in the afternoon. Then, just before heaving anchor, the battle alarm sounded.

As Jack ran up to his battle station he thought, *I hope someone up there heard my prayer. To come all this way and get blown to bits a few miles from our destination would be a horrible tragedy. But the Germans would love it. The ships are sitting ducks at anchor and easy targets for the cunning, persistent Luftwaffe.*

Ron arrived shortly thereafter, chewing on bubble gum. "Those goddamn Krauts never give up! We are just going to have to knock every plane out of the sky! Let's get to it, Jack." Fitz trudged up the staircase to the gun tub, his hot breath visible as he huffed and puffed. He thought out loud, "When will those Krauts leave us alone? Do they enjoy suicide missions?"

On this day, six of the ugly four-engine German FW Condor heavy bombers were coming at the anchored ships. Two came in low for a strafing run and headed directly for the *Esek Hopkins.*

Jack's heart pounded. *This is no place to die. Give me a break, God.*

The cannons on the *Esek Hopkins* erupted with violence. One of the Condors took a hit from a three-inch stern cannon and was blown out of the sky, with large fragments zinging overhead and striking a ship behind them. Smaller parts of the fuselage and wings flew in all directions, with some landing on the deck and bridge, not far from battle station number four.

Ron glanced at Jack. "Imagine getting killed by a fragment of a bloody German plane we shot down!"

The second Condor got past the shooting and unloaded three bombs with the *Esek Hopkins* as the target. They just missed astern. Ron was firing incessantly, but somehow his bullets were not on target —maybe because the Condors were slower than the Ju 88s which Ron had gotten acclimated to targeting. They heard an explosion behind them and jerked their heads around. Fortunately, it was not one of their ships, but a second Condor exploding from a direct hit from the cannon of another Liberty Ship. By this time, British Hurricanes from a local airfield appeared on the scene and began attacking and strafing the German aircraft. The remaining enemy planes departed from the scene in a hurry and headed west toward their bases in Norway. The Hurricanes chased them and took down at least one more Condor. Those Luftwaffe pilots had a lot of respect for the Hurricanes and did not stay around to challenge them. Today a winning score: three Condors shot out of the sky and no ships sunk.

The three waited in the gun tub, prancing and swinging their arms to stay warm for another thirty minutes. But there was no German follow-up. The all-clear alarm finally confirmed the attack was over. They swept the spent shells over the side and packed away the ammo and gun barrels along with their helmets and life-jackets. Jack did not have much appetite, but it was nearly dinnertime, and he followed his compatriots to the Forum to commiserate with the other mates.

As they trundled down the stairs, Ron noted, "Those bastards never give up. We are knocking the hell out of them, but they keep coming back for more. And right here off the coast of Russia. Do they know how many Russian and British fighter planes we have here? What is their objective? Are they trying to wear us down? It just seems downright dumb."

Jack quietly nodded in agreement. Fitz offered, "I think they are all suicidal. The whole damn country is full of suicidal people, starting with Hitler. Hopefully, in a year or two, they will achieve their ultimate objective, compliments of the United States."

The mess hall was nearly full, but relatively quiet. The crew members were enclosed in their own thoughts about the incessant attacks as they pushed food around on their plates.

Everyone had assumed it would be safer in Russia. Clearly, it was not. The laws of probability were against them. Eventually, the *Esek Hopkins* would get hit. The attack that afternoon was frightening. Yet somehow all the ships in the convoy dodged the grim reaper. There seemed to be no end to the madness.

Jack and Ron joined Sparks, Alex and Murray, while Fitz joined some other mates.

Sparks was in the midst of explaining how Archangel got attacked the night before. He started his story again for the new arrivals. "Just before the attack this afternoon, a Ruskie ship pilot came aboard to take us into port. He had been in Archangel the night before. He said the Germans started a bitch of an attack on the port last night. German intelligence apparently indicated our convoy would be tied up. Thank God the storm delayed us. The attack lasted less than an hour with the change in weather."

Ron shook his head, "I wonder how long our luck can hold out. I thought the Russians had a good air force and would offer more protection, for God's sake. Look at all the supplies we're delivering. It is in their self-interest to protect us."

Sparks observed, "In a normal world, you would be right. But this ain't no normal world. The pilot, Ivan something or other, who by the way does not speak the King's English very well, said things are pretty dismal in Archangel. I suspect the Russians are hanging on by a thread. Food shortages and the like. For all we know, they may be low on fuel and ammunition. I don't think Archangel is any Palm Beach."

Jack was pushing some cranberries around on his plate as he listened. It was easy to get depressed on this ship, in this country, during this war. Whenever he got down, he wondered what his family was doing back in sunny Baltimore. And he thought about Penny, her smile, her eyes, her soft warm skin and her freckles. Invariably, it cheered him up. Jack realized he should not allow himself to get caught up in self-pity, which for some, could easily become habit-forming.

He ruminated, "We are all here as volunteers and we have to make the best of what we have. It could be worse. We could be freezing in some POW camp without any food." His pals nodded in agreement.

Jack made an inquiry, "So, when does Ivan, our illustrious pilot, take us into the harbor?"

Sparks responded, "Captain Gleason is waiting on the bridge for orders from the Brits. There is apparently some repair work being done on the docks. But our pilot is itchy. He does not like wasting time sitting on American ships. He supposedly has the knowledge to guide us through the protective minefields laid by the Russians."

Ron and Jack said at the same time, "Let's hope so!"

On the bridge at 5:00 a.m. the next morning, Captain Gleason finally got clearance to heave anchor and head toward the harbor at Archangel. The engine was cranked up without a hitch.

Ivan, the Russian pilot, took over the helm while the Captain watched his every move. In theory, the pilot had temporary control of the ship. But should an emergency present itself, the Captain could overrule the pilot and take control. This rarely happened. Pilot Ivan proceeded with caution and the *Esek Hopkins* was the lead ship in the line of Liberty Ships coursing into Archangel Harbor. The buoys were not lit and were difficult to visualize. The first mate and Captain Gleason had their binoculars up the entire time and were struggling to make out the buoys and day marks.

Jack woke up when he felt the vibration of the engine starting up. He wanted to see the process of docking at their final destination. After all the time at sea, on this three-thousand-mile journey, he felt it was important to observe the docking exercise and see the port of Archangel.

In spite of the bitter cold, he made his way to the deck to absorb the whole experience. Just as he walked out, the ship shuddered, then stopped, and Jack was thrown off his feet. He rolled uncomfortably on the freezing cold, steel deck.

"God almighty! What the hell was that?" he cried out to no one. He got to his feet and raced to the side. A buoy was nearby just beyond the stern. They had run aground. He ran up to the bridge and entered in the midst of noisy, chattering chaos. The Captain was yelling at Ivan, who was raising his hands in protest and yelling back in Russian. Chief Cockrell took the wheel from the pilot. They all looked toward Jack as he entered. His presence seemed to temper the yelling. Chief Cockrell looked to Jack. "We seem to have run aground! Our pilot claims someone moved the buoy. Any sign of damage down below, Jack?"

"None that I could see, but I was on the deck," he replied.

The Captain asked Jack to find Williams, the second mate, and go down and check out the engine room and the bilges.

"Yes, sir," he said as he saluted a bit too officially. Jack turned and left the discord on the bridge. He bumped into Mark Williams on the way up and relayed the Captain's instructions.

Together they made their way to the engine room. They were back on the bridge within forty minutes to report that there was no sign of engine damage or water leakage. And all the cargo was intact.

Captain Gleason had taken control of the vessel and after several tries, he was able to reverse the engine with sufficient thrust to successfully back off the muddy bottom. He was aided by the incoming tide. All the convoy ships behind the *Esek Hopkins* had stopped in a long line. The sun was up by this time, and the channel buoys were easily visible now. The Captain was worried about the

Russian mines and had lost faith in the pilot, but he gave the wheel back and watched. The pilot had brought charts marking the mines, but they were torn and stained and difficult to read. The pilot looked at them infrequently. The second mate, Mark, scrutinized them carefully as they advanced toward Archangel.

"Coffee anyone?" yelled the Captain to no one in particular to ease the tension. Jack took the hint and ten minutes later returned with a tray including a pitcher and four cups and some rolls.

The ship was making steady progress at four knots. Along both sides were decrepit docks with slovenly boats of all shapes and sizes. Some were partially sunk. Sheds in the background had collapsed. As they got closer to the port of Archangel, the landscape did not improve.

Damaged buildings, mud roads, scattered military vehicles, bedraggled people, and smoke rising from old fires appeared to be the norm. Jack ran down to the main deck to assist in preparing the docking lines.

By 9:00 a.m. the Russian pilot identified their assigned dock and slowly pulled in along the lengthy quay as a few men on shore waved and indicated the ship's exact position. With surprising efficiency, the motley dock hands ran along the sides and cleated and secured the heavy lines thrown from the ship. Three cranes lingered on rail tracks parallel to the shoreline. They were full of rust and beat up. No doubt, German bombs made repairs difficult. Jack studied the cranes in their feeble condition and wondered if they were capable of lifting the heavy cargo from the *Esek Hopkins'* holds. They soon learned they were docked at a suburb of Archangel. The decrepit town was called Molotovsk.

Jack noted the date. It was September 21, 1942. What a journey. They made it in one piece in spite of the best the Germans could throw at them. Unfortunately, not every boat in the convoy could say that.

As the single accordion-like ladder was lowered from the side of the ship, three official-looking Russians approached the ladder and climbed up without requesting permission to board. On the bridge, the pilot glanced at the Captain and shrugged. "*Velcomen zu Archangel*, *Comrade.* I vill depart...now."

Gleason reluctantly thanked him for his service and chose not to engage in any further commotion about the grounding. The pilot scurried toward the ladder, and off the ship, apparently not interested in interacting with the Russian soldiers who had just boarded.

Other convoy ships were tying up in front of and behind the *Esek Hopkins.* Jack and Alex were on the main deck and stared down at the dishevelment on shore.

"Some worker's paradise," Alex remarked. "This place looks worse than typical land dumps in the US. I did not expect wide boulevards and fancy hotels, but this could be the entrance to hell. One thing is for sure, there will be no exciting shore-leave here."

Jack only shook his head slowly as he gazed down at the chaos below and wondered if he even wanted to leave the ship. Where were the cheering crowds and pretty girls with flowers?

Jack scolded himself. What was he thinking?

As the three Russians arrived at the top of the stairs, Jack followed them in their march across the deck toward the bridge. The crew was watching in surprise at the rudeness of the Russians. They walked around like they owned the place. They appeared determined to find their way to the bridge on their own, but when faced with several doors to enter, Jack stepped up boldly and introduced himself. The leader said in broken English that he was Major Fyodor Smalanov and he requested to be taken to the captain of the ship. Jack nodded and said, "Please, follow me."

Jack led them through the maze of corridors and up the metal staircase to the open door of the bridge. When Smalanov walked in and spotted the Captain, he marched toward him and slowly, reluctantly extended his large hand. He looked as if he would prefer to throw the Captain into prison, rather than shake the hand of this capitalist swine. But Smalanov obviously had advanced in the party, no easy task among a throng of cutthroats. It was by a certain earthy, practical wisdom that he understood his current duty.

Jack watched these robotic communist men with fascination. They were three rough-looking comrades. Each packed a sidearm. Smalanov was a particularly brutal-appearing character. Jack could not take his eyes off him. His flat green cap was pulled tightly on his large head. A gargantuan red star decorated the front. His face was aged, brown, and deep with cracks and wrinkles, especially at the borders of his mouth. He spoke with determination and authority. His English was heavily accented but understandable. His uniform stretched tightly over his stocky, six-foot-tall, solid frame. He commanded with a determined, deep cutting voice. When he spoke, it was clear he meant business and was not to be questioned. A few oversized medals and epaulets grazed on his chest.

Standing before the Captain, Smalanov tried to smile, but did not show his teeth. The Captain gazed directly into his black eyes and grudgingly shook his hand and introduced himself. The Russian brusquely thanked the Captain for having the courage to deliver the much-needed supplies to his homeland.

Captain Gleason nodded. "We are confident these precious arms will aid your gallant army in the ultimate defeat of the Nazis." Jack was impressed at the spark of political eloquence coming from the boss. Comrade Smalanov gave a reluctant bow and announced it was time to get to work.

"'Time is of the essence,' is the English term, I believe." Without asking, he pushed the charts aside from the crowded table and put down his bundles of paper. He gazed at the Captain, as if suddenly recalling some important information he must pass on, and with his heavy accent declared, "I must warn you, Captain, the Germans have no fear. They will continue to attack and bomb this port. Our air force is pressed for fuel but will offer the best protection possible. Our antiaircraft guns are accurate. Two nights ago, we had a significant attack. You must keep your gunners alert, especially at night. We are strict about keeping all lights out. Do you understand?"

The Captain looked at the two thuggish gunmen, then at

Smalanov. Was this a suggestion, a request, a demand, or an order? He stared straight into Smalanov's black eyes. "We have been dealing with German U-boats, and aircraft for the past five hundred miles. We are well acquainted with our duty."

Smalanov said nothing but put his papers in order. "I would like to see your cargo manifest, Captain."

For the next three hours Smalanov and his two associates checked the manifest against their list to document every piece of machinery, drum of oil, tank, aircraft, locomotive and morsel of cargo on the *Esek Hopkins.* The three Russians, along with Chief Mate Cockrell, then wandered around the holds and decks for another four hours. They inspected everything.

In addition, the Russians were compulsive about documenting every breathing human being on the vessel. They went over the crew list twice. They studied the photographs. They asked probing questions. Clearly, the Americans were dealing with a paranoid society, Jack concluded. Once they were satisfied the ship's muster was complete and accurate, they gave the Captain a batch of ID cards, which they referred to as a *propusk.* Smalanov told the Captain that the American officers must print each crew member's name on the card along with the name of the ship and pass them out. No one could depart from or return to the ship without the card.

They must be carried at all times while on Russian soil. Not doing so could result in prison time.

Smalanov nodded and stated that the cranes would begin to unload the cargo at sunrise the next morning. Finally satisfied, the three Russians departed. Captain Gleason and his officers were glad to be rid of them. The crew saw the *modus operandi* of the Russians, who acted as if the Americans were trying to steal from them the very supplies they were delivering.

For the time being, no one was allowed off the ship. The crew wandered around the deck, or stayed warm down below playing cards, snacking, or just wondering what to do once they got on shore. Someone heard there was lots of booze on shore; and cheap. Another noted the girls were readily available for the asking. One mate warned about the food and liquor: poisoning was a possibility.

Incongruously, at 5:00 p.m. the battle alarm sounded. Everyone looked at each other in puzzlement. They were at a Russian port. What the hell was going on? Were Smalanov's warnings on the up and up? Reluctantly they jumped and ran to their stations. Someone passed a Navy Armed Guard officer and asked him if they should stay on the ship or get to shore because of all the explosives on board. Without a thought, he told them to leave the ship.

Though he was not the captain, most took his advice and scuttled down the steps and pushed past the Russian guards. Meanwhile, Jack, Ron, Fitz, and a few others went to their stations and prepared their guns. After seeing most of his merchant marine mates scurry off, panic set in and Jack decided that he was not ready to sacrifice himself while most of the crew was hot-tailing it to shore. He scampered off. As a Navy Armed Guard, Ron stayed at his station. Fitz was puzzled and decided to stay on board, thinking it might be safer than the unknowns of the foreign shore. The Russian guards at the base of the stairs were in a state of confusion.

Everyone was searching the sky. No German raid materialized and after twenty minutes the crew wandered back and clambered aboard. The Russian guards had lost track of the crew and were upset they could not account for everyone who had left the ship. Not that there was much motivation for the crew to stay on shore.

About an hour later, the Captain made an announcement on the loudspeaker. He sounded upset. He ordered all Merchant Mariners and Navy Armed Guards to stay on board unless given permission for shore leave. He pointed out that they were guests of the Russians and they must follow rules and protocol. He warned that the *Esek Hopkins* may still get attacked while in port and it was important that the crew remain aboard to defend her. He was ashamed that so many men ran for shore. He then explained the propusk ID cards and informed the crew they would be handed out to everyone at breakfast the next morning. Click. Jack was ashamed. He should have thought it through before he scurried off. And he had abandoned his pal Ron and the other Armed Guards. Not good, Jack.

Captain Gleason justifiably was in a bad mood. In the early morning darkness, the Russian pilot had run the *Esek Hopkins* aground. Then as soon as the lines were secured, the three Russian robots burst on board with their obnoxious inquiries and searches. To complete the absurdity, the crew ran for the hills at the first inkling of an attack.

The crew looked among themselves sheepishly. There were many excuses they could have devised, but it made little difference. The boss had read them the riot act. They had failed in their duty. What else could go wrong?

CHAPTER 21

The Glamor of Archangel

FOR SOME REASON, IN SPITE of his justified anger, the Captain granted the merchant mariners shore leave the next evening. As promised, at breakfast, everyone had been given their *propusk* ID cards, which allowed the crew to depart from the ship and roam around on Russian turf. Maybe the Captain was just sick and tired of the crew and wanted to avoid hearing complaints. But the Navy Armed Guard had to stay on board. Those guys always had a tougher time getting to shore. Not all the merchant marines took advantage, however. Some were tired and wanted to catch up on shut-eye. Jack, Alex, and Sparks wanted to explore, so they took advantage of the leave.

Once they stepped off the ship's stairs and passed the two guards, who dutifully inspected their ID cards, they entered another world. First, there were no real paved roads, mostly mud and crud. After sloshing a few blocks through the goop, they entered the little "town" of Molotovsk. It was characterized indecorously by cracked wooden planks for sidewalks and sections of wooden streets. The "homes" and buildings looked like dysfunctional wood cabins. Garbage filled the alleys and roadways. The inhabitants were not much better. Many "residents" were political prisoners. Western items were in great demand. Jack was approached by a local who offered one hundred rubles (about twenty dollars US) for a pack of cigarettes (Jack had none). Articles of mariners' clothing fetched higher prices—like three thousand rubles for a coat. At first this seemed exhilarating until the three realized there was nothing they could do with the money.

They found a "bar" and wandered in through a beat-up, heavy wooden door onto irregular wooden planks. They were immediately recognized by the locals as Americans and got quick attention. They chose a small booth. Through a pair of unvarnished, swinging, creaky doors in the back of the room, a woman approached them. She was slender with blond hair, high cheekbones and blue eyes. At first glance she appeared to be in her late twenties. As she approached them and on closer inspection, she clearly had accumulated over one hundred thousand miles. She looked rough and hard. She was slender because she was emaciated. The blond hair was died and the skin on her cheeks was rough and scarred—likely from smallpox.

The cheap makeup could not cover the pain and exhaustion in her eyes. They were able to communicate what they wanted; three beers. It took ten minutes for the drinks to arrive. The prices were high, and as Americans, they certainly were overcharged. They paid in dollars, which brought a nearly toothless smile on the worn face of the waitress. There were a few men at tables gnawing on some bread and meat. A lone worker was seated at the bar. A few more customers came and went. It was curious, they all were female. They gazed at the Americans as they slowly walked past. They appeared to be plying their trade.

After a few long slugs on the beer, Jack whispered that he had a bad feeling. "If we stay much longer, we are going to get mugged," he predicted. Alex and Sparks nodded. They gulped down the remaining beer, got up, left a generous tip, and headed innocently for the door. Jack noted that the denizens in the bar looked menacingly at them as they departed. It was wise they left when they did.

The sun set around 6:00 p.m. on the gruesome scene, and the town was nearly black when they walked out of the bar. Occasional streetlights blinked on and off randomly. Fortunately, Alex had a good sense of direction, and they were able to slosh their way back to the *Esek Hopkins* before the streets got really dangerous in this fourth dimension of pain and destruction.

As they approached the long quay, they could discern the name *Nathanial Green* on the bow of the Liberty Ship berthed just behind the *Esek Hopkins*. None of them needed to be reminded that this was the ship sailing next to the *Mary Luckenbach* when she was vaporized by German bombs. Jack made a mental note to visit the *Nathanial Green* sometime in the daylight to see what damage she sustained and chat with the crew.

The two Russian guards demanded IDs as the three men arrived at the base of the stairs.

The Russians were brusque, rude, and disrespectful. Jack was not going to worry about the crude Russians. It was their country and the *Esek Hopkins* would only be here for two or three weeks.

The three banged their feet on the metal steps as they climbed up. By the time they arrived at the deck level, most of the mud had been freed from their boots. Sparks suggested they stop in the mess hall and tell everyone about their "wonderful" experience and the "lovely" scenery they had observed on their journey ashore. Alex declined and went off to crash, but Jack joined Sparks. There were only about eight cadets sitting around the mess hall when they arrived. During the next hour Jack and Sparks reveled in telling their mates what a dump this port was. They developed a protracted, sarcastic, hyperbolic story about the beauty of the waitress. Then to the bunks.

Jack dozed off quickly. An intolerable ringing in his brain aroused him. It was the emergency alarm. It was 2:00 a.m. He struggled to the head, splashed water in his face, and quickly got dressed. He had to ask himself if he was still at sea. No, no, he was in Russia. Was this going to happen every night? Until now, Jack thought his tremor was improving.

No wonder all those people in the village look so pathetic—they never sleep! His three roommates struggled out of their bunks. Only Alex did not seem surprised at the drills at night. He often said, "If I were German, this is what I would do. Constantly keep your enemy fatigued and on the edge."

Ron and Fitz were already at battle station number four with the gun loaded when Jack arrived. The sky was black, but aircraft could be heard in the distance. Suddenly tunnels of light from searchlights pierced the blackness and crisscrossed in the sky. The Russian shore batteries quickly lit up the blackness with an impressive barrage of exploding shells accompanied by obliterating noise. The light flashes and pounding had their impact on Jack's head and he soon developed an unadorned headache. No bombs fell, at least not near them. Maybe the Germans were chased away by the heavy firing. Finally, silence. As they waited, Jack took a few minutes to bring Ron and Fitz up to date on their "fun" in town. As soon as the all-clear alarm sounded, everyone wandered back to their bunks and crashed.

A mere two hours later they were back at their battle stations, with more fireworks, but no bombs, then all clear, then to bed; again. "Clearly the Germans are torturing us with sleep deprivation," Jack suggested as they headed to their bunks. Alex reminded Jack, "I told you so."

It was difficult to keep track of time. When Jack was aroused by the clacking of railroad cars and the groaning of cranes outside the ship, it was 6:00 a.m. on Tuesday, September 22. The political prisoners were starting one day late. In terms of sleep, it was a lost night. There was no chance of going back to sleep with that racket adjacent to his porthole. Jack decided to take a quick shower and make his way to breakfast. Group shower times were allowed at 6:30 and 7:30 a.m. on even days. Afterward, as he headed up to the mess, he thought about the people of Archangel, some of whom may not have the luxury of breakfast, let alone a shower. Neither Alex nor Sparks was present, but Ski sat next to Jack as he was finishing. Ski was looking like his former self with no black eyes and all sutures removed from his forehead.

Jack offered, "Glad to see you are healed."

Ski ignored the compliment and went on to other topics. "Say, I appreciated how you pushed me over when the German bastard was shooting at us. I have not talked to anybody about it. I prefer to keep it low-key. Know what I mean?"

Jack nodded as he consumed the last bite of scrambled eggs. "No problem. I don't talk about it. Some officers on the bridge saw it. And they laughed when they saw what happened to my shoe."

In an apparent offer of gratitude, Ski threw out a proposal. "Say, would you like to get into a poker game? On Mondays and Thursdays, me and some guys meet in the oil storage room at seven to do a little gambling. Only two-bit ante."

Jack did not enjoy cards, and the advice of second mate Mark Williams popped into Jack's memory: "Don't get into any gambling on board." So Jack wondered, was this invitation one that Ski presented as a gift or was it an opportunity to fleece Jack?

He replied, "Thanks, Ski, but I don't gamble. I better get up on deck now to make sure the crazy Russians don't screw things up unloading our ship."

It was a clear, crisp, cold morning with a lung-numbing temperature of 20 degrees F. His gray breath in front of him reminded Jack of how cold it was in the Russian fall season. He tightened his heavy, high-collared coat around his frame. There was a slippery layer of frost over all the decks, which made walking hazardous. The sight before him was not a pretty one.

The most startling thing was the age of the stevedores. Most could not have been over eighteen years old, and some may have been younger. They were prisoners and wore striped coats and pants, in various states of disarray. Many had no socks and frivolous shoes which barely covered their feet. A few older ones, perhaps in their twenties, were the bosses of the group. Four army guards with rifles oversaw the young men and their activities. The Liberty Ship looked like a prison camp. That was bad enough, but as Jack watched the youngsters unpack and lift off the cargo, he became alarmed. These folks were untrained and were little more than moving men.

They acted as if it was furniture they were pushing around. Did they not realize the ship was full of explosives? In addition, it was obvious they had little experience operating the old, worn shore winches. One time the ratchets got jammed and the cargo suddenly was suspended in the air and awkwardly bobbing up and down. Sometimes the ratchets did not latch, and a palate would slam down on the deck—or possibly back in the hold. While watching this chaos, Jack reflected on how cautious the American crew had been when they loaded the ship back in New Jersey. As Jack was contemplating, his side vision detected a sudden downward motion. It was a box of supplies which had inadvertently been set loose from a crane, and quickly dropped about ten feet into the hold with a stunning, frightening crash. Jack caught his breath, anticipating an explosion. The box ruptured and spilled out loads of canned foods. This was insanity.

Jack turned and double-timed it up to the bridge to find the Captain. The Captain was gazing out the forward window at the scrambled mess on deck. His binoculars were around his neck, his hat in his right hand, and his upper teeth squeezing on his lower lip. He did not notice Jack's entrance. Jack interrupted his revery, "Ah-hum, Captain."

Gleason turned and said, "Oh, Dodd. I saw you down on deck. What do you think?" This was a softball.

"Captain, I am greatly disturbed. Even if the Germans missed us, these idiots are going to blow us up! And they are just kids; and prisoners to boot! They can barely operate the winch. We should unload our own ship."

Gleason managed a smile. "You hit all the big points, Jack. I already have sent a message to Comrade Smalanov. The other day, he made it clear that the Russians would unload the ships. I had no objections, but it was based on an assumption that they were competent.

Which they are not. Smalanov may take all day to get here. But we can't wait. I have an idea that might light a fire under his ass. I want you to go down to the galley and get Jenkens to prepare a meal for the Ruskies. A nice breakfast with eggs, sausage, toast coffee, etc. A full breakfast. One of the guards speaks English. Tell him it is time for a break for the men—it is required for American workers. Invite them into the mess hall for a 'little' snack during the break. Once we get them in there, they can take their time. Get seconds, have a cigarette, even a little nap. Invite the guards in too. When Comrade Smalanov hears the boys are not at work, he will be here in an instant."

Jack's face lit up. He saluted, "Yes, sir! Consider it done, sir! I will notify Mr. Williams and Mr. Cockrell." Off he went.

The news was well received by the slovenly workers. They climbed down from the cranes and collected on deck. Jack counted fifteen. He led them into the dining hall as food was already being put on the tables. No cafeteria lines for these gentlemen. They sat down and began feeding themselves with their fingers; eating as if it may be their last meal. Mark Williams, Bruce Cockrell and Jack enjoyed the scene as the men silently stuffed themselves.

The four guards sat at a separate table—interesting class distinction in a classless society! Thirty minutes went by, and the prisoners were getting curious. Some shyly went to the counter for seconds, which were not refused. The guards got up and yelled something and motioned their guns toward the door. First Mate Mark Williams told the English-speaking guard to relax.

Americans are required to take at least a full hour for a rest period. Two of the guards became upset, including the English speaker. The other two seemed in no hurry. They got another cup of coffee, more donuts, and sat down.

Jack decided to report the scene to the Captain who had remained on the bridge. Just as Jack arrived, the Captain pointed to shore and said, "Dodd, look. Here comes the SOB. He looks hot too."

Jack and the Captain gazed out over the side. Comrade Smalanov was huffing and puffing hot air as he slugged through the muck and approached the ladder. A guard with a machine gun accompanied him. They passed the guards at the stairs without so much as a grunt. Smalanov stomped on deck. There was not a soul in sight. Even the American crew members made themselves scarce. No one came to greet Smalanov. He looked left and right and tried to recall the path to the bridge. He looked up and gestured to the bridge, but there was no one visible. He gazed down over the edge into the largest hold on the *Esek Hopkins*. Silence below. Smalanov gave an order to his aid, who looked at him strangely. Smalanov grabbed the man's automatic weapon, cocked it, and fired three rounds into the sky.

Captain Gleason frowned and said, "I guess I had better get down there and calm that madman. Jack, there is an M-1 semi-automatic rifle in that cabinet. Please take it out, make sure it is loaded, and stand by here at the helm." Jack followed the orders as the Captain calmly walked down.

In the mess hall, at the sound of the gunshots, most of the prisoners jumped up and looked at all the entrances, half expecting to get shot. The guards cautiously walked to the door—with their guns ready. No one moved. The only sound was of the men breathing.

The Captain calmly strolled on deck and gave a friendly wave to Smalanov, who was standing with legs akimbo and arms crossed. "Where are my prisoners?" he shouted.

The Captain quietly answered, "No need to get excited. Ask your comrade to disengage his weapon. Your men are in the mess. We simply offered them a short break and some coffee. Would you like to join them?"

Smalanov pulled his green cap with the red star from his large head and snapped it down against his thigh. "We have no time for this nonsense! This is not a vacation. Get them out and back to work immediately!" Second mate Williams arrived on deck.

The Captain replied, "Sure, no problem. Williams, would you

ask the prisoners to end their break and come out on deck, please? While I have you here, Comrade Smalanov, I would like to give you a report. Would you like to join me on the bridge?"

"No. I have not time for pleasantries! What report?" he growled.

Gleason approached him to avoid yelling. "Well, your prisoners do not know what they are doing. They have little or no experience with cranes or winches or pallets or any coordination of effort. They don't work well as a team. About an hour ago they dropped a pallet full of canned beans about ten feet into the hold. If that had been ammunition, this vessel would have blown to bits along with most of the port."

Smalanov raised his hand, indicating the Captain should stop. "I want to observe them at their jobs. Now."

As if from central casting, out stepped the prisoners. Most had looks of concern on their forlorn faces. They were searching for the source of the gunshots, or perhaps a dead body on deck. One or two appeared mirthful, while patting their tummies.

Smalanov shouted something in Russian and they all took off to their job sites. He followed them and screamed frequently. He yelled instructions. He gyrated with his hands. Some of the *Esek Hopkins* crew gathered around the perimeter and on the upper decks to watch the scene play out. The Russians proceeded to get back to work. The prisoners in the large hold took about thirty minutes to place lashings around the fuselage of a B-25 bomber. The wings were stored separately. On signal, the crane operator engaged the lift mechanism, and the olive-colored medium bomber slowly came out of the hold. When it reached the level of the deck, it slipped slightly in its sling. Then, a moment too soon, the crane operator moved it left and the tail struck the edge of the deck. The aircraft suddenly rotated ninety degrees in its sling, then slid backward out of the forward support. It was now precariously suspended only by the aft support sling and swinging dangerously back and forth. Smalanov screamed orders. First the crane operator raised it up. Then, confused, he lowered it back into the hold. More men went down below to reposition it safely in the hold. All the Americans on board held their breath.

Smalanov leaned over the edge of the hold and spewed instructions to the unfortunate denizens below.

The Captain went over to Smalanov and calmly informed him that some American crew members were going down to be certain everything was safe and secure. He directed Second Mate Williams to take a dozen deck cadets down.

Jack remained alone on the bridge holding the M-1 rifle as directed. Out of his side vision, he noted movement on the crane. The operator had scurried down the ladder and just hit the ground as Jack turned his head. The man took off for parts unknown. He was never seen again, dead or alive.

It took over an hour to unravel the mess and lift the aircraft fuselage out of the hold and onto a freight car adjacent to the *Esek Hopkins.* Amazingly, there was no discernable damage to the body of the B-25. During the final resolution of that crisis, Smalanov pulled the Captain aside and explained that these prisoners were the newest group under his command and had the least training. When Smalanov requested assistance, the Captain replied immediately that the American crew could have the entire contents of the ship onto the quay in a week with some help from the prisoners. Smalanov reluctantly agreed but demanded that three of his officers observe and document the transfer. Done!

The dinner that night was one of the most enjoyable of the entire cruise. The chatter went on long into the night with laughing, stories, and play-acting like Comrade Smalanov. Alex took the role of Smalanov and jumped on a table and pranced and danced and postured in exaggerated poses to everyone's delight. They loved Jack's story about the escaping crane operator. If the Ruskies ever found him, he would be summarily shot!

For the next seven days the cadets worked diligently to organize the unloading and use the prisoners as labor. No American complained. They all realized the unloading would be much safer under their control. And the days passed quickly. They worked in shifts nearly twelve hours a day. Everyone chipped in. The locomotive, aircraft, tanks, jeeps, ammunition, and food were loaded directly onto train cars adjacent to the ship. Once loaded, these railroad cars were moved out quickly and immediately transported to the front. No time was wasted. Within minutes new rail cars replaced the old. Jack was amazed how efficiently the Russians performed some tasks and how poorly others. The ship was unloaded without a hitch.

The *Esek Hopkins* was now sitting high in the water with no explosives and essentially no cargo remaining on board. The crew was proud and relieved. Most crew members enjoyed staying busy. And they mistakenly thought that this would get them home sooner.

On the evening of the seventh day, when the ship was finally empty, the crew had a celebration after dinner, which extended well past midnight. A few crew members were able to smuggle some local vodka on board. They did not break it out until the Captain had crashed around 10:00 p.m. It was strong stuff. Jack took a slug and spat it out. Alex took three small shots over ten minutes and fell flat on his face. Everyone enjoyed the opportunity to sneak the liquid contraband onto the ship. In their cheerfulness, the crew discussed what they would do with their free time. Everyone had a different solution. Most involved finding something to do on shore and related to girls and booze. No matter how pathetic a dump the port was, they would find some fun. And for some reason, during that week, the Germans had been relatively quiet. Heavy cloud cover certainly helped.

On Saturday, September 26, Jack and Ron decided to visit the *Nathanial Green* docked behind the *Esek Hopkins.* As they climbed up the long staircase and stepped on deck, they saw the residual destruction from the *Mary Luckenbach* explosion on September 14. In the holds, another batch of Russian prisoners was unloading the *Nathanial Green.* The prisoners were taking a ten-minute lunch break around 11:00 a.m. when Jack and Ron arrived. Jack observed that their meal consisted of a piece of black bread and a small block of white greasy material. No wonder the prisoners were so excited about the regular meal they had on the *Esek Hopkins.*

Ron knew some of the Navy Armed Guards on the *Nathanial Green.* They caught up with them for lunch in the mess hall. Alan, one of Ron's pals, was the ranking Navy officer on board. Alan pointed out that much of the debris from the explosion had been washed over by the weather and wind. Their captain wanted to preserve any personal effects found from the *Mary Luckenbach's* crew, like wedding rings, keepsakes, diaries, or even fragments of human remains. Very little was found in the debris.

Alan noted, "Tomorrow is Sunday and the Captain plans to have a service honoring those killed in the explosion. A sad but fitting way to bring an end to that disaster. Feel free to join us. It will start at 1000 hours."

There was considerable damage to the *Nathanial Green.* Many portholes were shattered and now covered with plywood. The radio antennas were damaged but had been replaced. The heat of the explosion had peeled gray paint off the sides. The two life rafts positioned on the top sides of the decks were fried, scalded, and barely recognizable. Several of the large air intake funnels were missing. All the 20mm machine guns on the starboard side were severely damaged and no longer usable. Replacement would have to wait until the ship returned to England. The smokestack in the center of the superstructure was absent. In short, the *Nathanial Green* was a wreck. She was lucky to have survived. And, miraculously, no one on board had been killed. The crewman who was blown overboard had been rescued. But there were many injuries to the crew, especially burns on faces and hands. Shirts and pants were shredded and baked by the heat.

At lunch they discussed potential causes for the explosion of the *Mary Luckenbach.*

Floating in the back of their minds, but left unsaid, was the thought of how to deal with such an occurrence if the *Esek Hopkins* was a future target. To a direct hit by a bomb, or well-placed torpedo, there was no answer.

Interestingly there was more than one opinion regarding the cause. During the horror of battle, sometimes memories are fogged and impressions incorrect. The general consensus was that two bombs struck the *Mary Luckenbach.* But Alan thought otherwise. He said the He 111s were flying between the ships. They were under intense fire. One of the planes was hit by a three-inch cannon, went into a roll, then crashed onto the deck of the *Mary Luckenbach.* Alan believed this was the cause of the huge explosion. Jack and two other men agreed the German plane was hit, but thought it rolled into the sea just short of the *Mary Luckenbach.* They felt the two bombs were the real culprits and from a different plane than the one which was shot down. The third idea was the simplest: a torpedo had a perfect strike in the midsection of the hull where the TNT was stored. Alan said their captain had seen two torpedoes coming toward the bow of the *Nathanial Green,* and he turned the ship sharply to starboard and shifted into neutral. The torpedoes narrowly missed their bow. The captain believed one, or both, of those torpedoes struck and destroyed the *Mary Luckenbach.* In any case, the destruction was total, and sixty souls were lost instantaneously.

Jack and Ron commented on how the *Esek Hopkins* trembled and shook from the explosion a half a mile away. Alan said the *Nathanial Green* and other ships close to the event were partially lifted out of the water as the shock wave depressed the surrounding ocean while a ten-foot tsunami wave was created and carried through the convoy in a vast expanding circle. Escort ships as far as three miles out felt the shock wave, then the tsunami. No one in the convoy would ever forget it.

Alan confirmed that he also saw two He 111s get knocked out of the sky by the enormous concussion. They were thrown laterally, flipped over, and smashed into the ocean. This may have been the only minor consolation. But this was not a good exchange: one American ship and all those lives for two German aircraft.

Jack and Ron were feeling melancholy as they departed the *Nathanial Green.* They decided to search for relief in the little town, which looked a fraction improved in the sunlight. The mud ruts were partially frozen. Trucks were bouncing around as they slowly made their way. Walking was a bit easier. They saw the pathetic population working on the ships, along the quay, along railroad tracks, and in the town. They were putting in twelve-hour days in freezing temperatures, then standing in line for an hour to get a piece of black bread. What a system!

The duo decided to visit the bar where they had gotten beers a few days before. During daylight hours the place was not quite as intimidating and there were more customers. They bumped into an American army officer standing at the bar, sipping on a beer. After collegial greetings the discussion turned to the convoys. The officer said that the Germans were broadcasting on the radio that they had sunk thirty-eight out of forty-two ships in the convoy. In fact, there were sixteen ships lost. Bad enough, but those lying Germans…

A short time later, a British officer strolled into the bar and spotted them. He walked over and waved, "Hello mates," with typical British flourish. Introductions were made, and toasts were offered once the newcomer got a beer. He had been in Murmansk, Russia, two weeks before. Murmansk was the other major drop-off port for American supplies. The Germans decided to bomb it to kingdom come. He said about fifty German fighter planes swarmed in one night. The Russians got their fighters in the air and a protracted dog fight ensued. The Russians acquitted themselves well, but while the Russian fighters were preoccupied, the Germans sent in a fleet of FW Condors and initiated an hour of heavy bombing. At least a third of the port was destroyed. That is why PQ 18 did not dock there even though it was a shorter trip. The Brit suggested Archangel was next on the list for a heavy bombing attack.

"Oh great," Jack mumbled, "wherever I go, the Germans follow."

The Brit added that food shortages were actually worse in Murmansk than in Archangel.

He suggested that hundreds, perhaps thousands had starved to death after the German attack. The roads and railways were destroyed. There was no way to import supplies and food. The only way to depart was by walking. "It was a bloody nightmare," said the officer.

"God almighty," Jack wondered aloud. "These damn Germans might just win this war. People are half starved here, but I have seen no bodies in the streets. Yet."

The Brit had one more bit of news. "Did you hear," he asked, "that two men were shot and killed on the street here this morning? No details yet available." They shook their heads but were not surprised. Life was very cheap in wartime Russia.

Jack had heard enough unsavory news, so after only one beer, he and Ron bid their farewells to the American officer and the Brit and walked farther along to see what else was in the vicinity. For the next hour they strolled past dilapidated wooden shacks and houses, past warehouses with holes in the roofs and general signs of destruction. As they got closer to Archangel, there was a cluster of buildings and another bar. As they stepped in, it appeared to be larger and more crowded than the first, and with better-looking women. They spotted a few crew members from the *Esek Hopkins* whom they joined and ordered another round of beers. A few Russian women were engaged in the little group. Their English was discernable. Everyone enjoyed the human interaction. All had agreed to take a break from discussing the war.

The afternoon passed in slow-motion. As the sun was setting, Ron decided to head back to the ship. Jack wanted to get one more beer. He was having fun hanging around members of the opposite sex and they seemed to enjoy his company. One short Russian lass liked Jack's bushy eyebrows. Eventually the group broke up and a couple crew members escorted some of the ladies of the night out into the darkness. Jack wondered if they had their rubbers with them.

A Russian officer at the bar was among the little group and spoke reasonable English. Once Jack finished his last beer, he said he was heading back to his ship. The Russian too was leaving and he said he had a truck and offered Jack a ride. Wisely, Jack took the offer. He had lost count of the beers and was not certain of the path back to the *Esek Hopkins.*

Once they got in the battered vehicle, Jack recognized the manufacturer of the truck, "Hey, this is an American truck. It's a Studebaker. Made in Detroit!"

The Russian smiled, showing his three brown teeth, and said only, "Not as tough as Russian trucks."

He dropped Jack off about a half a mile from the dock, where the road more or less disintegrated. No lights were on, but in the darkness, Jack could discern a railroad track nearby and he felt certain this would lead him to the *Esek Hopkins.* He was correct but he started walking in the wrong direction. After about five minutes, he was startled when he heard the loud, harsh, barking voice of a man speaking Russian. A huge brutish man directed a long rifle with an even longer glistening bayonet at Jack's chest. Beers or not, Jack shot his hands up. The rifle-bearing creature spoke no English. Fortunately for Jack, the brute wore a uniform, indicating he was in the Russian army and not a local criminal. The wheels started turning slowly in Jack's partially sotted brain. What was the Russian word for the ID in his pocket?

Pro—, *pro—*, something. Yes, that was it; *propusk*! Jack repeated it several times. The soldier kept the rifle pointed at Jack's chest and extended a gloved palm. Jack slowly lowered his left hand, and slowly reached into his back pocket to find the ID. He handed it to the large creature, who shined a red flashlight on the card. Fortuitously, the brute recognized the card. He grunted and handed the card back. He grasped Jack's shoulder and roughly turned him in the correct direction and gave him a shove. Jack put the card in his pocket and proceeded to walk away with his hands still pointing skyward. Once he was about a hundred yards away, he lowered his hands and picked up his pace. Breathing the bitter cold air deeply and squinting, he finally could discern the masts of Liberty Ships in the black haze. He was never so happy to lay eyes on the *Esek Hopkins.*

The next morning at breakfast Jack relived the experience to his Forum pals at the table.

They got a good chuckle. Alex noted that Jack was approaching a restricted area where the Russians were temporarily storing the supplies the convoy had brought. They certainly wanted no saboteurs. Jack was fortunate. He could have been the third killing in Archangel that day.

The next period in Archangel was not exactly fun. Many crew members had had unpleasant shore experiences and there was little to attract them back. Most of the women were unattractive, tough and full of diseases. The vodka was nearly lethal. The food on shore was ugly and tasteless, or worse. Several mates were admitted to the sick bay with severe stomach ailments. From the point of view of the crew, they had done their duty. They had delivered the precious goods across the ocean in spite of considerable odds against them. They had unloaded the ship with more efficiency and safety than the Russian prisoners. They felt it was time to cast off and get under way. They deserved, hoped and expected to sail back to their safe home waters expeditiously. But alas, it was not to be. The admirals had other plans.

And the Germans, after a respite of several days, decided to become pests again. The Luftwaffe pilots had developed an interesting new tactic. Since their airports were located along the northern shore of Norway, the flight time to Archangel was only about thirty minutes. The Russians did not possess the newly develop radar and the Germans knew it. The pilots decided to fly to about fifteen thousand feet, then cut off their engines and glide toward Archangel. At night they were not heard or seen. When they got close to their targets, they turned on the engines and started their bombing runs with little warning and no opportunity for the Russians to respond quickly with their own fighter planes and flack. The crew on all the ships at dock were beginning to feel like sitting ducks. Life got cheaper by the day.

Life was also cheap at the hands of the Russians. One morning, a Russian moron on the *Nathanial Hopkins* was caught smoking in the hold while there were still explosives on board. The word spread quickly up and down the quay. Within an hour a Russian officer climbed on board the *Nathanial Hopkins* and announced that anyone caught smoking in the holds would be shot along with anyone working with him in the hold. That word spread even faster. And everyone, Americans and Ruskies alike, knew this was no idle threat. Not a few mariners gave up smoking and donated their cigarette packs to the Dvina River that day.

In support of how serious the Russian military was about insubordination, there was a story which had circulated around the port about a local ship pilot. Apparently without orders, he decided to move a ship from one side of the river to the other. He got the skeleton crew to untie the vessel and they cast off. There were significant winds, and he was unable to control the ship. The ship was pushed sideways, struck two Russian skiffs, and then smashed into the docks on the opposite side of the Dvina River. In short order, Russian military units ran up to the docked ship. The pilot descended the ladder to meet his fate. Perhaps the whole episode had been a death wish. A Russian officer yelled in his face for a few minutes. The soldiers then escorted the pilot behind a warehouse, and he was shot by a firing squad on the spot.

Jack, Alex, and Sparks were growing tired of the boredom on the ship and, with some reluctance, decided to venture to shore once again. They heard from some crew members that there was a small playhouse a few miles from the ship in Archangel. They also had learned there was a streetcar line into Archangel with the last stop about a mile from the docks. So, for a different sort of entertainment, they decided to take in a show.

The theater was a moderate-sized wooden building with a small stage along the side wall. Refreshments were offered opposite the stage. The show was in Russian, and although Jack and company could understand nothing, they laughed and clapped along with the audience. The comedy must have been good because there was a long applause at the end. They had one beer then made their way to the streetcar and wandered home to their bunks.

The next day they learned there was one place in Archangel where the food was better than the usual fare. It was the Intourist Russian Hotel, which catered to non-Russians with cash. Crews on American ships were in that category. And the Intourist preferred dollars rather than other currencies. But items for consumption there were not cheap. A good dinner would include a salad consisting mostly of beets with lettuce fragments, an entree of a small potato or two and a fragment of meat or fish, along with a piece of cake for dessert. This would cost the fantastic sum of twenty dollars. But the salad was fresh, the potatoes tasty, and the meat or fish, though not excellent, was good considering the source. By Russian standards, the Intourist Hotel was five stars. To top things off, there was an impressive wood-paneled bar adjacent to the dining room and it was typically filled with Americans and Brits. And women. Once discovered, the hotel became the place to be.

Jack, Sparks, and Alex found themselves in the paneled bar at the Intourist one cold cloudy evening more than two weeks after arriving in Archangel. This initial foray confirmed this spot probably was the one place in Archangel where Western women would appear, rare as they were. They wondered how they had been kept in the dark about this spot for so long. It may have been the best kept secret in Archangel.

Even in this relatively nice, Western-style hotel, the Russians had peculiar customs. The first time Jack went to the bathroom he was in for a surprise. He entered a room with no door and went up to a fifteen-foot-long, low porcelain tub recessed in the floor where you peed.

About every sixty seconds a little water would trickle in and wash the pee to a drain at the end. As he peed, he heard a rustle behind him. There, along the wall, was a row of about twenty toilets with six-foot partitions on the sides but no doors. He turned to see a woman rising from the toilet, pulling up her skirt. Privacy was not a major concern in the Soviet Union. He gazed at her, not certain what the proper etiquette was. She was quite attractive and had beautiful, proportioned legs. She smiled at him and said with a crisp British accent, “Good evening.”

Flustered, Jack said, “Oh, hi,” as he pulled up his fly. He followed her to the only sink.

She offered, “The Ruskies are not very particular about their loo arrangements. In a way, very practical, don’t you think?”

Jack nodded as she shook her hands dry—there were no towels. She turned to exit, and said, “Enjoy.”

Jack was still trying to recover from the idea of shared toilets, and as he watched her shapely legs walk out the door, all he could come up with was, “Good evening.”

What an interesting place, he thought as he rinsed his hands and shook them dry. He walked toward the door as two women entered and nodded at him with a grin.

He wondered what else went on in there.

When he went back to the paneled bar, his pals were laughing as he approached. “So how do you like the shared accommodations? You are now a member of the ‘All in One Club!’”

Sparks chirped, “I am trying to figure out how to meet a woman in there for quick sex—maybe in the last stall.” A good chuckle.

Alex offered, “You just have to find the right woman.” Then Jack told them about the attractive British woman there during his visit.

Alex replied, “Yeah, she works with the top Brit officer in Archangel. Those officers have all the luck.”

Another round of beers helped pass the evening as they gandered at the rare women who were enjoying way too much attention. An American army officer from Texas stepped up and joined them. They enjoyed his Texas drawl. He repeated the story that the Germans were announcing on the radio that the Luftwaffe and U-boats had sunk thirty-eight ships of the convoy. Strange the Germans never revealed how many of their aircraft were lost.

It was nearing midnight, and the bar was thinning a bit. Jack was ready to head back to the ship. Just then, blaring air-raid sirens overwhelmed the chatter and laughter. A second of silence, then everyone proceeded toward a single small door on the far side of the paneled room. Everyone seemed to know where to go and the purpose of the door. Alex grabbed Jack's arm and pushed him along in that direction.

"That's the entrance to the air-raid shelter in the basement," he instructed.

The line of partially intoxicated revelers inched down a set of flimsy wooden stairs. Once at the bottom, Jack was stunned. The room was expansive with only one light bulb hanging from a fixture at the far end. It had a dank, moist feeling. The floor was dirt. People were packing in. The hotel staff and chefs were the last to enter. The single door was purposely left ajar.

Jack wondered if he might be better off in the street when the bombs started to fall. No one would like to be trapped in this place if the building were to collapse like a house of cards. And such a nice bar above.

They could hear and feel the distant thumping. Light flickered and flashed through the doorway. The basement dwellers were remarkably calm and rather quiet. What could one say? After about twenty minutes, the all-clear sirens sounded. Silently, in an orderly fashion, the basement cleared. It was as if everyone had been trained.

In a sense they had.

CHAPTER 22

Fireworks and Fun

THE STRESSFUL MONTH OF SEPTEMBER finally passed, and a distinctly colder October had arrived. Jack and his colleagues tried to stay busy on board the *Esek Hopkins.* Jack created a personal schedule to encourage reading of training manuals for two hours a day; most of them repeats. He would then exercise by stretching, followed by a walk around the deck for about an hour. This accomplished the combined goals of maintaining good muscle tone and inspecting the vacant ship to fulfill his deck cadet responsibilities. He then climbed to the bridge for coffee and chatting with the duty officer. Most nights he and his pals ate dinner on the *Esek Hopkins.* But there were unconfirmed stories from the galley that diminished food supplies from the Russians was becoming a significant problem. Rumors circulated that between-meal snacks were about to stop on board. Also, meal portions would soon shrink. Certain foods would stop, specifically steaks. Eggs were in short supply. Jack, Alex, and Sparks decided to visit the Intourist Hotel once a week for dinner to help out with the food shortage on board. Other crew members also were trying to catch one meal a day on shore.

The Luftwaffe's brief vacation did not last. But they had not yet initiated an intense bombing raid like they did at Murmansk. Perhaps there were more defensive guns at Archangel. Or perhaps the number of German planes and pilots was depleted. Nonetheless, the Luftwaffe did not want the city to get lonely or miss them. Jack estimated that, on average, there were three nighttime attacks per week on the city of Archangel and its suburbs. It was rumored the Russians had recently installed a primitive radar system. So, the ruse of German aircraft silently coasting into bombing missions was no longer viable. Jack recognized this was the reason there were often glaring searchlights and guns firing into the air before any sounds of aircraft permeated the black skies. Also, the Luftwaffe bombings seemed more random and less accurate. One thing was very clear: the Russians would do anything to keep the port of Archangel open. Clearly, the American supplies were having a positive impact on the Russian war efforts on the eastern front.

Through the onboard pipeline, Alex learned there was a functioning movie theater in the outskirts of Archangel. He, Jack, and Sparks decided to give it a whirl. A movie, no matter how pathetic, offered a much-needed break from their routine. They walked to the streetcar stop, rode into town, and got a respectable meal at the Intourist Hotel. The theater was about a twenty-minute walk from the hotel. By 7:00 p.m. they were seated in reasonably comfortable but dusty theater seats with only small amounts of debris on the floor, gazing at the small screen. After a few flickers, the show began. The dialogue was in Russian with no subtitles. Jack, always looking for the positive, hoped he might learn some Russian in this God-forsaken country, if he watched enough movies. This was his first shot. The trio occupied themselves by attempting to deduce the plot only from the scenes —much like the old silent movies, which Jack remembered from his youth. About an hour into the film the lights flickered on and off, and the film projector stopped. Everyone stood and started toward the exits.

As they followed suit, Jack pointed out to his colleagues, "If that was the end of the movie, that was a strange way to end it. I could never quite figure out the plot."

The attendees, in a winding, narrow line, spoke little and moved quickly to the only two doors leading outside. The trio stepped into the street, and immediately noted powerful search lights incongruously arcing above, like giant pencils scribbling in the air. As the first breath of icy air infiltrated their lungs, they were jolted by screaming air-raid sirens. Knowledgeable, experienced human forms scurried off the streets. The trio, with a streak of American independence, began walking down the center of the forlorn, scruffy road, in the general direction of the streetcar stop. Suddenly, long-barreled, black antiaircraft cannons hidden behind buildings and in wooded areas erupted viciously with stunning, intense bursts of light. The mighty shock waves jolted their heads and vibrated their eardrums, which were unaccustomed to such overwhelming intensity during their evolutionary development. The flashes were bright enough to offer an instant of daylight. The mind was not comfortable assessing the local geography for such short intervals. Windows rattled, dust jumped from the dirty road, and the trio picked up their pace. Had dogs been present, they would have howled; but alas, they had all been eaten. Alex, with his good directional sense, led the way. Perhaps his Greek heritage of self-discipline and determination in the face of adversity allowed him to ignore the flashing and pounding. The three were the only living creatures in the streets. Then, as if some diabolical entity targeted them as the last humans near the gates of hell, fragments, particles, and chunks of black, hot objects dropped randomly from the sky.

Alex extended his arms and hands protectively over his head and screamed, "Flack. Follow me!"

This new challenge propelled them into a sprint, first along the edges of buildings and then under a rickety wooden porch, which temporarily offered protection as items of all shapes and sizes plunked and bounced onto the dusty streets. Sparks begged them to stop so he could deal with a cough precipitated by the rapid intake of the icy, dusty air. They did. From this temporary, frail shelter they watched the unfolding fireworks. The intense pencils of light permeated high into the sky. Only occasionally did they illuminate an aircraft as it zipped through a circle of light. But this brief illumination helped the gunners determine altitude.

The explosions in the sky were bright, brighter than traditional American fireworks. Then came the loud boom of the exploding shells in the sky, hoping to obliterate the evil German flying machines. Distant cannon fire added to the cacophony. But none of this was equal to the nearby cannon eruptions. The three began to experience pulsing, pounding pressure on their facial skin and hair. It was a horrible unnatural sensory assault. The ground jolted with each firing. The percussion on the chest and face and inner ear was impossible to tolerate. Dust now filled the breathable atmosphere, sufficient to cause coughing and make it impossible to stop excessive blinking. They covered their faces with their gloves to filter the dust. On and on it went. Sparks inhaled a final dusty breath through his hands and announced he was ready to go. An instant before he spoke, Alex had already started running without notice to the others. He did not look back, but Jack and Sparks quickly began sprinting along edges of buildings, over logs, adjacent to pathetic, depleted bushes and hedges, following without thinking, hoping Alex knew the way.

In their panicked escape to somewhere, Jack began to wonder why there were no bomb strikes in their immediate area. Another sign of an omnipotent God looking over them. Suddenly, unexpectedly, there came a lull in the firing. The silence was intolerable, alarming, worrisome. Complete darkness descended. They slowed to a trot without vision and came to what appeared to be a large open square. Then, unannounced, and just as suddenly, all hell broke loose.

Around the square, there must have been half a dozen well-concealed cannons, which erupted almost simultaneously. The ground shook violently. Jack actually felt his feet depart from the earth and he fell when the earth reengaged. The trio had never been so shocked and frightened in their lives. The light flashes imprinted on their retinas the layout of the square and Alex led the way down a street he determined would take them to the trolley. The trotting was over; now they sprinted with uncertainty toward a house a few blocks away, even as the ground was jolting beneath their feet. The flimsy door was open and the house vacant. Once safely inside, they squatted on the floor and held their ears until there was a break in the shooting.

Sparks screamed, almost absurdly, "It's time to get the hell out of here!"

Off they went again. This time they ran the entire distance to the streetcar, likely a mile, with booming light flashes creating an instantaneous visual map in their minds, guiding their way. Incredibly, a streetcar was standing at its designated stop. Gasping for air, they ran up to the door, which was ajar. The booming was diminishing in intensity. The conductor was sitting calmly like he had nothing else to do. He waved them on. He announced something in Russian. They indicated no comprehension. He held up five fingers. They had no trouble finding a seat; the car was empty and dusty with debris decorating the cracked, uneven floor. They looked back and saw a red glow in the sky toward the far side of Archangel. Apparently, some bombs had connected and done their intended work. They looked at each other. Grit, debris, and particulate matter adhered to their faces, accentuated by the sticky dots of perspiration. They breathed hard. They said nothing. No one yet allowed themselves to feel safe. They wanted to believe what had just happened was the worst of it, but that was never a safe assumption in wartime Russia.

Sure enough, as predicted, after five minutes the streetcar grunted, growled, and lurched as it struggled to make its way. The path forward along the tracks was totally black with no streetlights, only gray dusty haze. Buildings, stores, vehicles, and the normal sights of a city were not discernable. The single, faint illumination was the dim, pale beam of light at the front of the rocking, clanking streetcar. Hopefully, someone kept the track clear of debris. During the four-mile trip, in spite of ten regular stops, only one additional passenger emerged from the gray mist of the shadows to climb aboard. Jack guessed it was a woman, but she was so bundled, it was not completely certain. Jack observed that the locals had become so acclimated to these air attacks and pounding antiaircraft responses that they had become fatalistic and barely seemed disturbed. The frequency and intensity of cannon fire declined as the bouncing trolly increased its distance from the center of the city. The three Americans still found the entire scene surreal, incredible, and unnerving.

Finally, Jack broke the silence. "Can you even imagine this nightmare back in our hometowns?" Fatigue had set in, and no one was inclined to respond.

The final one mile walk to the port was uneventful other than occasional flickers high in the night sky. The three were never so happy to see the friendly *Esek Hopkins.* They displayed their ID cards to the ever-present oafish guards and climbed up the gangway, exhausted physically and mentally. They clamored, breathless, into the mess hall. A few Navy guards were sitting around in deep conversation. No one was interested enough to even look at them. No sooner had they entered than one of the mates told them about a crewman on the *Exford* Liberty Ship who had committed suicide. The mate quietly commented, "You guys look like crap." He then continued with his story, saying the man had wrapped a portion of anchor chain around his neck and jumped overboard. Everyone on board appreciated the angst associated with being trapped on a ship with indiscriminate bombing all around. It was possible some of the crewmen in this convoy had considered taking their lives. But to carry it out was an enormous step from simply thinking about it. The level of desperation among the men could be high and not always detectable. With the somber mood in the mess, the trio decided to wait until the next day to inform their colleagues of their terrifying experience. They were beyond exhaustion and headed to their staterooms.

Jack gazed into the mirror in the shower room and was amazed at what he observed gazing back. He took a wet cloth and repeatedly washed until the imbedded dark spots and particulates on his facial skin were gone. His black hair was filled with debris. No showers were allowed at this hour, so he dipped his head into the sink and rinsed his hair several times. The sink filled with grit. As he washed, he reviewed the frightening events of that evening. His ears were still ringing. It was difficult to wrap his mind around the horror of it all. He looked into his brown eyes, his mind, his soul. What was he doing here? He had no idea of the degree of torment he would endure—for his country. He removed his shirt and washed off his chest as best he could. He managed to flex his legs upward and get his feet to the level of the faucet. He quickly rinsed his feet in the warm water. His mother called this process a "bird bath" when he was a kid. Yes, his sweet mother. Would he ever see her again? Or his home? Or his old life, which seemed a universe away? Was his old life even possible after these incomprehensible experiences?

Finally on his pillow, Jack compared the poor man's suicide to his own frightening experience and decided, on balance, the suicide was worse. A smile appeared on his exhausted face as the features, smell, and look of Penny fleetingly marched through his mind. A prayer then worked its way into his consciousness, and then, finally, sleep.

Most of his fellow mates slept well on board that night. Jack did not. Sometime during the night, in total darkness, he woke up in a sweat. It was another all too detailed, all too tangible, very frightening dream.

He stood on the main deck by himself, in the midst of a fire-fight, paralyzed with the thought that his luck had run out, sensing he was going to die alone, stunned as he saw hundreds of enemy bombers and fighters buzzing around the ship like terrifying evil insects, all with one goal: destroy Jack Dodd. Bullets were zinging, bombs were splashing all about and the insects were closing in. One bomber, an He 111, grew in dimension and speed. Jack could visual-

ize in uncanny detail, excessive detail, fine detail, the features of the pilot's faces, the pair of bristling, black machine guns aimed at him, the rivets on the aircraft, the twirling propellers as the craft unmercifully charged at him. The pilots were angry with revenge and hatred imprinted on their faces, all directed at him personally. He could see them push the throttle forward. Then a movement; a brief flicker on the deck was detected with his peripheral vision. There was another soul on the ship. He was running toward the side of the ship screaming above the harsh background noise, "Abandon ship, abandon ship." After an instant of confusion, Jack recognized him; it was Ski. He disappeared overboard. It was his last good deed offered to Jack. Time was up, the ship was going to die, with Jack on it. No escape this time. There were no weapons nearby, there was nothing he could do. Impossibly, the bomber slowed down, the sound slowed down, everything slowed down. Two decks up was a 20mm machine-gun tub. He tried to spring up the metal stairs. The harder he tried, the more difficult was the task. He turned to see how close the enemy was. The frightening, noisy aircraft seemed suspended in the air, less than a hundred feet away. He labored and struggled upward. When he finally arrived at the gun tub, he could find no ammo belts or magazines. He searched in vain as the bomber slowly advanced. It was one horrible, frustrating circumstance after another. Then his eyes were attracted to a floating object at a distant point on the horizon, an angel-like figure swiftly approaching the treacherous scene. In a white gown, drifting, gazing peacefully at the horror below, was his mother. He looked up hopefully. She was at peace; she simply smiled at Jack.

She was only an observer; she was unable to assist. Now bright flashes flickered from the bomber machine guns and bullets clanked on the steel deck around him. Jack could not find a life jacket. He gasped as he realized that if a bomb was dropped now, it could not miss. He gaped in terror and put his hands up as if to surrender. The bomber continued, traveling slower and slower, delaying his fate. The bomber was so close he heard the loud click as the bomb released, with a tiny spinning wheel on the tip, on a direct line to impact him personally, right between the eyes…

Surrounded by moisture, he was panting as he woke with a start. He wiped his face with the bed sheet. The dream had seemed more real than reality could ever be. Was this a form of payment for his changed psyche?

His mind raced, pondering how many real bullets had zinged past his head on this journey. How many torpedoes had missed the *Esek Hopkins*, how many bombs struck other ships, but not theirs? Coming home from the theater last night he easily could have been blown to many unidentifiable fragments; vaporized. Would this ever stop? And this trip was only half completed. Shaking, he climbed out of bed and whispered a few prayers as he got dressed. His roommates remained asleep. He quietly climbed the metal stairs and went out on deck to take in the frigid, damp air. He pondered his situation in life, his family, his upbringing, schooling, religion, friends. His mother was correct to worry about him. Not only for his survival, but what the experiences would do to him. He likely was not the same man who departed from Baltimore. He was not the same man who knew Penny. Jack rarely had dreams, but on this journey, he had powerful, ugly, confusing dreams. What was this experience doing to him, to his real self, his soul? He walked around the deck in deep thought for a long unaccountable time. Were other men digesting similar thoughts?

Jack had no appetite and he decided to skip breakfast. He slowly walked back to his room, his bunk. Only Alex was in the room, grunting as he got dressed. Jack entered and plopped on his bed and said nothing.

"What's up, my man? Have you eaten yet?" Alex cheerfully inquired. Jack wondered how Alex could be so bright after that horrible night they shared.

"No…I'm done," was Jack's reply.

Alex quickly perceived Jack's mood change and this double entendre. He probed subtly, by making a sideways inquiry. "Done what? Breakfast? Who was in the mess?"

"Just done…done with everything," Jack responded. He was barely audible. He leaned forward, like he was going to vomit. He rested his face in his hands.

This was not a job for Alex. It was beyond his pay grade. But he had seen this before.

And Jack was his friend.

"Hey, look up at me," he said firmly. Jack kept his face in his palms and shook his head no.

"Jack, what is this crap? Look here. What…you feeling sorry for, yourself?"

Finally, he yelled, "Look at me!" Alex reached down and pulled Jack's head up. His eyes were red, full of distress. An unusual frown occupied his handsome face. His mouth was down at the sides. He finally looked at Alex with pleading eyes.

Alex barked, "What? You something special? You don't deserve this? No, Jack. You are just a routine little piece of crap… Got it? A piece of crap…just like the rest of us. A lowly, smelly piece of crap, with this crappy crew, on this crappy ship, in this crappy ocean, in this crappy world. You think you are the only one? Everybody on this ship, in this war, is just as scared as you. Everybody has family, girlfriends, dreams… Everybody can choose to feel sorry for themselves. Or they can deal with it. Get up. Stand up," Alex barked. Jack did not move.

Alex, now therapist, consoler, aid, friend, grabbed Jack's head, pulled him forward off the bunk, and straightened him up. Alex towered over him.

"You hear me?" he shouted.

"Drop it," mumbled Jack.

Alex frowned, slowly rotated his head back and forth, and belted Jack with a hard right hook. Jack fell back on the floor with blood oozing from the left side of his mouth. He was surprised and stunned but jumped up with amazing alacrity and yelled, "You bastard," as he took a clumsy, inexperienced swing, which Alex easily deflected. Without hesitation, Alex nailed Jack with a strong left hook, which accurately hammered his right cheekbone. Jack fell to the floor again, dazed. Now blood was drifting from both sides of his mouth. Only one thought flicked through Jack's mind—the words of Chief Cockrell—"end a fight quickly." Jack jumped up and charged, directing his shoulder toward Alex's midsection. Alex turned and avoided the main thrust of the charge, and simultaneously grabbed Jack's shoulders and straightened him.

As he pulled back his large right fist, he said, "Jack, I hate to mess up those nice teeth of yours, but…"

At some point in this confused interval of space and time, their third roommate, Ross Engles, silently appeared. Wisely, Ross grabbed Alex's right arm from behind and defused, but did not stop his punch directed at Jack's bleeding face. Stunned at the blow, Jack started to fall backward again, but at the last second, caught himself and maintained his balance. Alex, with his free left hand, reached out and gave Jack a firm push on his chest, which propelled him backward and onto the floor for the third time.

Alex turned his attention to Ross. For an instant, Alex had a puzzled look on his face, which alarmed Ross. Alex did not want to injure him, since Ross had no need for Alex's therapy and should not have involved himself.

Ross interrupted Alex's mental calculus, "What the hell are you guys doing?" Before responding, Alex turned to be sure Jack was not attacking again. He paused, looked into Ross's eyes, and replied, "Jack and I just had a little disagreement over some toothpaste."

Ross appreciated the absurdity of the statement, but slowly responded, "I have some extra, and would be happy to share it with you guys."

Alex relaxed his fists and dropped his arms to his side. He turned to Jack, who remained sitting on the floor with smeared blood on his face and on his right hand, which he was using to wipe.

Ross walked slowly to Jack, not wanting to disturb the tenuous peace. Jack accepted his offered hand with his unblemished left hand and stood. Ross gazed at Jack's bloody and now swelling face.

"Lose any teeth?" he inquired. Jack explored with his tongue to account for them all and shook his head no. "I think we should take a walk down to the clinic and get to know Mr. Arnold. A little ice may help. Looks like you had a bad slip and fall on the stairs."

Alex stood aside as the pair left the room. He looked at his fists. As he walked to the bathroom to wash away the clumps of dried blood, he said to himself, "Maybe I should have stopped after two slugs. Ross likely saved those handsome teeth. But Jack is my friend."

Jack lay on the exam table with aching ice packs on each side of his face. He pondered what had just happened with his roommate and heretofore friend, Alex Salamis. What he had said and done was troubling and yet…

Jack skipped lunch and dinner; it was too painful to chew. At bedtime, Ross wanted to be present with Jack and Alex to be sure the "toothpaste" issue had been settled. The three stood in the center of their small stateroom.

Jack looked at Alex and extended his hand, and said, "Thanks, Alex. I appreciate now how you were trying to help."

Alex smiled and said only, "Hey, man, what are friends for?"

Ross gazed at them both with a puzzled look, and asked, "So all is good now?" Both men nodded to the affirmative. Yes, all was good.

Jack's injuries from his fall were minor headlines in the Forum. The more exciting news had been the adventures of the trio the night before. By the time Jack attended the morning mess the following day, everyone had heard in great detail, the horrifying experience of the trio. Even though no bombs fell close to them, they were the only crew members who had been in the city during the bombing attack. Their colleagues were excited for them, but also somewhat envious they had missed the show. Curiously, the three were viewed as "heroes." None of them felt like heroes. From on board, the crew had seen the searchlights and flashes of light and heard the cannons thumping, but it all seemed far away. One colleague, poking fun at Alex, asked, "Other than that, how was the movie?"

In spite of all the attention and distractions, the frightening dream circled around in the back of Jack's mind and continued to haunt him. Maybe he was not meant for this life. Maybe he was meant for a quiet life with a lovely woman like Penny. He could imagine loving her. Why didn't he tell her? Yet that little voice intruded once more.

She does not deserve a killer like you. She is too good for you.

He needed to suppress these thoughts. It was that self-pity thing battling in his head. Alex had cleared his mind. And his tremor was improving after the Alex affair.

He felt a strong urge to write to Penny. And he did.

The next morning, Captain Gleason made an announcement after breakfast. Since the bombers were ignoring the port and the ships, for the time being, he had decided to avoid sounding a general alarm when bombers attacked Archangel. But if the German attack pattern changed, the crew would man the guns as they had done at sea.

Not surprisingly, the fireworks did not end. Jack and his pals stayed on the *Esek Hopkins* the next few nights. Another air attack commenced one night over Archangel at 11:00 p.m. This time the German planes dropped flares on parachutes, which gave them a better view of their targets. As an evil side effect, when the flares hit the ground, they acted as incendiary bombs and caused many fires around Archangel. The Russian antiaircraft guns pounded away into the sky with determined, unremitting ferocity. Over the next hours, the flashing and thumping in the sky did not let up. It was difficult to speak, to hear, to read or even think. Men wondered how many aircraft were knocked out of the sky with all this racket.

With his face now healed and time on his hands, Jack was once again spending more time on the bridge. One day a telegram arrived, and Mark Williams showed it to him. It was from the British Admiralty thanking all the crews of the convoy for their bravery and dedication to fulfilling their mission. It ended with, "The prime minister wishes to associate himself with this message." As Jack pondered all the fireworks, the wasted time, the trials and tribulations of all the crews, he was glad someone appreciated the sacrifice they were making. And the prime minister, good old Mr. Churchill, was paying attention this time. And the better news was that the bombs were not dropping on the ships. Yet.

The area around Molotovsk and Archangel was a delta with many islands and interconnecting waterways. Fresh rumors on board suggested the *Esek Hopkins* soon was going to depart from Molotovsk. But this did not mean they were heading home. The ship was empty and sitting high in the water like it was when Jack first saw her back in Hoboken. These ships did not sail well in rough seas without being loaded with cargo. In fact, they were so unstable, there was a good chance they could capsize in storms like those they encountered on the inward leg of the voyage. From Mark, Jack learned they were going to load up with the one export available from this frozen, desolate land: lumber. This would be the important ballast for their journey home.

Indeed, it was on October 6 at 8:30 a.m. that the second mate of the *Esek Hopkins* sent orders below to crank up the engine. A Russian pilot arrived. He was required to move the ship. Captain Gleason remained on the bridge to monitor the process. With the aid of the Russian prisoner-stevedores on land, the cumbersome mechanics of untying the large lines from the bollards on shore had begun. Jack and his fellow deck cadets were responsible for dragging the three-inch lines on deck and stowing them. They were heavy with moisture, partially frozen and stiff and cumbersome. It typically took at least two men, with gloved hands, to get each line aboard. Once freed of all lines, the ship's crew waved farewell to the emaciated "comrades" on shore, and the Russian pilot slowly backed the *Esek Hopkins* out and into the channel. The crew felt "no love lost" as the ship turned to head out into the mine-free zone known so well to the pilot. Molotovsk and Archangel were certainly no respite from war. Not a man on board cared to visit these places again. The landscape was desolate, the people were thuggish and unrefined, and of course, the area was a bombing target for the Luftwaffe.

Jack whispered to himself, "Whatever steps are necessary to start home, let the process begin." Casting off was a promising first step.

The Russian pilot maneuvered the ship into one of the many streams and waterways separating the islands. He proceeded at a slow four knots. By late afternoon he had guided the *Esek Hopkins* to a dock about ten miles from Archangel. The Liberty Ship was the lonely inhabitant of this small, isolated port. In the distance were innumerable acres of densely treed forests, and piles of logs near the dock. Already trucks were pulling up with a fresh load as the stevedores caught the heavy lines and secured the empty vessel to the dock.

The sun was setting as they lowered the ladder, and a single Russian port warden came aboard to meet with the Captain. An hour later Captain Gleason announced on the loudspeaker system that the loading of lumber would begin at sunrise the next morning. He estimated the American vessels would be at this port for the next several weeks. Weeks! Collective groans. After all, how long could it take to fill the holds with logs? Sitting at this lonely, isolated port for another few weeks was not encouraging news to the crew. In fact, it was devastating news. After a brief period of optimism when they departed, Jack was quite upset. Exercise might offer a distraction, so he wandered around the deck as his mind whirred. He tracked down Mark, the second mate, and asked him how crew members could make their way to Archangel, some ten miles away. Jack reminded Mark that the crew would go mad if they were stuck on board in this wilderness for weeks. Mark made some inquiries and passed the good news to Jack within an hour. Jack was delighted to learn that three times a day there was a ferry boat from their dock to central Archangel for a minimal fee. He passed the word around to the crew. This fact alone improved the crew's state of mind and morale. They would be able to visit some of their old haunts, pathetic as they were.

Even though Jack was a mere deck cadet, his star continued to rise among his fellow mates. He seemed to get news quickly and usually it was valid. He also was recognized by the officers as the man who seemed to be the most interested in learning. They slowly, deliberately, gave him more tasks and responsibilities. He was targeted for advancement. And yet, he was ambivalent. Lately, he felt he would go on no more Liberty Ships. Too stressful, too difficult, too dangerous! He had avoided talking with Alex for a few days after their fight. But Jack recognized that his action was a sign of a true friendship. And the "episode" definitely cleared his mind.

After dinner that evening Jack visited the helm station to see if there was any new scuttlebutt. Once again, he had become a regular fixture on the bridge, and no one objected.

Sparks received some data on the wire from the British Admiralty. He knew it would make the crew happy and he asked Jack to spread the word. The Captain consented. The Brits had issued a statement for public consumption. It said that their convoy, PQ 18, had been the most heavily defended convoy in the war so far. They claimed there were a total of seventy-two escort ships defending the forty convoy vessels. All the men knew that seventy-two number was flexible; they were in increments, not all at the same time. The defending escort ships were British, American, and Russian. A total of forty-two German aircraft were shot down in defense of the convoy. In addition, six U-boats were sunk. And the Luftwaffe commander in Finland acknowledged that the Germans had suffered a "severe setback." In addition, the Brits estimated that some seven hundred torpedoes were shot at the ships over the one week of the prolonged attack. At one point on September 13, there may have been one hundred torpedoes in the water at the same time. On the downside, four Hurricanes had been shot down, but all the pilots were rescued. The convoy started with forty merchant ships. Twenty-eight made it to Russia. The exact number of crewmembers lost was not yet tallied.

Unexpectedly, Jack hugged Sparks and declared, "And I shot down at least one of those buggers. Yeah. I will tell the crew!" Finally, some positive news. He ran down to the mess hall and spread the word, with all the correct numbers, which circulated around the ship in minutes.

Ron appeared in the mess and spotted Jack and ran up and shook his hand.

"Great news, Jack," he exclaimed as he pumped Jack's hand. "We make a hell of a team! I wonder how many of those planes we hit, later crashed in the sea. Where is Fitz?"

Later that evening, Captain Gleason was reviewing the British reports with the officers. The meeting was informal, and Jack was allowed to sit in. The officers had studied the data and agreed with all of it except the torpedo count.

The Captain offered his analysis. "Each U-boat carried fourteen torpedoes. If there were only U-boats launching torpedoes, to have seven hundred torpedoes expended, there would have to have been fifty U-boats attacking them during the week. There's no way fifty U-boats were present. A more realistic number of U-boats in the attack was twelve. If each shot ten torpedoes, which is unlikely, the number would be one hundred and twenty expended. And that may be high, since six U-boats were sunk. And of the twelve convoy ships sunk, only about half were hit by torpedoes. The other half were struck by bombs. The German aircraft with torpedoes were likely more lethal than the U-boats. But each plane carried only one torpedo. No one estimated that there were six hundred torpedo-carrying aircraft. So, the reality is, there were not seven hundred torpedoes launched during the attacks. A more realistic estimate would be fifty torpedoes from U-boats and perhaps seventy from the bombers. Still, a frighteningly high number. It's amazing how low the ship losses were."

While this data was being analyzed, Jack was wondering who had time to count the torpedoes or even estimate the number. It sounded like an exercise in futility. The good news was that the *Esek Hopkins* had somehow survived...for the first half.

CHAPTER 23

Life is Cheap

EARLY THE NEXT MORNING, THE Russian stevedores gathered on the pier and started up the stairs onto the deck. To the crew's surprise, all the stevedores were women and girls! With no delay, the masts, rigging, and winches on the *Esek Hopkins* got busy, and bundles of logs were prepared and lifted from the pier and slowly, accurately delivered into hold number one. The ship's crew operated the cranes and helped secure logs while they watched the slender, muscular girls, like worker bees, efficiently wrestling with the huge, heavy bundles. They seemed more organized and capable than the males in Molotovsk, perhaps because the women were not prisoners. And they were not drunk. The towering vast holds of the ship did not intimidate the females and they began to neatly pack the chambers with logs and with enthusiasm.

It was difficult to determine what motivated these hardworking women. It certainly was not the pay. Patriotism might do it. More likely fear. Nothing distracted them, not even the men on board, who tried casually to make connections.

Late one morning, it began snowing. Tiny flakes poured from the sky. The hearty women continued their labors as the white flakes covered the dock and decorated their shoulders and caps. Nothing bothered them. They seemed happiest when they were singing their Russian folk songs. Tough women.

It took two or three days to fill each of five holds with logs and wood chips. By mid-October, the task of loading the *Esek Hopkins* was complete. The ship squatted deep in the freezing water like a stuffed hog. The crew hoped that now, at last, they must be closer to departure.

If they were, it was a well-kept secret. One morning the Captain read the contents of a letter over the loudspeaker. It was from Winston Churchill, who commended all the forces of PQ 18 for their bravery during the terrific German onslaught. The letter ended by noting that the "world is watching our heroism." *A little late, Winston, but a nice touch,* thought Jack. But, what else? No announcement about departure. Word filtered down from the bridge that the admirals were delaying. But why?

Agonizing boredom again set in. During his free time, Jack decided to take the ferry to Archangel alone so he could assess the length of time it took to arrive in Archangel and report to his colleagues. The trip took about an hour and the ferry docked, not at Molotovsk, but, near the center of Archangel. There appeared to be considerable new damage to the large docks, but a small ferry could tie up at many alternate sites. After disembarking, Jack walked around the center of town and noted more destruction than when he was last there. Some piles of bricks were still smoldering. *If this war ever ends, how are they going to clean up this mess,* he pondered. Fortunately, the Intourist Hotel appeared intact and there was considerable traffic in and out the front door. One wondered if this was a place where spying occurred on a large scale. Perhaps the Luftwaffe purposely did not bomb this spot.

Jack stopped in at their famous bar and bumped into a "limey" sailor. The mate was assigned to a minesweeper which also served as a rescue ship. He told Jack that during the three days of attacks on PQ 18, their ship alone pulled two hundred and fourteen survivors out of the sea. He also claimed that the Russian fighters had knocked out seventy Luftwaffe bombers on that last day of fighting. The Ruskies aggressively attacked the German aircraft shortly after they took off from the airfield in Norway. Jack was delighted to hear the story but wondered if the numbers were exaggerated each time the tale was told. Jack had become a bit more suspicious of the numbers thrown about after hearing their captain ratchet down the torpedo count from the earlier British reports.

As Jack strolled around, he noted that only a few stores were open in this dark, dismal place. But Jack spotted some used ice skates for sale in a store window. Since winter was quickly making its appearance, he purchased a pair for twenty-five rubles, which was less than one dollar.

Once he arrived on the *Esek Hopkins* with his new ice skates, there was hot scuttlebutt swirling. The night before one of the female Russian stevedores was machine-gunned in her legs by a Russian soldier. The reason for the shooting was unclear and her status was unknown. She certainly was not going to be able to function in this war with no legs. She might have been better off if they killed her. But maybe that was the point.

The October days quickly shortened, as the month dragged by slowly. All the talk on board revolved around the departure date. What could hold them up next? The *Esek Hopkins* was now sitting comfortably low in the water with the level at twenty-five feet on the bow.

Refueling might be the answer. On October 15, a British destroyer pulled up along the *Esek Hopkins* and tied up for the day. Was this a hopeful sign? No! The purpose was to refuel the destroyer. The entire crew was disappointed the fuel was not going in the other direction.

There was a little humor that afternoon. A British commander came aboard to chat with Captain Gleason. Jack was in the helm room and for some reason, with a twinkle in his eye, Gleason introduced Jack as Captain Dodd. The British officer started to salute Jack, but noticed he did not have on the appropriate stripes and possessed two lingering black eyes. He grinned at Gleason, then at Jack, and they all had a laugh. Perhaps Gleason really did like Jack.

Winter made its appearance early and the night temperatures were falling well below freezing. Ice was forming in thin sheets on the ship decks and walking became precarious.

Snow was reliably blanketing the scene. The waterways were freezing. Jack went on shore several times and tried out his ice skates on nearby ponds. On most days there was harsh wind from the arctic north with intermittent heavy snow. The only advantage of the wind was that it kept the snow from accumulating on the skater's pond. A few local kids using sticks and a rock tried to play a primitive form of hockey as Jack looked on.

Despite the blistering cold and wind, Jack took another ferry to Archangel on Saturday, October 17. He could round up no ship mates to join him. It was too cold. He needed some exercise and walked around town for a few hours. Despite the bad weather the city was more alive than in the past. The foul weather conditions were keeping the bombers away. Many kids were out playing in the snow, and some had skis and a sled. Jack was surprised to see so many children in this war-torn city. He had assumed they had been transferred inland to safer towns. Several kids approached him and indicated they wanted him to pull them on their sled. They called him *Americanski.* He complied and dragged them for at least a quarter of a mile amidst their screams and giggles. He needed the exercise and enjoyed it as his hot breath mixed with the frigid air. A brief snowball fight developed. Finally, he waved his arms in the air, as if to surrender and started off. They screamed for him to stay, but Jack had his fill and was huffing and puffing, so he said his goodbyes.

Not long after leaving the children, he came upon a barber shop and went in for a trim. The barber spoke a little English. He made a gallant attempt to thank Jack for helping out his country. He repeated, "*Spasibo, spasibo.*" Jack nodded a lot. The haircut turned out fairly well. Jack requested no trimming of his outstanding eyebrows. He joked with the barber that they helped keep his head warm. The barber did not seem to comprehend the effort at humor.

The sky remained overcast with snow on and off. Jack decided to get a room at the Intourist Hotel again rather than return to the morose ship. Good food was still available, and he entertained himself with two glasses of wine. He slept late on a bunk in a warm room with three other snoring men.

During breakfast in the hotel, Alex appeared, noisily stomping his boots as he entered the dining area.

"Hey, Alex, what brought you out on this winter morning?"

Alex waved and approached Jack's table as he peeled off layers of clothing.

"I guess I missed you!" he retorted with a chuckle. "I got tired of checkers and cards and needed to get off the ship. You should see the river. It's freezing up quickly. The ferry had to break through the thick ice. I am not sure how much longer we can make these trips. Unless we want to make the long walk on the ice."

After Alex ordered a hot chocolate, he reminded Jack that there was a meeting of all the Allied seamen that day at 1:00 p.m. in a local restaurant. Jack had completely forgotten. It was practically noon now. They chatted for a while, then started to the nearby restaurant for the meeting along with other gaggles of military men trudging to the same destination.

The large eatery had all the tables moved to the sides and the rows of chairs were filling quickly with Allied sailors. Some Russian officials and translators sat in chairs at the front of the room. They started on time with one of the Russian army officers addressing the group. A translator stood next to him with his own mic. They spouted out the usual appreciation for the Allied efforts to deliver supplies.

The next speaker was the mayor of Archangel who informed the group that some of the airplanes recently unloaded from the ships were already assembled and seeing action against the Nazis. In addition, the American Sherman tanks were participating in the battle of Stalingrad.

He predicted the huge German army would soon surrender there. Applause. His prediction turned out to be correct.

After all the speakers had finished, a small orchestra appeared and within minutes they were playing traditional Russian music. Then dancers appeared, and the orchestra played folk songs while the dancers put on a grand show of traditional Russian dancing. All were invited to join in. The few female dancers were kept busy dancing with American and British navy men. Jack liked to dance but there were too few women.

Jack and Alex started for the main door to work their way back to the Intourist Hotel. The mayor and his entourage had just preceded them and were walking into the street toward a shiny black sedan parked nearby. Out of nowhere, two loud shots rang out. Reflexively Jack and Alex ducked. Alex slid behind a concrete column just as four or five more shots rang out in quick succession. Jack crawled behind another column as chaos exploded. He peeped around the edge of the column to see a group of men looking down at two individuals flat on their backs. One appeared to be the mayor. Several men had pulled automatic weapons from their overcoats and were turning and inspecting everyone nearby. No one was assisting the men on the ground, suggesting no assistance was required. Jack looked up toward Alex and whispered above the screaming and yelling, "An assassination!" Alex nodded and pointed toward the back of the hall and whispered, "Slowly." Jack rose as slowly as he could and followed Alex. They purposely relaxed their arms at their sides and blended into the confused crowd, some going toward the front door and others heading toward the back of the building. The pair exited out a side doorway and casually glided into a side street. Outside stood the dance girls who were crying and nearly hysterical as troops surrounded them. Screaming sirens approached the scene. Alex nodded to the right, and they casually dismissed themselves from the turmoil. Jack unconsciously, unavoidably, started walking quickly, but Alex admonished him, "Walk slowly, man. We do not want to attract attention. Those guys will shoot first and ask questions later." Jack nodded and strolled like he was in an Easter parade with all the time in the world.

As they distanced themselves from the crime scene, Jack could no longer remain silent. "What the hell was that? And who got shot?" he asked.

"Not sure. But it looked like there were two dead men there. Likely the mayor got plugged, then the bodyguards killed the shooter. I counted two shots first, then five shots to kill the assassin. All close range. Neat job. Who knows why? Life is cheap here."

"Alex, do you and I attract trouble?" Jack asked with a grim laugh. Jack began to perspire as they gained distance from the turmoil. After all they had been through at sea, it was nearly as dangerous here in this rough, shattered, dismal city.

Alex and Jack made their way back to the Intourist Hotel, and to no one's surprise, the bar was packed. They joined up with some British and American sailors and started on a few beers. No one at the bar brought up the murders a half a mile away. But the rumor mill was going on about the female stevedore who was shot in the legs. Surprise, surprise, she was involved in a love triangle. Too bad one of her boyfriends had a machine gun. Supposedly he was arrested. Talk then centered on the meeting, the orchestra, and the dancing that afternoon. Apparently, no one yet knew about the murders. Alex whispered to Jack, "Let's keep it quiet for now. If we leak it, the bar will empty in a panic and folks run up to see the action."

Jack replied, "Got it. Should be interesting to see when the word gets out. The authorities might want to suppress it for now."

When the topic of females came up, which it always did, one of the Brits, a sailor named Harry, who had had a few beers too many, said he knew exactly where the female stevedores stayed. It was just a few blocks away. Cheers went up. With the men's inhibitions suppressed by alcohol, a handful of curious sailors followed Harry as he charged out of the bar into the cold. Jack went along to distract him from the earlier devastation. Somehow, he lost track of Alex.

Fortunately, the gaggle of rambunctious men headed in the opposite direction of the murder scene.

The dorm was located in a small run-down rooming house which had no signage. Seven sloshed men marched through the front door. There was no one at the front desk to offer resistance. Led by Harry, the group followed him up one flight of stairs and down a poorly lit hallway. He knocked on a random door as the team chuckled noisily. Several thought the whole thing was a joke. He was likely taking them to a men's dorm.

Surprisingly, a woman slowly cracked the door. Harry politely tried his Russian. Then impatiently, he pushed the door and they all flooded in. Their eyes popped open. The room had a large number of bunk beds, sparce on sheets and blankets. About half the bunks were occupied with women. Some of the occupants did not even wake up. They apparently went to sleep early so they could be up at 3:00 a.m. Many of the women were frightened by this motley group of men while others smiled. Perhaps an opportunity?

Well, what now? Harry was not joking; he had actually led them to the female dorm.

Several looked to him for leadership. Still under the effects of his numerous beers, he suggested they invite the ladies back to the Intourist Hotel for a drink. Several cheers rang out. He tried his Russian again with little success. One of the girls in a bunk knew English, and she was able to express to her roommates the desires of the unruly group of men. Four of the girls jumped up in various stages of dress and quickly threw on their shirts and work pants and boots to join the uninhibited characters. There were considerable Russian words flowing back and forth, but in the end, the four females joined their new male comrades and marched into the streets back to the Intourist Hotel for a few drinks.

On the way, two Americans excitedly were searching their pockets for their rubbers. One came up short. He looked at Jack.

"Hey, pal, can you spare a rubber. I could sure use a little entertainment tonight!" Good fortune looked upon the poor soul. Jack pulled out a rubber and handed it to the somewhat desperate chap. "Hey, man, you are the greatest! Thank you. I will pay you back someday." Jack laughed and replied, "All I want is a full report."

Jack could not help but smile as he watched the entire episode unfold. The motley swarm barreled into the bar and created a joyful scene among the patrons. The bartender could not pour the beers fast enough. Harry, swaying back and forth like a clock pendulum, ordered the first round. Jack got in line and grasped his free beer. The humorous scene helped distract Jack from the unsavory, traumatic scene earlier in the evening.

Not surprisingly, like the Sabine women, the four got all the attention, whether they desired it or not. One was not unattractive. She was one of the few Russians Jack had seen who had a decent set of teeth. Soon dancing started with "music" supplied by the women singing.

Laughter filled the room. It had been a long time since any of the sailors had such a fun night.

Jack was bushed. It was after midnight. He evacuated the scene before it got too raucous. He found the hotel manager and was able to talk his way into a room with nine other mates. All beds were occupied, but Jack was desperate. He climbed the steps slowly to the third floor as the musical laughter swirled up from below. He visited the public toilet to evacuate his bladder. As he walked in, a woman walked out. He gave her a big smile. Jack was thinking this might not be such a bad custom after all.

As Jack stumbled into the guest room, he saw an open space on the floor, along with a few blankets. A quick visual inspection confirmed all bunks were occupied. The single, poorly insulated window allowed a rudely cold breeze to squeeze through. Jack dropped to the chilly wooden planks like a sack of coal and surrounded himself in the blanket as best he could. His mind wandered. *What a day. It started innocently enough playing with kids in the snow, then to a meeting of allies, followed by a murder and ending with a raid of the ladies' dorm. Life certainly was interesting in Archangel. And cheap.*

He was delirious in short order. The loud snoring from his compatriots filled the space.

His last thought before being overtaken by the mist of sleep was, "Where is Alex?"

Alex was fine. He was cuddled up in a spare room at the stevedores' boarding house, under a blanket, with the Russian woman who possessed a "decent set of teeth."

CHAPTER 24

A Measure of Justice

THE NEXT FEW DAYS ON board the *Esek Hopkins* were a continuous stream of hours filled with abject boredom. Alex quietly raved about Natasha, the woman with the nice teeth. Clever Alex would find a way to meet her again. Neither Jack nor Alex heard any news about the murder they witnessed, and they maintained their vow of silence. Finally, three days later, the Captain mentioned to the officers that all crewmen going to shore should be especially careful and avoid any quarrels, fights or controversies because there was a report that the mayor of Archangel had been shot and killed by a local radical. The assassin was shot immediately by the mayor's bodyguards. Particularly disturbing, said Captain Gleason, was the fact that the mayor had been delivering a speech at a meeting of the allies. The police and KGB were on high alert. The officers passed this information quickly among the men of *Esek Hopkins.* Similarly, the officers and crews of all ships in the convoy were notified. Jack and Alex decided there was no reason to tell anyone about their presence at the murder. It made little difference.

As the days in Russia shortened, the crew became more anxious and disagreeable, especially with security now tighter on shore. Was this cruise to hell ever going to end? None of the men could imagine spending a winter iced in at this godforsaken place. If they did not get moving in the next two or three weeks, the entire fleet could be embedded for the length of the winter in one of the coldest spots on earth. The Russians did have ice breakers, but could they be relied on? Why not depart now, rather than risk getting trapped? There were many other practical reasons they should depart. One was the Russians could not reliably supply the ships with adequate food and potable water. They could barely feed themselves, much less several hundred British and American sailors. And the ships of PQ 18 were tied up like sitting ducks.

The spring of 1943 would likely see more German bombers, and even attacks on the port from surface ships. They could easily trap and destroy every ship in the port. After all, the *Tirpitz* could lob destructive seventeen-hundred-pound shells over twenty miles. Archangel could be leveled like Murmansk. Finally, they were wasting precious manpower and shipping capacity by sitting in port. The twenty-eight ships, each capable of hauling over eight thousand tons of supplies, meant that two hundred and twenty-four thousand tons of cargo space was sitting unused. And their well-trained, experienced crews were idling away trying to stay occupied when there was very little to do. They were sufficiently bored and restless to the point of causing trouble. One member of the Navy crew on the *Virginia Dare* had been taking apart a 20mm shell for some unknown reason when it exploded and tore his hand apart. Accidents happen when men feel useless. The number of "friendly" fist fights on some ships had increased in volume and brutality. What the men should be doing was hauling much-needed supplies from the US to other ports in the war-torn world.

The only possible reason to remain in port was to load up each and every merchant ship with the lumber as ballast. The *Esek Hopkins* was loaded to capacity by October 17. But no ship could depart until all the other ships were loaded. They must travel in convoys to survive the anticipated German attacks. No ship could or would sail alone. And of course, the escort ships had to be fueled up and have their full complement of ammunition.

The only other minor good reason for delaying departure was that the hours of daylight were shorter with each passing day. For the Luftwaffe, this reduced their window of attack. On the other hand, U-boats had a higher kill rate if they hunted in the dark.

This was the situation in the early winter of 1942 for the Liberty Ships and their crews trapped in Archangel.

Finally, a positive sign. A British corvette pulled up along the side of the *Esek Hopkins.*

This time, not to take on fuel, but instead to deliver huge numbers of three-inch and five-inch cannon shells along with three-hundred boxes of 20mm ammo. Then a negative: That same day, October 26, one of the crewmen was carried off the ship to go to a hospital in Archangel. They said he had yellow fever. Jack heard that was spread by mosquitoes. What mosquitoes? Jack hoped the crewman made it back before they departed. No one would want to spend the winter in Archangel in the midst of the war. And who knew about the hospital. Jack wondered if any doctors or nurses even spoke English.

Then the crew got word from the first mate that the Russian government was going to give the American and British crews a bonus of one month's pay. Great news for all, but everyone wondered where the Russians were going to get the money.

The next day Sparks got a news bulletin that the Japs had sunk two American aircraft carriers in the Pacific. One of them was the *Wasp.* A crewman on board had a cousin on the *Wasp.* That dreadful news made the entire crew regret their bellyaching.

On the same day some crew members returned from Archangel with news from a German broadcast. It claimed that the Allied convoy due next in Archangel was attacked off the island of Spitzbergen and seventeen ships had been sunk. The convoy was scheduled to arrive in Archangel around November 5. Another report indicated that all the German U-boats had been recalled from the East Coast of the US to concentrate their attacks on the convoys in the North Atlantic. The *Esek Hopkins* crew seemed quiet the next few days.

The following day, the Captain announced on the loudspeaker

that the German broadcast was propaganda. There was no Allied convoy at that time, in that place. The next convoy would not depart from Scotland until sometime in December. And the German U-boats had departed from the East Coast in July, not October. He completed his announcement by asserting, "The Germans are trying to get at our nerves."

It was working.

The days crawled by. Board games and gambling ramped up. By now, the crew seemed resigned to the fact that no amount of bellyaching would get them out of Russia faster. So, they tended to their duties and tried not to complain. The saying on board became, "Remember the *Wasp* and quit complaining."

Second Mate Williams directed Jack to busy himself with checking all the supplies in the four lifeboats. He told Jack that the medical officer wanted a quart can of Vaseline in each lifeboat. It turned out rubbing Vaseline on the hands, feet, and face could dramatically reduce the likelihood of frostbite. In addition, Jack was to confirm that each lifeboat had an adequate water supply, chocolate bars, and biscuits. There was a rumor that some crew members had taken the chocolate bars from lifeboats to use for enticing girls in Archangel. Jack confirmed that most of the chocolate bars indeed were missing. Chocolate was important for emergency survival by supplying energy and keeping sailors alert. He raided the galley and replaced most of the missing bars. In addition, Jack made certain that at least three Vaco suits were present in each lifeboat. He was following orders even though he believed it took too long to put the suits on. In an emergency, men were lucky if they got their life vests on. Jack did not see a single sailor jump in the sea with a Vaco suit on during the earlier attacks. Even so, the suits were supplied to each crewmember and were stored in the crewmember's stateroom. He also checked the state of the wooden mast and sail provided in each lifeboat along with the functioning of the two flashlights. Williams wanted each lifeboat to be in perfect order. So did Jack.

Although no one had officially given notice of a departure date, the officers seemed to be preparing for sailing. Then a rumor started, "on good authority," that the admirals had decided all the merchant ships were spending the winter in Archangel. Officers tried to put this rumor to rest quickly. But once a rumor starts, it can't be retracted.

Jack was well rested when he woke up on November 5. He was anxious to cast off, but for once, he had plans on this day and he was grateful this was not the chosen day. He dressed, exercised, had a quick breakfast and then went back to his stateroom to write a few letters home and one to Penny. He did not believe the rumor about spending the winter in Archangel and was convinced they would soon depart. Therefore, he took the ferry to Archangel to mail his letters. This was an act of faith, realizing there was probably only a fifty percent chance of successful mail delivery to the States, or to Scotland. Penny was on his mind. Again. He had received no mail from anyone. Most sailors had not.

As he clamored down the ship's stairs to go ashore, heavy snow started. He trudged toward the ferry dock, and to his surprise, standing there were Captain Gleason and the first mate. They were going to town to negotiate with the local authorities to obtain more food for the *Esek Hopkins.* The ship had run out of eggs two weeks earlier and the crew noticed the smaller portions and absence of desserts and cakes. If they were soon casting off, the ship would need to stock up. After the three settled on the ferry, there was little talk during the one-hour trip due to the wind, the chill, and the heavy snow. The temperature was forecasted to go as low as ten degrees that night. Once in town they split, and Jack mailed his letters at the dilapidated post office. He then went shopping in spite of the blizzard-like conditions. One store was practically giving away a pair of skis and as crazy as it seemed, Jack decided to purchase them. He donned them once outside and tried to ski back to the ferry dock. He had no previous experience with skis, and it was a struggle with several clumsy falls. Jack quickly realized the falls were easy: it was the getting up part which was difficult.

November dragged on. The weather got worse.

The Germans stopped flying.

Meanwhile, the war continued at sea. German U-boats would not return to port simply because the weather turned cold. The water temperature below the surface was quite a bit warmer than the surface air. Captain Hymmen, aboard *U-408*, still had eleven torpedoes on board. He had not fired one since their successful attack on the Convoy PQ 18 on September 13. Since PQ 18 had arrived in Archangel, no new convoys had passed through the North Atlantic.

Boredom also permeated the crew of *U-408*. The submarine spent all its time on the surface unless the wave and wind action prohibited it. But even on the surface, the life of the crew changed very little. In the cold of winter, it was nearly impossible to go out on the narrow deck. Only on calm, windless days was that possible. Even then, the cold would not allow more than a few minutes outside. And once on deck, there was little to do except breathe in some fresh air and stretch. With no convoys passing to Archangel, this quadrant of the Atlantic was quiet enough for the Kriegsmarine to allow U-boats to alternate returning to port to change crews, refuel, get provisions, and take on new torpedoes. Since Hymmen had expended only three torpedoes, his ship was last on the list to return to port from this sector. That date was approaching soon: November 10.

Hymmen's vessel was performing the required crisscross pattern over a one-hundred-mile quadrant on Thursday, November 5. At noon, there was a two-foot chop and clear skies as they held their course due south at one hundred and eighty degrees. The requisite two officers were stationed on the open twelve-foot conning tower keeping watch. Each had powerful binoculars. This repetitive routine had long ago lost its excitement. Radio communications from Kriegsmarine headquarters confirmed that no enemy ship or convoy had been spotted in their sector for weeks. They were northeast of Iceland and still within the Arctic Circle. This final swing south would complete their mission and direct them home.

The two officers were shivering in the cold air and remained in active conversation while clapping their gloved hands to help stay warm. Puffs of their condensed breath quickly vaporized in the breeze as they discussed the anxiously awaited home-cooked meals and compared it to the tiresome, ugly food available on board. And a bath; everyone longed for a clean bath. The only background sound was that of the waves slapping against the side of *U-408* as she pushed through the cold Arctic seas at eight knots. Captain Hymmen was below, in his tiny cabin, lying on the only private bunk on the *U-408*, reading Goethe.

On November 5 at 11:15 a.m. a US Navy PBY twin-engine amphibious aircraft took off from Egilsstadir Airport on the east coast of Iceland. With seven crew members aboard, she was on a routine search mission for U-boats. The aircraft was specifically designed for submarine search-and-destroy missions. She carried four depth charges under her wings. The Navy pilots called these planes the "Angels of Death." The name was justified. During the war, they were responsible for forty confirmed U-boat sinkings and many more damaged. They had a range of two thousand five hundred miles and could fly as high as fifteen thousand feet. They were not designed for speed; they topped out at only one hundred and ninety-six miles per hour. But for typical search-and-destroy missions they cruised at one hundred and twenty-five miles per hour, which was perfect for sub chasing. These humble-looking seaplanes were not to be trifled with. Each had a Browning 50-caliber machine gun in the nose, a pair in each side cupola, and another aft which could aim downward. They were quite capable of defending themselves. The acronym PBY stood for "Patrol Bomber Y." The Y was code for the manufacturer, Consolidated Aircraft. Over three thousand were produced. As sea planes, they also were used to rescue downed pilots or crews from sunken ships. And because of their long range they were excellent reconnaissance aircraft.

The pilot, Russ Miller, did not think they would go on a mission that day because of low cloud cover and intermittent snow. But, by 10:00 a.m. a breeze from the northwest blew all the weather out to sea. Their plan was to cover a large grid east of Iceland. They were to return to base by 3:00 p.m., just before sunset. Russ loved the twin-engine PBY. She was the most versatile plane he had ever flown. It was in her DNA to take off from water or land. She was tight to fly and followed commands perfectly. He loved his time in the air.

They taxied down the runway and, after tower clearance, Russ slammed the throttle full down and the pair of twelve hundred horsepower Pratt & Whitney engines roared and thrust her down the bumpy concrete runway and into the clear blue sky.

Before takeoff, Russ was told there were no American or British ships scheduled to be sailing in their district, so anything observed under-way was considered German. There had been little activity in the recent past since Convoy PQ 18 passed by about five weeks earlier. Only occasional small fishing boats were encountered. In fact, Russ had not attacked any enemy vessels since September 15. And that was a miss.

An hour into their flight, on a southern tack, the copilot, Max Caldwell, spotted a thin white line straight ahead about twelve miles away. It clearly was a surface ship of some kind and was cruising a course directly south at about eight to ten knots, judging by her long wake. Russ quickly dropped the altitude to two thousand feet. "Definitely a U-boat," observed Max as he called in for clearance to attack.

"Headquarters says go for it. No friendlies in the area." Within one minute they could see the sub begin to submerge. They were about two miles away. Russ dropped the altitude to fifty feet to improve the odds of a strike.

On the intercom, Max suggested they drop two cans on the first pass.

Russ replied, "Agreed. Set depth for forty feet. Phil, drop when you are ready." The bombardier replied, "Roger that. I have her in my sights."

A few seconds later, "Two released."

Russ reminded the rear gunner to give them a sighting on how close the cans were.

He replied through the intercom, "Splash slightly forward of descent point. Looks close to the shadow."

About five seconds later, Phil observed, "Both detonations went off. Some black in the fountain."

Russ was banking the PBY hard to port. He strained to his left to see the last of the water columns collapse into the sea. "I think we were close. I'll line up for a second run."

All seven crew members had eyes riveted on the sea.

The two German officers on the conning tower of *U-408* were commenting on how pleasant it was without the frigid waves crashing in their faces. During a pause in their conversation, one looked into the sky.

"Do you hear that?" as he turned in a complete circle.

"You have good ears. I hear nothing but waves and wind," his fellow officer said. "Look, behind us."

A tiny dot was on the horizon descending on a course directly astern. The officer reflexively pushed the alarm button and they both scrambled down through the narrow round hatch. The angle of the U-boat had already turned downward as they hit the deck inside. At the sound of the dive alarm, the crew reflexively scurried toward the front of the U-boat, through the narrow passageways to add weight forward and help the vessel submerge quicker.

Captain Hymmen was at the helm station as the officers hit the deck. "*Was haben Sie*? (What do you have?)

The officer who first heard the aircraft exclaimed, "A plane diving on us. It looked like a PBY. Coming in directly behind us."

Captain Hymmen showed appropriate concern on his wrinkled face. Now he and his crew were on the other side of the battle.

He barked, "Dive to one hundred and twenty meters. Secure all stations. Engage backup lighting. Electric motors at full." The twin diesel engines had already been turned off. The bow tilted down further. Then complete silence. They were about twenty-five feet below the surface when their sonar detected the splashes above.

Seconds later the two depth charges exploded with extreme violence at their designated depth of forty feet. *U-408* was moving quickly downward at a steep angle. At the depth of forty feet the aft third of the submarine was within twenty feet of the exploding depth charges on either side of the hull. The drop was near perfect.

Hymmen's last human sensation was one of exploding pain in his ears and crushing pressure on his skull.

Russ Miller continued his wide turn to port and developed a plan to run a parallel track over the sub from the same direction as the first pass. In his mind, he envisioned a large oval racetrack. He turned to port again to get into the home stretch. Now straight ahead, two miles out, he could see the disturbance in the sea where they dropped the first cans.

"Phil, you ready to drop the next load?" asked Russ.

Phil replied, "Ready, sir. I will look for the shadow. By now she could be at one hundred feet or more." Beyond one hundred feet, even in clear water, subs were difficult to visualize from the air.

Max said as he was squinting, "I see some debris in the water. And it looks like some oil."

As they closed in on the site, Russ confirmed the observation of his copilot. "Yup, looks like we only wasted two cans. Phil, hold your fire. Can you confirm?" The intercom became garbled as everyone seemed to speak at once. A couple of guys cheered. There was no question. As they flew directly over the area at fifty feet, black oil was seen bubbling up from below with huge volumes of debris bobbing on the waves. Then body parts and damaged life vests appeared. The photographer snapped photos with the onboard camera.

Max looked at Russ and inquired with a smile, "Should we look for another U-boat or head home?"

Predictably Russ declared, "I feel pretty good. Let's head home and beat the sunset. A cold beer would be nice."

There were no objections.

At the moment the depth charges exploded, Jack Dodd had just fallen down for the third time while struggling to get to the ferry dock with his new skis. Had he and his fellow shipmates known, they would have been pleased and gratified that the U-boat which sank two of their fellow merchant ships on September 13 had paid its final bill and was now ruptured, crushed, and resting awkwardly on the sandy bottom of the sea.

CHAPTER 25

An Altercation

ANOTHER MONTH WAS SLOWLY DISAPPEARING before his eyes. Jack was beginning to think they *would* spend the winter holed up on the *Esek Hopkins*, iced in at this godforsaken port. He continued his daily routine of exercise, reading, letter writing, deck duties, then free afternoons. His skis allowed a new form of entertainment. Periodically he took the ferry to Archangel where he located a decent slope near the dock. Some kids showed up after school and were able to communicate their training skills to their new amateur skiing friend. Jack appreciated this and started bringing little gifts. Sometimes he would stay for dinner at the Intourist Hotel. He enjoyed interacting with other American and British crew members who also were frequenting the bar and entertaining the ladies.

Jack was now composing at least one letter per day. His notes were characteristically short. The rotation each day was first to his mother, then Penny, then his sisters and brothers. With time, his guilt regarding how he may have changed was slowly diminishing. Most certainly because he was no longer shooting at aircraft. In addition, his tremor had disappeared.

In one sense, it was sad that each letter was similar, with a brief outline of his mundane existence and the doldrums of the pathetic port, the progressive food shortages, and the air attacks. There was not much else to tell. If his sisters compared letters, they would quickly realize they were much the same. Tough luck: he was fulfilling his duty to write. And on his end he had received only one letter, and that was from his mother four weeks ago. Letters to the crew followed a circuitous and cumbersome route. It often took weeks for mail to arrive from the States. And the mail bag was dumped on board only once or twice a week while tied up in Archangel. Clearly, it was not a priority for the authorities. Even the Captain grumbled about the absence of mail.

With his considerable spare time, and surrounded by utter boredom on most days, Jack was feeling more comfortable fantasizing and comforting himself with thoughts about Penny. He was still second-guessing himself. Should he have made a commitment to her? Could it possibly have worked out? Should his notes to her be more affectionate? The circular thinking always returned to the same end point. He was caught up in a dreadful world war and could be dead on short notice. She lived three thousand miles from his home. It made more sense for her to find a mate closer to her home. Still…

The Luftwaffe apparently was satisfied that they had damaged the city and docks enough that they could reduce the bombing runs. The officers on board were convinced they had run out of pilots and aircraft. When an occasional reconnaissance plane appeared overhead, and the Russians were kind enough to greet them with heavy cannon fire.

On Sunday, November 8, after a full day of skiing with the local youngsters, Jack was greeted with some good news when he arrived back on the ship. An Allied convoy of about five hundred warships and landing craft had deposited American troops in northern Africa. This was Operation Torch, the first act of aggression by the U.S during the war. Jack was overjoyed to hear some positive news. Everyone was chattering about it in the Forum. The US troops were now actively aiding the British who were fighting against the clever desert fox, German General Erwin Rommel. Jack wondered if he would ever get a Liberty Ship to that part of the world. At least he would not be freezing.

Captain Gleason had been spending more time ashore. Something was up. Finally, a tanker ship tied up adjacent to the *Esek Hopkins* and pumped fuel aboard. More boxes of supplies and ammunition appeared, which Jack and the crew happily loaded in the holds. Then on Saturday, November 14, Russian authorities climbed aboard to search the ship and count the crew. More local paranoia. God forbid some Russian should escape. The whole country was like a vast prison. Then all shore leave was canceled. The final sign that departure was imminent was when the Russian pilot showed up on the bridge at 7:00 p.m.

The next morning, November 15, Jack made it his business to be on the bridge early. Captain Gleason had spent the night on shore and was not present when second mate, Mark Williams arrived, followed by the Russian pilot, one Sergi. The pilot gave orders to start the engine and make preparations to cast off. Mark and Jack protested, but Sergi said an ice breaker was creating a path as they spoke. He promised they would retrieve the Captain downstream.

Since the pilot had the authority, they were bound to follow his instructions. The lines were released and recovered on board with no fanfare, and Sergi backed the *Esek Hopkins* out into the channel without the Captain. Jack stationed himself on the port wing while Mark was on the starboard wing. Bruce Cockrell arrived on the bridge and stood by the pilot at the helm. The river in this area curved back and forth. Sergi seemed to be traveling a bit fast for the circuitous route. As they rounded one sharp bend to the right, the *Esek Hopkins* swung to port.

Unfortunately, there was a British merchant ship, the *Empire Snow*, tied up on the left side of the channel. Chief Cockrell, Mark, and Jack yelled to Sergi to slow. He ignored the command. The ship continued too fast on a dangerous course, sliding laterally toward the British ship. A layer of ice on the surface cracked and split as the *Esek Hopkins* drifted out of the channel toward the docked merchant ship. Several hands on the *Empire Snow* began to wave and yell at the crew on the deck of the *Esek Hopkins*. Finally, Sergi put the engine in reverse, but too late. Mark screamed to the men on the bow to drop the starboard anchor in hopes it would hold the bow and avoid a collision. Again, too late. Time seemed to slow as the ships were destined for a crash in accordance with the basic laws of physics. All the players watched silently. The port anchor, still in its resting position, first struck the *Empire Snow* with a frightening grating, metallic sound. It punched a hole in the starboard quarter of the hapless British ship, which then crushed into the dock and bounced back, striking the *Esek Hopkins* a second time. The two collisions stopped the momentum of the *Esek Hopkins*.

Everyone near the bow of each vessel ran forward to assess the damage. There was a seven-foot hole on the side of the *Empire Snow*. Fortunately, the penetration was high up and there was no danger of flooding. Sergi ordered the starboard anchor to be pulled and he backed the *Esek Hopkins* away as if it were a bumper car at an amusement park. No one could find any damage to the *Esek Hopkins*, other than paint missing from the anchor. Men on the *Empire Snow* confirmed they saw no damage. Sergi was pleased, signaled to the engine room to go forward, and they continued down the path through the broken ice.

Bruce was practically screaming at Sergi, who ignored him. Jack was fascinated by how indifferent Sergi was following the accident. In the US, both ships would have stayed in port for weeks while an investigation was carried out. The guilty party would have been fined or reprimanded or lost his pilot's license. In Russia, they just kept on sailing. Fortunately, no one was injured. Jack pondered what Captain Gleason would say about the pilot's reckless action.

Jack recalled this was not the first collision for the *Esek Hopkins*. If these minor collisions were the only injury to the ship during this adventure, he would be grateful to God in heaven.

Jack positioned himself outside on the port wing as they cruised out the Dvina River.

The cold breeze blew through his black hair. His lashes fluttered in the wind as he squinted in the distance. In a sense, Jack felt somewhat forlorn. When the *Esek Hopkins* cast off there was no band, no cheering crowds, no flags waving, no fanfare of any kind; only the few emaciated female stevedores who untied the lines waved briefly, then went back to work. And the Captain was not even on board. But on another level, he was happy. The ship had successfully delivered its cargo to Russia and the crew was all in one piece. Only a single crew member was absent.

He was retained in the hospital with "yellow fever." The medical officer, Mr. Arnold, told Jack that he thought the man actually had hepatitis from a virus. That too could turn a man's skin yellow. Jack was glad to have that issue clarified, since there were no mosquitoes in Archangel this winter. Jack did not know the man well, but hoped he had a safe journey home.

As they cruised away, Jack gazed back in the distance at the forlorn spectacle of Archangel. If he never saw the place again, that would be fine. And now the journey home. Three thousand miles—unless they were directed elsewhere. Perhaps Scotland? But Jack was ready for home —for a break. It was time. With furrowed brow, he then wondered what else could go wrong. He knew the Germans were not going to leave them alone. He prayed there would be a full complement of escort ships to protect them. During the inbound trip, the escorts had been crucial in keeping merchant ship losses down. But now they were carrying only lumber. Who cares? Hmm. Maybe the Germans would *not* care. Why trade their precious airplanes for a few ships full of wood?

As the river widened, Sergi found a broad area with deep water and ordered the anchor to be dropped. Here the ship would wait for Captain Gleason's return. The crew waited anxiously for his arrival. They felt naked without him. They would rebel if another captain was assigned to *Esek Hopkins*. That rumor flashed through the crew, causing considerable consternation. He got them here, only he could get them home. Late in the afternoon he was delivered by skiff, as if some sort of savior. The crew actually gathered on the port side and cheered as he climbed up the ladder. When he arrived on deck, he looked curiously at the crew and asked, "What's wrong?" Bruce Cockrell chuckled. "The crew missed you Captain and they just wanted you to feel welcome back home."

The Captain nodded and smiled. "I am not leaving you lads. You won't get off that easy. Now back to your stations."

The same skiff that brought the Captain, took Sergi back. As they exchanged positions on the small boat, the Captain simply nodded to Sergi. Gleason had already learned about the collision. He was not pleased. The one consolation was that Sergi got the ship through the minefields.

When Captain Gleason arrived on the bridge, Bruce, Mark and Jack filled him in with the details. As the Captain digested all they outlined to him, he stroked his chin with a thoughtful "Hmm. Maybe I am lucky I was not on board. I will not be called to any investigation. And I don't plan to delay our departure." Smiles and relief all around.

The next morning, they pulled in the anchor and motored out to get a place in line with the new convoy. Excitement filled the air. The crew was finally headed home. They learned there were thirty-one ships in the convoy, and the *Esek Hopkins* was placed in the third of five rows and the fourth in from the port side. They also learned that there still were two crew members in Archangel besides the man with yellow fever. The two men worked in the engine room and could not be left behind. The ship would not go back to Archangel, but a British destroyer would pick up the men and speed out for drop-off.

Just as the sun was setting, the destroyer pulled up and throttled back to match the *Esek Hopkins'* speed of eight knots. Lines were exchanged between the ships. Everyone from both vessels watched as the transfer took place. Once the lines were secured, each individual crewman jumped into a basket and was slowly pulled to the *Esek Hopkins* as the basket swayed back and forth in the breeze. Each held on for their lives. They had life vests on, but if either had fallen between the ships, they would have been pulled under and either drowned or been ground up by the props.

The transfers were successful. But then something unexpected happened. As the lines were retrieved, for some reason, the destroyer drifted very close to the *Esek Hopkins* and a destroyer davit struck one of the lifeboats on the side of *Esek Hopkins*, leaving a substantial hole. It was lifeboat number two, which, by chance, was the one Jack was assigned to in the event of an emergency. Jack realized that the lifeboat was now worthless until the hole was repaired. He decided he might as well do it himself — tomorrow in the light of day. In addition, the *Esek Hopkins* sustained a few dents and scrapes on the starboard side. Jack wondered if this was some type of metaphysical payback for the *Esek Hopkins* punching a hole in the British merchant ship the day before. The destroyer pulled away with no apparent injury.

As the convoy formed up, two Russian fighters were seen above them. They kept watch until the ships got out of the White Sea. The crew learned that evening that the immediate destination was Reykjavik, Iceland.

The next morning, Jack and his snoring roommates were jarred by the loud cracking of nearby cannon fire. They quickly learned this was a drill on a nearby cruiser and soon the *Esek Hopkins* crew was out on deck testing their own guns. Jack, Ron, and Fitz collected at machine gun station number four and had a renewed level of excitement as they practiced loading and firing.

The days grew noticeably shorter. For some reason the crew got more rambunctious as the nights grew longer and more depressing. Perhaps it was because they were leaving unpredictable Russia, and they could quarrel on board with no risk of ending up in a Russian prison. Or perhaps it was just some newly felt sense of freedom. In any case several fights broke out. Most were brief, minor, and of little significance. But one was not. It involved Ski.

Over the course of the long journey, Ski had managed to irritate several deck cadets over minor incidents. But one built up and boiled over. The cadet, one Myron Stilsky, another Pole, got fed up with Ski's inordinate remarks at dinner and challenged him in front of ten others in the mess. They agreed to settle things down in a small space next to the engine room which was void of logs. Immediately. The two quarrelers and another ten men excitedly headed down to the engine room. The space was cleared of debris to accommodate the boxers. No gloves were used. There was little delay as Ski fired a quick jab and nailed Myron's nose, causing him to fall with blood covering his face.

"You bastard, I wasn't even ready."

"Come and get some more," Ski challenged.

Myron stood slowly, watching every move, expecting another punch as he gained his full stature. Myron was slightly taller but more slender than Ski. He made a faint, which momentarily threw Ski off balance. Myron then made a full roundhouse swing with his right arm and nailed Ski square and hard on his left cheekbone. Observers grimaced as they heard a faint cracking sound. Ski was on his back, spitting blood.

The chief engineer, Steve Littlejohn, saw and heard the commotion and climbed the narrow metal stairs, up past the oscillating piston rods and grinding engine noises, to the main deck, then up to the bridge. Puffing for breath he barged into the helm station to confront the seated Captain, sipping on a cup of coffee, along with Chief Mate Cockrell gazing forward with binoculars and Jack at the helm under the careful supervision of the Captain.

Littlejohn declared between breaths, "Captain, there is an ugly fight down in storage bin number twelve next to the engine room." The Captain stood and ordered, "Cockrell, get down there!"

The Chief handed the binoculars to Jack and took off down the metal stairs, with Littlejohn not far behind. The Captain took the wheel from Jack and said, "Dodd, get Sparks in here to back up, and you go down and be my eyes and ears. And stay out of trouble."

Sparks heard his name and appeared from the back hall. Jack took off. He was not sure exactly where storage bin number twelve was but as he scampered down the engine room stairs, despite the monotonous groaning and grinding of the mechanical rotating parts, he could hear yelling from the adjacent space. He wormed his way, avoiding getting any article of clothing caught in the machinery. By now there must have been twenty men packed in watching the tumult. The Chief had just arrived and held Ski tightly by the arms from behind, as Myron, still on his knees, surveyed the situation. Both men had bloody hands, bloody faces, and bloody mouths with red tint outlining their white teeth. Myron stood with evil emanating from his bruised, swollen eyes. A laceration dripped blood down his forehead.

"Back off, Myron," billowed the Chief as Ski powerfully squirmed left and right to escape his grip. "This little social club meeting is over."

Jack told a mate to get some clean wet rags. He ventured into the ring to see if he could help Chief Cockrell. At this instant, Ski jerked and loosened himself from the Chief and charged for one more swing at Myron. Myron saw it coming and ducked. The Chief momentarily lost his balance and stumbled. Jack lurched toward Ski to push him away. Myron turned swiftly and swung just as Jack appeared and hit Jack over the left orbit, missing Ski entirely. Chief Cockrell recovered and advanced toward Myron and nailed him full face with a jackhammer jab using his clublike fist and knocking him forcefully into the crowd. Jack was holding his face as Ski advanced toward Myron, but the Chief intercepted him with a powerful, bloody blast which collapsed him into a pile on the floor.

The Chief stood, like a triumphant gladiator, in the center of the ring and bellowed, "Anyone else have something to say?" The men backed up and began to scurry for the stairs before they could be remembered.

The Captain was monumentally pissed off. And everyone avoided him—for days. Ski spent four nights locked in the brig and Myron locked in a tiny clinic room. Jack was treated with ice packs and pain meds and, fortuitously, required no sutures. Poor Jack. Two blows in a week. The only sequalae was a prominent black left eye and bright red blood around the white of his eye.

Ralph Arnold, the medical officer, if he was good at anything, he certainly was not good at closing wounds. It later showed on both Ski and Myron, who ended up with ugly, thick, irregular facial scars. Perhaps it added some authenticity to Ski's unhappy demeanor. Ski also ended up with a non-displaced fracture of the left cheekbone which required the new sulfa antibiotic now available on board but in short supply. Myron lost an incisor, which left an impressive gap when he smiled. There was no dentist on board. A mate found the tooth and Myron kept it as a souvenir. Even though there were about fifteen witnesses, the rumor mill churned and seemed to change with each passage around the ship. Myron started it, no, Jack, no, the Chief. It was over a woman, no, money, no, an unsavory claim about someone's mother.

On and on. Since Jack had been sent by the Captain to be his eyes and ears, he prepared a three-page report which more or less accurately described the boxing part of the incident. He handed it to the Captain the next day. The Captain thanked him and for the second time asked Jack how he managed to get a black eye while given specific instructions to "stay out of trouble." Jack's answer did not suffice.

Even the Chief was on the Captain's poop list for slamming the two fighters. But Jack's written report helped the Chief. Jack opined that had the Chief not intervened, the fight may have gone on much longer with more serious injuries. And Jack would never forget watching the Chief's single crushing blows, which disabled both contestants.

When Ski was let out of the brig, he bumped into Jack in a hallway. He made a friendly enough comment to Jack. “Hey. Funny how you got belted by Myron. Not me. I would never have missed.”

Jack replied, “No big deal. Have you learned a lesson about fighting? Two fights on this trip and two scars to show for it.” Jack moved on before Ski could respond.

After breakfast one day, after Myron was out of the brig, he approached Jack. “Sorry about the punch, bub. I was aiming at Ski, the SOB.”

“No worries. It’s just a bruise. Nothing broken. No hard feelings,” Jack replied.

Jack was spending less time on the bridge until Captain Gleason got out of his funk. The next spell of foul weather helped distract the Captain.

CHAPTER 26

Confusion

TO PASS THE TIME, JACK wrote new letters to Penny, his mom, sisters and this time to his brothers who would certainly enjoy the part about the fight. He described the altercation in some detail but left out the part about his black eye. The one thing which kept the crew's spirits up was the knowledge that someone at home thought about them and cared for them. It was a continuing source of hope.

On board ship, the most annoying thing about Jack's black eye was how everyone chuckled whenever they looked at him. Part of it may have been because he got it while trying to break up the fight. It was not "properly" earned. And this time it was one eye and easily seen from across the room as it developed into a deep purple color. Jack thought it was strange that his black eyes were not as impressive when he was struck by Alex. Perhaps the application of ice so quickly helped that time. He became too self-conscious and adamantly refused to be photographed.

The next day was relatively calm and clear, so Jack, black eye and all, spent several hours repairing the hole in lifeboat number two with assistance from three other deck cadets. The final result was pleasing to all. Bruce Cockrell inspected the job and was impressed.

That night, as the ship plugged along at eight knots, the moon was full and the skies were the clearest Jack had seen during the entire journey. He strolled out on deck to take in the calm seas and glistening reflected light. The moon was so bright he could read his watch. He thought what a juicy target the *Esek Hopkins* must be for a U-boat on this bright night, even with her lights out. But all remained quiet.

On November 20, clouds arrived, and winds picked up, and all the distractions of the fight on board were pushed aside. By noon they were in another howling storm, with the men inside getting shuffled around like jumping beans as waves crashed over the bow. The convoy made a course adjustment north and the waves started hitting them on the port beam. This was the worst of all since the wind and waves made the ship rock left and right, creating the most havoc down below. Jack reassured himself that all they had in the holds was lumber and wood chips. No chance of explosion. And that heavy core mass absolutely offered protection from capsizing.

In the morning the visibility was better, but they had lost visual contact with their fellow ships. On the bridge, this fact made everyone very uncomfortable as they watched high waves pound their little ship. Alone. Shared misery was somehow reassuring.

Jack could not sleep and sure enough, at 5:00 a.m., the battle station alarm sounded. Ron and Fitz beat him to gun station number four. It was pitch black as they gazed into the sky.

Then a light flickered in his peripheral vision. It was an unidentified ship behind them. The Captain had sounded the alarm because he thought the ship was a U-boat or enemy surface ship.

The light flickers were a message. Jack was not proficient at translating Morse code, so, uninvited, he trotted down one flight to the bridge to learn more. The unknown ship had commanded, "Identify yourself."

The Captain told the signalman to reply only "*Esek Hopkins.*" The other ship sent, "When did you last see the convoy?" Captain Gleason ordered the mate not to respond.

Then a signal came, "What course are you steering?" Again, the Captain wanted to remain silent.

The last signal said, "Steer one hundred eighty-five. Keep in touch."

There was no further communication from them, and they soon drifted out of sight. The officers on the bridge were split on whether the vessel was friendly or enemy. They had never identified themselves. Therefore, most likely an enemy. The Captain did not sail at one hundred and eighty-five degrees either. That would have taken them south. They were on a two-hundred-and-eighty-degree course to the northwest.

For the next hour the crew froze and shivered at their battle stations, while showered with sheets of freezing salt water. But nothing came of it. If it was an enemy U-boat, they left the *Esek Hopkins* alone. Maybe they decided not to waste a valuable torpedo on a ship filled with lumber. Maybe they were out of torpedoes and did not want to attack an armed merchant ship with their single deck cannon. At the breakfast mess, everyone had the jitters and their own ideas about the mystery ship's identity. Was this trip home going to be more hazardous than the inbound journey? And where were the escorts? Jack was not the only one sleeping poorly.

By midafternoon, when the weather had cleared a bit, they spotted another Liberty Ship in the haze. Two hours later a pair of Allied destroyers appeared. What a relief to see the escorts. A signal conversation ensued. The destroyers had lost all traces of the other ships in the convoy. Oh, joy! At sunset, one of the destroyers instructed the *Esek Hopkins* to turn south to avoid U-boats in a wolfpack ahead. Wow, the Captain certainly was happy to encounter the destroyers. Otherwise, they likely would have been easy pickings by the wolfpack. In addition, the escorts informed the Captain that there were minefields in the vicinity and the *Esek Hopkins* should stay in sight of the destroyers. Perhaps that unidentified ship had given them good advice.

Jack said under his breath, "No wonder we are all getting gray!"

Later that night, the Captain was using the sextant to take a sighting on a star through the breaks in the clouds. Gleason felt they were traveling south for too long. They had lost contact with the destroyer. Jack took the helm for a while as the Captain sat at the chart table and did some course plotting and calculations. After about thirty minutes, he began cursing and told Sparks to wake up the first and second mates. In about five minutes they stumbled up to the bridge, still half asleep.

"Look where we are! Our dead reckoning has taken us way off course." He pointed to the chart. Jack had never seen him so angry. "I want you to double-check my calculations. If I am correct, we are about sixty miles from the coast of Norway. We are lucky the Luftwaffe is not bombing us right now!"

By 1:00 a.m., after all agreed on the *Esek Hopkins'* position, the Captain changed course to two hundred and ninety degrees to carry them toward Iceland. On a chart, the plot of their earlier course looked like they were drunken sailors. Gleason ramped up the RPMs and they got to eleven and a half knots, the maximum speed for the ship. They had lost all contact with Allied ships. Unfortunately, the wind and wave action picked up, making the ride even rougher. Going into the wind and waves, their true speed over ground was likely four knots.

By daybreak, they spotted a cruiser. She identified herself as HMS *Onslaught.* She ordered the *Esek Hopkins* to modify the course to two hundred and forty degrees. Gleason complied. The winds and waves seemed worse now that they were heading straight into them. The *Esek Hopkins* may have dropped her effective speed to one knot—(only one nautical mile every hour).

Jack commented to the Captain, "If this storm doesn't let up, we may never get to Iceland." He did not respond.

The big brass in the Admiralty were always changing their minds. This time the HMS *Onslaught* caught up with the *Esek Hopkins* and flashed new orders. After a brief stayover in Iceland, the convoy would proceed to Loch Ewe, Scotland. In addition, Captain Gleason was told he was to be the lead ship for the convoy. That made him temporary "commodore" of the fleet. A few other merchant ships were seen on the horizon. They would follow *Esek Hopkins* to Iceland.

Sounded good. Except the convoy would be going through a large German minefield. So, the *Esek Hopkins* would be the "guinea pig." Still, the Captain accepted without hesitation.

The cruiser eventually pulled in front of the *Esek Hopkins* and led the ships in a straight line through the minefields. Other ships in the convoy began to collect aft of *Esek Hopkins.*

Over the next few days, the storm slowly subsided. In the meantime, Jack and the deck cadets saw a number of mines bobbing in the ocean. Jack wondered how many were bobbing just below the surface.

It was November 26, Thanksgiving Day, when they spotted the hazy gray coast of Iceland to starboard. Their progress had been abysmally slow. They were instructed to enter a deep, protected fjord and drop anchor. Once the anchor was set, Jack, and a few mates, stood on deck as the sun set in the west and the large full moon rose in the east. Above in the sky the Northern Lights danced and shimmered. Jack was unable to take his eyes from the amazing, colorful dancing of electrons low in the sky. He had never observed them before.

That night the crew enjoyed a traditional Thanksgiving dinner which included apple pie for dessert. Everyone on board was thankful they had made it this far and many mumbled private prayers. The main topic of discussion at dinner revolved around the probability of arriving home for Christmas.

As much as Thanksgiving brought back fond memories of the family in Baltimore, of the two holidays, Jack would prefer to be with his family on Christmas. At moments like this, he missed the home team. And Penny. What was she up to? Had she received any of his letters? A thought occurred to him. *What would he dream about if he had never met Penny?*

Collectively, the entire crew aboard the *Esek Hopkins* had much to be thankful for. At the end of the meal, the Captain came to the mess and gave a short collegial speech, thanking the deity along with the dedicated crew.

By noon the next day, they pulled up the anchor and joined ten other ships anchored at Iceland to create a mini convoy. They had departed from Russia with thirty-one ships.

Eventually they heard a rumor that four had been "captured." Whatever that meant. None of the officers were discussing the fate of the other seventeen ships. It was all wrapped in mystery.

Had they been lost in the storm? Or proceeded to a different destination? Jack was never let in on that secret.

Their immediate destination was Loch Ewe, Scotland. Jack was happy they were going to an English-speaking country for a change. But it was more than that. A sense of ennui surrounded his thoughts as he wondered if by some chance, he might find a way to visit Penny. He now realized that whenever he heard the word "Scotland," his mind automatically flipped to fond memories of Penny. *Penny, Penny, Penny.* Was there some tiny opportunity to visit with her? But what would he do? Climb in bed with her? Feel her soft freckled skin, inhale her sweet breath? Have his pleasure with her? Then what? Repeat the tearful goodbyes? Tell her he loved her? Reminisce all over again? Once more, wish he had not left her? Again? Nothing had changed. Except he had survived over half of this portion of his wartime odyssey. And there was no sign the war was closer to ending.

At his next opportunity on the bridge, he unobtrusively checked a map and realized there was no chance to see Penny. Loch Ewe was over one-hundred-fifty miles north of Glasgow.

There was only one thing he could do to placate his yearnings. Write another letter. The mail bag would be dropped off in Scotland. Even though there were a few letters to her already in the mail quay, one now, confirming the ship's day in Scotland, would be more impactful, even if she read it long after his departure. He would compose a heartfelt note once they anchored in Loch Ewe.

The journey to Scotland was not without incident. There were several general alarms and sub sightings along the way resulting in many depth charges from the escorting destroyers. But there were no torpedo attacks on the little convoy. In addition, to help rid the mind of depression, there were more sunny days and slightly less freezing weather as they cruised southward toward the British Isles.

Before sunrise, the *Esek Hopkins* anchored in Loch Ewe, Scotland. Within an hour, a skiff arrived with a chattering group of British officials who climbed aboard and roamed about the boat shaking hands and congratulating the crew. The congratulations apparently were for surviving the journey to Archangel. During the chattering the officials passed on some unhappy news. They informed the crew that the HMS *Avenger* escort aircraft carrier, which had accompanied their convoy to Russia, had been sunk by a U-boat in the Mediterranean Sea. So sad, thought Jack. He felt as if he had lost an old friend. The Hurricane fighters from that carrier had likely saved Jack's life and all those aboard the *Esek Hopkins* along with most of the Liberty Ships in PQ 18.

They remained at anchor for two days. There was no shore leave. On the first day, Jack began his letter to Penny. Short declarative sentences. It went:

Dearest Penny,

I think of you every day. I am near you now. I can almost see you before my eyes. I truly long for you. We are anchored at Lock Ewe. There is no shore leave. Yet I feel your presence. Still, I am sad. This may be the closest we are forever. My ship casts off for the States tomorrow. I hope you are well. So far, I have received no letters from you. As you recall, our mail service is terrible. Even the Captain complains. They may arrive all at once next week.

I have written to you almost daily. Silly little notes. They help me with our connection, no matter how fragile. I cannot know if we will ever see each other again. I hold out hope. I miss you.

With great affection,

Jack

He sealed it quickly. He wanted to end with "I love you," but could not make himself write those words. It was too risky. For now, that would have to do.

Other than doing routine maintenance on board, there was not much happening on the now dreary vessel. Jack found himself gazing through delicate mist at the exceptional beauty of the mountains and valleys along the Scottish coast, which maintained their green luster even in this winter weather. His ennui was shattered when a fuel ship scooted up and threw lines up to the main deck. He helped secure the heavy ropes as the transfer of fuel began; enough fuel to complete their journey across the ocean to the East Coast. Enough fuel to say goodbye to Scotland. Forever.

It was December 4 when the Captain ordered the anchor pulled, and slowly and skillfully, he steamed out of Loch Ewe to head west among a dozen other merchant ships. For some reason, into Jack's memory, popped a recollection that this day was the birthday of his brother, Bill, who was thirty years old. Too bad Jack was not home to help celebrate. At age thirty, during wartime, and with Bill's busy schedule, there was not likely to be much of a party.

As the cluster of lumber-laden merchant ships entered the Atlantic, the weather became overcast, and building winds and waves from the west pushed against the bows of the steel hulls. On the first night out, as visibility deteriorated, two Liberty Ships collided. Without radar, or lights, night travel in rough weather was a high-risk adventure. No details were immediately available, but neither ship was seriously damaged, and there were no injuries. Some natural instinct in Captain Gleason's experience kept them safely positioned in the convoy.

During the first three days, as they struggled and bounced west against the elements, there were no battle stations called, no torpedoes detected and no enemy aircraft seen in the skies, yet there were occasional underwater thuds of depth charges in the area. The escorts were paying attention.

Jack realized that another important day revealed itself on Sparks' calendar. December 7, 1942, marked the one-year anniversary of the attack on Pearl Harbor. He brought it up before the Forum at the morning mess. That event was the reason they all were on the *Esek Hopkins,* all in the military, all sacrificing and dying for their country. There ensued a great deal of chatter and philosophizing and all agreed that they, and the entire US population, were justified in hating the Japs for starting this catastrophic conflict. And the Germans. These strong feelings helped alleviate the misery and struggles they had endured. There was no end in sight.

The next day, the winds mounted, and another nasty North Atlantic storm hit with particular fury. The *Esek Hopkins* was plowing straight into the overpowering wind and massive pyramids of ocean. Huge waves washing over the bow of the ship actually knocked away one of the forward lifeboats along with a davit. The lost lifeboat quickly bobbed and bounced into the distance among the tips and troughs of the seas. It was out of sight within a minute. The remaining davit was dangling and randomly banging against the side. Jack and two other deck cadets were assigned by Captain Gleason to resolve the issue. Gleason's order pulled Jack away from the comfort of the helm station and put him in considerable danger. Was the Captain still unhappy with him?

The Captain commanded, "Either cut that damned davit away or secure it to the hull to stop that infernal pounding."

Besides Jack, the Captain ordered Murry Wayburn and Alex Salamis to accomplish the objective. As Jack departed from the bridge, First Mate Cockrell told him to collect the men and meet him in the mess in ten minutes.

Alex and Murray were not happy with Jack's news. "Captain's orders!" Jack yelled as he walked away. "We meet Cockrell in the mess, now."

Murray quipped, "We should stop meeting like this Jack."

They encountered Cockrell outside the mess hall gazing out a forward port hole while the davit randomly slammed persistently and loudly as the ship bounced and rocked like a pitiful toy.

"Well lads, this is no quick fix." Alex noted with inappropriate nonchalance. He added. "Looks like a suicide mission!"

Murray shook his head, "Why can't this wait for calmer seas?"

"Captain's orders, that's why." Cockrell stated firmly with no leeway in his voice.

The men quickly determined that to remove the davit would require a welder and that was impossible under the existing storm conditions. The only choice was to secure the davit tightly to the side of the ship. A plan of action evolved which began with finding six lines; two per man. They collected life vests and body harnesses. A ten-foot line was secured to each body harness which was tightened around each man. Life vests were then secured. Heavy gloves were next. As they dressed, they discussed the safest and most efficient way to accomplish the goal. They would exit the steel door one at a time as the bow peaked on the top of a wave. This gave them about five seconds to go out onto a relatively dry deck and secure their lifeline to a steel post or a stanchion near the damaged davit. Once the three were secured, they were to grasp the dangling hook on the end of the davit line, secure it to a stanchion, and tighten the winch to hold the davit in one position. If other lines were needed to secure it, they were to add them with the extra line each man carried. Each man nervously practiced tying a bowline. Each man was scared.

Alex volunteered to go first. Cockrell manned the steel door on the side of the ship. He nodded to Alex and opened the door as the bow started its upward arc and volumes of ocean swiftly sloshed past the opening. Alex, like a jaguar, gingerly exited onto the deck which was still covered with two inches of swirling ocean water. The men watched through the porthole as he made his way across the deck to the swinging davit and secured his line to the nearest stanchion. Success! He waved for the next man as the bow descended unremorsefully. They all watched the next crest of water pour over the deck as the bow descended in its never-ending cycle. Alex hugged the davit. The water smashed him and buried him up to his chest. He shook his head like a wet cat and gave a "thumbs up" sign.

Jack elected to go last so he could learn from the other two. Cockrell told Jack to keep an eye on Alex through the blurry porthole. Murray said he was ready and nodded to Cockrell, who waited for the mass of water to pour off the deck. Cockrell pushed hard on the door, and Murray exited, trying to imitate the successful journey of his predecessor. Murray carefully made his way to the davit with rope in hands. His wet, nervous hands were not functioning optimally in the cold. He struggled to attach his lifeline to the stanchion. The bow descended forcefully. A massive wave descended over the deck. Murray looked up at the now shoulder-high wave with panic in his eyes. Too late. He released the line and wrapped his arms around the stanchion and turned his back toward the bow just as the wave struck. Meanwhile, Alex was knocked off his feet and was completely submerged for a few long seconds. His lifeline held. Alex struggled to stand, and he searched for Murray. He was still there, squeezing the steel pipe for all he was worth. The bow ascended, the wave rinsed away, and Murray was able to secure his lifeline.

Jack was next. The anxiety showed on his face after seeing Murray nearly get washed overboard. Cockrell saw it but knew the solution. He yelled, "Ready, go!" He pushed open the heavy steel door as the bow arced upward toward the heavens. No time for analysis. Jack stopped thinking and squeezed out the door. Cold wind and pellets of hard rain and sea water bombarded his face. The salty brine burned his eyes. He blinked and squinted as he made his way through the swirling wind gusts. His motion was crab-like. Just as the bow began its descent and waves began to pour over the deck, he quickly secured his lifeline to a stanchion adjacent to his colleagues. As the bow plowed into the next trough, the three men felt lighter than air and their stomachs rose in their bellies. Water surged over the bow and crashed on the deck striking the three men waste high with a powerful surge. All three lifelines yanked hard as the sea pushed the men backward. Jack felt as if a powerful monster had grabbed his body and had its way with him. It was frightening to feel so trivial.

Now the hard part. As if rising from the dead, the bow accelerated upward. As it neared its apogee, the davit block and steel hook swung violently, nearly striking Alex. The three men ducked. It banged into the side of the ship with an annoying crash. This was going to be more difficult than they had calculated. With the ship's constant motion left and right, to and fro, the hook was never still. They took turns reaching up to grasp the hook, but none could hold it.

Calculating the timing was difficult. The swing pattern was not regular, and they could take their best shot only when the bow was ascending.

From the bridge, Captain Gleason, Mark Williams, and Sparks silently watched the tense act play out below them. Gleason now wondered if he should have waited for calmer weather before giving the order.

The screaming loud wind and constant irregular motion continued. After a number of misses, Jack yelled out, "I will create a large bowline on my rope. When the hook swings past I will try to lasso it. Then we can secure it and add additional lines."

The others nodded. Jack rapidly created the bowline with a two-foot loop at the end. He gave the line to Alex, the tallest, who after three attempts caught the swinging hook. From there it was all downhill. Murray slowly released the winch as the Jack and Alex pulled the hook closer to the deck. With their extra lines they securely tied down the hook so there was essentially no motion and no crashing noise.

Now the last part of the operation: return. Jack waved that he wanted to go first. Again, it was all about the timing. Jack squinted back to see if he could discern Chief Cockrell at one of the circular portholes. He was there. Waving. As the bow started to rise up, Jack released the lifeline and slowly, carefully took long strides along the wet deck until he arrived at the door, which Cockrell swung open. Jack grasped the rim and pulled himself in and crashed on the floor. One down.

Then Murray successfully repeated the process. Alex got the timing perfectly but ran too fast and as he turned toward the open door, slipped, and slammed into a stanchion. Somehow his legs slid through, but the stanchion cables held his upper body as his feet dangled overboard.

The bow was already down, and a large wave was rushing across the deck creating a precarious situation. Cockrell yelled, "Dodd, hold the door!" Without waiting another instant, Cockrell lurched out, grabbed Alex around his waist, yanked him up, and threw him through the open door in the midst of the powerful wave. Cockrell's mass and strength paid off. They both collapsed on the floor as water poured in. Alex was stunned and coughed up some water, but he was all in one piece. Jack and Murray pulled hard against the mass of water to get the door secure.

Mission accomplished.

Both Neptune and Poseidon were watching over them with kind eyes on this day.

CHAPTER 27

Clarity

JACK WAS PHILOSOPHICAL. "CHALK UP one more near-death experience. Overboard in this mess you would never be seen again, even with a life jacket on. I have already been through nine lives!" The next two meal sessions in the Forum were preoccupied with discussion and analysis of the danger on deck during storms and their new hero, Chief Cockrell.

The storm subsided the next morning. As the skies cleared, none of the other Liberty Ships or escorts were in sight. The *Esek Hopkins* was sailing alone once again.

Jack was on the bridge when Sparks received a warning that there was U-boat activity in an area they were approaching. Captain Gleason made an announcement over the loudspeaker to that effect. He ordered all crew members to don their life jackets until further notice. To a U-boat, the *Esek Hopkins* was a juicy morsel puttering along by herself--nearly defenseless. Then, to further agitate the crew, the shrill klaxon blasted. Everyone ran to their stations and prepared their guns for an attack. A single aircraft was spotted flying westward. The officers tracked it with binoculars and determined it was an American Liberator bomber. The all-clear alarm sounded. They relaxed and ventured down below. Very good news! They were inching closer to the East Coast.

That afternoon, while plugging along at eight knots by themselves, they encountered an Allied convoy proceeding eastward in the opposite direction. One of their escort destroyers approached the *Esek Hopkins* to confirm we were friendlies. The crew watched the convoy in the distance, wondering what they had in store as they headed for Russia. The *Esek Hopkins'* crew members all were so happy they were proceeding in the opposite direction. That same day, Sparks got word that the *Esek Hopkins* was to rendezvous with the rest of the convoy at a particular course setting. It was the first communication they had from their compatriots in two days. The next morning the convoy was spotted, and it took all day to catch up and get into their assigned position. Jack and the crew felt a bit more relaxed being among friends. And friends with lots of guns.

Each day that passed offered the crew more encouragement that it was possible they might make it home safely, and as a bonus, before Christmas. It was December 15, and they were beyond mid-ocean on their journey. The weather alternated between clear blue, breezy skies and brisk winds, black low clouds, and snow. Jack was tiring of this foul, unstable weather and the tiresome scene of water in all directions. He needed to get back on land for a while. As they approached the Gulf Stream off the East Coast, they encountered a patch of dense fog. The air was cold, but the water temperature was sixty-six degrees. This differential created impermeable hazy conditions of zero visibility. But it was another sign they were getting close. By the next morning the officers on the bridge were estimating how far they were from the famous Ambrose Light Tower. This seventy-six-foot light marked the outer entrance to New York Harbor. Even the term "New York" was music to their ears.

At last, early on the morning of December 24, 1942, the convoy cruised into New York Harbor with running lights ablaze as the sun peeped over the eastern horizon. Jack could spot car headlights on shore. By 7:30 a.m. they were positioned between Staten Island and Brooklyn, and it was there they were instructed to drop anchor. Jack scanned the scene from the port wing of the bridge and had a deep sense of gratification, quiet satisfaction, and relief. He recalled his first sight of the Statue of Liberty at the onset of the trip to Russia. He and the crew had completed their journey on the steady, reliable *Esek Hopkins*. She held up well in all types of weather and all types of combat. She carried them over sixty-five hundred miles. Remarkably, there were no casualties. What a delight to be in the safe waters of the United States. One's outlook on life took a complete turn. Like a new beginning. No one was bombing, strafing, or targeting them with torpedoes. The crew was instantly more relaxed and carefree. They had made it home, and home for Christmas.

Or had they?

The crew was always at the bottom of the news chain.

The Captain went ashore on a launch soon after anchoring. Jack retreated to his room and began packing his bags while he and his roommates filled the room with chatter, pulling clothes from storage boxes and searching for gear. Jack came across a small fragment of folded paper. He realized what it was even before he opened it. He sniffed it. Nothing related to Penny was detectable. As he unfolded it, he looked at Penny's handwriting. His thoughts wandered to the day they spent together when she wrote it. Her soft, freckled skin, her generous smile, the first night of secret, silent love making… like a flickering film…bits and pieces of a drifting relationship… He refolded the note and placed it in his breast pocket.

The Captain did not return to the ship until six o'clock that evening. The crew had packed their bags and were wandering aimlessly around the decks looking for something to occupy their time. All thoughts were on departure. Who would meet them? Some had relatives or friends in New York. How would they travel to their homes?

But it was not to be. The loudspeaker system clicked on. Gleason announced the new plan: they were to anchor for the night in New York Harbor and then sail for Baltimore at 4:00 a.m. on Christmas morning. Everyone let out a loud groan of disappointment.

Boos emanated from the distraught assemblage. A few down below kicked the mess table, accompanied by outbursts of cussing. Many began to migrate back to their rooms, grumbling all the way with duffel bags dragging behind them. But, at some level, after this precarious journey, they had gotten acclimated to disappointments. For Jack it was good news, bad news. Good he would be in his home port to disembark; bad he would miss Christmas with family. On board they put up a tiny tree made from rolls of toilet paper, with paper cut-out decorations. A handful of mates sang a few Christmas carols after dinner. Many stayed in their rooms as a form of protest.

Jack was not able to sleep, so he went up to the bridge just as the local pilot arrived around 3:30 a.m. The pilot and Gleason chatted for a few minutes, then the pilot ordered the engine to be fired up. Once it was hot enough to put into gear, he ordered the anchor drawn up by the windlass and proceeded out toward the ocean by 5:00 a.m. Captain Gleason stood watch and checked every move with occasional nods of approval. Convinced that the ship was in good hands, and nearly out of the harbor, the Captain went to his room to clean up. Not thirty minutes had passed when a drastic jolt shook the ship, accompanied by a horrendous scraping sound and groaning and creaking from the hull. Furnishings, crew, officers and Jack flew forward and stumbled into the bulkhead. The Captain was on the throne and came running to the bridge while buckling his trousers. The handful of men on the main deck were thrown down and all gazed up at the bridge, wondering who was in charge. The ship came to a frightening, rapid, final halt. Aground! Again! Merry Christmas!

Jack wondered out loud, "What good are these pilots if they can't get us out of their own harbor?"

Captain Gleason was steaming and incandescent as he glared right through the hapless pilot with threatening eyes. No one wanted to be on the other side of that angry stare. A few unchaste words escaped from the Captain's mouth in the direction of the pilot, who wisely said nothing but offered only a meek apology, complaining that the buoys were out of position.

The Captain ordered the ship to be inspected and the crew assessed for injuries. Jack scampered off to round up some deck cadets to complete the Captain's command. The ninety-minute check-out of the lower compartments showed no sign of damage, but most of the hull was not amenable to inspection because of the obstructing logs and wood chips. Jack reported that no damage was found. And there were no significant injuries, only a few bruises and one small laceration on one of the cook's legs.

High tide assisted with the dilemma when it peaked at 9:00 a.m. As the tide incrementally lifted them, and the entire crew was ordered to the ship's stern, with aid from two local tugs, they were able to gradually, grudgingly back off. How embarrassing and frustrating. The Liberty Ships that were following them in the convoy, passed by them on this last leg of their journey. A few sister ships tooted their whistles as they passed and mates on deck pointed thumbs down to the embarrassed crew. Pilots and the *Esek Hopkins* did not get along!

Jack reminded Chief Cockrell, who was watching every move the pilot made at the wheel, that local pilots were steering the ship when the *Esek Hopkins* collided with the barge and tug in Halifax, and again when she struck the British merchant ship in Archangel. Pilots ran her aground twice, once in Archangel and now in New York Harbor. Cockrell only nodded and grimaced. The pilot wisely remained silent.

Within an hour, the pilot launch arrived and the ladder from the side of *Esek Hopkins* was lowered. The now timid pilot bowed without a word as he departed from the bridge. The launch pulled under the ladder and the pilot jumped safely from the *Esek Hopkins.* Off they went. The pilot hoped the officers would forget his name. However, it was his responsibility to report the grounding to the Coast Guard, which he did. And, as required, his name was memorialized in the ship's log.

The *Esek Hopkins* continued under way with calm seas and the sun favorably looking down on a cool, crisp, clear morning as the ship quietly slid down the New Jersey coast. Jack stood on the outdoor bridge extension and watched the shoreline slowly pass by. Soon enough, along the coast there were signs of previous U-boat attacks from earlier in the year. Jack saw three partially submerged merchant ships. It sent a shiver down his spine. Maybe there was no truly safe place in the world from those clever Germans. Then, as if by command, Sparks announced to the bridge staff that he had just received a report of a U-boat on the surface heading toward the East Coast.

"Oh God." Jack turned and said to Sparks, "We might get sunk right here, just like those poor guys. We need to wipe out every single U-boat in the sea!"

Silence reigned; there was no response from anyone else on the bridge. But no U-boats would get this ship, at this time, on this journey.

With Chief Cockrell now at the helm, they turned to starboard around Cape May, New Jersey, headed up the Delaware Bay into the Chesapeake and Delaware Canal to port. But true to form, they stopped and anchored overnight due to dense fog. What else could delay them? Neptune or Poseidon clearly wanted to tease and torment the crew.

By 11:00 a.m. the next morning, the fog lifted, and they entered the northern Chesapeake Bay and headed south toward their final destination. They turned to starboard and sailed up the familiar Patapsco River toward the port of Baltimore. Jack was excited as they approached the lovely city of his birth. But there was no available dockage anywhere in Baltimore, so the *Esek Hopkins* spent one last night anchored near Martin Airport in Middle River.

Over the past week, Jack's tremor had slowly dissipated as the ship left behind all the sleeplessness, worry, and terror. Yet he sensed some strange new feelings of unease. But why? He was going home. Had his family changed? Had he changed? He knew he was a different man than when he departed. Would they perceive it? How different was he really? Was he a different soul after the bombing, strafing, torpedoes, and death around him day after day? He could not be the same person.

He wanted to act as if he was unchanged. But how could he do that? He was not a performer. And had his brief, but intense, delightful relationship with Penny changed him for the better? Most certainly it had. As these thoughts swirled through his mind, he recognized that perhaps she had been like a savior to him. After all, in stressful times, thinking about her acted as a much-needed safety valve.

Finally, with the crew growing surly and talking "mutiny" if there were any more delays, the ship tied up on December 27, at the Port Covington dock and Jack Dodd and the crew of the *Esek Hopkins* set foot safely on American soil for the first time in six months, and eleven days.

Ron Sewell and Jack bumped into each other as they exited the ship. The pair immediately picked up their conversation where it last ended. How was the *Esek Hopkins* able to survive all those German aircraft attacks? Ships were sunk all around them, yet there were no injuries on their lucky vessel.

The best Jack could come up with was, "The gods were with us on this journey. All of us. No matter how many bullets the Germans shot at us, they all missed. Except the one that destroyed my shoe. It was like we had some invisible shield around us." They promised to keep in touch.

Once on *terra firma,* the crew was required to enter a warehouse to submit their hour accounts, sign papers, and collect their Merchant Marine pay. Jack dragged along his cumbersome, olive green, duffel bag. As the crew members completed paperwork and made their way toward the exit, with pockets full of cash, backs were slapped, hugs exchanged, and a few tears shed. Mailing addresses were passed back and forth with promises to maintain correspondence.

Ski found Jack in the crowd and marched up to him with an intimidating look on his face, almost making Jack ready for a fight. He struggled with words, but finally got out, "Thanks Dodd, thanks for helping me out. That thing at the Academy was stupid. Made no sense. Don't think too bad of me."

Jack extended his hand and offered, "Things have a way of working out. Sometimes in strange ways. No worries, Ski." Jack inspected the lumpy, partially healed scar on Ski's face and noted, "Well, you will always have a souvenir from our voyage. Something to tell your grandchildren. Good luck."

Jack felt a tapping on his left shoulder. He turned to face his roommates, Alex, Ralph and Ross. They all shook hands.

Jack inquired, "What are you going to do with all that cash, Alex?"

"It's already spent. If I can escape from Baltimore. I am heading back to New York. We still friends?"

Jack smiled, "Those punches cleared my head. Yes, still friends. And thanks."

Ross understood. Only poor Ralph was out of the loop and could not follow the nature of the conversation. They all exchanged addresses and postulated whether or not they would sign up on another merchant ship.

Jack offered, "I think I will. In spite of all the battles, controversy, stress, horrible ports—except Scotland—the experience was at some level, educational and maturing. I need some rest, but I think I may go out again. But not to Russia this time. Someplace where it's warm. Let's keep in touch, guys. Maybe we will catch up on the next ship."

They all agreed and said they likely would sail again.

Jack spotted the Captain, bent over and alone, stuffing something in his duffel bag. Jack approached him and spoke first, "Captain Gleason, I wanted to thank you." Gleason stood straight and extended his hand.

"Jack Dodd. Well, I should thank you. You worked hard and learned a great deal, I expect. It was nice having you on board. It was quite a journey, no?"

"Yes, sir, it was. I will never understand how we survived all those attacks by the Germans. And why other ships got hit and we did not. I think God had something to do with it. And seeing the mess in Archangel makes me have a greater appreciation of the good old USA."

Gleason observed, "Every time I set my feet back on US shores, I have those same thoughts. There is no place like this in all the world. And don't forget that. And be sure to tell your grandchildren that too. Say, do you plan to make additional cruises? I think you have an aptitude for this life. You could move up the ranks in the Merchant Marine if you want. I would be happy to write you a reference letter."

"Why yes, sir. I want to take a few months off, but I think I may stick with it. I appreciate your comments," Jack replied.

"Say, before I depart, I wanted to ask you how things are between you and that fellow...what's his name...Ski? That was really brave of you to push him to safety when the Ju 88 was firing at us. Incidentally, I put that in my cruise log. I hope he appreciates what you did," said Gleason.

"Yes, sir, things are fine between us. I didn't even realize who it was until we crashed on the deck. Any cadet would have done the same."

Just then Chief Cockrell walked up and greeted them. He looked at Jack and noted with a laugh, "Well, your black eye is healing nicely. You should come up with a good story for your family."

"I will think of something more interesting than an accidental poke," Jack replied. Then, "Chief, it has been a true educational experience working with you. I learned so much...thank you."

At his point the Captain shook hands again and peeled off, as did the Chief. Jack watched them somewhat forlornly as they briskly walked out through the opening in the wire fence toward the street. He wondered if he would ever see them again. Somehow, he felt he should have had more to say to the Captain. After all, Gleason had accomplished all his goals: he delivered the desperately needed supplies to Scotland and Russia; he avoided getting sunk, in spite of the enemy's best efforts; and he returned his crew home safely through all kinds of weather and turmoil. As the Chief had said to Jack on his first day on board, "You are lucky to be on this ship with Captain Gleason." Jack never forgot him.

In his revery, he heard in the distance a distinctive voice calling his name, "Jack, Jack Dodd. Thank God you are home in one piece."

He looked up to see Mary Hogan Dodd, his lovely white-haired mother, walking quickly toward him. She grabbed him with a strong, long hug as she kissed his cheek. Her eyes were filled with tears. She was accompanied by Jack's oldest brother, Howard, who grasped his hand. The arrival of the *Esek Hopkins* had been announced in the *Baltimore Sun* newspaper the day before. Jack was totally surprised to be greeted by his mom and brother.

His mother inspected her youngest son. "You have aged," she observed without hesitation, as only mothers can get away with. "And how did you get that black eye?"

Howard chirped, "He must have run into a fist. I hear boxing is popular on Merchant Marine ships. What does the other guy look like?"

Jack smiled. "Well, Mom, I have been through a lot, and I have seen a lot. I can tell you all about it when we get home. And Howard is right about the black eye. There are lots of opportunities to earn one. In this case, I was just trying to stop a fight. And the other two guys look a lot worse. And Howard, I did my best to follow your advice. I paid attention, I learned a lot and I tried to stay out of trouble, mostly with success. Now, I can't wait to see the family, and get into my own bed. By the way, Mom, I kept my promise to you; I made it home safely."

She looked at her youngest son and smiled. "Don't you know? You made it home because of my prayers."

For that, Jack had no retort. But he wondered if she was correct. It was not chance or probability or fate at all. Those torpedoes, those exploding ships around him, those bombs, those bullets zinging past his head were all calculated and planned. It was divine will. After all, his mother was always right.

As the Dodds walked away, Jack turned back once more to gaze at the *Esek Hopkins.* He could not hold back the tears. He would not see that ship again, but he would never forget her and his incredible sea experience like no other. His mind swirled with emotion. As the trio headed toward Howard's parked car, Jack checked his breast pocket to see if the folded paper was still there. In the process, he noticed that the tremor in his hands was no longer present. In his mind he decided that he had left the tremor on board the ship as a final gift.

As they motored home in Howard's quiet, blue Packard sedan with spotless, white-walled tires, Jack asked if he had received any mail. His mother sensed the question had something more attached to it than was on the surface.

She answered, "No, Jack. The only letters we received from overseas were those from you. We received about ten of your letters. It meant so much for us to read them. Your sisters were so thrilled." A pause. "Were you expecting a letter?"

Ironically, at the very instant she spoke, their mailman was dropping three letters into the mail basket on the front porch of their home. One letter, in a small ivory envelope, with neat handwriting in blue ink, revealed a return address from Scotland.

As he accelerated his quiet Packard onto Park Heights Avenue, Howard interrupted his mother's question. "I bet he met a nice young lady in Scotland."

Jack smiled, a long thoughtful smile, and with a twinkle in his eye replied, "You are right, Howard. You are exactly right."

~Finis~

Postscript

JACK DODD CONTINUED IN THE Merchant Marine until January 19, 1945. The Germans surrendered on May 5, 1945. Jack advanced during those three and a half years to Second Mate which was the third position in command of a merchant ship. He sailed on five vessels after the *Esek Hopkins*. They departed from the ports of New York; Beaumont, Texas; New Orleans; and Philadelphia. Five of the six cruises took him overseas. One was a US coastal trip.

Jack later married Margaret (Mimi) Berlinger and had three children, all of whom went into health care. His son Michael Howard Dodd became a dentist, his daughter Margaret became a psychiatrist and his second daughter, Deborah, a nurse. Jack died in 1990 from complications of diabetes and aspiration pneumonia.

Captain Edward J. Gleason was a fictional character based on the real captain of the *Esek Hopkins*. He continued in the Merchant Marine. His luck ran out on his next cruise where his ship was sunk by a U-boat and he was lost at sea.

The *Esek Hopkins* survived the war but was scrapped in 1967 in Kearny N.J.

Addendum

AS NOTED IN THE TEXT, the west coast was not the only area for constructing Liberty Ships. A total of eighteen shipyards began the manufacturing process. They extended from Portland, Maine to Jacksonville, Florida on the east coast and along the Gulf coast from Panama City, Florida to Houston, Texas. Liberty Ships were pumped out in numbers difficult to fathom. By September 1945 at the end of the war, about twenty-seven hundred Liberty Ships had been manufactured by US shipyards. The facility which produced the most ships was the Bethlehem-Fairfield Shipyard in Baltimore, where the *Esek Hopkins* was built. That yard accounted for three hundred eighty-five Liberty Ships. They also produced the very first Liberty Ship, the *Patrick Henry*, and it was there that President Roosevelt went to give the name Liberty Ship to these new vessels. And it was there that Jack Dodd witnessed the Roosevelt speech.

In early January 1942, before the mass production techniques kicked in, it took about one hundred seventy days to complete a Liberty Ship. By the spring of that year, production time was cut in half. A year later, a ship was completed in forty-six days. The shipyards were operating in three eight-hour shifts which allowed twenty-four hours of construction per day. As noted, the employees got one day off after working seven. On Sept 23, 1942, at the Kaiser yard in Portland, Oregon, President Roosevelt watched the launch of the seventy-fifth Liberty Ship, the *Joseph N. Teal.* Incredibly, this vessel was completed in ten days. The fastest construction time was achieved two months later, at the same Kaiser shipyard, when the *Robert E. Peary* was completed and launched in the record time of four days, fifteen hours, and twenty-nine minutes. This record time was the result of competition with other shipyards to see who could build ships the fastest. At one level this achievement was a publicity stunt to demonstrate to the enemy Axis powers how the US could out-produce them. The average production time for a Liberty Ship was about forty days.

There were many reasons for the amazing production rate of these four hundred and forty-foot merchant ships. One important factor was Henry Kaiser's philosophy of allowing workers to give input regarding any component of production. This allowed improvements to get immediate responses from management. Kaiser also encouraged continuous improvement of each aspect of production, no matter how trivial. Over time, these little things added up, and had a significant impact on production. In addition, each shipyard developed a sense of a unified community, a sort of family, in a single effort to defeat the enemy.

Another major change in production was the elimination of rivets in connecting steel plates in the hulls. Riveting was time-consuming and technically difficult. Instead, steel plates were welded together with no loss of strength. It has been estimated that each Liberty Ship had some forty-three miles of welding seams to secure the hundreds of steel plates.

Perhaps the most important issue was that each ship was designed to be identical in configuration and parts. Therefore, everything could be mass-produced, and the parts were all exactly the same and interchangeable no matter where the ships were manufactured. Damaged parts were easily replaced. Everything from doorknobs to the steam engine were identical, and once the specs were drawn up, they could be produced in a variety of locations.

Even before Pearl Harbor, the Roosevelt administration came to the realization that the country would have to convert to a war footing. Part of that conversion was to produce merchant ships faster than the Axis powers could sink them. In fact, that is exactly what happened. U-boats sunk an incredible two thousand two hundred and eighty-two merchant ships during the war. In addition, they sunk one hundred and seventy-five war ships. Without rapid production of Liberty Ships by the United States, it is very likely that the war in Europe would have been lost.

The Germans paid dearly. During the early years, relatively few U-boats were sunk.

Once Allied convoys were accompanied by escort ships and detection techniques improved, U-boats were sunk faster than they could be produced. Data shows there were eight hundred and forty-two U-boats built during the war. By the time of the German surrender in April 1945, seven hundred and ninety-three of them had been sunk; a ninety-four percent loss rate. During the war years between 1939 and 1945, it is estimated that the mortality rate for the U-Boat crews was seventy-four percent, the highest in the German military service. Near the end of the war, when the crew on a U-boat departed from port, as a practical matter, they were on a suicide mission.

Ultimately, this race was won by the Allies.

The seamen of the Merchant Marine were not members of any branch of the US military.

They were employed and paid by corporations which owned the ships, and those ships were operated under the authority of the US Commerce Department. In some quarters, the merchant seamen were viewed as inferior to members of the military because they were considered unfit for service since many could not pass the rigorous navy physical exams. There was some level of friction on board many liberty ships between the Merchant Mariners and the US Navy Armed Guards. The pay was slightly higher for the Merchant Mariners and the shore leave policy was more liberal than for the Navy Armed Guards.

After the war, the friction continued. The Merchant Mariners received no VA Hospital benefits (they had to pay out of pocket for any war-related injuries), no GI school loans, no assistance with job training or job searches, no GI home loans, no medals or burial rights, and no membership in military social clubs. They were not even permitted to partake in military parades. Yet they were injured, they suffered, and they died next to their Navy compatriots. They were just as patriotic and just as dedicated to the hazardous task of delivering critical supplies to our allies. They were just as important in winning the war as any other member of the US military. Even the Russians honored our Merchant Mariners with awards, medals and parades—in the Soviet Union! In 1988, by an act of Congress, some of these injustices were rectified. This was a little late for most of these patriots.

Acknowledgments

MANY THANKS TO MY COUSIN, Dr. Michael H. Dodd, who was kind enough to pass on to me the organized data his father collected during his trip to Russia, which formed the backbone for this historical fiction.

Thanks also to my wife, Maureen, for her valuable suggestions, along with her patience while I was engaged in research, writing and editing. There are many friends to whom I owe thanks including Rick Sheahan for his encouragement to start this project; Indy Pommers for his assistance in reviewing and critiquing the manuscript; Kathy Miller for proofreading, comments, and encouragement; and Bill Museler who offered useful suggestions regarding naval history.

I am most thankful for the time and effort spent by my editor, Katherine Pickett. Her valuable insights and sensible revisions helped improve this manuscript significantly.

And many thanks to Harley Patrick and his staff at Hellgate Press for their help getting this manuscript into book form.

Finally, I greatly appreciate the many volunteer crew members of the Liberty Ship *John W. Brown*, who answered my numerous questions during my visits to that ship. The *John W. Brown* is docked in Baltimore Harbor and is one of only two remaining Liberty Ships in the United States. The vessel is restored and available for public tours on Wednesdays and Saturdays. Twice a year it sails into the Chesapeake Bay for amazing cruises which are open to the public. Check for details at: *ssjohnwbrown.org*.

About the Author

CAPTAIN MICHAEL DODD GREW UP in the port city of Baltimore, Maryland, on the Chesapeake Bay. The area is known as "The Land of Pleasant Living." He spent many years sailing and cruising on the beautiful waters of the Bay. In 2016 he obtained a USCG 50 ton captain's license for inland waters.

Captain Dodd's love of the water is reflected in his first book, *Chesapeake Bay Odyssey: 23 Ports of Call with Historic Perspectives.*

He is a retired physician and lives near Annapolis with his wife, Maureen.

Captain Dodd's websites are:
seastoriesbydodd.com and *boatingabcs.com*

www.hellgatepress.com

Made in the USA
Middletown, DE
02 August 2024

58397120R00203